THE FINAL SHOWDOWN

Brisco turned, stepping one pace away from the bar. "Well, Tom," he said quietly, his voice just loud enough to carry over the sound of the music, "I've come foryuh."

Riveted to the spot, Tom Blazer felt an instant of panic. Brisco's presence here had the air of magic, and Tom was half frightened by the sheer unexpectedness of it. Sounds in the saloon seemed to die out, although they still went full blast, and Tom stared across that short space like a man in a trance, trapped and faced with a fight to the death. There would be no escaping this issue, he knew. He might win, and he might lose, but it was here, now, and he had to face it. Tex Brisco stood there, staring at him.

"Yuh've had yore chance," Tex said gently. "Now I'm goin' to kill yuh!"

The shock of the word *kill* snapped Tom Blazer out of it. He dropped into a half crouch, and his lips curled in a snarl of mingled rage and fear. His clawed hand swept back for his gun....

—"The Trail to Crazy Man" by Louis L'Amour

THE GOLDEN WEST

LOUIS L'AMOUR
ZANE GREY
MAX BRAND

THE GOLDEN WEST
Edited by
Jon Tuska

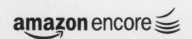

Published by AmazonEncore
P.O. Box 400818
Las Vegas, NV 89140

ISBN-13: 9781477842331
ISBN-10: 1477842330

TABLE OF CONTENTS

Foreword

A short novel is a story too short to be a novel—forty thousand words or less—and too long to be a short story. It was a literary form that once was encouraged and flourished when there were numerous fiction magazines published weekly, monthly, or quarterly in the United States, and it is a form at which numerous American writers excelled. Although a great many authors have written excellent Western fiction, beginning with Mark Twain and Bret Harte, only three managed as a result of their Western stories to attract a sufficient readership to become wealthy. Zane Grey, Max Brand, and Louis L'Amour were the three, and their work has endured with generations of readers throughout the world. For this collection I have selected a short novel by each of these authors, consisting of stories I regard as among their best work.

F. L. Lucas, a literary historian who taught at Cambridge, published a book of common sense and uncommon wisdom in 1951 titled LITERATURE AND PSYCHOLOGY, so much so that I have had cause to re-read it often. Surveying Western literature, in the broader sense of that adjective, he arrived at perhaps the essential element that unifies the themes of these short novels when he concluded: "I believe that the future may need from writers something more than 'objectifying futility'. I believe that it may need from literature (if it has not by then been degraded to a state-department) all its power to fortify and inspire human endurance, and from psychology all its capacity to understand and to control the infinite complexities and perversities of human character."

Jon Tuska
Portland, Oregon

Tappan's Burro

Zane Grey

Zane Grey (1872–1939) was born Pearl Zane Gray in Zanesville, Ohio. He was graduated from the University of Pennsylvania in 1896 with a degree in dentistry. He conducted a practice in New York City from 1898 to 1904, meanwhile striving to make a living by writing. He met Lina Elise Roth in 1900 and always called her Dolly. In 1905 they were married. With Dolly's help, Grey published his first novel himself, BETTY ZANE (Charles Francis Press, 1903), a story based on certain of his frontier ancestors. Eventually closing his dental office, Grey moved with Dolly into a cottage on the Delaware River, near Lackawaxen, Pennsylvania. It is now a national landmark.

Although it took most of her savings, it was Dolly Grey who insisted that her husband take his first trip to Arizona in 1907 with C. J. "Buffalo" Jones, a retired buffalo hunter who had come up with a scheme for crossing the remaining bison population with cattle. Actually Grey could not have been more fortunate in his choice of a mate. Dolly Grey assisted him in every way he desired and yet left him alone when he demanded solitude; trained in English at Hunter College, she proof-read every manuscript he wrote and polished his prose; she managed all financial affairs and permitted Grey, once he began earning a good income, to indulge himself at will in his favorite occupations, hunting, fishing, sailing, and exploring the Western regions.

After his return from that first trip to the West, Grey wrote a memoir of his experiences titled THE LAST OF THE

Zane Grey

PLAINSMEN (Outing, 1908) and followed it with his first Western romance, THE HERITAGE OF THE DESERT (Harper, 1910). It remains one of his finest novels. The profound effect that the desert had had on him was vibrantly captured so that, after all of these years, it still comes alive for a reader. In a way, too, it established the basic pattern Grey would use in much of his subsequent Western fiction. The hero, Jack Hare, is an Easterner who comes West because he is suffering from tuberculosis. He is rejuvenated by the arid land. The heroine is Mescal, desired by all men but pledged by the Mormon church to a man unworthy of her. Mescal and Jack fall in love, and this causes her to flee from Snap Naab, for whom she will be a second wife. Snap turns to drink, as will many another man rejected by heroines in other Grey romances, and finally kidnaps Mescal. The most memorable characters in this novel, however, are August Naab, the Mormon patriarch who takes Hare in at his ranch, and Eschtah, Mescal's grandfather, a Navajo chieftain of great dignity and no less admirable than Naab. The principal villain—a type not too frequently encountered in Grey's Western stories with notable exceptions such as DESERT GOLD (Harper, 1913)—is Holderness, a Gentile and the embodiment of the Yankee business spirit that will stop at nothing to exploit the land and its inhabitants for his own profit. Almost a century later, he is still a familiar figure in the American West, with numerous bureaucratic counterparts in various federal agencies. In the end Holderness is killed by Hare, but then Hare is also capable of pardoning a man who has done wrong if there is a chance for his reclamation, a theme Grey shared with Max Brand.

Grey had trouble finding a publisher for his early work, and it came as a considerable shock to him when his next novel, RIDERS OF THE PURPLE SAGE (Harper, 1912), arguably the greatest Western story ever published, was rejected by the same editor who had bought THE HERITAGE OF THE DESERT. Grey asked the vice president at Harper & Bros, to read the new novel. Once he did, and his wife did, it was accepted for publication. It has never been out of print since.

RIDERS OF THE PURPLE SAGE is dominated by dream imagery and nearly all of the characters, at one time or another, are preoccupied with their dreams. For its hero Grey created the gunfighter, Lassiter, another enduring prototype, the experienced Westerner in contrast with the Eastern neophyte, Lassiter with his "leanness, the red burn of the sun, and the set changelessness that came from years of silence and solitude...the intensity of his gaze, a strained weariness, a piercing wistfulness of keen, gray sight, as if the man was forever looking for that which he never found." In this, as well, Lassiter is the prototype for all those searchers and wanderers found in Grey's later stories, above all John Shefford in THE RAINBOW TRAIL (Harper, 1915) and Adam Larey in WANDERER OF THE WASTELAND (Harper, 1923).

Hermann Hesse went East for inspiration in his dreaming; Zane Grey went West. "Yes," Hesse wrote in DEMIAN (S. Fischer, 1919), "one must find his dream, for then the way is easy. However, there is no forever-enduring dream. Each dream surrenders to a new one, and one is able to hold fast to none of them." In RIDERS OF THE PURPLE SAGE, life itself, the outer world, and human evil do not permit dreams to last indefinitely. Bishop Dyer dreams. Jane Withersteen dreams. Venters and Bess dream. Lassiter lives in a dream of vengeance. Lassiter in his relationship with Jane and her ward, Fay, fulfills an ancient dream of a family and, through his actions, fulfills his own dream by destroying Bishop Dyer. At the close, Lassiter, Jane, and Fay are alone, sealed in Surprise Valley. Hermann Hesse and Frederick Faust who wrote as Max Brand became familiar with Jungian ideas, and each for a time consulted with Jung. Grey could know nothing of the process of individuation in 1912 but what he grasped intuitively. For him, personal rebirth into a state of wholeness, the restoration of the Garden of Eden and a state of innocence, came after the expenditure of passion and the vanquishing of evil. This would remain the psychodrama underlying many of Zane Grey's finest Western stories.

Grey's success for a time exceeded even his wildest dreams. The magazine serials, the books, the motion pictures—and Grey at 108 films still holds the world's record for cinematic derivations based on the works of a single author—brought in a fortune. He had homes on Catalina Island, in Altadena, California, a hunting lodge in Arizona, a fishing lodge in the Rogue River area in Oregon.

Whatever his material prosperity, Grey continued to believe in the strenuous life. His greatest personal fear was that of growing old and dying. It was while fishing the North Umpqua River in Oregon in the summer of 1937 that Grey collapsed from an apparent stroke. It took him a long time to recover use of his faculties and his speech. Cardiovascular disease was congenital on Grey's side of the family. Despite medical advice to the contrary, Grey refused to live a sedentary life. He was convinced that the heart was a muscle and the only way to keep it strong was to exercise it vigorously. Early in the morning on October 23, 1939, Dolly was awakened by a call from her husband. Rushing to his room, she found Grey clutching his chest. "Don't ever leave me, Dolly!" he pleaded. He lived until the next morning when, after rising and dressing, he sat down on his bed, cried out suddenly, and fell over dead.

Tappan's Burro

Even more than with Bret Harte, there has always been a tendency among literary critics to dismiss Zane Grey, although, unlike Harte, Grey at no point enjoyed any great favor with them. Part of this attitude may have come about because he was never a realistic writer. This he could not be, since he was one who charted the interiors of the soul through encounters with the wilderness. If he provided us with characters no more realistic than are to be found in Balzac, Dickens, or Thomas Mann, they nonetheless have a vital story to tell. "There was so much unexpressed feeling that could not be entirely portrayed," Loren Grey once commented about his father, "that, in later years, he would weep when re-reading one of his own books." Zane Grey's Western romances, particularly those from 1910 through 1930, are not the kind of Western fare of gunfights and confrontations that his paperback publishers perversely have always tried to make of them. They are psycho-dramas about the spiritual odysseys of the human soul. They may not be the stuff of the real world, but without such odysseys the real world has no meaning.

I

Tappan gazed down upon the newly born little burro with something of pity and consternation. It was not a vigorous offspring of the redoubtable Jennie, champion of all the numberless burros he had driven in his desert prospecting years. He could not leave it there to die. Surely it was not strong enough to follow its mother, and to kill it was beyond him.

"Poor little devil!" soliloquized Tappan. "Reckon neither Jennie nor I wanted it to be born....I'll have to hold up in this camp a few days. You can never tell what a burro will do. It might fool us an' grow strong all of a sudden."

Whereupon Tappan left Jennie and her tiny, gray, lop-eared baby to themselves and leisurely set about making permanent camp. The water at this oasis was not much to his liking, but it was drinkable, and he felt he must put up with it. For the rest the oasis was desirable enough as a camping site. Desert wanderers like Tappan favored the lonely water holes. This one was up inside the bold brow of the Chocolate Mountains where rocky wall met the desert sand, and a green patch of paloverdes and mesquites proved the presence of water. It had a magnificent view down a many-leagued slope of desert growths, across the dark belt of green and shining strip of red, that marked the Río Colorado, and on to the upflung Arizona land, range lifting to range until the saw-toothed peaks notched the blue sky.

Locked in the iron fastnesses of these desert mountains was gold. Tappan, if he had any calling, was a prospector. But the lure of gold did not bind him to this wandering life any more than the freedom of it. He had never made a rich strike. About the best he could ever do was to dig enough gold to grubstake himself for another prospecting trip into some remote corner of the American Desert. Tappan knew the arid Southwest from San Diego to the Pecos River and from Picacho on the Colorado to the Tonto Basin. Few prospectors had the strength and endurance of Tappan. He was a giant in build, and at thirty-five had never yet reached the limit of his physical force.

With hammer and pick and magnifying glass, Tappan scaled the bare ridges. He was not an expert in testing minerals. He knew he might easily pass by a rich vein of ore. But he did his best, sure at least that no prospector could get more than he out of the pursuit of gold. Tappan was more of a naturalist than a prospector, and more of a dreamer than either. Many were the idle moments that he sat staring down the vast reaches of the valleys, or watching some creature of the wasteland, or marveling at the vivid hues of desert flowers.

Tappan waited two weeks at this oasis for Jennie's baby burro to grow strong enough to walk. The very day that Tappan decided to break camp he found signs of gold at the head of a wash above the oasis. Quite by chance, as he was looking for his burro, he struck his pick into a place no different from a thousand others there and hit into a pocket of gold. He cleaned the pocket out before sunset, the richer for several thousand dollars.

"You brought me luck," said Tappan to the little gray burro, staggering around its mother. "Your name is Jenet. You're Tappan's burro, an' I reckon he'll stick to you."

Jenet belied the promise of her birth. Like a seed in fertile ground, she grew. Winter and summer Tappan patrolled the sand beats from one trading post to another, and his burro traveled with him. Jenet had an especially good training. Her mother had happened to be a remarkably good burro before Tappan had bought her. Tappan had patience; he found leisure to do things, and he had something of pride in Jenet. Whenever he happened to drop into Ehrenberg or Yuma or any freighting station, some prospector always tried to buy Jenet. She grew as large as a medium-size mule, and a three hundred pound pack was no load to discommode her.

Tappan, in common with most lonely wanderers of the desert, talked to his burro. As the years passed, this habit grew until Tappan would talk to Jenet just to hear the sound of his voice. Perhaps that was all that kept him human.

"Jenet, you're worthy of a happier life," Tappan would say, as he unpacked her after a long day's march over the barren land. "You're a ship of the desert. Here we are, with grub an' water, a hundred miles from any camp. An' what but you could have fetched me here? No horse, no mule, no man! Nothin' but a camel, an' so I call you ship of the desert. But for you an' your kind, Jenet, there'd be no prospectors, an' few gold mines. Reckon the desert would be still an unknown waste. You're a great beast of burden, Jenet, an' there's no one to sing your praise." And of a golden sunrise, when Jenet was packed and ready to face the cool, sweet fragrance of the desert, Tappan was wont to say: "Go along with you, Jenet. The mornin's fine. Look at the mountains yonder callin' us. It's only a step down there. All purple an' violet! It's the life for us, my burro, an' Tappan's as rich as if all these sands were pearls." But sometimes, at sunset, when the way had been long and hot and rough, Tappan would bend his shaggy head over Jenet, and talk in a different mood. "Another day gone, Jenet, another journey ended...an' Tappan is only older, wearier, sicker. There's no reward for your faithfulness. I'm only a desert rat, livin' from hole to hole. No home! No face to see! Only the ghost of memories. Some sunset, Jenet, we'll reach the end of the trail. An' Tappan's bones will bleach in the sands. An' no one will know or care!"

Tappan's Burro

When Jenet was ten years old, she would have taken the blue ribbon in competition with all the burros of the Southwest. She was unusually large and strong, perfectly proportioned, sound in every particular, and practically tireless. But these were not the only characteristics that made prospectors envious of Tappan. Jenet had the common virtues of all good burros magnified to an unbelievable degree. Moreover, she had sense and instinct that to Tappan bordered on the supernatural.

During these years Tappan's trail criss-crossed the mineral region of the Southwest. But as always the rich strike held aloof. It was like the pot of gold buried at the foot of the rainbow. Jenet knew the trails and the water holes better than Tappan. She could follow a trail obliterated by drifting sand or cut out by running water. She could scent at long distance a new spring on the desert or a strange water hole. She never wandered far from camp so that Tappan would have to walk far in search of her. Wild burros, the bane of most prospectors, held no charm for Jenet, and she had never yet shown any especial liking for a tame burro. This was the strangest feature of Jenet's complex character. Burros were noted for their habit of pairing off, and forming friendships for one or more comrades. These relationships were permanent. But Jenet still remained fancyfree.

Tappan scarcely realized how he relied upon this big, gray, serene beast of burden. Of course, when chance threw him among men of his calling, he would brag about her, but he had never really appreciated Jenet. In his way Tappan was a brooding, plodding fellow, not conscious of sentiment. When he bragged about Jenet, it was her great qualities upon which he dilated. But what he really liked best about her were the little things of every day.

During the earlier years of her training, Jenet had been a

thief. She would pretend to be asleep for hours just to get a chance to steal something out of camp. Tappan had broken this habit in its incipiency. But he never quite altogether trusted her. Jenet was a burro. Jenet ate anything offered her. She could fare for herself or go without. Whatever Tappan had left from his own meals was certain to be rich dessert for Jenet. Every mealtime she would stand near the campfire, with one great long ear drooping, and the other standing erect. Her expression was one of meekness, of unending patience. She would lick a tin can until it shone resplendently. On long, hard, barren trails Jenet's deportment did not vary from that where the water holes and grassy patches were many. She did not need to have grain or grass. Brittle-bush and sage were good fare for Jenet. She could eat greasewood, a desert plant that protected itself with a sap as sticky as varnish and far more dangerous to animals. She could eat cactus. Tappan had seen her break off leaves of the prickly pear cactus and stamp upon them with her fore hoofs, mashing off the thorns, so that she could eat the succulent pulp. She liked mesquite beans, leaves of willow, and all the trailing vines of the desert. She could subsist in an arid wasteland where a man would have died in short order.

No ascent or descent was too hard or dangerous for Jenet, provided it was possible of accomplishment. She would refuse a trail that was impossible. She seemed to have an uncanny instinct both for what she could do, and what was beyond a burro. Tappan had never known her to fail on something that she stuck to persistently. Swift streams of water, always bugbears to burros, did not stop Jenet. She hated quicksand, but could be trusted to navigate it, if that were possible. When she stepped gingerly, with little inch steps, out upon thin crust of ice or salty crust of desert sinkhole, Tappan would know that it was safe, or she would turn back.

Tappan's Burro

Thunder and lightning, intense heat or bitter cold, the sirocco sandstorm of the desert, the white dust of the alkali wastes, these were all the same to Jenet.

One August, the hottest and driest of his desert experience, Tappan found himself working a most promising claim in the lower reaches of the Panamint Mountains on the northern slope above Death Valley. It was a hard country at the most favorable season; in August it was terrible. The Panamints were infested by various small gangs of desperadoes—outlaw claim-jumpers where opportunity afforded and out-and-out robbers, even murderers, where they could not get the gold any other way. Tappan had been warned not to go into this region alone, but he never heeded any warnings. The idea that he would ever strike a gold claim big enough to make himself an attractive target for outlaws seemed preposterous and not worth considering. Tappan had become a wanderer from the unbreakable habit of it. Much to his amazement he struck a rich ledge of free gold in a cañon of the Panamints, and he worked from daylight until dark. He forgot about the claim-jumpers, until one day he saw Jenet's long ears go up in the manner habitual with her when she saw strange men. Tappan watched the rest of that day, but did not catch a glimpse of any living thing. It was a desolate place, shut-in, red-walled, hazy with heat, and brooding with an eternal silence.

Not long after that Tappan discovered boot tracks of several men adjacent to his camp, and in an out-of-the-way spot that persuaded him that he was being watched by claim-jumpers who were not going to jump his claim in this torrid heat, but meant to let him dig the gold and then kill him! Tappan was not the kind of man to be afraid. He grew wrathful and stubborn. He had six small canvas bags of gold and did not mean to lose them. Still he grew worried. *Now*

19

what's best to do, he pondered. *I needn't give it away that I'm wise. Reckon I'd better act natural. But I can't stay here longer. My claim's about worked out. An' these jumpers are smart enough to know it. I've got to make a break at night. What to do?*

Tappan did not want to cache the gold, for in that case, of course, he would have to return for it. Still he reluctantly admitted to himself that this was the best chance to save it. Probably these robbers were watching him day and night. It would be most unwise to attempt escaping by going up over the Panamints. "Reckon my only chance is goin' down into Death Valley," soliloquized Tappan grimly. This alternative was not to his liking. Crossing Death Valley at this season was always perilous and never attempted in the heat of day. At this particular time of intense torridity, when the day heat was unendurable and the midnight furnace gales were blowing, it was an enterprise from which even Tappan shrank. Added to this were the facts that he was too far west of the narrow part of the valley, and, even if he did get across, he would find himself in the most forbidding and desolate region of the Funeral Mountains.

Thus thinking and planning, Tappan went about his mining and camp tasks, trying his best to act natural. But he did not succeed. It was impossible while expecting a shot at any moment to act as if there was nothing on his mind. His camp lay at the bottom of a rocky slope. A tiny spring of water made verdure of grass and mesquite, welcome green in all that stark iron nakedness. His campsite was out in the open, on the bench near the spring. The gold claim that Tappan was working could not be seen from any vantage point, either below or above. It lay back at the head of a break in the rocky wall. It had two virtues—one that the sun never got to it, and the other that it was well hidden. Once there, Tappan knew he could not be seen. This, however, did not diminish his growing uneasiness. Something sinister hung over him. The solemn stillness was a menace. The heat of the day appeared to be increasing to a degree beyond his experience. Every few moments Tappan would slip back through a narrow defile in the rocks and peep from this covert at the camp. On the last of these occasions, he saw Jenet out in the open. She stood motionless. Her long ears were erect. In an instant Tappan became strung with thrilling excitement. His keen eyes searched every approach to his camp, and at last in the gully below to the right he saw two men crawling along from rock to rock. Jenet had seen them enter that gully and was now watching for them to appear.

Tappan's excitement succeeded to a grimmer emotion. These stealthy visitors were going to hide in ambush, and kill him as he returned to camp. *fenet, reckon what I owe you is a whole lot,* mused Tappan. *They'd have got me sure. But now.* ...Tappan left his tools and crawled out of his covert into the jumble of huge rocks toward the left of the slope. He had a six-shooter. His rifle he had left in camp. Tappan had seen only two men, but he knew there were more than that, if not actually near at the moment, then surely not far away. His only chance was to worm his way like an Indian down to camp. With the rifle in his possession he would make short work of the present difficulty.

Lucky fenet's right in camp! thought Tappan. *It beats hell how she does things!*

Tappan was already deciding to pack and hurry away. At this moment, Death Valley did not daunt him. Yet the matter of crawling and gliding along was work unsuited to his great stature. He was too big to hide behind a little shrub or a rock, and he was not used to stepping lightly. His hobnailed boots could not be placed noiselessly upon the stones. Moreover, he could not step without displacing little bits of weathered rock. He was sure that keen ears not too far distant might have heard him, yet he kept on, making good progress around that slope to the far side of the cañon. Fortunately he headed up the gully where his ambushers were stealing forward. On the other hand this far side of the cañon afforded but little cover. The sun had gone down behind a huge red mass of the mountain. It had left the rocks so hot Tappan could not touch them with his bare hands.

He was about to stride out from his last covert and make a run for it down the rest of the slope, when, surveying the whole amphitheater below him, he espied the two men coming up out of the gully, headed toward his camp. They looked in his direction. Surely they had heard or seen him. But Tappan saw at a glance that he was closer to the camp. Without another moment of hesitation he plunged from his hiding place, down the weathered slope. His giant strides set the loose rocks sliding and rattling. The robbers saw him. The foremost yelled to the one behind him. Then they both broke into a run. Tappan reached the level of the bench and saw he could beat either of the robbers into the camp. Unless he were disabled! He felt the wind of a heavy bullet before he heard it strike the rocks beyond. Then followed the *boom* of a Colt. One of his enemies had halted to shoot. This spurred Tappan to tremendous exertion. He flew over the rough ground, scarcely hearing the rapid shots. He could no longer see the man who was firing, but the first one was in plain sight, running hard, not yet seeing he was out of the race. When he became aware of that, he halted and, dropping on one knee, leveled his gun at the running Tappan. The distance was scarcely sixty yards. His first shot did not allow for Tappan's speed. His second kicked up gravel in Tappan's face. Then followed three more shots in rapid succession. The robber divined that Tappan had a rifle in camp. He steadied himself, waiting for the moment when

Tappan's Burro

Tappan had to slow down and halt. As Tappan reached his camp and dived for his rifle, the robber took time for his last aim, evidently hoping to get a stationary target. But Tappan did not get up from behind his camp duffel. It had been a habit of his to pile his boxes of supplies and roll of bedding together and cover them with a canvas. He poked his rifle over the top of this and shot the robber. Then, leaping up, he ran forward to get right of the second one. This man began to run along the edge of the gully. Tappan fired rapidly at him. The third shot knocked the fellow down. But he got up, and, yelling as if for succor, he ran off. Tappan got another shot off before he disappeared.

"Ahuh!" grunted Tappan grimly. His keen gaze came back to survey the fallen robber, and then went out over the bench, across the inside mouth of the cañon. Tappan thought he had better utilize time to pack instead of pursuing the second robber. Reloading the rifle, he hurried out to find Jenet. She was coming into camp.

"Shore you're a treasure, old girl!" ejaculated Tappan.

Never in his life had he packed Jenet, or any other burro, so quickly. His last act was to drink all he could hold, fill his tin canteens, and make Jenet drink. Then, rifle in hand, he drove the burro out of camp, around the corner of red wall, to the wide gateway that opened down into Death Valley.

Tappan looked back more than he looked ahead, and he had traveled down a mile or more before he began to breathe easier. He had escaped the claim-jumpers. Even if they did show up in pursuit now, they could never catch him. Tappan believed he could travel faster and farther than any man of that ilk. But they did not show up. Perhaps the crippled robber had not been able to reach his comrades in time. More likely, however, the gang had no taste for a chase in that torrid heat.

Tappan slowed his stride. He was almost as wet with sweat as if he had fallen into the spring. The great beads rolled down his face, and there seemed to be little streams of fire trickling down his breast. Despite this, and his labored panting for breath, not until he halted in the shade of a rocky wall did he realize the heat. It was terrific. Instantly, then, he knew he was safe from pursuit, but he knew also that he faced a greater peril than that of robbers. He could fight evil men, but he could not fight this heat.

So he rested there, regaining his breath. Already thirst was acute. Jenet stood nearby, watching him. Tappan imagined the burro looked serious. A moment's thought was enough for Tappan to appreciate the gravity of his situation. He was about to go down into the upper end of Death Valley—a part of that country unfamiliar to him. He must cross it, and also the Funeral Mountains, at a season when a prospector who knew the trails and water holes would have to be forced to undertake it, but Tappan had no choice. His rifle was too hot to hold, so he stuck it in Jenet's pack, and, burdened only by a canteen of water, he set out, driving the burro ahead. Once he looked back up the wide-mouthed cañon. It appeared to smoke with red heat veils. The silence was oppressive.

Presently he turned the last corner that obstructed sight of Death Valley. Tappan had never been appalled by any aspect of the desert, but here he halted. Back in his mountain-walled camp the sun had passed behind the high domes, but here it still held most of the valley in its blazing grip. Death Valley looked a ghastly glaring level of white over which a strange, dull, leaden haze dropped like a blanket. Ghosts of mountain peaks appeared dim and vague. There was no movement of anything. No wind! The valley was dead. Desolation reigned supreme. Tappan could not see far toward either end of the valley. A few miles of white glare merged at last into leaden

24

pall. A strong odor, not unlike sulphur, seemed to add weight to the air.

Tappan strode on, mindful that Jenet had decided opinions of her own. She did not want to go straight ahead or to right or left, but back. That was the one direction impossible for Tappan, and he had to resort to a rare measure—that of beating her—but at last Jenet accepted the inevitable and headed down into the stark and naked plain. Soon Tappan reached the margin of the zone of shade cast by a mountain and was not so exposed to the sun. The difference seemed tremendous. He had been hot, oppressed, weighted. It was now as if he was burned through his clothes and had walked on red-hot sands.

When Tappan ceased to sweat and his skin became dry, he drank half a canteen of water, and slowed his stride. Inured to the desert hardship as he was, he could not long stand this. Jenet did not show any lessening of vigor. In truth, what she showed now was an increasing nervousness. It was almost as if she scented an enemy. Tappan never before had such faith in her. Jenet was equal to this task.

With that blazing sun on his back, Tappan felt he was being pursued by a furnace. He was compelled to drink the remaining half of his first canteen of water. Sunset would save him. Two more hours of such insupportable heat would lay him prostrate.

The ghastly glare of the valley took on a reddish tinge. The heat was blinding Tappan. The time came when he walked beside Jenet with a hand on her pack, for he could no longer endure the furnace glare. Even with closed eyes he knew when the sun sank behind the Panamints. That fire no longer followed him. The red left his eyelids.

With the sinking of the sun the world of Death Valley changed. It smoked with heat veils, but the intolerable constant burn was gone. The change was so immense that it seemed to have brought coolness.

In the twilight—strange, ghostly, somber, silent as death—Tappan followed Jenet off the sand, down upon the silt and borax level, to the crusty salt. Before dark, Jenet halted at a sluggish belt of fluid—acid, it appeared to Tappan. It was not deep, and the bottom felt stable, but Jenet refused to cross. Tappan trusted her judgment more than his own. Jenet headed to the left and followed the course of the strange stream.

Night intervened—a night without stars or sky or sound, hot, breathless, charged with some intangible current! Tappan dreaded the midnight furnace winds of Death Valley. He had never encountered them. He had heard prospectors say that any man caught in Death Valley when these gales blew would never get out to tell the tale, and Jenet seemed to have something on her mind. She was no longer a leisurely complacent burro. Tappan imagined Jenet seemed stern. Most assuredly she knew now which way she wanted to travel. It was not easy for Tappan to keep up with her, and ten paces ahead of him she was out of sight.

At last Jenet headed the acid wash, and turned across the valley into a field of broken salt crust, like the roughened ice of a river that had broken and jammed, then froze again. Impossible it was to make even a reasonable headway. It was a zone, however, that eventually gave way to Jenet's instinct for direction. Tappan had long ceased to try to keep his bearings. North, south, east, and west were all the same to him. The night was a blank—the darkness a wall—the silence a terrible menace flung at any living creature. Death Valley had endured them millions of years before living creatures had existed. It was no place for a man.

Tappan was now three hundred and more feet below sea

level, in the aftermath of a day that had registered one hundred and forty-five degrees of heat. He knew when he began to lose thought and balance—when also the primitive directed his bodily machine—and he struggled with all his will power to keep hold of his sense of sight and feeling. He hoped to cross the lower level before the midnight gales began to blow.

Tappan's hope was vain. According to record, once in a long season of intense heat, there came a night when the furnace winds broke their schedule and began early. The misfortune of Tappan was that he had struck this night.

Suddenly it seemed the air sodden with heat began to move. It had weight. It moved soundlessly and ponderously, but it gathered momentum. Tappan realized what was happening. The blanket of heat generated by the day was yielding to outside pressure. Something had created a movement of the hotter air that must find its way upward to give place to the cooler air that must find its way down. Tappan heard the first low, distant moan of wind, and it struck terror in his heart. It did not have an earthly sound. Was that a knell for him? Nothing was surer than the fact that the desert must sooner or later claim him as a victim. Grim and strong, he rebelled against the conviction.

That moan was a forerunner of others, growing louder and longer until the weird sound became continuous. Then the movement of wind was accelerated and began to carry a fine dust. Dark as the night was, it did not hide the pale sheets of dust that moved along the level plain. Tappan's feet felt the slow rise in the floor of the valley. His nose recognized the zone of borax and alkali and niter and sulphur. He had gotten into the pit of the valley at the time of the furnace winds.

The moan augmented to a roar, coming like a nightly storm through a forest. It was hellish—like the woeful tide of

Acheron. It enveloped Tappan, and the gale bore down in thunderous volume, like a furnace blast. Tappan seemed to feel his body penetrated by a million needles of fire. He seemed to dry up. The blackness of night had a spectral whitish cast; the gloom was a whirling medium; the valley floor was lost in a sheeted, fiercely seeping stream of silt. Deadly fumes swept by, not lingering long enough to suffocate Tappan. He would gasp and choke—then the poison gas was gone in the gale. But hardest to endure was the heavy body of moving heat. Tappan grew blind, so that he had to hold to Jenet and stumble along. Every gasping breath was a tortured effort. He could not bear a scarf over his face. His lungs heaved like great leather bellows. His heart pumped like an engine short of fuel. This was the supreme test for his never-proven endurance, and he was all but vanquished.

Tappan's senses of sight and smell and hearing failed him. There was left only the sense of touch—a feeling of rope and burro and ground—and an awful insulating pressure upon all his body. His feet marked a change from salty plain to sandy ascent and then to rocky slope. The pressure of wind gradually lessened; the difference in air made life possible; the feeling of being dragged endlessly by Jenet at last ceased. Tappan went his limit and fell into oblivion.

When he came to, he was suffering bodily tortures. Sight was dim. But he saw walls of rocks, green growths of mesquite, tamarack, and grass. Jenet was lying down, with her pack flopped to one side. Tappan's dead ears recovered to a strange murmuring, babbling sound. Then he realized his deliverance. Jenet had led him across Death Valley, up into the mountain ranges, straight to a spring of running water.

Tappan crawled to the edge of the water and drank guardedly, a little at a time. He had to quell the terrific craving to drink his fill. Then he crawled to Jenet and, loosening the ropes of her pack, freed her from its burden. Jenet got up, apparently none the worse for her ordeal. She gazed mildly at Tappan, as if to say: "Well, I got you out of that hole."

Tappan returned her gaze. Were they only man and beast, alone in the desert? She seemed magnified to Tappan, no longer a plodding, stupid burro.

"Jenet, you...saved my life," Tappan tried to enunciate. "I'll never...forget."

Tappan was struck then to a realization of Jenet's service. He was unutterably grateful. Yet, the time came when he did forget....

II

Tappan had a weakness common to all prospectors, but intensified in him. Any tale of a lost gold mine would excite his interest, and well-known legends of lost miners always obsessed him. Peg-Leg Smith's lost gold mine had lured Tappan to no less than half a dozen trips into the terrible, shifting sand country of southern California. There was no water near the region said to hide this mine of fabulous wealth. Many prospectors had left their bones to bleach white in the sun and at last be buried by the ever-blowing sands. Upon the occasion of Tappan's last escape from this desolate and forbidding desert he had promised Jenet never to undertake it again. It seemed Tappan promised the faithful burro a good many things. It had become a habit.

When Tappan had a particularly hard time or perilous adventure, he always took a dislike to the immediate country where it had happened. Jenet had dragged him across Death Valley, through incredible heat and the midnight furnace winds of that strange place, and he had promised her he would never forget how she had saved his live, nor would he ever go back to Death Valley! He crossed the Funeral Mountains, worked down through Nevada, and crossed the Rio Colorado above Needles, and entered Arizona. He traveled leisurely, but he kept going, and headed southeast toward Globe. There he cashed one of his six bags of gold and indulged in the luxury of a completely new outfit. Even Jenet appreciated this fact, for the old outfit could scarcely hold together.

Tappan had the other five bags of gold in his pack, and after hours of hesitation he decided he would not cash them and trust the money to a bank. He would take care of them. For him the value of this gold amounted to a small fortune. Many plans suggested themselves to Tappan, but in the end he grew weary of them. What did he want with a ranch, or cattle, or an outfitting store, or any of the businesses he now had the means to buy? Towns soon palled on Tappan. People did not long please him. Selfish interest and greed seemed paramount everywhere. Besides, if he acquired a place to take up his time, what would become of Jenet? That question decided him. He packed the burro and once more took to the trails.

A dimly purple, lofty range called alluringly to Tappan. The Superstition Mountains! Somewhere in that purple mass laid the famous treasure called the Lost Dutchman gold mine. Tappan had heard the story often. A Dutch prospector had struck gold in the Superstitions. He had kept the location secret. When he had run short of money, he would disappear for a few weeks, and then return with bags of gold. His strike assuredly had been a rich one. No one ever could trail him or get a word out of him. Time passed. A few years made him old. During this time he conceived a liking for a young man and eventually confided that someday he would tell him the secret of his gold mine. He had drawn a map of the landmarks adjacent to his mine, but he was careful not to put on paper directions how to get there. It chanced that he suddenly fell ill and saw his end was near. Then he summoned this young man who had been so fortunate as to win his regard. Now this individual was a ne'er-do-well, and upon this occasion of his being summoned he was half drunk. The dying Dutchman produced his map and gave it with verbal directions to the young man. Then he died. When the recipient of this fortune recovered from the effects of liquor, he could not remember all the Dutchman had told him. He tortured himself to recall names and places. The mine was up in the Superstition Mountains. He never remembered quite where. He never found the lost mine, although he spent his life at it and died trying. The story passed into legend as the Lost Dutchman Mine.

Tappan had his try at finding it. For him the shifting sands of the southern California desert or even the barren and desolate Death Valley were preferable to this Superstition Range. It was a harder country than the Pinacate of Sonora. Tappan hated cactus, and the Superstitions were full of it. The huge saguaro stood everywhere, the giant cacti of the Arizona plateaus, tall like branchless trees, fluted and columnar, beautiful and fascinating to gaze upon, but obnoxious to prospector and burro.

One day from a north slope, Tappan saw afar a wonderful country of black timber that zigzagged for many miles in yellow winding ramparts of rock. This he took to be the rim of the Mogollon Mesa, one of Arizona's freaks of nature. Something called to Tappan. He was forever victim to yearnings for the unattainable. He was tired of heat, glare, dust, bare rock, and thorny cactus. The Lost Dutchman gold mine was

31

a myth. Besides, he did not need any more gold.

Next morning Tappan packed Jenet and worked down off the north slope of the Superstition Range. That night about sunset he made camp on the bank of a clear brook, with grass and wood in abundance—such a campsite as a prospector dreamed of but seldom found.

Before dark Jenet's long ears told of the advent of strangers. A man and a woman rode down the trail into Tappan's camp. They had poor horses and led a pack animal that appeared too old and weak to bear up under even the meager pack he carried.

"Howdy," said the man.

Tappan rose from his task to his lofty height and returned the greeting. The man was middle-aged, swarthy and rugged, a mountaineer, with something about him that relegated him to the men of the open whom Tappan instinctively distrusted. The woman was under thirty, comely in a full-blown way, with rich brown skin and glossy dark hair. She had wide-open black eyes that bent a curious, possession-taking gaze upon Tappan. "Care if we camp with you?" she inquired, and she smiled.

That smile changed Tappan's habit and conviction of a lifetime. "No, indeed. Reckon I'd like a little company," he said.

Very probably Jenet did not understand Tappan's words, but she dropped one ear, and walked out of camp to the green bank.

"Thanks, stranger," replied the woman. "That grub shore smells good." She hesitated a moment, evidently waiting to catch her companion's eye, then she continued. "My name's Madge Beam. He's my brother, Jake. Who might you happen to be?"

"I'm Tappan, lone prospector, as you see," replied Tappan.

Tappan's Burro

"Tappan! What's your front handle?" she queried.

"Fact is, I don't remember," replied Tappan, as he brushed a huge hand through his shaggy hair.

"Ahuh? Any name's good enough."

When she dismounted, Tappan saw that she was a tall, lithe figure, garbed in rider's overalls and boots. She unsaddled her horse with a dexterity of long practice. She carried the saddlebags over to the spot Jake had selected to throw the pack.

Tappan heard them talking in low tones. How strange he felt it was that he did not react as usual to an invasion of his privacy and solitude! Tappan had thrilled under those black eyes, and now a queer sensation of the unusual rose in him. Bending over his campfire tasks, he pondered this and that, but mostly the sense of the nearness of a woman. Like most desert men, Tappan knew little of women. He had never felt the necessity of a woman. A few that he might have been drawn to had gone out of his wandering life as quickly as they had entered it. No woman had ever made him feel as this Madge Beam. In evidence of Tappan's preoccupation was the fact that he burned his first batch of biscuits, and Tappan felt proud of his culinary ability. He was on his knees, mixing more flour and water, when the woman spoke from right behind him.

"Tough luck you browned the first pan," she said. "But it's a good turn for your burro. That shore is a burro. Biggest I ever saw." Thereupon she picked up the burned biscuits and tossed them over to Jenet, then she came back to Tappan's side, rather embarrassingly close. "Tappan, I know how I'll eat, so I ought to ask you to let me help," she said with a laugh.

"No, I don't need any," replied Tappan. "You sit down on my roll of beddin' there. Must be tired, aren't you?"

33

"Not so very," she returned. "That is, I'm not tired of ridin'." She spoke the second part of this reply in a lower tone.

Tappan looked up from his task. The woman had washed her face, brushed her hair, and had put on a skirt—a singularly attractive change. Tappan thought her younger. She was the handsomest woman he had ever seen. The look of her made him clumsy. What eyes she had! They looked through him. Tappan returned to his task, wondering if he was right in his feeling that she wanted to be friendly.

"Jake an' I drove a bunch of cattle to Maricopa," she said. "We sold it, an' Jake gambled away most of the money. I couldn't get what I wanted."

"Too bad! So you're ranchers. Once thought I'd like that. Fact is, down here at Globe a few weeks ago I came near buyin' some rancher out an' tryin' the game."

"You did?" Her query had a low, quick eagerness that somehow thrilled Tappan, but he did not look up. "I'm a wanderer. I'd never do on a ranch."

"But if you had a woman?" Her laugh was subtle and gay.

"A woman! For me? Oh, Lord, no!"

"Why not? Are you a woman hater?"

"I can't say that," replied Tappan soberly. "It's just...I guess...no woman would have me."

"Faint heart never won fair lady."

Tappan had no reply for that. He surely was making a mess of this second pan of biscuit dough. Manifestly the woman saw this, for, with a laugh, she plumped down on her knees in front of Tappan, and rolled up her sleeves over shapely brown arms.

"Poor man! Shore you need a woman. Let me show you," she said, and put her hands right down upon Tappan's. The touch gave him a strange thrill. He had to pull his hands

34

away, and, as he wiped them with his scarf, he looked at her. He seemed compelled to look. She was close to him now, smiling in good nature, a little scornful of man's encroachment upon the housewifely duties of a woman. A subtle something emanated from her—more than kindness or gaiety. Tappan grasped that it was just the woman of her, and it was going to his head.

"Very well, let's see you show me," he replied, as he rose to his feet.

Just then, her brother Jake strolled over, and he had a rather amused and derisive eye for his sister. "Wal, Tappan, she's not over fond of work, but I reckon she can cook," he said.

Tappan felt greatly relieved at the approach of the brother, and he fell into conversation with him, telling something of his prospecting since leaving Globe and listening to the man's cattle talk. By and by the woman called: "Come an' get it!" Then they sat down to eat, and as usual with hungry wayfarers they did not talk much until appetite was satisfied. Afterward, before the campfire, they began to talk again, Jake doing the most of it. Tappan conceived the idea that the rancher was rather curious about him and perhaps wanted to sell his ranch. The woman seemed more thoughtful, with her wide black eyes on the fire.

"Tappan, what way you travelin'?" Beam finally inquired.

"Can't say. I just worked down out of the Superstitions. Haven't any place in mind. Where does this road go?"

"To the Tonto Basin, Ever heard of it?"

"Yes, the name isn't new. What's in this basin?"

The man grunted. "Tonto once was home for the Apaches. It's now got a few sheep an' cattlemen, lots of rustlers. An', say, if you like to hunt bear an' deer, come along with us."

"Thanks. I don't know as I can," returned Tappan irreso-
lutely. He was not used to such possibilities as this suggested.

Then Madge Beam spoke up. "It's a pretty country. Wild
an' different. We live up under Mogollon Rim. There's minerals in the cañons."

Was it what was said about minerals that decided Tappan
or the look in her eyes?

Tappan's world of thought and feeling underwent as great
a change as this Tonto Basin differed from the stark desert so
long his home. The trail to the log cabin of the Beams
climbed many a ridge and slope and foothill, all covered with
manzanita, mescal, cedar, and juniper, at last reaching the
cañons of the rim where lofty pines and spruces lorded it over
the under forest of maples and oaks. Although the yellow
Mogollon Rim towered high over the site of the cabin, the al-
titude was still great, close to seven thousand feet above sea
level.

Tappan had fallen in love with this wild wooded and
cañoned country. So had Jenet. It was rather funny the way
she hung around Tappan, mornings and evenings. She ate
luxuriant grass and oak leaves until her sides bulged.

There did not appear to be any flat places in this country.
Every bench was either uphill or downhill. The Beams had no
garden or farm or ranch that Tappan could discover. They
raised a few acres of sorghum and corn. Their log cabin was
of the most primitive kind, and outfitted poorly. Madge
Beam explained that this cabin was their winter abode, and
that up on the rim they had a good house and ranch. Tappan
did not inquire closely into anything. If he had interrogated
himself, he would have found out that the reason he did not
inquire was because he feared something might remove him
from the vicinity of Madge Beam. He had thought it strange

the Beams avoided wayfarers they had met on the trail and had gone around a little hamlet Tappan had espied from a hill. Madge Beam, with woman's intuition, had read his mind and had said: "Jake doesn't get along so well with some of the villagers. An' I've no hankerin' for gun play." That explanation was sufficient for Tappan. He had lived long enough in his wandering years to appreciate that people could have reasons for being solitary.

This trip up into the rimrock country bade fairly to become Tappan's one and only adventure of the heart. It was not alone the murmuring clear brook of cold mountain water that enchanted him, nor the stately pines, nor the beautiful silver spruces, nor the wonder of the deep, yellow-walled cañons, so choked with verdure and haunted by wild creatures. He dared not face his soul and ask why this dark eyed woman sought him more and more, and grew from gay and audacious, even bantering, to sweet and melancholy, and sometimes somber as an Indian. Tappan lived in the moment.

He was aware that the few mountaineer neighbors who rode that way rather avoided contact with him. Tappan was not so dense but he saw that the Beams would rather keep him from outsiders. This was perhaps owing to their desire to sell Tappan the ranch and cattle. Jake offered to sell at what he called a low figure. Tappan thought it just as well to go out into the forest and hide his bags of gold. He did not trust Jake Beam, and liked less the looks of the men who visited this wilderness ranch. Madge Beam might be related to a rustler and be the associate of rustlers, but that did not necessarily make her a bad woman. Tappan guessed that her attitude was changing, and she seemed to require his respect; all she wanted was his admiration. Tappan's long unused deference for a woman returned to him, and he saw that Madge Beam was not used to deference. When Tappan saw that it was having some strong softening effect upon her, he redoubled his attentions. They rode and climbed and hunted together. Tappan had pitched his camp not far from the cabin, on a shaded bank of the singing brook. Madge did not leave him much to himself. She was always coming up to his camp on one pretext or another. Often she would bring two horses and make Tappan ride with her. Some of these occasions, Tappan saw, happened to occur while visitors were at the cabin. In three weeks Madge Beam changed from the bold and careless woman who had ridden down into his camp that sunset to a serious and appealing woman, growing more careful of her person and adornment, and manifestly bearing a burden on her mind.

October came. In the morning white frost glistened on the split-wood shingles of the cabin. The sun soon melted it, and grew warm. The afternoons were still and smoky, melancholy with the enchantment of Indian summer. Tappan hunted wild turkeys and deer with Madge, and revived his boyish love of such pursuits. Madge appeared to be a woman of the woods and had no mean skill with the rifle.

One day they were high on the Mogollon Rim with the great timbered basin at their feet. They had come up to hunt deer, but got no farther than the wonderful promontory where before they had lingered.

"Somethin' will happen to us today," Madge Beam said enigmatically.

Tappan never had been much of a talker, but he could listen. The woman unburdened herself this day. She wanted freedom, happiness, a home away from this lonely country, and all the heritage of woman. She confessed it broodingly, passionately, and Tappan recognized truth when he heard it. He was ready to do all in his power for this woman and believed she knew it, but words and acts of sentiment came hard to him.

"Are you goin' to buy Jake's ranch?" she asked.

"I don't know. Is there any hurry?" returned Tappan.

"I reckon not. But I think I'll settle that," she said decisively.

"How so?"

"Well, Jake hasn't got any ranch," she answered, and added hastily, "no clear title, I mean. He's only homesteaded one hundred an' sixty acres, an' hasn't proved up on it yet. But don't you say I told you."

"Was Jake aimin' to be crooked?"

"I reckon...an' I was willin' at first. But not now."

Tappan did not speak at once. He saw the woman was in one of her brooding moods. Besides, he wanted to weigh her words. How significant they were! Today more than ever before she had let down. Humility and simplicity seemed to abide with her, and her brooding boded a storm. Tappan's heart swelled in his broad breast. Was life going to dawn rosy and bright for the lonely prospector? He had money to make a home for this woman. What lay in the balance of the hour? Tappan waited, slowly realizing the charged atmosphere.

Madge's somber eyes gazed out over the great void, but full of thought and passion, as they were, they did not see the beauty of that scene. Tappan saw it, and in some strange sense the color and wildness and sublimity seemed the expression of a new state of his heart. Under him sheered down the ragged and cracked cliffs of the Mogollon Rim, yellow and gold and gray, full of caves and crevices, ledges for eagles and niches for lions, a thousand feet down to the upward edge of the long green slopes and cañons, and so on down and down into the abyss of forested ravine and ridge, rolling league on league away to the encompassing barrier of purple mountain ranges. The thickets in the cañons called Tappan's eye back to linger there. How different from the scenes that had used to be perpetually in his sight! What riot of color! The tips of the green pines, the crests of the silver spruces, waved about masses of vivid gold of aspen trees, and wonderful cerise and flaming red of maples, and crags of yellow rock covered with the bronze of frost-bitten sumac. Here was autumn and the colors of Tappan's favorite season. From below breathed up the roar of plunging brook; an eagle screeched his wild call; an elk bugled his piercing blast. From the rim wisps of pine needles blew away on the breeze and fell into the void. A wild country, colorful, beautiful, bountiful! Tappan imagined he could quell his wandering spirit here, with this dark-eyed woman by his side. Never before had nature so called him. Here was not the cruelty of the flinty hardness of the desert. The air was keen and sweet, cold in the shade, warm in the sun. A fragrance of balsam and spruce, spiced with pine, made his breathing a thing of difficulty and delight. How for so many years had he endured vast open spaces without such eye-soothing trees as these? Tappan's back rested against a huge pine that tipped the rim and had stood there, stronger than the storms, for many a hundred years. The rock of the promontory was covered with soft, brown mats of pine needles. A juniper tree, with its bright green foliage and lilac-colored berries, grew near the pine and helped to form a secluded little nook, fragrant and somehow haunting. The woman's dark head was close to Tappan, as she sat with her elbows on her knees, gazing down into the basin. Tappan saw the strained tensity of her posture, the heaving of her full bosom. He wondered, while his own emotions, so long deadened, roused to the suspense of that hour.

Suddenly she flung herself into Tappan's arms. The act amazed him. It seemed to have both the passion of a woman

40

and the shame of a girl. Before she hid her face on Tappan's breast, he saw how the rich brown had paled, and then flamed.

"Tappan...! Take me away...take me away from here ...from that life down there," she cried in smothered voice.

"Madge, you mean take you away...and marry you?" he replied.

"Oh, yes...yes...marry me, if you love me. I don't see how you can...but you do, don't you? Say you do."

"I reckon that's what ails me, Madge," he replied simply.

"*Say* so, then!" she burst out.

"All right, I do," said Tappan with heavy breath. "Madge, words don't come easy for me...but I think you're wonderful, an' I want you. I haven't dared hope for that, till now. I'm only a wanderer. But it'd be heaven to have you...my wife...an' make a home for you."

"Oh...oh!" she returned wildly, and lifted herself to cling around his neck and to kiss him. "You give me joy...oh, Tappan, I love you. I never loved any man before. I know now ...an' I'm not wonderful...or good. But I love you."

The fire of her lips and the clasp of her arms worked havoc in Tappan. No woman had ever loved him, let alone embraced him. To awake suddenly to such rapture as this made him strong and rough in his response. Then all at once she seemed to collapse in his arms and began to weep. He feared he had offended or hurt her and was clumsy in his contrition.

Presently she replied. "Pretty soon...I'll make you beat me. It's your love...your honesty...that's shamed me. Tappan, I was party to a trick to...sell you a worthless ranch. I agreed to...try to make you love me...to fool you ...cheat you. But I've fallen in love with you, an', my God, I care more for your love...your respect...than for my life. I can't go on with it. I've double-crossed Jake, an' all of them.

41

Dear, am I worth lovin'? Am I worth havin'?"

"More than ever, dear," he said.

"You will take me away?"

"Anywhere…anytime, the sooner the better."

She kissed him passionately, and then, dislodging herself from his arms, she knelt and gazed earnestly at him. "I've not told all. I will someday. But I swear now on my very soul… I'll be what you think me."

"Madge, you needn't say all that. If you love me…it's enough. More than I ever dreamed of."

"You're a man. Oh, why didn't I meet you when I was eighteen instead of now…twenty-eight, an' all that between. But enough. A new life begins here for us. We must plan."

"You make the plans, an' I'll act on them."

For a moment she was tense and silent, head lowered, hands shut tightly. Then she spoke. "Tonight we'll slip away. You make a light pack that'll go on your saddle. I'll do the same. We'll run off…ride out of the country."

Tappan tried to think, but the swirl of his mind made any reasoning difficult. This dark-eyed, full-bosomed woman loved him, had surrendered herself, asked only his protection. The thing seemed marvelous. She knelt there, those dark eyes on him, infinitely more appealing than ever, haunting with some mystery of sadness and fear he could not divine.

Suddenly Tappan remembered Jenet. "I must take Jenet," he said.

That startled her. "Jenet…who's she?"

"My burro."

"Your burro. You can't travel fast with that pack beast. We'll be trailed, an' we'll have to go fast. You can't take the burro."

Tappan's Burro

Then Tappan was startled. "What! Can't take Jenet? Why, I...I couldn't get along without her."

"Nonsense. What's a burro? We must ride fast...do you hear?"

"Madge, I'm afraid I...I must take Jenet with me," he said soberly.

"It's impossible. I can't go if you take her. I tell you, I've got to get away. If you want me, you'll have to leave your precious Jenet behind."

Tappan bowed his head to the inevitable. After all, Jenet was only a beast of burden. She would run wild on the ridges and soon forget him and have no need of him. Something strained in Tappan's breast. He had to see clearly here. This woman was worth more than all else to him. "I'm stupid, dear," he said. "You see I never before ran off with a beautiful woman. Of course, my burro must be left behind."

Elopement, if such it could be called, was easy for them. Tappan did not understand why Madge wanted to be so secret about it. Was she not free? But then he reflected that he did not know the circumstances she feared. Besides, he did not care. Possession of the woman was enough.

Tappan made his small pack, the weight of which was considerable owing to his bags of gold. This he tied on his saddle. It bothered him to leave most of his new outfit scattered around his camp. What would Jenet think of that? He looked for her, but for once she did not come in at mealtime. Tappan thought this was singular. He could not remember when Jenet had been far from his camp at sunset. Somehow Tappan was glad.

After he had his supper, he left his utensils and supplies as they happened to be and strode away under the trees to the trysting-place where he was to meet Madge. To his surprise she came before dark, and, unused as he was to the complexity and emotional nature of a woman, he saw that she was strangely agitated. Her face was pale. Almost a fury burned in her black eyes. When she came up to Tappan and embraced him almost fiercely, he felt that he was about to learn more of the nature of womankind. She thrilled him to his depths.

"Lead out the horses an' don't make any noise," she whispered.

Tappan complied, and soon he was mounted, riding behind her on the trail. It surprised him that she headed downcountry and traveled fast. Moreover, she kept to a trail that continually grew rougher. They came to a road, which she crossed, and kept on through darkness and brush so thick that Tappan could not see the least sign of a trail. At length, anyone could have seen that Madge had lost her bearings. She appeared to know the direction she wanted, but traveling upon it was impossible owing to the increasingly cut-up and brushy ground. They had to turn back and seemed to be hours finding the road. Once Tappan fancied he heard the *thud* of hoofs other than those made by their own horses. Here Madge acted strangely, and, where she had been obsessed by a desire to hurry, she now seemed to have grown weary. She turned her horse south on the road. Tappan was thus able to ride beside her, but they talked very little. He was satisfied with the fact of being with her on the way out of the country. Woman-like perhaps, she had begun to feel the pangs of remorse. Sometime in the night they reached an old log shack by the side of the road. Here Tappan suggested they halt, and get some sleep before dawn. The morrow would mean a long hard day.

"Yes, tomorrow will be hard," replied Madge, as she faced Tappan in the gloom. He could see her big dark eyes on him. Her tone was not one of a hopeful woman. Tappan pondered over this, but he could not understand because he had no idea how a woman ought to act under such circumstances. Madge Beam was a creature of moods. Only the day before, on the ride down from the rim, she had told him with a laugh that she was likely to love him madly one moment and scratch his eyes out the next. How could he know what to make of her? Still, an uneasy feeling began to stir in Tappan.

They dismounted and unsaddled the horses. Tappan took his pack and put it inside. Something frightened the horses. They bolted down the road.

"Head them off," cried the woman hoarsely.

Even on the instant her voice sounded strained to Tappan, as if she were choked, but, realizing the absolute necessity of catching the horses, he set off down the road on a run. He soon succeeded in heading off the horse he had ridden. The other one, however, was contrary and cunning. When Tappan would endeavor to get ahead of it, it would trot briskly on. Yet it did not go so fast but what Tappan felt sure he would soon catch it. Thus, walking and running, he got quite a long distance from the cabin before he realized that he could not head off this wary horse. Much perturbed in mind Tappan hurried back.

Upon reaching the cabin, Tappan called to Madge. No answer! He could not see her in the gloom or the horse he had driven back. Only silence brooded there. Tappan called again. Still no answer! Perhaps Madge had succumbed to the weariness and was asleep. A search of the cabin and the vicinity failed to yield any sign of her, but it disclosed the fact that Tappan's pack was gone.

Suddenly he sat down, quite overcome. He had been duped. What a fierce pang tore his heart! But it was for loss of the woman—not the gold. He was stunned and sick with bitter misery. Only then did Tappan realize the meaning of love and what it had done to him. The night wore on, and he sat there in the dark and cold and stillness until the gray dawn told him of the coming of day.

The light showed his saddle lying where he had left it. Nearby lay one of Madge's gloves. Tappan's keen eye sighted a bit of paper sticking out of the glove. He picked it up. It was a leaf out of a little book he had seen her carry, and upon it was written in lead pencil:

I am Jake's wife, not his sister. I double-crossed him and ran off with you and would have gone to hell for you. But Jake and his gang suspected me. They were close on our tail. I couldn't shake them. So here I chased off the horses and sent you after them. It was the only way I could save your life.

Tappan tracked the thieves to Globe. There he learned they had gone to Phoenix—three men and one woman. Tappan had money on his person. He bought horse and saddle, and, setting out for Phoenix, he let his passion to kill grow with the miles and hours. At Phoenix he learned Beam had cashed the gold—twelve thousand dollars. So much of a fortune! Tappan's fury grew. The gang separated here. Beam and his wife took the stage for Tucson. Tappan had his trouble in trailing their movements. Gambling dives and inns and freighting posts and stage drivers told the story of the Beams and their ill-gotten gold. They went on down into Tappan's country, to Yuma, and El Cajon, and then San Diego in California. Here Tappan lost track of the woman. He could not find that she had left San Diego, nor any trace of her there. But Jake Beam had killed a Mexican in a brawl and had fled across the line.

Tappan gave up the chase of Beam for the time being and lent his efforts to finding the woman. He had no resentment toward Madge. He only loved her. All that winter he searched San Diego. He made of himself a peddler as a ruse to visit houses, but he never found a trace of her. In the spring he wandered back to Yuma, raking over the old clues, and so on back to Tucson and Phoenix.

This year of dream and love and passion and despair and hate made Tappan old. His great strength and endurance were not yet impaired, but something wonderful died out of him. One day he remembered Jenet. "My burro!" he soliloquized. "I had forgotten her...Jenet!"

Then it seemed a thousand impulses merged into one and drove him to face the long road toward the rimrock country. To remember Jenet was to grow doubtful. Of course, she would be gone. Stolen or dead or wandered off! But then, who could tell what Jenet might do? Tappan was both called and driven. He was a poor wanderer again. His outfit was a pack he carried on his shoulder. But while he could walk, he would keep on until he reached that last camp where he had deserted Jenet.

October was coloring the cañon slopes when he reached the shadow of the great wall of yellow rock. There was no cabin where the Beams had lived—or claimed they lived—or a fallen ruin, crushed by snow. Tappan saw the signs of a severe winter and heavy snowfall. No horse or cattle tracks showed on the trails.

To his amazement, his camp was much as he had left it. The stove fireplace, the iron pots appeared to be where he had left them. The boxes that had held his supplies were lying here and there, and his canvas tarpaulin, little the worse for wear or the elements, lay on the ground under the pine where he had slept. If any man had visited this camp in a year, he had left no sign of it.

Suddenly Tappan espied a hoof track in the dust. A small

track—almost oval in shape—fresh! Tappan thrilled through all his being. "Jenet's track, so help me God," he murmured.

He found more of them, made that morning, and, keen now as never before on her trail, he set out to find her. The tracks led up the cañon. Tappan came out into a little grassy clearing, and there stood Jenet, as he had seen her thousands of times. She had both long ears up high. She seemed to stare out of that meek, gray face, and then one of the long ears flopped over and drooped. Such perhaps was the expression of her recognition.

Tappan strode up to her. "Jenet...old girl...You hung 'round camp...waitin' for me, didn't you?" he said huskily, and his big hands fondled her long ears.

Yes, she had waited. She, too, had grown old. She was gray. The winter had been hard. What had she lived on when the snow lay so deep? There were lion scratches on her back and scars on her legs. She had fought for her life.

"Jenet, a man can never always tell about a burro," said Tappan. "I trained you to hang 'round camp an' wait till I came back. Tappan's burro, the desert rats used to say! An' they'd laugh when I bragged how you'd stick to me where most men would quit. But brag as I did, I never knew you, Jenet. An' I left you...an' forgot. Jenet, it takes a human bein'...a man...a woman...to be faithless. An' it takes a dog or a horse or a burro to be great. Beasts? I wonder now. ...Well, old pard, we're goin' down the trail together, an' from this day on Tappan begins to pay his debt."

III

Tappan never again had the old wanderlust for the stark and naked desert. Something had transformed him. The green and fragrant forests and brown-aisled, pine-matted woodlands, the craggy promontories and the great colored cañons, the cold granite-water springs of the Tonto seemed vastly preferable to the heat and dust and glare and the emptiness of the wastelands. But there was more. The ghost of his strange and only love kept pace with his wandering steps, a spirit that hovered with him as his shadow. Madge Beam, whatever she had been, had showed to him the power of love to refine and ennoble. Somehow he felt closer to her here in the cliff country where his passion had been born. Somehow she seemed nearer to him here than in all those places he had tracked her.

So, from a prospector searching for gold, Tappan became a hunter seeking only the means to keep soul and body together. All he cared for was his faithful burro Jenet, and the loneliness and silence of the forestland. He learned that the Tonto was a hard country in many ways, and bitterly so in winter. Down in the brakes of the basin it was mild in winter, the snow did not lay long, and ice seldom formed. But up on the rim, where Tappan always lingered as long as possible, the storm king of the north held full sway. Fifteen feet of snow and zero weather was the rule in dead of winter.

An old native once said to Tappan: "See hyar, friend, I reckon you'd better not get caught up in the rimrock country in one of our big storms. Fer if you do, you'll never get out."

It was a way of Tappan's to follow his inclinations, regardless of advice. He had weathered the terrible midnight storm

49

Zane Grey

of hot wind in Death Valley. What were snow and cold to
him? Late autumn on the Mogollon Rim was the most perfect
and beautiful of seasons. He had seen the forestland brown
and darkly green one day, and the next burdened with white
snow. What a transfiguration! Then, when the sun loosened
the white mantling on the pines, and they had shed their bur-
dens in drifting dust of white and rainbowed mists of melting
snow, and the avalanches sliding off the branches, there
would be left only the wonderful white floor of the woodland.
The great rugged brown tree trunks appeared mightier and
statelier in the contrast, and the green of foliage, the russet of
oak leaves, the gold of the aspens turned the forest into a
world enchanting to the desert-scared eyes of this wanderer
of the wasteland.

With Tappan the years sped by. His mind grew old faster
than his body. Every season saw him lonelier. He had a
feeling, a vague illusive thing, that instead of his bones
bleaching on the desert sands, they would mingle with the
pine mats and the soft fragrant moss of the forest. The idea
was pleasant to Tappan.

One afternoon he was camped in Pine Cañon, a timber-
sloped gorge far back from the rim. November was well on.
The fall had been singularly open and fair, with not a single
storm. A few natives happening across Tappan had remarked
casually that such falls sometimes were not to be trusted.

This late afternoon was one of Indian summer beauty
and warmth. The blue haze in the cañon was not just the
blue smoke from Tappan's campfire. In a narrow park of
grass not far from camp, Jenet grazed peacefully with elk
and deer. Tappan never heard the sound of a rifle shot.
Wild turkeys lingered there, to seek their winter quarters
down in the basin. Gray squirrels and red squirrels barked
and frisked, and dropped the pine and spruce cones, with

50

thud and *thump,* on all the slopes.

Before dark a stranger strode into Tappan's camp, a big man, of middle age, whose magnificent physique impressed even Tappan. He was a rugged, bearded, giant, wide-eyed and of pleasant face. He had no outfit, no horse, not even a gun.

"Lucky for me I smelled your smoke," he said. "Two days for me without grub."

"Howdy, stranger," was Tappan's greeting. "Are you lost?"

"Yes an' no. I could find my way out down over the Mogollon Rim, but it's not healthy down there for me. So I'm hittin' north."

"Where's your horse and pack?"

"I reckon they're with the gang that took more of a fancy to them than me."

"Ahuh...you're welcome here, stranger," replied Tappan. "I'm Tappan."

"Ha! Heard of you. I'm Jess Blade, of anywhere. An' I'll say, I was an honest man till I hit the Tonto."

His laugh was frank for all its note of grimness. Tappan liked the man and sensed one who would be a good friend and bad foe.

"Come an' eat. My supplies are peterin' out, but there's plenty of meat."

Blade ate, indeed as a man starved, and did not seem to care if Tappan's supplies were low. He did not talk. After the meal, he craved a pipe and tobacco. Then he smoked in silence, in slow-realizing content. The morrow had no fears for him. The flickering, ruddy light from the campfire shown on his strong face. Tappan saw in him the drifter, the drinker, the brawler, a man with good in him, but over whom evil passion or temper dominated. Presently he smoked the pipe out, and with reluctant hand knocked out the ashes and returned it to Tappan.

"I reckon I've some news thet'd interest you," he said.

"You have?" queried Tappan.

"Yes, if you're the Tappan who tried to run off with Jake Beam's wife."

"Well, I'm that Tappan. But I'd like to say I didn't know she was married."

"Shore. I remember. So does everybody in the Tonto. You were just meat for thet Beam gang. They had played the trick before. But accordin' to what I hear, thet trick was the last fer Madge Beam. She never came back to this country. An' Jake Beam, when he was drunk, owned up thet she'd left him in California. Some hint at worse. Fer Jake Beam came back a harder man. Even his gang said thet."

"Is he in the Tonto now?" queried Tappan, with a thrill of fire along his veins.

"Yep, thar fer keeps," replied Blade grimly. "Somebody shot him."

"Ahuh!" exclaimed Tappan with a deep breath of relief. There came a sudden check to the heat of his blood.

After that, there was a long silence. Tappan dreamed of the woman who had loved him. Blade brooded over the campfire. The wind moaned fitfully in the lofty pines on the slope. A wolf mourned as if in hunger. The stars appeared to obscure their radiance in haze.

"Reckon thet wind sounds like storm," observed Blade presently.

"I've heard it for weeks now," replied Tappan.

"Are you a woodsman?"

"No, I'm a desert man."

"Wal, you take my hunch and hit the trail fer low country."

This was well-meant and probably sound advice, but it alienated Tappan. He had really liked this hearty-voiced stranger. Tappan thought moodily of his slowly in-growing mind, of the narrowness of his soul. He was past interest in his fellow men. He lived with a dream. The only living creature he loved was a lop-eared lazy burro, growing old in contentment. Nevertheless, that night Tappan shared one of his two blankets.

In the morning the gray dawn broke, and the sun rose without its brightness of gold. There was a haze over the blue sky. Thin, swift-moving clouds scudded up out of the south-west. The wind was chilled, the forest shaggy and dark, the birds and squirrels were silent.

"Wal, you'll break camp today," asserted Blade.

"Nope. I'll stick it out yet a while," returned Tappan.

"But, man, you might get snowed in, an' up hyar thet's serious."

"Ahuh! Well, it won't bother me, an' there's nothin' holdin' you."

"Tappan, it's four days' walk down out of this woods. If a big snow set in, how'd I make it?"

"Then you'd better go out over the rim," suggested Tappan.

"No. I'll take my chance the other way. But are you meanin' you'd rather not have me with you? Fer you can't stay hyar."

Tappan was in a quandary. Some instinct bade him tell the man to go, not empty-handed, but to go! But this was selfish and entirely unlike Tappan, as he remembered himself of old. Finally he spoke. "You're welcome to half my outfit...go or stay."

"Thet's mighty square of you, Tappan," responded the other feelingly. "Have you a burro you'll give me?"

"No, I've only one."

"Ha! Then I'll have to stick with you till you leave."

No more was said. They had breakfast in a strange silence. The wind brooded its secret in the treetops. Tappan's burro strolled into camp and caught the stranger's eye.

"Wal, thet's shore a fine burro," he observed. "Never seen the like!"

Tappan performed his camp tasks. Then there was nothing to do but sit around the fire. Blade evidently waited for the increasing menace of the storm to rouse Tappan to decision, but the graying over of sky and the increase of wind did not affect Tappan. What did he wait for? The truth of his thoughts was that he did not like the way Jenet remained in camp. She was waiting to be packed. She knew they ought to go. Tappan yielded to a perverse devil of stubbornness. The wind brought a cold mist, then a flurry of wet snow. Tappan gathered firewood, a large quantity. Blade saw this and gave voice to earnest fears, but Tappan paid no heed. By nightfall, sleet and snow began to fall steadily. The men fashioned a rude shack of spruce boughs, ate their supper, and went to bed early.

It worried Tappan that Jenet stayed right in camp. He lay awake a long time. The wind rose and moaned through the forest. The sleet failed, and a soft steady downfall of snow gradually set in. Tappan fell asleep. When he awoke, it was to see a forest of white. The trees were mantled with blankets of wet snow—the ground covered two feet on a level. The clouds appeared to be gone, the sky was blue, the storm over. The sun came up warm and bright.

"It'll all go in a day," said Tappan.

"If this was early October, I'd agree with you," replied Blade. "But it's only makin' fer another storm. Can't you hear thet wind?"

Tappan only heard the whispers of his dream. By noon the

snow was melting off the pines, and rainbows shone everywhere. Little patches of snow began to drop off the south
branches of the pines and spruces, and then larger patches,
until by mid-afternoon white streams and avalanches were
falling everywhere. All of the snow, except in shaded places
on the north sides of trees, went that day, and half of that on
the ground. Next day it thinned out more, until Jenet was
finding the grass and moss again. That afternoon the telltale
thin clouds raced up out of the southwest, and the wind
moaned its menace.

"Tappan, let's pack an' hit it out of hyar," appealed Blade
anxiously. "I know this country. Mebbe I'm wrong, of
course, but it feels like storm. Winter's comin' shore."

"Let her come," replied Tappan imperturbably.

"Say, do you want to get snowed in?" demanded Blade,
out of patience.

"I might like a little spell of it, seein' it'd be new to me," replied Tappan.

"But, man, if you ever get snowed in hyar, you can't get
out."

"That burro of mine could get me out."

"You're crazy. Thet burro couldn't go a hundred feet.
What's more, you'd have to kill her an' eat her."

Tappan bent a strange gaze upon his companion, but
made no reply. Blade began to pace up and down the small
bare patch of ground before the campfire. Manifestly he was
in a serious predicament. That day he seemed subtly to
change, as did Tappan. Both answered to their peculiar instincts, Blade to that of self-preservation, and Tappan to
something like indifference. Tappan held fate in defiance.
What more could happen to him?

Blade broke out again, in eloquent persuasion, giving
proof of their peril, and from that he passed to amazement,

55

and then to strident anger. He cursed Tappan for a nature-loving idiot. "An' I'll tell you what," he ended. "When mornin' comes, I'll take some of your grub an' hit it out of hyar, storm or no storm."

But long before dawn broke that resolution of Blade's became impracticable. Both were awakened by the roar of a storm through the forest, no longer a moan, but a marching roar with now a crash, and then a shriek of gale! By the light of the smoldering campfire Tappan saw a whirling pall of snow, great flakes as large as feathers. Morning disclosed the setting in of a fierce mountain storm, with two feet of snow already on the ground, and the forest lost in a blur of white.

"I was wrong!" called Tappan to his companion. "What's best to do now?"

"You damned fool!" yelled Blade. "We've got to keep from freezin' and starvin' till the storm ends an' a crust comes on the snow."

For three days and three nights the blizzard continued, unabated in its fury. It took the men hours to keep a space cleared for their campsite, which Jenet shared with them. On the fourth day the storm ceased, the clouds broke away, the sun came out, and the temperature dropped to zero. Snow on the level just topped Tappan's lofty stature, and in drifts it was ten and fifteen feet deep. Winter had set in with a vengeance. The forest became a solemn, still, white world. But now Tappan had no time to dream. Dry firewood was hard to find under the snow. It was possible to cut down one of the dead trees on the slope, but impossible to pack sufficient wood to the camp. They had to burn green wood. Then the fashioning of snowshoes took much time. Tappan had no knowledge of such footgear. He could only help Blade. The men were encouraged by the piercing cold forming a crust on the snow. But just as they were about to pack and venture forth, the weather moderated, the crust refused to hold their weight, and another foot of snow fell.

"Why in hell didn't you kill an elk?" demanded Blade sullenly. He had changed from friendly to darkly sinister. He knew the peril, and he loved life. "Now we'll have to kill an' eat your precious Jenet. An' mebbe she won't furnish meat enough to last till this snow weather stops an' a good freeze'll make travelin' possible."

"Blade, you shut up about killin' an' eatin' my burro Jenet," returned Tappan in a voice that silenced the other.

Thus instinctively these men became enemies. Blade thought only of himself. For himself, Tappan had not one thought. Tappan's supplies ran low. All the bacon and coffee were gone. There was only a small haunch of venison, a bag of beans, a sack of flour, and a small quantity of salt left.

"If a crust freezes on the snow an' we can pack thet flour, we'll get out alive," said Blade. "But we can't take the burro."

Another day of bright sunshine softened the snow on the southern exposures, and a night of piercing cold froze a crust that would bear the quick step of a man.

"It's our only chance...an' damned slim at thet," declared Blade.

Tappan allowed Blade to choose the time and method and supplies for the start to get out of the forest. They cooked all the beans and divided them in two sacks. Then they baked about four pounds of biscuits for each of them. Blade showed his cunning when he chose the small bag of salt for himself and let Tappan take the tobacco. This quantity of food and a blanket for each, Blade declared, was all they could pack. They argued over the guns, and in the end Blade compromised on the rifle, agreeing to let Tappan carry that on the possible chance of killing a deer or elk. When this matter had been decided, Blade significantly began putting on his rude

57

snowshoes that had been constructed from pieces of Tappan's boxes and straps and burlap sacks.

"Reckon they won't last long," muttered Blade.

Meanwhile, Tappan fed Jenet some biscuits, and then began to strap a tarpaulin on her back.

"What ya doin?" queried Blade suddenly.

"Gettin' Jenet ready," replied Tappan.

"Ready...fer what?"

"Why, to go with us."

"Hell!" shouted Blade, and he threw up his hands in helpless rage.

Tappan felt a depth stirred within him. He lost his late taciturnity and his silent aloofness fell away from him. Blade seemed on the moment no longer an enemy. He loomed as an aid to the saving of Jenet. Tappan burst into speech. "I can't go without her. It'd never enter my head. Jenet's mother was a good faithful burro. I saw Jenet born way down there on the Rio Colorado. She wasn't strong, an' I had to wait for her to be able to walk. She grew up. Her mother died, an' Jenet an' me packed it alone. She wasn't no ordinary burro. She learned all I taught her. She was different. But I treated her same as any burro, an' she grew with the years. Desert men said there never was such a burro as Jenet. Called her Tappan's burro, an' tried to borrow an' buy an' steal her. How many times in ten years Jenet has done me a good turn I can't remember. But she saved my life. She dragged me out of Death Valley. An' then I forgot my debt. I ran off with a woman an' left Jenet to wait as she had been trained to wait. I knew she'd wait at that camp till I came back. She'd have starved there! Well, I got back in time...an' now I'll not leave her here. It may be strange to you, Blade, me carin' this way. Jenet's only a burro. But I won't leave her."

"Man, you talk like thet lazy lop-eared burro was a

58

woman," declared Blade in disgusted astonishment.

"I don't know women, but I reckon Jenet's more faithful than most of them."

"Wal, of all the stark starin' fools I ever run into, you're the worst."

"Fool or not, I know what I'll do," retorted Tappan. The softer mood left him swiftly.

"Haven't you sense enough to see thet we can't travel with your burro?" queried Blade, patiently controlling his temper. "She has little hoofs, sharp as knives. She'll cut through the crust. She'll break through in places, an' we'll have to stop to haul her out...mebbe break through ourselves. That would make us longer gettin' out."

"Long or short, we'll take her."

Then Blade confronted Tappan as if suddenly unmasking his true meaning. His patient explanation meant nothing. Under no circumstances would he ever have consented to an attempt to take Jenet out of that snow-bound wilderness. His eyes gleamed. "We've a hard pull to get out alive. An' hard-workin' men in winter must have meat to eat."

Tappan slowly straightened up to look at the speaker. "What do you mean?"

For answer, Blade jerked his hand backward and downward, and, when it swung into sight again, it held Tappan's worn and shining rifle. Blade, with deliberate force that showed the nature of the man, worked the lever and threw a shell into the magazine, all the while his eyes fastened on Tappan. His face seemed that of another man, evil, relentless, inevitable in his spirit to preserve his own life at any cost. "I mean to kill your burro," he said in voice that suited his look and manner.

"No!" cried Tappan, shocked into an instant of appeal.

"Yes, I am, an' I'll bet, by God, before we get out of hyar

you'll be glad to eat some of her meat!"

That roused the slow-gathering might of Tappan's wrath. "I'd starve to death before I'd...I'd kill that burro, let alone eat her."

"Starve and be damned!" shouted Blade, yielding to rage.

Jenet stood right behind Tappan, in her posture of contented repose, with one long ear hanging down over her gray, meek face.

"You'll have to kill me first," answered Tappan sharply.

"I'm good fer anythin'...if you push me," returned Blade stridently.

As he stepped aside, evidently so he could have unobstructed aim at Jenet, Tappan leaped forward and knocked up the rifle as it was discharged. The bullet sped harmlessly over Jenet. Tappan heard it *thud* into a tree. Blade uttered a curse. As he lowered the rifle, in sudden deadly intent Tappan grasped the barrel with his left hand. Then, clenching his right, he struck Blade a sudden blow in the face. Only Blade's hold on the rifle prevented him from falling. Blood streamed from his nose and mouth. He bellowed in hoarse fury: "I'll kill you fer thet!"

Tappan opened his clenched teeth. "No, Blade...you're not man enough."

Then began a terrific struggle for possession of the rifle. Tappan beat at Blade's face with his sledge-hammer fist, and the strength of the other made it imperative that Blade use both hands to keep his hold on the rifle. Wrestling and pulling and jerking, the men tore around the snowy camp, scattering the campfire, knocking down the brush shelter. Blade had surrendered to a wild frenzy. He hissed his maledictions. His was the brute lust to kill an enemy that thwarted him. But Tappan was grim and terrible in his restraint. His battle was to save Jenet. Nevertheless, there mounted in him the hot

60

physical sensations of the savage. The contact of flesh, the smell and sight of Blade's blood, the violent action, the beastly mien of his foe changed the fight to one for its own sake. To conquer this foe, to rend him and beat him down, blow on blow!

Tappan felt instinctively that he was the stronger. Suddenly he exerted all his muscular force into one tremendous wrench. The rifle broke, leaving the steel barrel in his hands, the wooden stock in Blade's. It was the quicker-witted Blade who used his weapon first to advantage. One swift blow knocked down Tappan. As he was about to follow it up with another, Tappan kicked his opponent's feet from under him. Blade sprawled in the snow, but was up again as quickly as Tappan. They made at each other, Tappan waiting to strike, and Blade raining blows aimed at his head, but which Tappan contrived to receive on his arms and the rifle barrel he brandished. For a few minutes Tappan stood up under a beating that would have felled a lesser man. His own blood blinded him. Then he swung his heavy weapon. The blow broke Blade's left arm. Like a wild beast he screamed in pain, and then, without guard, rushed in, too furious for further caution. Tappan met the terrible onslaught as before and, snatching his chance, again swung the rifle barrel. This time, so supreme was the force, it battered down Blade's arm and crushed his skull. He died on his feet—ghastly and horrible change!—and, swaying backward, he fell into the upbanked wall of snow and went out of sight, except for his boots, one of which still held the crude snowshoe.

Tappan stared, slowly realizing.

"Ahuh, stranger Blade!" he ejaculated, gazing at the hole in the snowbank where his foe had disappeared. "You were goin' to kill an' eat…Tappan's burro!"

Then he sighted the bloody rifle barrel, and cast it from

him. It appeared then that he had sustained injuries that needed attention, but he could do little more than wash off the blood and bind up his head. Both arms and hands were badly bruised and beginning to swell. Fortunately no bones had been broken.

Tappan finished strapping the tarpaulin upon the burro, and, taking up both his and Blade's supply of food, he called out: "Come on, Jenet!"

Which way to go? Indeed, there was no more choice for him than there had been for Blade. Toward the Mogollon Rim the snowdrift would be deeper, and impassable. Tappan realized that the only possible chance for him was downhill. So he led Jenet out of camp without looking back once. What was it that had happened? He did not seem to be the same Tappan that had dreamily tramped into this woodland.

A deep furrow in the snow had been made by the men packing firewood into their camp. At the end of this furrow the wall of snow stood up higher than Tappan's head. To get out on top without breaking the crust presented a problem. He lifted Jenet up and was relieved to see that the snow held her, but he found a different task in his own case. Returning to camp, he gathered up several of the long branches of spruce that had been part of the shelter, and, carrying them out, he laid them against the slant of snow he had to surmount, and by their aid he got on top. The crust held him.

Elated and with revived hope, he took up Jenet's halter and started off. Walking with his rude snowshoes was awkward. He had to go slowly and slide them along the crust. But he progressed. Jenet's little steps kept her even with him. Now and then one of her sharp hoofs cut through, but not to hinder her particularly. Right at the start Tappan observed something singular about Jenet. Never until now had she been dependent upon him. She knew it. Her intelligence apparently told her that, if she got out of this snow-bound wilderness, it would be owing to the strength and reason of her master.

Tappan kept to the north side of the cañon where the snow crust was strongest. What he must do was to work up to the top of the cañon slope, and then keep to the ridge, travel north along it, and so down out of the forest. Travel was slow. He soon found he had to pick his way. Jenet appeared to be absolutely unable to sense either danger or safety. Her experience had been of the rock confines and the drifting sands of the desert. She walked where Tappan led her, and it seemed to Tappan that her trust in him, her reliance upon him, were pathetic.

"Well, old girl," said Tappan, "it's a horse of another color now...hey?"

At length he came to a wide part of the cañon, where a bench of land led to a long gradual slope, thickly studded with small pines. This appeared to be fortunate and turned out to be so, for when Jenet broke through the crust, Tappan had trees and branches to hold while he hauled her out. The labor of climbing that slope was such that Tappan began to appreciate Blade's absolute refusal to attempt getting Jenet out. Dusk was shadowing the white aisles of the forest when Tappan ascended to a level. Yet he had not traveled far from camp, and that fact struck a chill upon his heart.

To go on in the dark was foolhardy. So Tappan selected a thick spruce, under which there was a considerable depression in the snow, and here made preparation to spend the night. Unstrapping the tarpaulin, he spread it on the snow. All the lower branches of this giant of the forest were dead and dry. Tappan broke off many and soon had a fire. Jenet nibbled at the moss on the trunk of the spruce tree. Tappan's meal consisted of beans, biscuits, and a ball of snow that he held over the fire to soften. He saw to it that Jenet fared as well as he. Night soon fell, strange and weirdly white in the forest, and piercingly cold. Tappan needed the fire. Gradually it melted the snow and made a hole down to the ground. Tappan rolled up in the tarpaulin and soon fell asleep.

In three days Tappan traveled about fifteen miles, gradually descending, until the snow crust began to fail to hold Jenet. Then whatever had been his tasks before, they were now magnified. As soon as the sun was up, somewhat softening the snow, Jenet began to break through, and often, when Tappan began hauling her out, he broke through himself. This exertion was killing even to a man of Tappan's physical prowess. Besides the endurance to resist heat and flying dust and dragging sand seemed another kind than that so needed to toil on in this snow. The endless snowbound forest began to be hideous to Tappan—cold, lonely, dreary, white, mournful, the kind of ghastly and ghostly winterland that had been the terror of Tappan's boyish dreams! He loved the sun, the open. This forest had deceived him. It was a wall of ice. As he toiled on, the state of his mind gradually and subtly changed in all except the fixed and absolute will to save Jenet. In some places he carried her.

The fourth night found him dangerously near the end of his stock of food. He had been generous with Jenet. But now, considering that he had to do more work than she, he diminished her share. On the fifth day Jenet broke through the snow crust so often that Tappan realized how utterly impossible it was for her to get out of the woods by her own efforts. Therefore, Tappan hit upon the plan of making her lie in the tarpaulin, so that he could drag her. The tarpaulin doubled once did not make a bad sled. All the rest of that day Tappan hauled her. And so all the rest of the next day he toiled on, hands behind him, clutching the canvas, head and shoulders bent, plodding and methodical, like a man who could not be defeated. That night he was too weary to build a fire, and too worried to eat the last of his food.

Next day Tappan was not dead to the changing character of the forest. He had worked down out of the zone of the spruce trees; the pines had thinned out and decreased in size; oak trees began to show prominently. All these signs meant that he was getting down out of the mountain heights. But the fact, hopeful as it was, had drawbacks. The snow was still four feet deep on a level, and the crust held Tappan only about half the time. Moreover, the lay of the land operated against Tappan's progress. The long, slowly descending ridge had failed. There were no more cañons, but ravines and swales were numerous. Tappan dragged on, stern, indomitable, bent to his toil.

When the crust no longer held him, he hung his snowshoes over Jenet's back and wallowed through, making a lane for her to follow. Two days of such heart-breaking toil, without food or fire, broke Tappan's magnificent endurance. But not his spirit! He hauled Jenet over the snow and through the snow, down the hills and up the slopes, through the thickets, knowing that over the next ridge perhaps was deliverance. Deer and elk tracks began to be numerous. Cedar and juniper trees now predominated. An occasional pine showed here and there. He was getting out of the forestland. Only such mighty hope as that justified could have kept him on his feet.

He fell often, and it grew harder to rise and go on. The hour came when he had to abandon hauling Jenet. It was necessary to make a road for her. How weary, cold, horrible the white reaches! Yard by yard Tappan made his way. He no longer perspired. He had no feeling in his feet or legs. Hunger

65

ceased to gnaw at his vitals. His thirst he quenched with snow—soft snow now, that did not have to be crunched like ice. The pangs in his breast were terrible, cramps, constrictions, the piercing pain in his lungs, the dull ache of his overtaxed heart.

Tappan came to an opening in the cedar forest from which he could see afar. A long slope fronted him. It led down and down to the open country. His desert eyes, keen as those of an eagle, made out flat country, sparsely covered with snow, and black dots that were cattle. The last slope! The last pull! Three feet of snow, except in drifts, down and down he plunged, making way for Jenet! All that day he toiled and fell and rolled down this league-long slope, wearying toward sunset to the end of his task, and likewise to the end of his will.

Now he seemed up and now down. There was no sense of cold or weariness, only direction! Tappan still saw! The last of his horror at the monotony of white faded from his mind. Jenet was there, beginning to be able to travel for herself. The solemn close of an endless day found Tappan arriving at the edge of the timbered country where wind-bared patches of ground showed long, bleached grass. Jenet took to grazing.

As for Tappan, he fell with the tarpaulin under a thick cedar, and with strengthless hands plucked and plucked at the canvas to spread it, so that he could cover himself. He looked again for Jenet. She was there, somehow a fading image, strangely blurred. But she was grazing. Tappan lay down and stretched out, and slowly drew the tarpaulin over him.

A piercing cold night wind swept down from the snowy heights. It wailed in the edge of the cedars and moaned out toward the open country. Yet the night seemed silent. The stars shone white in a deep blue sky, passionless, cold, watchful eyes, looking down without pity or hope or censure. They were the eyes of nature. Winter had locked the heights in its snowy grip. All night that winter wind blew down, colder and colder. Then dawn broke, steely, gray, with a flare in the east.

Jenet came back where she had left her master. Camp! She had grazed all night. Her sides that had been flat were now full. Jenet had weathered another vicissitude of her life. She stood for a while, in a daze, with one long ear down over her meek face. Jenet was waiting for Tappan, but he did not stir from under the long roll of canvas. Jenet waited. The winter sun rose, in cold yellow flare. The snow glistened as with a crusting of diamonds. Somewhere in the distance sounded a long-drawn discordant bray. Jenet's ears shot up. She listened. She recognized the call of one of her kind. Instinct always prompted Jenet. Sometimes she did bray. Lifting her gray head, she sent forth a clarion: *Hee-haw hee-haw-haw. . . hee-haw how-e-e-e-e!*

That stentorian call started the echoes. They pealed down the slope and rolled out over the open country, clear as a bugle blast, yet hideous in their discordance. But this morning Tappan did not awaken.

Jargan

Max Brand

Fredrick Schiller Faust (1892-1944) was born in Seattle, Washington. He wrote over 500 average-length books (300 of them Westerns) under nineteen different pseudonyms, but Max Brand—"the Jewish cowboy," as he once dubbed it— has become the most familiar and is now his trademark. Faust was convinced very early that to die in battle was the most heroic of deaths, and so, when the Great War began, he tried to get overseas. All of his efforts came to nothing, and in 1917, working at manual labor in New York City, he wrote a letter that was carried in *The New York Times* protesting this social injustice. Mark Twain's sister came to his rescue by arranging for Faust to meet Robert H. Davis, an editor at The Frank A. Munsey Company.

Faust wanted to write—poetry. What happened instead was that Davis provided Faust with a brief plot idea, told him to go down the hall to a room where there was a typewriter, only to have Faust return some six hours later with a story suitable for publication. That was "Convalescence," a short story that appeared in *All-Story Weekly* (3/31/17) and that launched Faust's career as an author of fiction. Zane Grey had recently abandoned the Munsey publications, *All-Story Weekly* and *The Argosy,* as a market for his Western serials, selling them instead to the slick-paper *Country Gentleman.* The more fiction Faust wrote for Davis, the more convinced this editor became that Faust could equal Zane Grey in writing a Western story.

The one element that is the same in Zane Grey's early

Western stories and Faust's from beginning to end is that they are psycho-dramas. What impact events have on the soul, the inner spiritual changes wrought by ordeal and adversity, the power of love as an emotion and a bond between a man and a woman, and above all the meaning of life and one's experiences in the world conspire to transfigure these stories and elevate them to a plane that shimmers with nuances both symbolic and mythical. In 1920 Faust expanded the market for his fiction to include Street & Smith's *Western Story Magazine* for which throughout the next decade he would contribute regularly a million and a half words a year at a rate of 5¢ word. It was not unusual for him to have two serial installments and a short novel in a single issue under three different names or to earn from just this one source $2,500 a week.

In 1921 Faust made the tragic discovery that he had an incurable heart condition from which he might die at any moment. This condition may have been in part emotional. At any rate, Faust became depressed about his work, and in England in 1925 he consulted H. G. Baynes, a Jungian analyst, and finally even met with C. G. Jung himself who was visiting England at the time on his way to Africa. They had good talks, although Jung did not take Faust as a patient. Jung did advise Faust that his best hope was to live a simple life. This advice Faust rejected. He went to Italy where he rented a villa in Florence, lived extravagantly, and was perpetually in debt. Faust needed his speed at writing merely to remain solvent. Yet what is most amazing about him is not that he wrote so much, but that he wrote so much so well!

By the early 1930s Faust was spending more and more time in the United States. Carl Brandt, his agent, persuaded him to write for the slick magazines since the pay was better and, toward the end of the decade, Faust moved his family to

Max Brand

Hollywood where he found work as a screenwriter. He had missed one war; he refused to miss the Second World War. He pulled strings to become a war correspondent for *Harper's Magazine* and sailed to Europe and the Italian front. Faust hoped from this experience to write fiction about men at war, and he lived in foxholes with American soldiers involved in some of the bloodiest fighting on any front. These men, including the machine-gunner beside whom Faust died, had grown up reading his stories with their fabulous heroes and their grand deeds, and that is where on a dark night in 1944, hit by shrapnel, Faust expired, having asked the medics to attend first to the younger men who had been wounded.

Faust's Western fiction has nothing intrinsically to do with the American West, although he had voluminous notes and research materials on virtually every aspect of the frontier. THE UNTAMED (Putnam, 1919) was his first Western novel and in Dan Barry, its protagonist, Faust created a man who is beyond morality in a Nietzschean sense, who is closer to the primitive and the wild in nature than other human beings, who is both frightening and sympathetic. His story continues, and his personality gains added depth, in the two sequels that complete his story, THE NIGHT HORSEMAN (Putnam, 1920) and THE SEVENTH MAN (Putnam, 1921).

Those who worked with Faust in Hollywood were amazed at his fecundity, his ability to plot stories. However, for all of his incessant talk about plot and plotting, Faust's Western fiction is uniformly character-driven. His plots emerge from the characters as they are confronted with conflicts and frustrations. Above all, there is his humor—the hilarity of the opening chapters of THE RETURN OF THE RANCHER (Dodd, Mead, 1933), to give only one instance, is sustained by the humorous contrast between irony and naïveté. So many of Faust's characters are truly unforgettable, from the most familiar, like Dan Barry and Harry Destry, to such marvelous creations as José Ridal in BLACKIE AND RED (Chelsea House, 1926) or Gaspar Sental in THE RETURN OF THE RANCHER.

Too often, it may appear, Faust's plots are pursuit stories and his protagonists in quest of an illustrious father or victims of an Achilles' heel, but these are premises and conventions that are ultimately of little consequence. His characters are in essence psychic forces. In Faust's fiction, as Robert Sampson concluded in the first volume of YESTERDAY'S FACES (Bowling Green University Popular Press, 1983), "every action is motivated. Every character makes decisions and each must endure the consequences of his decisions. Each character is gnawed by the conflict between his wishes and the necessities of his experience. The story advances from the first interactions of the first characters. It continues, a fugue for full orchestra, ever more complex, modified by decisions of increasing desperation, to a climax whose savagery may involve no bloodshed at all. But there will be psychological tension screaming in harmonics almost beyond the ear's capacity."

Faust's finest fiction can be enjoyed on the level of adventure, or on the deeper level of psychic meaning. He knew in his heart that he had not resolved the psychic conflicts he projected into his fiction, but he held out hope to the last that the resolutions he had failed to find in life and in his stories might somehow, miraculously, be achieved on the higher plane of the poetry that he continued to write. Yet Faust is not the first writer, and will not be the last, who treasured least what others have come to treasure most. It may even be possible that a later generation, having read his many works as he wrote them (and they are now being restored after decades of

Max Brand

Inept abridgments and rewriting), will find Frederick Faust to have been, truly, one of the most significant American literary artists of the 20th Century. Much more about Faust's life, his work, and critical essays on various aspects of his fiction of all kinds can be found in THE MAX BRAND COMPANION (Greenwood Press, 1996).

I

It was the spring of the year. In the summer Jargan worked. In the autumn he traveled. In the winter he slept. In the spring Jargan slowly awakened. It may be wondered at, this schedule of living. People asked how Jargan could afford it, since he had no established fortune behind him on which he might draw at will. He never deigned to burn his hands with a rope or to ride herd or to wander behind a burro loaded down with a prospector's pack. If he did none of these things, how was it that Jargan, in the course of a short summer, could lay up such supplies that he lived in luxury during the rest of the year? In his season of travel he went whither he would, letting his fancy of the moment blow him away as freely as the wind blows a dead leaf. When the winter came and the mountain nights began to grow crisper and longer, Jargan invariably turned up again at Big Horn, and rented again that big room with the south windows and the great old four-poster bed, and dropped at a gesture, one might say, into a long period of inertia. During all of that time he ate of the fat and he drank of the cream, and ever he paid in cash. So it was, also, in the spring of the year. He began to awaken; his clothes became gorgeous; a light appeared, burning in his eyes far back from the surface—and men began to take heed of him when he passed.

How could he afford such a régime? Certainly he was not existing upon the stored savings of a long life of previous labor, for Jargan had attained only to the blissful age of twenty-one. Yet for three years he had done nothing. He was eighteen when he dropped into Big Horn and amused the good folk with his soft, deep voice and his soft, dark eyes—

73

Max Brand

and Red Larsen, attempting to make game of him, had been corrected with a gun and bullets of .45 caliber.

So the worthy citizens of Big Horn swallowed the laughter that they had prepared at the expense of Jargan. They swallowed it and converted it into a choked silence. Thereafter, Jargan was undisturbed. For three years no man had lifted a hand against him. For three years they had pondered the sudden death of that famous gunfighter, Red Larsen, and as a result of their thoughtfulness Jargan slept on in peace.

The source of his livelihood was discovered before he had been long in town. The sight of his fat wallet had inspired a gentleman newly out of the East and pardonably proud of the dexterity of his fingers. He sat down with Jargan for a three-day session at stud, and the things he did with those cards were beyond speech, beyond credence. Yet at the end of that period he was horribly broke, and Jargan, at the end of the third day's session, showed him a simple little trick with a deck of cards and then gave him five hundred dollars to take him home again. The wise man out of the East went back sadder and wiser.

That long contest opened the eyes of Big Horn to the fact that it had in its midst a gambler of the first water. "He could make greenbacks blossom out of a Scotchman's pocketbook," said the English bartender in the hotel bar. "But look at the hands God gave him! Look at the head start he was furnished with!"

Indeed, they were remarkably long, straight-fingered hands, with nails as neatly cared for and skin of as tissue-like a delicacy as any woman's. He did not even waste them upon the making of Bull Durham cigarettes. Instead, he carried "tailor-made" smokes in a long, flat, golden case. That case was as much out of keeping with the rest of Jargan's attire as a five-carat diamond would be out of place on the shirt front of

Jargan

an old clothes dealer, but it was in perfect keeping with his hands, and sometimes, when the heavy, sweet-scented smoke of his Egyptian tobacco arose, the man who sat on the opposite side of the gaming table would be hypnotized into forgetfulness of everything save those long, soft hands, the burning cigarette, and the pale, smiling, handsome, dull-eyed face. His gaudy cowboy outfit for the nonce disappeared.

The last puff from one of those expensive cigarettes was now blown languidly forth, and Jargan snapped the butt high into the air and turned his head a little to watch its course. It was the blue, blue time of the evening of that spring day. In the West there was still a strong blur of color, but all the rest of the sky was deepest blue, and the mist in the pretentious square around which Big Horn was built was blue, also, and the statue of Columbus in the center of the square was withdrawn to a greater distance by that same blue haze.

In the beginning, Big Horn was founded with great hopes. It was to be a rich metropolis. Its central life was to turn around this square. But alas for great hopes!—the metropolis failed to grow. There were not even enough houses completely to surround the square. They merely outlined its magnificent dimensions with sketchy strokes, here and there.

Having watched the falling of the yellow-burning cigarette butt against the thickening twilight, Jargan allowed his careless eye to roam over the houses of the square. They were not beautiful, and Jargan loved beauty, but he endured in Big Horn partly because it had something more than one narrow, dust-blown street to look out upon, and partly because it lay in a region of golden sunshine, eternally warm sunshine. The sun was necessary to Jargan's happiness. Without it, he withered like a tropical plant. He had been known to walk bareheaded through its noon blaze, and yet his skin remained pale.

75

Indeed, he was an exotic, a strange fellow, and he was so equipped by nature that at every pore he could drink up physical pleasure. Just as he enjoyed the white-hot noonday, so, also, he found enjoyment in the magic closing of the day, and the falling of evening like a fog, so that voices up and down the street sounded small and far away, and there was no rhyme or reason to anything but sleep in this gracious world.

He had lain there smoking with closed eyes; thin wisps of dust trailed through the air, from time to time. But even this was not unpleasant to him, for he could detect the strange, biting tang of the alkali in that dust, an odor that whipped up into his mind the terrible picture of the dead desert. Jargan had crossed such a desert on a dying horse, his own life fainting in a wounded body, and far away the pursuers dancing in small black dots on the horizon mirage. Now the scent of the alkali brought that old torture burningly home to him, but on the other hand he had only to turn his head a little in order to hear the cool clinking of the glassware in the bar where men were drinking, and from which, again, other odors stirred, of a newly wetted floor and of many drinks in the making. To him, then, the square was not altogether ugly, so he stared at it after his cigarette had fallen into the dust beside the hotel verandah.

Yonder two children were playing ball and running with a mad abandon that made a faint sweat start on the brow of Jargan. His heart was in more perfect accord with yonder peak-hatted fellow who lounged beside the great statue of Columbus that a rich and drunken miner had donated in a careless moment. The man was standing, but his slouching attitude indicated that he was upon his feet with the minimum of effort. He was making a cigarette that he placed between his lips. Then he produced a match.

The smooth brow of Jargan gathered in the slightest

76

frown. Something annoyed him in that sight. He did not know what. The man's hand moved in a wide arc as he struck the match against the base of the statue. Then he lit his ciga-rette. The evening was sufficiently dim to make the flare of the match quite visible even at that distance.

Jargan frowned more deeply. He was expectant of some-thing else, but what? The fellow now walked away, and Jargan followed him with intent eyes. He crossed the square. He came up the hotel steps. He walked down the verandah, a tall, slender-hipped, wide-shouldered man with the dark skin and the smoky eyes that betray Indian blood. He looked like a Mexican. He might very well be from south of the Río Grande. Yet there was a difference. He had an excessive and stiff-necked dignity, for one thing. Altogether, he impressed Jargan as being a novelty among cowpunchers in spite of the catholic conformity to custom of his outfit.

Jargan rolled back in his chair again. It was his special chair that no other man in Big Horn presumed to sit in, even when Jargan was not on the verandah. It was made with a long, low-reclining back, and there was an extension in front upon which he could rest his legs. Now he stretched his arms along the wide arms of the chair and felt the comfortable sup-port pressing against him.

Closing his eyes, he wondered if he would be fool enough to answer the impulse that bade him go to the center of the square and stand beside the statue of Columbus. For he knew, now, why it was that the scratching of that match had excited in him a mysterious expectancy. Now he recalled that, at about that hour, but usually in the midst of some group of talkers in the square, this same tall, peak-hatted man had stood beside the statue and lit a match by scratching against the pediment. Always before, he had had quite a struggle to light the match against the glazed surface of the stone.

Max Brand

Vague questions formed in the mind of lazy Jargan. Why did the same man always go there at the same hour? Why did he light his match in the same way? Once, Jargan recalled now, it had required seven strokes to light the match! How odd that he could recall such details, but often, when the conscious mind is blank, the unconscious mind will be working for us.

Jargan, with a deep, deep sigh, raised from the floor beside him his peak-crowned hat, pushed himself up to a sitting position, deposited the hat upon his head, and rose to his feet with a faint moan of effort. He stretched himself. There was an inch more than six feet of him, and he stretched it all. Who has watched a cat prepare for a mouse hunt by unlimbering each muscle in all its lithe body? Just so Jargan extended his arms above his head and slowly writhed until there was not a fiber of him that had not been pulled and tested. Then he dropped his arms, gave one shrug that snapped everything into place, and looked about him as though he were seeing the two other men on the verandah for the first time.

They had observed his complicated method of getting up with a silent interest. Yet they did not venture a smile even when his back was turned. Some men are never ridiculous, just as some animals never are. A dog's antics may throw a spectator into fits of laughter, but who laughs at a cat? Even when it plays, there is a touch of grim earnestness about its movements, and it seems to be merely practicing with its sharp claws and its needle teeth, waiting for real work to commence. Men smile, too, at a clumsy bear, for all his might, but who will smile at the lounging grace, the ineffable malice of a panther hardly a tenth of the bear's size? As for Jargan, he tripped going down the steps from the verandah, but there was something in the light-footed deftness of his recovery that again kept the two men who looked at him from smiling.

78

He sauntered across the square. Not until he was twenty steps away did the two turn to one another with a silent, grave glance of consultation, and yet neither of them had ever seen Jargan before!

They watched him turn and come to a pause at the base of the lordly statue of the Genoese. Then one of them cursed softly.

"Yes," said the other, as though a perfectly understandable comment had been made, "he looks like he might be about nine parts man!"

II

From beside the granite base of the statue, Jargan had turned and was surveying the facade of the building. He was really not far away, but the dull light gave an effect of distance. The two on the verandah were retired to indistinct blurs under the shadow of the roof. The two lights in the barroom windows made all the rest of the hotel ghostly dim. All the face of the hotel was masked in shutters except for two rooms. One of those was in the corner, his own familiar room. The other was on the far corner.

He decided that he must do the thing for which he had come. He took out a cigarette and selected a match. The match he racked against the slick surface of the granite. It did not light, but he did not repeat the motion. Instead, he stared, fascinated, at the window of the room in the far corner of the building, for a lamp had suddenly appeared at it. The lamp was raised straight up, and then it was carried across the window in a stroke that completed the figure of a cross. It then disappeared, only dimly illuminating the square of the window from the interior of the room.

Jargan walked back to the hotel. He was a vastly different Jargan from the one who had idled on the verandah of the hotel. The forgotten cigarette was crumbled between his first and middle fingers. He walked with a longer and a lighter stride. When he reached the steps of the verandah, he went up them with one bound, landing without a jar on the floor above.

In the doorway he paused. Throwing back his head, he looked over the square, flashed a glance at the two silent smokers on one side, and then turned into the interior of the building. He ran to the floor above, hurried down the hall, and tapped at the door of that corner room from which the light had showed.

He heard the murmur of a man and a woman speaking together, and then the door was opened by a woman in a white nursing costume. In the uncertain light and by the heavy shadow that fell across her face, he could see nothing of her features, but when she spoke and asked him what he wanted in a harsh voice, it was as though the speaking enabled him to see her more clearly. It was a broad, heavy-jowled face with pinched-up eyes and a low forehead, as forbidding a countenance as he had ever seen. Her little, pig-like eyes were glittering at him as she asked her question for the second time.

"Who are you? And what are you staring at now?"

He could think of no answer. Why, indeed, had he come up to this room he did not know, except that he had followed a blind impulse, and now he was completely upset by meeting a woman. Women were rare in that hotel. Indeed, men are the travelers in the West. The women remain at home.

"You've got the wrong place. This is the room of Mister Carpaez."

She withdrew and closed the door, while Jargan went slowly down the hall, halting every few steps. It was all very

80

queer. There could be no doubt now that the man who lit his cigarette at the base of the Columbus statue had, perhaps by the number of strokes of the match against the statue base, conveyed a signal to the people in this room of the hotel, and that the signal had been answered by the movement of the lamp in the window.

Downstairs he found the proprietor of the hotel, Jud Haskins, a typical cowpuncher, except that he had lost a leg and, without the necessary member, had been forced to find an occupation on foot instead of in the saddle. Labor and ten years of patience had brought him this reward. From his little office he directed the operations of Big Horn's only hotel.

The sight of Jargan at the door brought him out of his chair and hobbling on his wooden leg across the floor. "What's up, Jargan?" he asked. "Anything wrong? Have they been burning your bacon again?"

According to the experience of the past three years, it was a full three weeks earlier than Jargan's usual time of complete awakening, and yet here he was with his black eyes on fire, like midsummer when he was in one of his moods of desiring action.

"Nothing wrong, partner," said Jargan. "But...I'm thinking of stirring about a little. It's in the air, ain't it?"

"Why," said Haskins, "I dunno but you're right. Only, you usually take it easy a little longer than this, don't you? You 'most generally wait till the hot days before you think of showing your nose outside much. Ain't that the fact?"

"Hot weather's got nothing to do with it," answered Jargan. "But agent that's full of hell-fire and dollars all summer gets to remembering that he's past thirty and nothing saved in the winter. I've seen 'em that wouldn't bet one to ten on their own weight between Christmas and Saint Patrick's Day, that would give you odds on the color of your own hair on the Fourth of July. That's why I lie around and take it easy, Jud. I don't want to waste my energy!"

He smiled at the hotel proprietor, and the latter smiled brightly back at him. They had long ago decided that each other was worthy of great respect. Jargan, who usually talked not at all of his own affairs, had waxed free of tongue with Haskins, and, what Haskins heard, he locked up in the secret vaults of his memory. Sometimes he had a terrible, cold feeling that Jargan was purposely testing him by making him the confidant of many facts about his past, waiting for the time when Haskins might repeat a single syllable of what he had been told, for if once a single story were launched abroad, it would be quickly traced to Haskins. Although his wooden leg did not at all interfere with his admirable gun play, yet he had no desire to meet Jargan when the latter was on the war path. To add to his reticence, he had learned that a full half of the yarns Jargan told were the rankest inventions. One could never tell when to believe the gambler. For instance, he might be speaking Gospel truth now, when he declared that he liked hot weather simply because it loosened the strings of the pocketbooks of others. Or again, it might be that it was the first explanation that came handy to the tongue of the formidable youth.

"The fatheads and the suckers crawl out of the shade when the sun goes north," went on Jargan, "and I'm waiting to ring the bell and call them into the pasture where the greenest grass is growing." He laughed joyously. He seemed quite incapable of feeling shame or remorse because of his profession.

"Let me tell you something," said the proprietor.

"Go as far as you like," answered Jargan. "I'll listen all day to any man. I learned how to pull a gun by sitting in the sun an hour watching the motions of a cat's paw when she was playing with a mouse. Ever watch a cat's paw, Haskins?"

"Don't suppose I've ever studied it."

"You've missed something. I'd rather sit and watch a cat's paw work than dance with the swellest girl that ever had freckles."

"If it comes down to that, it doesn't mean much," suggested Haskins. "You ain't much of a time waster when it comes to girls."

Jargan threw back his head and laughed. He went through all the motions of the heartiest laughter, but the only sound was a deep, soft chuckle. "Girls?" he said. "I like 'em all. The only reason that I don't start on one trail and stick to it is because I find the sign of so many other trails crossing it." His black eyes gleamed and shone upon Haskins.

"And now what's brought you here?" asked the latter.

"To pass the time of day with you," said the gambler.

"Don't lie to me, son," said Haskins. "When you make a move that ain't called for and plumb necessary, cats will stop eating canned salmon when the tin is off! Loosen up, Jargan, and tell me what you want!"

Again Jargan laughed, positively rolling about, so profound seemed his enjoyment in the insight of his host. But he grew sober again in a trice. "Went down the hall," he said, "and saw a woman at the door of the room in the far corner. Who's in that room, Haskins?"

The proprietor cursed softly in astonishment. "You are a queer one," he declared. "You mean to say that you don't know anything about Carpaez?"

"Not a word."

"Why, the whole town has been talking about nothing else for two weeks."

"Maybe, but I've been asleep."

"Sit down, then, son, and I'll tell you a yarn that'll make your mouth water."

83

III

"It was about five year back that the *don* showed up," said Haskins. "He come with his son out of nowhere…meaning that he'd never been seen before in these parts. He was a shade over six feet tall, I guess, and he was built like a lion. He had a gray mustache that come out to curling points on each side, and he had a black beard that come to a point, too. His eyebrows come up to a speck over each eye, so he had the look of one of these pictures of the devil. He had the manners of a grand duke. Not one of them flash-in-the-pan four-flushers that kowtow to the boss and give the hired man hell. No, sir, he talked to the blacksmith like he was a prince in disguise.

"*Don* José Carpaez…that's his name. He had a boy along with him, a kid at the tail end of his teens, full of pepper and vinegar. The lads around Big Horn, because he talked fancy English with a foreign twang to it, thought they'd ride him a bit. But they found out he had two hard fists and knew how to use 'em. His idea of a little daily morning exercise was beating up a couple of husky cowpunchers, and the old man would lick his chops when he seen the kid come prancing in for breakfast with one eye turning purple and black. 'My son,' he said to the kid, Juan, 'all brave men fight, but only brave fools get black eyes.'

"Well, that all come about five years ago, when old Carpaez come through Big Horn looking for a place to settle down. He had a wad of money with him, and he had the bad luck to fall into the hands of Guy Johnson. Little old Johnson got hold of him, talked him dizzy, spun him around, and woke him up owning the worst stretch of rocks and sand that ever went by the name of range land. Well, sir, it would've busted your heart to see the old boy cheated like that, and him never guessing it. He builds a little house, buys some cattle, and settles down as pleased as can be.

"That was five years ago, and you ain't seen him in the time you been here because after the first two years he had so damned little cash to spend that he never came to town. All he done was to mortgage his soul to send his son away to college. Juan Carpaez is somewhere in the East, stepping around with the best of them, but the old man is starving on his ranch. Every vacation time, when Juan comes home, old José has been splurging to make the kid think that everything was going along well. In the meantime, Guy Johnson had mortgages wrapped around the old *don* up to the neck. He was just on the edge of giving the strings a pull and squeezing Carpaez out, when there comes along a crash of another kind altogether.

"How come you ain't heard of it, I dunno. But you sure sleep sound while you're sleeping, Jargan! It was three weeks back. Jack Hargess and his brother Bill were riding down the Montgomery Road right past the Carpaez place, and they heard a crackling of guns blowing down the wind. So they up with their hosses and went hell-bent for the house. They hit it and tore inside, and they found that four gents had just busted down the door to old Carpaez's bedroom.

"The old bulldog had tackled them with a knife. He'd been blazing away with his revolver and doing not much more than make noise for quite a spell, but when it come to knife work, he was right at home. He tore into them four skunks and messed 'em all up. Then the Hargess boys tangled with the merry-go-round. At the first yip they let out, the four turned and ran for it.

"Two of 'em got plumb away, but two had been so sliced up by Carpaez's knife that they couldn't make no respectable time, and the Hargess boys just nacherally salted them away with lead so's they'd keep from that day till they landed in hellfire. One was Josh Hampton...you remember him that was sent up for robbing little Millbury?"

"Don't recollect it," said Jargan.

The other sighed. "You got no talent for gossip," he declared. "Anyway, Josh was a bad one. He was spoiled right to the center. The one that dropped with Josh was a dark-skinned gent with a streak of soot in his eyes. You know what I mean, Jargan? Negro blood, I guess, mixed up with the white. There was nothing on him to show where he came from...no name...no nothing.

"When the Hargess boys turned around to *Don* José, they found the cheery old devil sitting on the floor with his back against the wall, smoking a cigarette and leaking blood like his skin was turned into a sieve. He thanked them hearty for what they done, and then they tied him up. Before they finished, he was fainting, and it looked so serious that they sent a rush order for Doc Chalmers to come out from town.

"Doc came out, give him a look, and said that everything would be hunky-dory if he had a little rest and quiet and good food, and the Hargess boys decided that he'd have them things if they had to cook for him themselves. But the next day along comes Guy Johnson, asking for money that was overdue, with the law to back him up and foreclosure in his brain...the yaller hound!

"The Hargess boys told him plumb liberal what they thought about him, a gent that would talk of throwing a sick man out of his own house. Then they rigged up a buckboard and they took old Carpaez into town and fixed him up in my second-best room...you having the first. They wired to Juan, away off in his college, and they let him know what had happened, and he wired back that he was coming on the jump.

86

Jargan

"But he ain't showed up yet. And it seems like the old man is grieving a good deal about the length of time that it takes Juan to come. Anyway, he ain't getting well the way he ought to, hanging on and taking about as many steps backward as he takes forwards. And that's the whole story, Jargan. The woman you met at the door? That's the nurse, Mary Chapel. You see, the Hargess boys are doing this job up brown. They're paying all the bills, and they sent clean to Salt Springs for this nurse.

"They say that the old Spaniard is the gamest old sport that ever used a knife and that he's going to live on the fat of the land if they can help him to it. Since he got to getting worse lately, they've rented the room next to his, and one of them stays there regular. That's the sort of white men the Hargess boys are, and I guess it won't do 'em no harm in these parts. If one of 'em wanted to run for sheriff tomorrow, I figure it would be unanimous, the way the boys would elect him. Now, Jargan, what's interested you in this deal?"

Jargan smiled. "What interests me?" he answered. "I'll tell you, son, I'm going to save up this yarn and tell it again to my Sunday school class. It'll do 'em all good."

So he turned away and sauntered through the door while the proprietor, grinning and shaking his head, looked after him.

Jargan went into the barroom. His coming caused a slight stir, for he was not one to advance unnoticed in any society, even when stern, strong-hearted whisky was a rival in holding the public eye. But what interested Jargan was that the stir his coming started was so very slight and ended so soon, for, as a rule, his advent into the barroom in the spring meant a fat addition of business to the hotel and the bartender. Not that he was a particularly hard drinker himself, but because he treated generously left and right. So he took it for granted that the first drink he had bought in the matter of two or three months would bring a clustering group around him, but there was no such movement, and Jargan was angered to the soul.

He was, to tell the truth, rather a vain fellow. He loved admiration. He literally bloomed under it. But the anger of Jargan disappeared when he saw that the reason he was neglected was on account of the presence of that tall, smoky-eyed fellow in the peak-crowned hat who had so often made the signal from the base of the statue of Columbus. He had taken the tactically commanding position in the exact center of the bar, and he held forth in a slow and rather pompous style, speaking English after the fashion of one who thinks in a foreign language and then translates the exact words, but never into smooth and easy idiom.

"They were four or five centimeters long, sirs. That is, an inch and a half, say. Great, stupid heads, great soft bodies... *phaugh!*" He cast up his long, eloquent hands, raised his eyes, and shuddered in his aversion. "But who could stop to look at one of the creatures? No, no! The ground had become alive! The dead earth had turned into the hopping, crawling things. Wherever you went, the ground poured after you. You could not escape...wherever you stood, there they were already, not by thousands or millions or billions...no, but they covered the ground as grass covers it.

"'What devil sends them?' we ask. We look up. The air is astir with hawks and with eagles. They sweep down. They eat till they are full. They rise again and fly. They eat again and again, but what they eat is nothing. It is not even a morsel crumbled from the loaf.

"Yonder a horse goes thirsty to the watering trough and, instead of drinking, starts throwing his head up and down. All horses are fools. This one is only more foolish than others. I go to see why it will not drink. And there...the watering trough has no water! It is solid with the crawling locusts. *¡Dios! ¡Dios! ¡Madre! ¡Madre!* The water is alive! Boots with polished surface are what one must wear. Otherwise they crawl over you...instantly you are covered, and the horrible little smell...." He made another gesture.

"And where," said Jargan, "did all this happen?"

The tall man came out of his trance of disgust at the recollection and cast a glance of sharp rebuke at the interrupter and the interruption. The others, also, glowered upon Jargan.

"It's the Argentine he's telling about," said one eager listener. "He's talking about the locusts. They eat every doggone thing, Jargan. They'd even eat up cactus."

This was communicated in hardly more than a whisper, and Jargan hardly heard. He was staring fixedly at the man from Argentina, while his mind went from one picture to another, this handsome, smoke-eyed, lazy fellow at the bar, and the pig-faced woman in the room above. What was there between them?

IV

Perhaps there was no connecting link outside of his imaginings, yet he had fairly ample proof that the man communicated with the woman, and that he dared not make those communications by word of mouth but kept at a distance and delivered his message by the means of signs. The secrecy of that method implied guilt. He was sharply recalled to himself by the purring and angered voice of the man of Argentina saying: "You see little in my words...you see much in my face. What is it that you see, sir?"

Jargan's lips parted as he smiled. They exposed two even rows of teeth of the most perfect regularity, the most dazzling whiteness. Not a spark of mirth appeared in his black eyes, but in his fingertips and in the bones of his arms there arose a mighty volition, tingling and aching and urging him to fight. In another instant he would have launched an insult, but in the interval he caught sight of the pale, agonized face of the bartender. He remembered that the poor devil had opened the place on shares with the hotel owner, and that all of his capital was invested in the furnishings. Suppose a gunfight wrecked the place?

"Go on with your yarn, partner," said Jargan kindly. "I ain't going to bother you none." He turned and left the barroom.

He was not displeased with himself. It rather tickled his vanity to see that he could make such a ready concession to another man, a stranger, without shaming himself in the eyes of the men of Big Horn. That murmur which arose as he left the bar was a murmur of relief, and before the man from the Argentine was five minutes older he would understand that, in the person of Jargan, he had narrowly missed a grim danger.

By the time he had finished his supper in the noisy dining room, big Jargan had well-nigh forgotten the entire episode of the man, the lit match, the woman. It was not his affair. He lingered a little over the story of old Carpaez, but this, also, was of diminishing interest. When he went up to his room, he was ready to sleep. Summer, after all, had not yet come.

Before sleeping, he sat for a time in front of the window and stared out over the straggling square of Big Horn's lights, and above these at the black mountains molded softly against a blue-black sky, and higher still to the bright mottling of stars. Such moments as these brought immense peace and content to the strange soul of Jargan.

There were times when he felt that his talents were wasted

in the West. There were times when he envisioned himself in the midst of the gamblers of Manhattan, with the stakes climbing high and the hours getting small. One such night might make his fortune. But he knew that he could never snuff out of his nostrils the smell of sun burning on the desert, neither could he ever get from his mind the cold shining of the stars at night. The mountain desert had made him, and he could never escape.

That was small punishment to Jargan. It only meant that he had to shake off his dreams of cities and millions, now and again. He did it tonight without effort and had risen from the window to turn to his bed when he stopped with his hand upon the covers to turn them back. He stood up straight, frowning. One part of his brain had been working all this time in protest at his indolence. One part of his soul was in revolt, and now that revolt began to work into his conscious brain. Something was wrong. Something was decidedly wrong.

Then he saw the connecting link that tied the man of the Argentine and the woman of the brutal face to the story of *Don* José Carpaez. For had he not been told that one of the assailants of Carpaez was a dark-skinned man, a stranger who had never before been seen in these parts? Yes, a dark-skinned man with smoky eyes. Such a description might have served for the man he had seen in the barroom, and had there not been two who fled in safety from the attack of the Hargess boys? The sense of sleepiness was banished from the mind of Jargan. If the man from the Argentine had attacked old Carpaez once, might he not attempt to attack again, and this time through the medium of the nurse? How that woman could be a bedside nurse, how any patient could recover under the surveillance of those glittering little evil eyes, were mysteries to Jargan. It became vitally necessary that he look in upon her at her work. He wanted to see her as she leaned above the sufferer. He must see her in that capacity, and then he would be able to draw his own conclusions.

He leaned from the window. The roof of the verandah began not three feet below. It was utterly simple to double up his legs, pass his long body through the window, and then work down the shelving roof until he came to the far corner. There, he flattened against the wall and looked about him on the street. Horsemen were coming and going regularly. Voices called here and there. By starlight and by lamplight combined, he could make out forms, almost faces. It seemed incredible that they should not see him as clearly, but he remembered that he was completely withdrawn from the light and that he stood against the drab wall unrelieved. Only a noise or a shaft of light would call attention to him.

Relieved in that respect, he turned toward the window. What he saw was partially veiled or wholly cut off by the blowing back and forth of the thin curtain, but he made out a bed and upon it the profile of a white-headed, white-mustached man of fifty-five. His features were now greatly emaciated, so that the cheek bones thrust out prominently; the eyes seemed puffed, and the hands that lay crossed upon his breast were almost colorless. Certainly there was cause for the anxiety of those two good men, the Hargess brothers, who had placed him here under the doctor's care. If ever Jargan had seen a man at death's door, this was one.

Bill Hargess was even now reading a newspaper at one side of the room, but presently, covering a great yawn, he dropped the paper and rose. Jargan heard him directing Mary Chapel to call him if the patient showed signs of sinking. Then he turned to an adjoining door and disappeared. Jargan looked after him with oddly mingled emotions.

Bill Hargess and his brother represented the force that was most hostile to the gambler in Big Horn. More than once they had suggested that it would be well to persuade a character as notorious as Jargan to seek other quarters, and, although they had not yet been able to persuade the sheriff, the time might very well come when they could succeed. Hitherto, Jargan had hated them wholeheartedly, with the feeling that they were blunt-headed fellows incapable of understanding an artist. Now he revised his opinion. There was something to them. This unsuspected bigness of heart in them opened his eyes. He began to respect them more. Indeed, like all of those who prey upon society, he despised those who did not fight against him.

No sooner was Bill Hargess gone than the woman approached the bed, leaned over, and raised the hand of the sick man. When she released it, it fell back heavily, limply, upon his breast. This fall barely induced him to open his heavy eyes and stare up at her. She attempted to smile. It was a mirthless grimace that kept Jargan shivering even after she had turned her back and started for the door.

That glimpse of her evil face determined him upon radical action of some sort. He only waited to plan a reasonable course. In the meantime, he had watched with interest the maneuvers of a great black cat that was curled up on the feet of the *don*. As the woman left the room, it rose, arching its back with hair on end, but a signal from Mary Chapel, as she closed the door, had caused it to sink back into its former position.

Its head was not now lowered in sleep, however. After looking about for some time, it turned its great yellow eyes fully upon the window at which Jargan stood, while its tail began to curl from side to side. It gave the uncanny effect of lying upon guard during the absence of its mistress from the room, and it seemed to have instantly detected the presence of an enemy. If Jargan had been filled with dislike by the appearance of Mary Chapel, he was now inspired to a perfect horror of loathing. Not once did the great cat, fully half again as large as any Jargan had ever before seen, stir from its place. Its big round head remained raised high, and the eyes were staring steadily. When Jargan looked into them for an instant, he felt almost hypnotized. The yellow was not fixed and steady. It was a swirling light, and, after he gazed at those eyes for a moment, the beast seemed to increase in size, seemed to draw nearer.

Jargan forced his head to one side and found himself panting as he looked away into the pure and open air of the night. When he looked back again, Mary Chapel was returning with a steaming pitcher in one hand and a tall glass in the other. The heavy, sweet aroma blew to Jargan outside the window.

Leaning by the bed, she raised old Carpaez a little and presented the glass to his lips. The steaming liquor burned his skin apparently. At least, he winced away with a muffled exclamation, and Mary Chapel, allowing him to sink back onto the pillow again, stood over him with a scowl of perfect malignancy. The blood of Jargan ran cold again, but the horror for the sake of Carpaez was turned to fear for his own safety.

The black cat had crossed the bed to its mistress and rubbed against her with arched back until she looked down to it. Then it leaped to the floor, went straight to the window beyond which Jargan stood, and, leaping onto the sill, whined in Jargan's face.

V

For a moment, nearly yielding to a vast wave of commingled disgust and horror and fear, Jargan was on the point of jerking out his revolver and dashing the butt against the head of the creature. Instead, he shrank back, and, hearing the steps of the woman approaching rapidly, he glided around the corner of the building just as Mary Chapel thrust her head out of the window.

"What's up here?" grumbled the nurse. "What d'ye see, Betty dear? What d'ye see?"

A faint *meow* from the cat answered this appeal, and the cold sweat started on Jargan's forehead. It was as if the woman and her strange pet could actually exchange thoughts in their speech.

After a moment he heard her steps retreat, and again Jargan returned to his post of vantage. Mary Chapel was now on the far side of the room, but the black cat, from on a chair nearby, kept a steady pair of gleaming eyes fixed upon the window. The instant Jargan appeared, it stood up, arched its back, and lashed its sides with its tail. Nearer at hand, on a little stand just beside the window, stood the glass of chocolate where the wind could blow across it and cool it. Above it rose a slender glass vase which the kindness of the Hargess boys kept filled with green stuff. A gust of wind brushed heavily against the foliage, tilted the vase a little, and, when the pressure was released, the vase settled back with a faint and musical chatter against the top of the stand.

It was the glass of chocolate upon which Jargan fixed his eyes with the most interest. The pale and set features of Mary Chapel as she had offered that drink to the invalid were again present to his mind, and again that sensation of coldness and of unspeakable loathing, which had passed over him so many times in the past few moments, swept up his body. Of course, there might be nothing in his singular fears. Yet he reached through the window, despite the fact that the black cat, at sight of his hand, actually spat and raised an angry paw. Mary Chapel, leaning over to pick the newspaper from the place where it had fallen on the floor, muttered: "What, Betty? What, girl?"

But before she had straightened and turned to look, Jargan had tipped the vase so that it fell in and struck the glass of chocolate. Both went crashing to the floor.

Jargan, fleeing instantly to the corner of the house, heard the angry outcry of the nurse. A little later there was the sound of glass being swept up. He was about to return to his place when he heard the voice of the woman crying loudly: "Betty, you fool, stop licking up that stuff! Where is the wise devil in you now?"

Apparently the cat had been tasting the chocolate as it lay in shallow pools upon the floor, but that harsh warning from the woman confirmed the fears that had been forming in the mind of Jargan. He stole down the roof once more and went directly beneath the window, stooping low. As he passed it, his shoulder was caught and strongly held.

He turned with a start and above him was the convulsed face of Mary Chapel, gone white with fear and devilish with passion. At sight of Jargan she released her grip with a gasp.

"You!" she said. "You!" She turned and glanced quickly into the interior of the room, as though dreading that they might be spied upon. She turned back to him as he rose. "It was you, then, that knocked over the vase?" she asked.

"It was the wind. Not me."

"No?" All the while her eyes were working quickly back and forth and up and down as though she were trying to look around a corner and see the truth about him. "Who are you?" she said eagerly, at last. She wound her nervous fingers into his shirt and held him. "Will you talk? Who are you in this game, Jargan? Why ain't I been told about you?"

Jargan laid a finger on his lips. "D'you want the whole town to see us talking together like this?" he asked.

She started back but returned almost at once. "Tell me one thing," she said. "Is it the little fellow, the little fellow with the yellow hair and the blue eyes, that's sent you here?"

"That's him," said Jargan.

She shrank back and shook her man-size fist in his face. "Damn you," she breathed. "Damn you for making a fool out of me." She jerked the window down and then the shade behind it.

Jargan, realizing that he had fallen into a simple trap, was still determined that his share in this unknown drama was not finished. He hurried down the roof to his own window, dragged himself through it, and then hurried down the hall until he came to the Carpaez's door. He tried the knob. It was fast. He knocked heavily.

"Who's there?" gasped a husky voice from the room.

He waited, grinding his teeth.

"Here," he heard the woman saying. "It's cooler now. Drink this. This'll hearten you!"

Against the door, on the inside, there was a quick, light scratching sound as though the great black cat were striving to get out at him. It was the crowning horror.

"Don't drink!" shouted Jargan. "Don't drink, Carpaez!"

At the same time he drew back the width of the door, crouched, and then hurled himself forward, bunching his body behind his right shoulder. That cushion of muscle struck the door near the lock. Behind it all his powerful body was driving. The impact tore the steel lock through its surrounding wood. It flung the door wide and sent it crashing back against the wall. Jargan plunged to the center of the room.

What he saw was Carpaez, lifted in bed on the arm of Mary Chapel, with a fresh glass of chocolate at his lips. At sight of him she recoiled, trembling with fury. Big Hargess came to the door of his room, rubbing the sleep out of his eyes, and to him she pointed out Jargan.

"Are you going to allow that, Mister Hargess?" she whined. "Are you going to let a drunken gambler like Jargan break in on me and...?" Her voice broke. It was rage that made her mute, but it sounded very like fear.

Hargess was wild with anger at once. He stalked up to Jargan. "I've heard about your damned intrusion before," said the rancher. "But this is the first sample of it that I've seen. I'll throw you out of the room unless you go now, Jargan. I'll throw you out, and I'll have you rolled in tar later on by the boys! Now get out!"

Jargan drew a great breath. Hargess was a big man, a great-shouldered, thick-chested giant of a man, and a fight with him would be a pleasure to be remembered for many a long year. There would be no gun work. Hargess was notably one who made his way by the dint of heavy fists liberally bestowed. All the long, striking muscles up and down the arms of Jargan writhed into bunches and slipped away again like running water over ridges of rock. But yonder was the pale-faced old man, peering about him with faint eyes and saying in a feeble and yet dignified voice: "My friends...my dear friends...you take too much trouble on my behalf...."

The fighting lust dissolved from the heart of Jargan. He pointed to the sick man. "Hargess," he said, "look yonder at Carpaez."

"I've seen him, and what the devil of it?" said the other, hotter and hotter as it was apparent that the gambler was backing down. "I'm going to have an explanation in full for this outrage, Jargan. Why did...?"

"Damn you!" exploded Jargan. "You can have all the explanations you want later on. But I'll tell you what I've come here to see...that Carpaez doesn't drink that chocolate!"

Hargess blinked at him. "You've gone crazy, Jargan. Or are you joking?"

"Joking? I tell you, Hargess, if he drinks that, he'll be dead before morning!"

There was a gasping breath from Hargess. He turned to Mary Chapel and found her drawn back against the wall with the black cat pressed against her feet and spitting viciously at the two men who seemed to be threatening the mistress.

"I dunno what's in his head, Mary," said the rancher. "What's he driving at?"

"He's crazy," said Mary Chapel. "You've called him that yourself, and you're right."

"Crazy or not," said Jargan, "it don't cost much to have somebody find out what's in that chocolate. I want that pitcher!"

But as he stepped forward to take it, Mary Chapel caught the pitcher from the table and cast it through the window. It broke with a crash on a stone in the street.

"If there's going to be suspicions," she cried, "I'll not stand for it!"

"Stand for what, Mary?" asked the rancher. "There's sure no harm in what he just asked to have done. If that chocolate was all right...."

"All right?" screamed Mary Chapel. "And what d'ye think might be wrong with it? Am I one to have folks spying at what I do with my own hands?"

"Look at the cat!" exclaimed Jargan. "That cat licked up some of the chocolate that fell on the floor. You see where it lay before Miss Chapel wiped it up? The cat licked up some of that up. Now watch it!"

The black cat drew itself suddenly rigid, and then fell in convulsions upon the floor. Mary Chapel, with a wail, dropped on her knees and tried to take the poor creature in her arms. But her hand was ripped open by the claws of the beast, which had to be wrapped in a towel and carried out in this fashion, the nurse keeping up a running fire of imprecations upon Jargan and of appeals to a merciful heaven to spare the life of her cat. Her footfalls died away as she fled downstairs to get hot water for her sick pet. Hargess, bewildered and horrified, would have kept her in the room, but Jargan held him back.

"It's no use holding her," said Jargan. "Let her save her cat if she can. Our main job is to see if we can save Carpaez."

"Save him? From what? What the devil is it all about, Jargan? My head's spinning."

"What's sickened the black cat, Hargess?"

"Poison?" cried the rancher. "You mean to say that she-devil has been…?"

"I don't say anything," said Jargan. "But it looks tolerable to me as though the old boy was being slowly poisoned. This evening they got hurry-up orders, and they planned to finish him up quick. That chocolate was the stuff that was to turn the trick. They had him weakened down to a point where they could kill him at one wallop, and nobody would think much of it. It would look natural enough. There'd be no *post mortem*."

Hargess dropped upon one knee by the bed, the better to peer into the face of the sick man. The brow of Carpaez was wrinkled and clouded with a frown, but the stimulus of the violent scene that had passed in the room had brought his mind out of the cloud that had enwrapped it. One hand touched the arm of Hargess on one side of his bed. The other fell upon the hand of Jargan on the opposite side, and the skin, to the gambler's sensitive touch, was icy cold and thick and harsh.

"My dear friend Hargess," said the invalid, "you have done already too much for me. My own son has forgotten me in this time of need…but you have done too much. You shall not imperil yourself for me as you have just been doing. I

100

saw you struggling…with someone coming to attack me. …" He laid his hand across his forehead. "My mind goes a blank there," he said faintly. "I can remember no more. Except that there was danger, and that you were here, Hargess. Therefore I knew that I must be safe."

Big Hargess reached across the bed and closed the hand of the sick man upon that of the gambler. "You feel the hand of that man?" he asked.

"Yes." Carpaez nodded.

"It's the hand of another friend," said Hargess. "It's the hand of a man that's just saved your life, and, unless I read the sign plumb wrong, it's the hand of a gent that you'll see a lot more of before you're through with him."

"My brain is spinning," whispered Carpaez. "I shall know how to thank him in the morning. But now…."

His hands relaxed. His eyes closed. He had fainted.

VI

The morning, if it did not bring to *Don* José Carpaez the strength to know and to thank the man who had saved his life, brought to his door a big youth in his early twenties with the brown face and the strong, steady eye and the elastic step of an athlete who has trained in the open. Aside from that, his appearance was by no means prepossessing. His clothes seemed to have been, at one time, good in make and material and fashionable in cut, but time and hard usage had ruined them. Great grease stains blotched the coat and trousers. His collarless shirt was turned in at the throat, and, although the throat itself was clean enough to suggest a recent washing, the shirt was black with grease and grime. The once swaggering hat was battered to a shapeless pulp that flopped awkwardly upon his head. The toe of one shoe was gouged open, very much as though a barb of wire had caught in it and slashed it wide; the heel had been completely ripped away from the other.

This was the man, nevertheless, who knocked loudly upon the door of Carpaez's room the next morning. That door was opened by Jargan. Down the hall Jargan heard a mumbling of angry voices. He guessed that the tattered stranger had worked considerable havoc with the outposts before he was able to break through the lines and reach this point.

"Who are you?" said Jargan.

"It's more to the point to say...'Who are you?'" said the other, panting. "Let me through the door!" He thrust out a big, square, lower jaw.

Thereupon Jargan discovered that they were of a like bigness. Sweeping the form of the other, he discovered likewise the athletic mold of the newcomer, and Jargan smiled upon him, a smile that showed his white teeth but left his black eyes unlit. "Son," said Jargan, "didn't your mamma never teach you not to talk so fast? Before you start to bust in here, tell me why you're coming."

The latter glanced over his shoulder. Footsteps were hurrying toward him. Angry voices were growing louder.

"Here," he said, "is a good reason."

Without turning his head, he smote Jargan squarely on the point of the jaw. Although taken brutally and most unfairly by surprise, Jargan was in the act of jerking his head back when the blow landed with sufficient force to knock him flat upon his back. The big young stranger leaped into the room. Had he stepped wide of Jargan, all would have been well. But he stepped too close, and that was a great mistake. There are certain tribes of cats that fight with more deadly effect when lying upon their backs than when on all fours. While Jargan, lying prone, might not be as effective as when he stood erect, he was still not out of the battle. The man of the ragged clothes had stepped almost literally upon an intermeshing of barbed wire. The first step entangled him. The second brought him crashing to the floor.

As he fell, with an oath of surprise and anger, he tried for a strangle hold, whipping his left forearm under Jargan's right shoulder, and then clamping his left hand upon the throat of the other, but the surface of Jargan's skin seemed to be oiled. The hand slipped from his throat at the first shrug of a shoulder. Before the stranger could draw breath, the surprising fellow had writhed into a new position, half propped upon his left elbow while he smote up with his right fist, a sharp and cruel blow.

It did not stun the big stranger, but it set him back upon the floor. Before he could move again, the battle was taken out of the hands of Jargan. Half a dozen men, headed by the hotel proprietor, dived through the door, spilled at random over the newcomer, and flattened him under a pile of bodies.

Jargan rose and pitched them right and left until he came to the form of the man of the ragged clothes, now with most of the wind pressed out of him. Jargan lifted him to his feet and dragged him into the hall, followed by the others. There, too numb and breathless to fight back, the youth leaned against the wall, panting heavily, and stared at Jargan.

Jargan stared back. Upon the side of his jaw a sore place was aching. He was aware that a lump was forming. He knew, still further, that had the blow landed a fraction of an inch nearer the point of his chin, he would have collapsed upon the floor and not recovered for some time. Therefore he viewed the tall young man with growing respect.

"What in hell," said Jargan slowly, "is the meaning of all this?"

"He busted up to the desk," said the owner of the hotel, "and he said he wanted to see José Carpaez. I told him that he couldn't do it, because Carpaez was sick and because you were in charge and wouldn't let anybody but the doctor come near. He wanted to know who the devil you were, and, before I could tell him, he bolted for the stairs. I hollered to Jordan and Kilpatrick, here, to stop him. They tackled him together, but he turned into gunpowder, blew up, and kept on going!"

A growl from Jordan and another from Kilpatrick verified this portion of the tale.

"They stopped him long enough for some of the rest of us to catch up. We nailed him again on the stairs. There was another blowing up, and he got clean up here. For a fighting fool I ain't seen his like in some years!"

Jargan moistened his lips and regarded the stranger with a beneficent eye. "We were just warming up to our work," he said. "You sure spoiled a nice party by busting in between us that way. Now, son, tell us what's your rush to see old Carpaez?"

"Why should I explain?" said the other haughtily. But his dignity was impaired by his lack of wind, and presently he gasped: "I am Juan Carpaez...let me in to him!"

Here Haskins interpolated an incredulous exclamation, and, stepping close, he jerked the other around until the light from the window at the end of the hall struck full upon his face. Then he stepped back, shaking his head.

"I dunno," said Haskins. "It might be. I ain't seen him in three years, and he's sure growed a lot. What sign have you got that you're young Carpaez dressed up like a hobo in a play?"

"Here, Haskins," said the other. "Look at this. Perhaps you remember?" Drawing up his coat sleeve, he displayed on the forearm a great curved scar, several inches in length.

Jargan

"By the Lord," said Haskins, "I remember it now. That was where that crazy fellow sliced you four years back. Carpaez, I'm sure sorry that I've treated you this way, but it was the clothes that fooled me. I'd always seen you dressed up slick...and I ain't seen you at all for three years!"

"It's nothing at all," said the latter. He shook hands heartily with Haskins. "I ought to thank you for taking such good care of my father that nobody can break in on him. Now I suppose I may see him?"

He turned triumphantly upon Jargan, only to find that worthy was in the act of lighting a cigarette. He completed that act, blew a wedge of sweet-scented smoke toward the ceiling, and then snapped the burned match to a distance. "You may not," said Jargan complacently. "I got no orders from the doctor to let you in. Your dad's sick, kid. You hear? He's been busting his heart for three weeks because you ain't showed up. Now that you've come...well, I'll wait for doctor's orders before...."

"I'll see you damned before I let you keep me out of that room," said Juan Carpaez.

His bright blue eyes burned and snapped at Jargan, but the gambler merely dropped one hand upon his hip, just above the butt of his revolver, and he continued smoking.

"There's been about enough noise, I reckon," he said. "I've heard you damn me, son, and I won't need to write that down in a book to remember it. But you and me can have our arguments later on. Right now, you and the rest of the bunch are going to clear out of this hall. Noise may kill the old man as sure as bullets."

That last sentence brought a quick change in the manner of Carpaez. All the violence disappeared. Without a word of protest, he allowed Jargan to go back into the room alone and close the door. Young Juan Carpaez remained in the hall with

105

Haskins, entreating him to say what had happened and what the condition of his father was now. The others had now gone downstairs. Haskins took Juan up to the end of the hall and there confided the whole strange story.

"It's a fairy book yarn, Carpaez," he said. "You never heard of Jargan. You went away to school before he landed in these parts and began to make history every summer. Anyway, Jargan seen some sort of a signal flashed by a gent named Nuñez Mendoza to the hotel and saw the answer flashed from the window of your father's room. It looked queer to Jargan, so he started investigating, and the long and short of it was that he seen Mary Chapel, the nurse that was taking care of your father, bring in some chocolate that Jargan managed to spill off the table, because he figured there was something wrong with it. Then he tore around to the room, busted the door in…it's only got a latch right now…and stopped the nurse from giving your father a drink of the stuff that was left in the pitcher. A rumpus started. In the middle of it, the cat got convulsions and died. Carpaez, the chocolate was poisoned! Mary Chapel was arrested. The doc came and gave your father a blood test and found that he was soaked full of arsenic. That was why he hadn't got well of his wounds! Then they started to look for Nuñez Mendoza, but Nuñez had slipped out. He came back in the middle of the night, sliced through the wall of the jail, and let Mary Chapel out, and both of them are clean gone this morning. Right now your father has about an even break to get well or to not get well. What they figure is that Mendoza bribed Mary Chapel to use the poison slow and sure, so's nobody would ever suspect that it had anything to do with your father. But he got tired of waiting. Last night he decided to finish things up quick, and she mixed a knockout dose. Just by luck Jargan happened to catch the flash of that signal. That's the short of why Jargan won't let folks bust in on your father. He's taken this case into his own hands, and Jargan has a pretty good pair of hands, as you'll be apt to learn later on."

"He should have knocked me on the head with the butt of his gun," said the youngster miserably. "The quickest way to get rid of me would have been the best way. What a fool I've been."

"The main thing," said Haskins solemnly, "is why you ain't showed up all this time?"

"Because I've had to fight my way every mile that I came west and south," said Juan Carpaez. "But that's a long yarn."

VII

As a matter of fact, it was so long a tale that it did not come forth for a whole week. At the end of that time, Juan and Jargan sat in the sunshine that streamed through the windows of the bedroom and saw the doctor raise a finger at them. They followed his gesture into the hall.

"He's through the thick of it," he told them. "He's sleeping soundly. From now on that constitution of his will bring him back to his old self rapidly. Stay away from him. Stay out here and don't go in until you hear a sound from him."

It was while they walked up and down the corridor that young Carpaez told the story. As soon as the telegram from Bill Hargess came to him, he had hastily left college and, with a wallet filled with cash, had taken a night train for New York, there to get an overland to the West. When he wakened in the morning, he found that his money had been stolen in the hotel. He could not delay even to complain. He decided to beat his way across the country on the trains. Other men had done it before him, and he believed that he could give as good an account of himself as they had done, but he had not traveled a day on the rods before he discovered that he was being dogged across the continent by two villainous-looking fellows.

One misfortune followed another. In one terrible experience he was nearly knocked off the rods by a stone tied to the end of a rope and allowed to trail under the car by some enemy lodged on the top of it. He escaped from that peril only to be arrested on a charge of vagrancy at the next town he reached. There he was lodged in jail for five days before he managed to break out and resume his journey. Finally he had reached Big Horn, sadly worn and battered, to be sure, and raging with a desire to retrace his steps, as soon as possible, and find the two who had hounded him on the way West, and pay them in full.

Jargan listened to the narrative with a growing interest. He had found much to like in the other during the week of intimate association while they watched over old Carpaez. Now, as he learned the truth about that slow journey home and as he looked into the brown face and the keen blue eyes of the other, he felt, for the first time in his life that he had found a man whom he would be glad to have as his partner. Hitherto he had played a lone hand, but, very gradually, he began to see that there might be a value in close companionship.

"It sort of looks," he said thoughtfully, "as though there was a gang working to get rid of both you and your father. Look here, Juan, did you ever fall foul of a gent named Mendoza from the Argentine?"

"From the Argentine? I don't remember. We left there five years ago and came here. There may have been a Mendoza there who was an enemy, but I don't think so. My father had only two enemies in Argentina."

Jargan

"Two?" said Jargan, intensely interested.

Carpaez looked earnestly at his friend. "I have told my father," he said, "that I would never repeat the story, but surely we have no secrets from you, Jargan. When he is well, he will be the first to tell you with his own words. I'm only anticipating him by a few days. It goes back to the time when my father was a rich man in Argentina. Very, very rich. His land grant came from Spain in the days when they gave land according to the cattle that one brought into the country. The first Carpaez to come to Argentina brought great shipments of cattle, so he got great square leagues of land. His *estancia* became big and rich. Those who followed him increased the camp. It seemed as though every Cordoba was bound to prosper in our new country...."

"Cordoba?" echoed Jargan.

The other frowned, but then continued. "You may as well know all the truth. Cordoba is our name and not Carpaez. When my father left Argentina, he took the new name. The Cordobas who lived like princes in Argentina...he could not bear to have them beggars in other places by the same name, so he took that of Carpaez. The Cordobas, then, grew rich in Argentina. They had numberless cattle. They owned blooded horses, a great home in Buenos Aires, railroad stock...in fact, there was nothing into which their hands did not dip. As the fortune increased, it became necessary that a closer financial genius be used to manage it. My father, you see, was no financier. When he was still a young man and came into the estate, he took in two young secretaries. The idea was simple and beautiful. One was to act as a check upon the other. Each had bookkeepers that kept the accounts of the estate. If one took a false step, it would be discovered in the accounting rendered by the other. The majordomos of the *estancia,* the managers of the various properties, made their reports to the two secretaries, Ricardo Romero and Guillermo Solis, and Solis and Romero made their reports and recommendations separately to my father.

"It seemed perfect, and my father, who hates business, sat back and forgot about his properties. So it went smoothly, wonderfully smoothly, for year after year while Romero and Solis became middle-aged men of family, still in the same positions, drawing down larger and larger salaries, growing rich. One would have said that they were growing rich because they had made such wise selections for the investment of money, but the investments they had made here and there for my father were not so good. Just how peculiar they were, he did not notice for many years. You see, they could cover the fact that they had employed vast quantities of the money by the way they presented their accounts. My father hardly glanced at these. All he knew was that he could draw out as much cash as he pleased whenever he pleased. That was enough for him. Also, he knew that more land had been added to the estate. That was also enough for him. Only an accident made him wish to come to the assistance of a friend who had suffered tremendous losses. It was Carbal? Perhaps you remember the rebellion of Carbal? No? Well, it was not such a great thing. But Carbal rebelled. Some of his family had been treated badly, and Carbal began an uprising. His poor little rebellion was overthrown at once, and he was forced to flee from the country and became a penniless man abroad. But my father knew him well. He determined to buy the estate of Carbal when the government sold it, and then he would work the property and send the entire income to poor Carbal…a very generous idea, eh?

"But when he attempted to get the money, he discovered that he had not enough, and that it would be hard to get enough. He looked about and found that here and there upon his estate mortgages had been plastered. In fact, he had from time to time signed the documents that his secretaries placed before him. He had thought nothing about them. Now, alarmed, he began a close investigation, and he discovered that he had been plucked to the extent of millions of dollars by his secretaries. He looked up their resources. He found that both of them were very rich men. They had grown by magic while managing his estates. He went over their books, but the books of one agreed perfectly with the books of the other. Of course, it is plain to see what they had done. They had simply put their heads together and decided that what was simply a good living if they remained honest and apart would become a gold mine if they worked in co-ordination. So they had worked together to plunder the estate of Cordoba.

"Ricardo Romero was the leader. He is a man of iron, a big, broad, smiling man of iron. He is full of laughter and cold-blooded wiles. He is fond of birds and little children. He is always playing games...that is Romero. That is that devil! Romero was the man who planned everything and showed Solis what must be done if they were to get rich. The honesty of Romero appeared only in the equality of the division of the spoil which he made with Solis. Each of them received exactly one half.

"As for Solis himself, he is quite a different sort. He is a thin-faced, fish-eyed hypocrite. He is devout. He prays much. He has built churches. He is that sort of thief, you see, Jargan? He talks little. He appears to think much. That is *Señor* Guillermo Solis. But he is as black a devil as Romero!

"When my father began to press on and discover the truth about them, and saw how they had pulled the wool over his eyes and how they had crucified their benefactor, he became enraged. You don't know my father when he is enraged,

Jargan. He is fifty-five, or nearly that now, and his hair is white with his troubles. But his strength is still tremendous when he is angered. He is a fighter. He flies for the throat like a bulldog. Yes, he is like a lion, that father of mine. I remember that terrible passion that came over him when the blow fell and he made the discovery, although my mother and I did not know it at the time. We could hear him stamping up and down his room. Once he threw a chair the length of the room, and it was found smashed to splinters. Sometimes we heard him groan. He came out with hollow eyes and rushed to find Solis and Romero, to denounce them and throw them into prison. But at the door of his house, he was stopped. He was arrested by an officer of the law on the charge of treason.

"That night the news came of the charges. The devilish Solis and the fiend Romero had informed the government of the intentions of my father to give money to support Carbal, and in so doing afford succor to an enemy of the state. The newspapers made a furor over it. It was said that my father had merely been waiting until the revolt of poor Carbal showed some headway. Then he intended to throw all of his vast resources upon the side of the rebels. There was a wave of popular anger, supported by the malicious lies published by two papers financed by Romero and Solis, and the trial of my father ended in his sentence to confiscation of his estate and a nominal term of three months in prison. It was held that the loss of his property would not be punishment enough.

"So he was sent to prison. My mother died of grief and shame, and the estate was sold to the highest bidder...or, rather, bidders...who happened to be Solis and Romero, buying the property with the money they had gained through speculation in its management. Jargan, do you speak Spanish?"

"Yes."

Jargan

"Then you know that only in Spanish are the words found in which to describe such demons. My father left Argentina at the end of his term of imprisonment and went to Spain, where he sold the old estates of the Cordoba family and, with the money and a new name, came to the United States. Here he expected, even at his age, to make a new beginning out of an old ruin, but all fortune has been against him. Now he lies barely past the point of death in a room and on a bed that the charity of strangers has furnished for him."

Juan dropped his face in his hands. Jargan, to whom such violent betrayal of emotion was distasteful, made his eyes a blank, incapable of seeing through the screen of cigarette smoke. There was a Latin flexibility and impetuosity of temper in the young Cordoba with which he could never be in sympathy, but under the surface he knew there was a solid manliness that he respected with all his heart.

"Juan," he said after a moment, when Cordoba again looked up, "where do you think we'll be a month from today?"

The other shook his head.

"Somewhere out to sea," said Jargan. He threw his cigarette out the window and shrugged his shoulders. "Without a hoss," he said, "I dunno how I'll make out, but you and me and the *don* have sure got to start trailing for Argentina."

"Never!" exclaimed Juan. "My family has been disgraced there! Never, Jargan!"

"Hell!" said Jargan. "Never is quite a spell. If a gent beat me out of a man-sized wad of money like that...or even if it was five-cents' worth of pipe tobacco...I'd go back and foller his trail till I wore my feet off. But that ain't the real point of what I'm saying. The real point, partner, is that there's something stirred up down in Argentina that'd be good for you to see."

113

"You do not know us, Jargan," said the Spaniard. "We shall never return to be shamed before our countrymen. Besides, they have cast us off, and therefore we cast off them!"

"Rot!" said Jargan. "That sounds pretty, but it don't mean nothing, partner. A country may throw off a man, but a man can't never forget his country. Ain't that right? You've dreamed about Argentina a pile of times, eh?"

Juan sighed.

"What I'm driving at is this," went on Jargan. "You and your father pull up stakes and leave the Argentine and try to forget about it and settle down plumb peaceable. Nobody bothers you for five years. At the end of that time, you and your dad are looked up, and *pronto* a lot of bad luck begins to come your way. They try to knife your father first, and then they try to poison him. At the same time they work at the other end of the line and try to kill you while you're on your way south. Don't you make something out of that, Cordoba?"

The latter frowned, and then shook his head. "It means that we have enemies, yes," he said. "But what else, Jargan?"

"And where have you any enemies except in Argentina?" asked Jargan, almost in disgust. "The gents around these parts swear by your father. But you notice that Mendoza comes from the Argentine and that he seems to have run the work to kill your father. No doubt he had his hand in sending the two on your trail, too. That checks up with this result... Solis and Romero, them two skunks down in the Argentine, have got afraid of you again, so they've sent out spies to locate you and finish the two of you. They nearly done it, the first crack out of the box. But you can rest easy that they'll try again. Why? Because there's something happened down in the Argentine that would make it uncomfortable for them if you got wind of it!"

"What?" exclaimed Cordoba.

"That's why," said Jargan, "we're going to be on the ocean in a month from today. Your father will be well by that time …or well enough to travel, anyway. We'll head south to see the look on the faces of Romero, Solis, and company when they take a slant at the three of us breezing out onto that *estancia,* or whatever you call it."

"Travel to the Argentine? Without a penny?" groaned Juan.

"Bah!" said Jargan. "I've played chances at ten to one. Don't you think this is worth a play?"

VIII

It was still a day or so less than a month from that moment when Jargan stepped into the room of a hotel in New Orleans and shied his hat across to a chair. He then brought out his usual cigarette, lit it, and fanned a cloud of smoke from before him.

"It is as I feared," said *Don* José Cordoba. "There has been no good fortune. The money has not been picked up."

The *don* had, as Jargan prophesied, almost recovered. He was still a little pale, perhaps, but his face had filled out, his eyes were clear, his step was firm and active. "The money *has* been picked up," said Jargan. "There's no doubt about that. But it's been picked up out of my pocket, *Don* José, and there'll be quite a spell in between before it's put back. That's the way they work."

Don José made a graceful gesture of surrender. "It is money lost in my service," he said. "It is a debt that I shall see repaid to the last penny, *señor.*"

Jargan regarded him with calm disapproval and answered

115

not a word to this remark. "There's a hoss boat," he said, "that's leavin' this afternoon for Buenos Aires. It's a tramp freighter, the *General Slawson,* command of Captain Joséph Humphries, and it's carrying a load of hossflesh headed for Argentina. Partly they're high-blooded devils and partly they're mustangs. The yarn goes that somebody down in Argentina wants to toughen up the breed in one direction and give it more speed in the other direction...hosses for work and hosses to race, you see?" He paused. The father and son had interchanged glances during this singular speech, but they made no comment. If Jargan had gone mad and begun to rave, they would have listened with unalterable control of their facial muscles. "The point," explained Jargan, "is that we can get aboard that boat and run down to Buenos Aires on her. We have not the coin to buy passage. There ain't any other cabin passengers, anyways. But there's a need of some men to handle hosses. *Don* José, could you wrangle hosses for a couple of weeks going south?"

"I?" said the other in his deep, gentle voice. "I shall be glad to attempt it, *señor.*"

So it was settled.

That morning they had arrived in the city of many colors to wait for a boat that was to touch port in a few days and then start for Buenos Aires, but the pocket of Jargan, containing all the available wealth of the party, had been picked as they walked the street that day and their total resources were now nothing. So Jargan had sent his two friends to their hotel room and sallied forth alone to look over the resources of the town.

He had been successful, indeed, in locating a gambler of his acquaintance, but the fellow was hopelessly broke, and Jargan had passed on until he located a battered old tramp freighter at the docks, just taking aboard the last of its cargo

Jargan

of horses for Argentina. There he had glimpsed and heard the ravings of a huge man with an apoplectic face, and learned that it was the captain, Joseph Humphries, and that his irritation came from the desertion of several of his intended crew at the last moment.

So the three of them, lugging their suitcases, came down to the dock together, three big men, all of exactly one height. From the front, the dignity of *Don* José's white mustaches and flowing white hair gave him an added importance. It seemed to Jargan, now that the Spaniard's health was returning, he had never seen a man with such natural gentility. As they came onto the dock, he thought with a qualm of the contrast between the red-faced, roaring captain and the reserved gentleman of Argentina.

"*Don* José," he said, "I forgot one thing. I should have told you that the reason the captain's men left him was because he beat one of 'em almost to death."

Don José turned his fearless blue eye upon Jargan and smiled. "He will not strike me more than once, I think," he said.

Jargan shook his head. "Here's the point," he explained. "On dry land nobody could do it and keep a whole hide. But out at sea they tell me it's different. The captain is king. He can do what he wants. He can string you up by the neck if he feels like doing it. Afterward he'd have to account for it when he struck port. The trouble is that, when he gets to port, he's always got two-thirds of his crew ready to swear their lives away for him."

Don José sighed. Then he resolutely shook his head. "There is a black side to everything," he said. "We shall do very well aboard that boat, if we can secure the work."

Securing the work proved to be ridiculously simple. There were not even questions about their ability to handle horses.

117

"A man is a man, and a hand is a hand," observed Captain Humphries as they signed the book of the ship in his cabin. "Take 'em forward and show 'em quarters. Then take 'em aft and show 'em the work."

The boatswain obeyed. He conducted them first to the cramped and dirty quarters of the forecastle, where they put their luggage on the bunks that were assigned to them. Jargan cast a troubled glance at *Don* José, but the latter smiled and dropped his hand on the shoulder of Jargan.

"There is one thing for which we can be grateful," he said. "It is that Mendoza has not reached the boat. We shall sail free from him, and, therefore, we shall leave our bad luck behind us. *Señor*, I am happy enough to sing." And sing he did, when they had changed their clothes for overalls and started back into the hold of the ship.

They found the horses packed closely around the outer portion of the deck, with their heads pointed inward. There was not room for them to lie down, and they were packed cunningly so that, when the ship rolled, they would wedge together and not fall. The circumference of the ship was divided here and there by stout partitions, between each of which there was a number of horses. The animals were tethered to the fence that ran immediately before them. Distributed in this manner, the feeding and watering meant an immense labor by hand. For this labor the captain had signed a crew of ruffians of the first water. Jargan, familiar since his childhood with rough men, felt that he had never seen such a choice aggregation. Each one represented a different country: France, England, Russia, Germany, India, Japan— black, white, yellow, and brown; the color made no difference. Strength of hand and thickness of skin were the main essentials.

There was no delay in beginning the work. Instantly they

118

started in with the first feeding, while a riot of noise, stamping, neighing, and snorting, broke out up and down the decks. It was a shipment very largely of tough Western mustangs with enough dashes of good blood to give them looks, as a rule, but with the durable muscle of their wild ancestors and the temper of devils, confined as they were in this strange and terrible stable with a thousand unknown smells striking their nostrils. In the whole line, Jargan noticed only one quiet horse. He pointed out to a Mexican, carrying hay beside him, a tall, gray stallion with a single stall. The stallion curiously watched the motions of the men passing near him, but he neither neighed nor stamped or pawed. He was a keen contrast with a raging black stallion in a similar stall at the far end of that corridor. Jargan pointed out the contrast to the Mexican.

The latter merely grunted. "Two devils," he said. "That's the mustang *El Pantera*." He turned and pointed to the gray. "And that is a great outlaw. That is *Asesinato!*"

Even the stout nerves of Jargan thrilled. "The Panther" and "Murder" were strange names for horses. They explained themselves. *El Pantera* was lashing himself into a fury because other horses were being fed before him. *Asesinato,* the beautiful gray, merely watched with pricked ears. Even as Jargan watched, he saw that the pricked ears were a hypothetical sham. A man carrying hay passed too near the lifted head. Instantly the ears went flat back. The head darted out, snakelike, and the teeth snapped on a fold of shirt. *Asesinato* jerked his head down; the sleeve was ripped from the shirt, but the shrieking sailor managed to cast himself upon the deck and escape further damage. Before he had raised himself to his feet, *Asesinato* had pricked his ears cheerfully once more. Jargan set his teeth. He had never seen such malevolence in a horse. There was exactly the beautiful head that made children want to step up and pat the velvet muzzle, but if a child

119

ever attempted that, it would be a murder, that was all. *El Pantera,* at the far end of the corridor, writhing and prancing, with his eyes bloodshot and his ears flattened, was far less terrible than this silent demon.

Strength fascinates the strong, and Jargan looked with a hungry interest at *Asesinato.* It seemed to him that he could remember tales of such a beast going the rounds of the fairs and the roundup shows as an outlaw, an outlaw that no man had ever ridden for five solid minutes, an outlaw that strove always to kill the man whom he had thrown. He was roused from his trance by the booming voice of the boatswain in his ear: "What the hell is this? A beauty show or a ship? Start moving!"

Jargan favored the big boatswain with one of his mirthless smiles. Had they been on shore a speech half as violent would have gained the ship's officer a sound thrashing, but Jargan was by no means minded to spoil the passage before it began. He obeyed the order without a word.

The ship began to move while they were still at work. The time-honored custom of permitting all hands to loiter on deck while the ship drifts out from the dock was not honored on board the *General Slawson* with Joseph Humphries in command. When they finally were allowed to go on deck, the *General Slawson* was sliding far down the river. Jargan turned to *Don* José, who leaned on the rail at his side, and found that the latter, although sweating profusely, was neither completely exhausted nor out of temper with the work he had had to do.

"The first step home," said the man of Argentina, "is always a happy step. But look yonder, my dear friend!"

He pointed to a gasoline launch that was skimming down the river and that now sheered sharply in toward the side of the *General Slawson.* Standing up in the boat, he saw no less of a person than Nuñez Mendoza, his hat off, his black hair blowing in the wind, waving gracefully toward stout Joseph Humphries as the latter stood on the deck. In another moment Mendoza had reached the side, and there was a hasty parley between him and the captain, a waving of money, a lowering of the rope ladder. Then, while Mendoza climbed up the ladder, his trunk was hoisted aboard with a rope.

"Mendoza!" had, of one accord, broken from the lips of Jargan and Juan Cordoba.

Don José looked fixedly at the well-tailored fellow as he stood talking with the captain. "And that is Mendoza?" he said at last. "Well, it is bad enough to have the devil with one on dry land, but what will it be to be cooped up with him on the same boat at sea?"

IX

It seemed unquestionable that the malignant purpose of Mendoza had brought him to the ship to plague them on their journey to the Argentine, but for the next three days little was seen of him. Only now and again he appeared on the deck with the captain, with whom he seemed to have become a boon companion. The two could be seen swaggering back and forth at interims, but most of the time they spent in the cabin, gambling and, so the cabin boy reported, drinking. Juan Cordoba suggested that no real malice had actuated Mendoza in taking passage upon that boat, but merely a real desire to get back to his own country. That suggestion, however, could not live in the face of Jargan's report of the facts: on a passenger boat Mendoza could have started three days later than the horse boat and yet landed at Buenos Aires three days sooner.

Max Brand

The *General Slawson* plowed slowly through the tropic waters, wallowing along with a thick blanket of smoke pressing down over her bow as the trades fanned her, or the smoke blew to the side as the speed of the boat equaled the fainter strength of the wind. Every day it became hotter. The air seemed heavy and was hard to breathe even on deck. Below it was stifling. In that atmosphere the horses became down-headed and stood with flagging ears, the sweat coming down their sides. Through all that sickening weather as they crossed the equator, the work of the crew did not abate.

The old sailors, stripped to the waist and usually with bare feet, stood the trial better than the rest. Jargan was well enough. A pale spot sometimes showed in the hollow of his cheek, and blisters covered the palms of his hands, but he had within him an exhaustless well of nerve energy ready at his command. Juan Cordoba did nearly as well, but with *Don* José it was different. The long sickness had too newly left him. He was by no means back to normal, and he began to sink rapidly. It was in vain that Juan and Jargan attempted to help him and actually do almost his entire share of the work. Merely to stay below during the great heat and breathe the damp, hot air was too much for the older man. Half fainting, he bore it all without a word of complaint, while the boatswain sought him out with curses and forced him on to greater efforts. Always he would murmur to Jargan: "It will soon be over, Jargan. Do nothing for my sake, dear friend. One blow, and we are all ruined."

Presently the object of Mendoza was plain to them. He had corrupted the captain to his purpose, and the captain had simply instructed the boatswain to see that *Don* José did his full share of the work. He knew that sooner or later the elder Cordoba would sink under the effort, and then the first sign of brutality on the part of the boatswain would bring an attack from Juan or, still more probably, Jargan. The moment a blow was struck, the situation would change and the captain, if he wished, might even declare that a state of mutiny existed, throw them all in irons, and then—but the possibilities were limitless. It only required that the boatswain should center his attention on *Don* José.

It became a problem of endurance. The answer to the problem could only be of one nature. On the seventh day out, *Don* José reeled as he walked, and Jargen attempted to expostulate with the boatswain. The latter laughed in his face.

"Sick, is he?" he said. "A damned bluff, I'd call it! I've seen 'em try it before. No, he don't go to the doctor. He stays here!"

Don José stayed. It was only a matter of hours, now, before he dropped to the deck. The boatswain plied him with curses and threats, not really aimed at him but in the hope of leading Juan or Jargan to an outbreak. Only the pleading of the old man kept them in hand.

The outbreak came, against all expectancy, in a crisis of another sort. It was the one cheery time of day. The sun was hardly up. The heat had not yet begun to burn. The whole crew was cool and comfortable at the work of washing down the decks. In the midst of that work there was a call from below in the form of a shrill whinny, and then a cry from the boatswain.

"All hands below!"

They rushed down below to the first deck, and in the corridor they found a scene of wild confusion. A Babel of earsplitting neighs and stampings filled the air. In the center of the corridor *El Pantera* and *Asesinato* reared on their hind legs like two humans and were beating with forehoofs and tearing with their teeth. They whirled, separated, and rushed together again. Jargan saw blood streaming down the crest and

123

shoulder of *Asesinato,* while the other seemed as yet un-harmed. Some of the men started forward with ropes, but the boatswain called them back. He turned with a demoniac face toward *Don* José.

"Go put them horses back in their places!" he commanded. "On the jump!"

Don José drew a deep breath, hesitated, and then started forward without a word. Jargan stopped him with a hand on his shoulder. "Look here, bo's'n," he said, "my partner here can't handle a rope. Let me at them two and I'll have 'em tied in a minute!"

He had started forward, but the boatswain shouted to him to keep back. He had issued his orders. They were not to be changed. With a string of curses he forced *Don* José to continue.

Down the passage *Don* José went, steadily enough, although reeling a little when the deck shelved unexpectedly as the ship heeled in the wind and waves. In his hand he carried the lariat that means so much in the grip of the expert and means nothing at all to the amateur. The boatswain stepped forward and blocked the passage of any of the others who might offer to assist the older man.

The battle of the two stallions was progressing about evenly when *Don* José, coming near, threw the noose, not for the hoofs of one of the horses, as he might have thrown it, but ignorantly toward the head, hoping to choke one down. Even so, the noose fell wide of its mark and merely whipped across the back of *Asesinato.* The horse whirled to face the new attack, slashed out with heels that caught the black in the chest and crushed it back, and then darted at *Don* José with ears flattened and snaky head thrust forward.

The Spaniard plunged to one side, and *Asesinato,* slipping on a wet place on *the* deck, floundered to the boards. He was up again with the uncanny agility of a cat, a marvelous thing to view in a horse, and wheeled toward *Don* José again. The final kick had taken all the spirit of battle out of *El Pantera*. He stood back in a far corner with the blood streaming from his breast, watching the new combat with fierce but frightened eyes.

It was at that moment that Jargan leaped forward. He smashed through the press of sailors before him. The boatswain whirled toward him with set face and burly fist poised. "Keep back, you swine!" he commanded. "I'll crack your skull for you if you try to get past! Orders are orders. Keep back or I'll have you hanged for mutiny!"

Jargan, tearing himself clear of the others, leaped in with a driving fist that cracked the big boatswain cleanly on the jaw. His head snapped back, and he went down. Jargan raced on down the passage as *Asesinato,* regaining his footing after his first misspent charge, was wheeling to beat down *Don* José.

Still the latter, although only armed with a rope of whose management he knew nothing, stood his ground. He was reeling with weakness. His knees buckled under his weight. Yet he showed no symptoms of being about to fly. Jargan went past him like a catamount, snatching the rope from his feeble hands, and darting on at the great gray horse. He had no time to make the noose. All he could do was to thrash the rope across the face of the charging demon, and then leap back and flatten himself against the wall as the flying danger went past.

Asesinato wheeled again. Now, having missed his charge twice, he had a red eye of fury. There is nothing more terrible than a maddened horse, and Jargan, in that crowded space, knew that the chances were working five to one against him. In the foreground he saw *Don* José, gallantly and foolishly, throw up his arms with a shout of dismay and rush forward, as

125

if those naked hands could be of any help to Jargan in his battle with the murderous stallion. In the distance, among the shouting, surging mass of sailors, some of whom had picked the boatswain from the floor, he saw Juan Cordoba whip out a flashing revolver to kill the horse, and saw the weapon torn from his hand by the others. He saw and heard these things in one of those photographic flashes of the mind. Then he threw his rope. He did not aim at the head. Instead, he threw for the flying hoofs of the gray. As he threw, he could only pray for luck. His own skill, indeed, was hardly greater than that *of Don* José. In his childhood he had used a rope as a game, and since childhood he had scorned such a laborious means of making a livelihood. Now he had to look back to the skill that had been his ten years before.

Luck favored him. He saw the noose flick out on the deck. He jerked back frantically and saw it twitch up around diagonal foreleg and hind leg, just as he had hoped. At the same time he cast himself to the side, face down upon the floor. The white teeth of *Asesinato* met at his shoulder. Had he trusted only to his plunging hoofs, *Asesinato* would have broken the back of Jargan, but, instead, he chose to sink his teeth into the fallen man. The result was that he caught only the shirt, ripped cleanly from Jargan's body, and allowed the latter to spin to his feet and fling his whole weight against the end of the rope before *Asesinato* himself could whirl. The legs of the stallion were knocked out from under him. He fell with stunning force upon his side. The next instant he was hopelessly enmeshed in the rope.

X

Very loud and very pleasant was the ringing cheer of the sailors as Jargan completed his victory, an involuntary outburst. But what meant more to him was the hand of *Don* José on his shoulder and the silence of the Spaniard. When they turned toward the others, they saw that the boatswain was just returning to his senses, staggering like a drunkard. Captain Humphries was coming through the crew, and behind him the sneering face of Nuñez Mendoza.

If the boatswain were staggering as though drunk, the captain was in fact drunk. His usually red face was now fairly purple. One glimpse of the boatswain and of the blood that was trickling down the back of the latter's head where it had struck the deck and Captain Humphries roared with fury: "The man that strikes my officer strikes me! Get Jargan. Tie him and throw him in the hole. And the other? Where's the other? Where's the young snake? Where's Juan? Here he is... take him, too, and throw him in for good measure! Damn them, I'll teach them discipline!"

Behind the captain, halting midway on the flight of steps from above, appeared the cripple, Peter, Captain Humphries's small son. Jargan, as his glance roved about, seeking some escape, now looked at him. He saw that the youngster was white with excitement, perhaps with fear. The glimpse of poor little Peter was enough to warn him that Humphries would stick at nothing if he were resisted now. The story was short and ugly. After the death of his wife, Humphries had taken his only child on board his boat with him. On the very first cruise Peter had stumbled in the way and had been kicked out of it by his father. The result was a smashed bone in his leg that the doctors could not properly mend, and poor Peter was now crippled forever. He clung to the stairs with his withered arms and looked in terror down upon the crowd of men where his brutal father was thundering. If such a thing had happened to Peter for no crime at all, what would happen to Jargan for what the captain called open mutiny?

The very perfection of the captain's rage saved the skin of Jargan for the time being. Humphries wanted some grim and soul-satisfying torture, and he could not think of a sufficient one on the spur of the moment. Therefore, he ordered his men to take Jargan to the hole, and Juan Cordoba with him. Each was taken by the arm and shoved roughly away down the passage, past the heads of the frightened, restless horses until, passing down to the bottom of the ship, a trap door was raised and a dark, foul-smelling pit was exposed to them, and they were ordered down into it.

The healthy bronze of Juan Cordoba paled several shades, but Jargan merely shrugged his shoulders and addressed his last word to the Mexican who made one of the party. "Pedro," he said, "some of the boys are going to want to take it out of *Asesinato*'s hide for breaking out of his stall. If you keep them away from him, you get that gun of mine that you've admired. Understand?"

Pedro nodded, and grinned wickedly. "I know," he said. "You want to save him till you can get at him yourself, eh?"

Jargan regarded the other quietly for a moment. There was no use, he saw, in attempting an explanation, so he simply agreed with a nod and then led the way down into the black pit below them.

In the meantime, Captain Humphries, left with a red-hot temper and no means of lessening its heat at hand, began to regret that he had sent the two men away. Yet he must wait and devise a punishment that would be remembered and trembled at as long as he sailed the sea. On smaller pretexts than this he had indulged his love of cruelty. Now he had found a treasure trove. One man had struck a ship's officer, another had drawn a revolver, and he could find sailors who would swear, at his bidding, that the revolver had been aimed at the fallen boatswain. He could go further. He could declare that it was the beginning of a mutiny and that the attack was planned to be carried on to the rest of the ship's officers.

Jargan and Juan Cordoba were absolutely at his mercy. The captain was a specialist in pain. To him this prospect was as entrancing as the discovery of a pot of gold to a miner. But must he rage in quiet? He rolled his eyes to find an object on which to vent the first flush of his anger. The object he selected was *Don* José Cordoba, who now came unsteadily down the passage in front of the men who were leading the gray and *El Pantera* back to their original places.

"Come here!" shouted Humphries. He turned to the boatswain. "Bring him here!"

The boatswain darted one gratified glance at his master, and then strode down the deck, caught *Don* José by the arm, and jerked him forward until he confronted the captain.

"Now," roared Humphries with a string of oaths, "we'll find out how far a damned work-away can try to run a ship where I'm captain! To begin with, what in hell d'you mean by starting a mutiny?"

Don José was very weak, but now he managed to draw himself to his full height, and he smiled straight into the eyes of Humphries and said not a word.

"Answer me!" thundered Humphries.

Don José shrugged his shoulders.

"Then take it, damn you!" bellowed the captain, striking the man from Argentina full in the face.

Down he fell, a loose and heavy form, knocked completely senseless. The captain started forward as though he would jerk Cordoba to his feet for the pleasure of knocking him down again. He was checked by a loud and wailing shriek from behind and turned to see little Peter, clinging to the rail with one withered hand while the other was thrown up before his eyes to shut out the memory of what he had seen.

Captain Humphries cursed beneath his breath. Then, in a stride, he was through the crowd, barely in time to catch Peter in his arms as the little fellow pitched down in a faint. Throwing the light burden of the child over his arm and shouting for the doctor, Captain Humphries raced up to the open air of the deck above. There he placed Peter on the boards and, dropping to his knees, opened the shirt of the boy and began fanning him with his hat, at the same time thundering forth with another call for the doctor.

The latter came, sweating in haste.

"He's dead!" panted Joseph Humphries. "Doc, I've killed him! Lord God, I've damned myself...I've killed him!"

The doctor was a little man. He was hardly half the bulk of Captain Humphries, but he was the one man who spoke his mind to the big fellow. He was the one man in the world whom the captain feared.

"You haven't killed him...this time," said the doctor, after a summary examination. "But another little trick like this one and you'll have to wrap him in canvas and put a weight at his feet and drop him overboard. You hear me? One more...."

The captain held up his hand and turned a convulsed face toward the doctor. "Don't say it, Doc," he muttered. "It wasn't Peter that I hit. I...I...I didn't even know he was near me!"

Jargan

"Pick him up," commanded the doctor curtly, "and take him into your cabin. I'll work over him there and see what can be done."

In the captain's cabin he worked until little Peter opened his eyes, which seemed deathly big and black in the midst of his pale, pinched face. One glimpse of his father, at one side of the room, brought another shriek from his lips, and he pressed both hands across his eyes. "He killed him," gasped Peter. "He...he killed him, Doctor!"

Not one of the crew of the captain's ship would have believed their eyes had they seen it, but Captain Humphries dropped upon his knees and lifted the hands of Peter from his eyes. "Pete!" he protested. "That hound ain't killed. He tried mutiny. He tried murder, Pete, but I didn't kill him. I...I only knocked him down!"

The eyes of Peter remained tightly shut and now he shuddered. "Doctor," he whispered.

"Well?" queried the doctor.

"Please...send Dad away!"

The doctor turned savagely on the captain. "Get out!" he said.

Like a beaten dog the captain rose. He hesitated in the middle of the cabin. "Doc," he said, "I'll fix up the man and send him up here. D'you think that would help Pete?"

"Do you want him to?" the doctor asked the boy, and received an affirmative nod.

Captain Humphries fairly fled from the cabin and astonished the sailors among whom he burst a moment later on the deck below. *Don* José was in the act of picking himself up from the deck, where he had been permitted to lie, no one daring to aid the captain's victim. Now he was lifted in the stout arms of Humphries himself.

"Get some water!" thundered the captain. "Get some

131

plaster for his cut lip. Hurry, damn you! Are you made of wood, you?"

The sailors scattered as though by magic. Only Nunez Mendoza remained near. His face had grown black at this turn of events. "Remember this, Humphries," he said, as soon as he was sure that no other person would overhear him, "if you change your mind about finishing Cordoba, I can still change my mind about the money!"

That speech brought only a glare and another roar from the captain. "Damn you and your money! Get out of my sight!"

Mendoza, like a man stunned, went.

XI

It was in the after cabin that the captain and the doctor conferred later on. From the captain's own cabin there came a murmur of voices, the deep, smooth voice of a man and the edgy, uneven voice of little Peter.

"Hark to 'em," said big Humphries. "Hark to 'em, and Pete chattering like a magpie, God bless him! What does he see about the Spaniard to make him talk?"

"He sees the mark of your fist on his face," said the doctor.

Humphries writhed his ponderous bulk around as though to strike the doctor. One blow of that massive hand would have crumbled the spare frame of the doctor, but the blow did not fall. "Maybe that's it," he admitted then, sadly and humbly. "Maybe that's what's loosened his tongue, but... listen!"

A burst of shrill laughter sounded in the forward cabin.

"Listen to that, Doc! Listen to that! I ain't heard him laugh like that for a couple of years. Not since...."

He stopped and winced. Plainly he inferred that the blow he had struck the child had stopped all of Pete's laughter. Now he went to the door, dropped to his knees, and peered shamelessly through the keyhole. He returned after a moment to the doctor. His face was full of pain as he spoke.

"He's sitting on the Spaniard's knee," he said. "He's got Pete's head against his shoulder. He's telling him a yarn about something or other. Anyway, Pete's eyes are closed, and he's smiling." He paused, then began to walk up and down the cabin, his heavy boots clumping to and fro, to and fro, while the doctor looked out the window with eyes that were dull with the distance of the ocean's horizon. "He must be a pretty good man!" exclaimed the captain. He stopped before the doctor as though the discovery had shaken him to his feet. "He talks to Pete like he was fond of him. Yet he knows that Pete's my son, and he knows that my fist knocked him down. Doc, how's that possible?"

The doctor made no reply. He busied himself in the filling of his pipe. When he came to the lighting of it, the sudden sound of laughter from the forward cabin, fresh, thrilling laughter, made him drop the match from his fingers.

The captain resumed his walking and he resumed his mumbling talk at the same time. "I had the other two turned loose out of the hole," he said.

He shot a scowling glance across the cabin at the doctor, as though defying the little man to smile at him for having changed his mind. When he observed that the doctor was not inclined toward mirth, he sighed with relief. "I turned 'em out. They're both queer," said Humphries. "What d'ye think the fighter is doing?"

"Jargan?" queried the doctor.

"Who else? Yes, him. He's back working on the gray

horse. First he bandaged the black. After that, he got to working on *Asesinato*."

The doctor sat bolt upright and began to puff away at his pipe with the most furious speed.

"I had the Mexican watch 'em," explained the captain. "Seems that Jargan offered the Mexican his revolver, if he'd keep the boys away from *Asesinato* while he was in the hole. Now...."

The doctor spoke through a thick cloud of smoke. "Why did they send two man-killers like the black and the gray in the first place?" he asked.

"A little sharp American business," said the captain. "The Argentine firm asked for tough mustang blood. This is what they get."

The doctor smoked silently again.

"He says now," continued the captain, "that there's nothing wrong with *Asesinato*...never was anything wrong with him. Says there's nothing wrong with any horse, but it's all with the men who've handled 'em. Sounds like fool talk, eh? Might as well say that men are good or bad just according to the way you treat 'em...."

"Well?" broke in the doctor. "Well? Why not say that?"

The captain glowered at him, and then, changing his expression, ground his fist across his forehead. "I've never been able to figure just how you work things out, Doc," he growled. But he seemed strangely subdued and strangely worried. Every now and then, when the sharp burst of Pete's laughter came from the next cabin, he would stop in his pacing as though struck.

"After all," said the doctor, "it seems to me that you have really nothing against Jargan and the others."

The captain shrugged his shoulders. He had never been able to conceal the shady sides of his character from the terrible little doctor. "He's made of money," confessed Humphries. "He flashed a roll of bills thick enough to choke a mule, heavy enough to knock down a horse. It made me dizzy to look at it. What could I do? What could I do, Doc?"

The doctor clung to his role of silence. He had seen it work before; now he noticed that the big captain writhed before it.

"All I had to do," Humphries said, "was to see that none of the three of 'em got ashore in the Argentine. Understand? There wasn't much to that, was there?"

"Perhaps a little accident to the three of them on the way, eh?" suggested the doctor smoothly.

The captain started and glanced at the other. "No more of that!" he said, breathing hard.

The doctor smiled quietly. "I've got a suggestion, if you really want to right yourself. You've played a dirty hand in this game."

Humphries shook his head like a badgered bull, but he endured the punishment of the doctor's stinging tongue.

"I can show you the way out," said the doctor, "and it's a way that you'll like."

"Start talking, then."

"Mendoza is a pretty strong fellow, don't you think?"

"What's that got to do with it?"

"A handy man in a fight of any kind, I should say."

"I don't follow you, Doc."

"This cabin, I should say, has nothing in it that can be easily damaged?"

"Doc, what are you driving at?"

"Just at this...Mendoza has done Jargan and the other two wrongs. Mendoza has told you that the three are all criminals. From what you've seen of the one they call *Don* José, you think they're all white men. You want to give Jargan a chance to get back. Well, Captain, my idea is that you take

135

'em both to this cabin, turn 'em loose in here, and lock the door from the outside. They'll make an adjustment of some kind then, I think."

XII

All that had happened on that ship, this day, had been inexplicable to Jargan. Now, in the middle of the afternoon, he sat cross-legged on the deck in the little passageway in front of the gray man-killer, *Asesinato*. In fact, *Asesinato* could have reached the head of the man with his teeth at any time, but he was occupied in quite another fashion. He had at first thought that the wheat heads that were held by Jargan must be a delusion and a snare, some new and cunning way of tormenting him. Eventually he had snatched at a little wisp of the carefully selected heads that Jargan held and had found that they were really not poison.

After that, he fell to studying the tall stranger. He had never been a headlong horse. An Indian had raised *Asesinato,* and long lessons of Indian patience and Indian cruelty had been taught the horse. Instead of being maddened by what he learned, *Asesinato*'s mind had been developed. He had learned to study the men near him. He had learned to tempt them toward his beautiful head by means of pricking his ears. Now he had set about studying Jargan. Inside of an hour, he had decided that this man who was so strong, so fearlessly willing to fight him, was also kind, gentle of hand and spirit. In short, *Asesinato* made up his mind that this fellow, although in appearance a man, was in reality of a far nobler species. In another hour it came to pass that Jargan sat under the fence in easy reach of *Asesinato* and fed the man-killer out of the palm of his hand.

Jargan

It is marvelous how much a horse can learn about a man by touching his hand with that sensitive, almost prehensile upper lip. *Asesinato* learned in that fashion, and by snuffing out a great breath upon the hand of Jargan, then glaring half angrily, half in terror, into the face of the man to see if a blow was suspended in the air. But there were no blows, only a steady and soothing voice that cast around the gray a cloud of trust and content. He knew that he had been very bad that morning. He knew that in the ordinary course of events heavy blows of a whip should be his measure for having broken from his assigned place. Instead of that, in due time here was this man, whose fingers he had learned to trust, busily washing out the wounds that *El Pantera* had made and then closing the places with wonderfully soothing bandages.

Sympathy, which speaks in a hundred languages without words, was now eloquent enough to speak from Jargan to the wild horse, or, in reality, to a horse not wild at all, but simply over-domesticated. Men, when they train horses, count upon implanting an instinctive fear in the beasts. Instead, now and again, they only succeed in implanting instinctive hatred. This was the case with beautiful *Asesinato*. He had well earned his name.

It was at this pleasant work that the message from the captain came to Jargan. It was delivered by the boatswain, his bruised face more murderous in expression than ever. Jargan was wanted above, and Jargan, rising from his place, patted the nose of the gray in farewell and followed. On the forward part of the deck he passed *Don* José, walking back and forth with little Pete hobbling at his side. *Don* José waved toward him, but there was no time to exchange a word. He could only guess, from the liberty of *Don* José, that all was not as bad as it might be, and that his own liberty was something more than a temporary thing. Juan, he knew, had been assigned to the fire room to pass coal. Perhaps he was about to be given a similarly onerous position.

Presently the boatswain knocked at the door of a cabin. The voice of the captain himself called loudly to enter, and Jargan opened the door and stepped into the presence of the captain and none other than Nuñez Mendoza. The boatswain closed the door and left them together.

Mendoza had started a little at the sight of Jargan, but he settled back in his chair and waited.

The captain explained at once. "It looked to me," he declared, "that you two ought to be able to get together and talk things over friendly. I don't want any stabbings in the back on a ship I command. So I've brought you together. I'm going to go over you and make sure that you have no weapons of any kind on you. Then I'm going to walk out and let you talk."

Mendoza sprang from his chair with an exclamation, but the roaring oath of Humphries convinced him that he would not alter his position. Of his own volition he gave up a revolver and a heavy-handled knife of grim dimensions. Then the captain walked out and left them together.

Their maneuvers were not unlike those of two panthers, forced into one cage. Keeping as far from one another as the dimensions of the cabin permitted, they found chairs and sank into them gingerly, keeping on the edges of their seats, ready to spring into action at a moment's notice.

"Seems to me," began Jargan, "that there ain't going to be any cause for trouble between us, Mendoza."

"Of course not, *señor*," said Mendoza. He spread out the palms of his hands in a gesture of sublime affability. "From the first we have thought well of each other."

The lips of Jargan parted and showed his white teeth in that mirthless smile of his. "That's right," he answered. "All we need, if we're going to get on together, is for you to tell me

Jargan

just why you were sent up to murder José and Juan Cordoba."

"So?" said Mendoza, lifting his brows in polite wonder. "The name is not Carpaez?"

Jargan grinned again, lifted himself out of his chair with an easy motion, and stepped to the center of the room. There he sat upon the edge of a little round table that was fixed to the floor. "Are we going to get together, Mendoza?" he asked.

The Argentinian had likewise left his chair. He leaned against the cabin wall. "I cannot tell what you mean, *señor*," he murmured.

"This," said Jargan. "I want the whole news. I want to know why you came, and who hired you."

"Hired me?" cried Mendoza.

"You hound!" snarled Jargan, all his surface good humor suddenly leaving him. "If you won't talk, I'll choke it out of you." He flung himself headlong across the cabin.

To meet that rush, however, he noticed that the man from the Argentine did not so much as stoop to dodge or to prepare to cast his own weight against that of Jargan. Instead, he stood bolt erect, with his right hand held a little behind him and a strange, cruel smile upon his lips. Then that right hand jerked up with a flash of bright steel dripping from it. Jargan, with a shout of dismay and rage, saw that he was running on certain death. He had barely time, at the last moment, to check his impetus a little and lunge to the side.

The knife slithered down his arm as Mendoza stabbed hastily. Then, as he leaped in, Jargan flung himself back across the little round table in the center of the room. He was safe for an instant, at least.

"Call for the captain," snarled Mendoza, "before I stick you like a pig, and then kick the blood out of you faster while you wallow on the floor."

139

Jargan, stepping back as he circled the table, laid his hand on the back of a chair.

"No, no." Mendoza smiled. "The chairs are fastened to the floor, my friend."

"Right for you," answered Jargan. "They're fastened to the floor, but the floor is old, and...." As he spoke, he threw his whole strength against the chair. There was a squeaking and ripping as the rusted bolts tore through the wood. The heavy chair came loose in Jargan's hands. At the first sight of that maneuver, Mendoza had sprung forward with his knife extended like a rapier. He was in time only to receive the mass of the chair crashing against his body. His knife flew to the side. He toppled back and landed half stunned against the wall.

Fear of death was the stimulus that brought him struggling to his feet, but it was only to feel the fingers of Jargan writhe into his hair, jam his head back against the wall, and then the point of his own knife tickled the hollow of his throat.

"Do you talk?" panted Jargan.

"*Señor*," said Mendoza, "I have never intended anything else from the first."

Jargan stepped back. "Mendoza," he said, "you've got nerve enough to be an honest man! Why in hell don't you change your part one of these days?"

"Because I have been tempted," said Mendoza, panting a little but still maintaining his white-lipped smile. "I have been tempted by the example of the famous gambler, *Señor* Jargan."

Jargan could only reply by shrugging his shoulders.

XIII

They sat in a semicircle, Jargan and *Don* José, and Juan, sooty from the fire room, facing Mendoza and waiting for his story. It was typical of Mendoza that, now that he was cornered, he showed neither shame nor perturbation. He continued smoking, as calm as ever, and his thoughtful eye showed either he was arranging his story or selecting the proper words for an artistic opening to the tale that was to unriddle the mysteries behind that attempted murder in Big Horn.

"When a man grows old," began Mendoza at length, "he is very apt to grow foolish, also. I have seen the strongest of men in their youth grow stronger still in middle age and then slowly crumble as they become old. For my part, I shall die in the prime of my middle life."

"Or, perhaps, even sooner," said *Don* José with the most courteous of bows.

Mendoza smiled with a touch of deviltry in his eyes. "You are right, *señor*. Perhaps even sooner." He raised his eyes, and waved some smoke toward the ceiling as though sending a greeting toward the infinite. "To come into my story, age was the undoing of no less a man than Guillermo Solis."

There was a light exclamation from both of the Cordobas.

"You," said the Argentinian to *Don* José, "can perhaps best appreciate how truly great a man he was."

"Yes," said *Don* José, "I can appreciate how...great he was."

"Seeing that he began as nothing?"

"Exactly, and is now rich."

"And respected."

"True," said *Don* José, his voice hardening a little, "re-

141

spected, also! Well, well, go on, *señor*."

Mendoza smiled upon them all in a paternal fashion. "As a matter of fact," he continued, "many people have given too great a portion of the credit to Ricardo Romero. But you, *señores,* will agree with me that Solis is the artful and profound spirit who saw into the future."

"Exactly," said *Don* José.

"I am verging toward the point, my friends. I began by saying that *Don* Guillermo had begun to grow old, but I gave you no hint as to how very old he suddenly became. *Señores,* that great man suddenly stepped out of the world and became attached to a religious order."

Don José started, then settled back. "Nothing in the world, I had thought, could surprise me. But this, I confess, does. Continue, my friend."

"When he entered the holy order, conscience entered him, you see."

"Ah."

"I mean exactly that. He became, of a sudden, one filled with remorse for past sins. He thought of many things. He said that the building of churches alone could not possibly atone for what he had done to one man above all others, that when he rapped at the gate of heaven, the very mention of one name would bar him from entrance. You follow me, *señores?*"

"Even to heaven," said *Don* José.

Mendoza smiled again. "But, though Guillermo Solis, now *Padre* Guillermo, was willing to confess his sins to himself, he was not willing to publish them to the world unless there existed a sufficient reason for such publication...unless, in fact, you or your son were still alive. He determined then that he would select a man at once clever enough and silent enough to keep his goal from the world and send him out to find the Cordobas. I, *señores,* was the man whom he so honored with his choice. He sent for me. He unburdened himself of a strange story, which all of you know already. He told me that the supposed traitor, José Cordoba, was in truth a virtuous man. Having completed the tale, he let me infer that, if I in turn repeated the story, my days in this world would not be long. I accepted the munificent terms on which the work was tendered to me. I went home. I packed my necessaries. I purchased a ticket for Spain, where it was reasonably certain that you were living, and I was about to leave when I received a message that brought me into the presence of that other great man, Ricardo Romero. Although Solis may once have been the greater of the two, the more inspired, there is no real comparison between their strengths now.

"I saw Romero, I say, and he told me, in short, that he knew every word that had passed between me and the good Solis. How he learned, the devil alone can tell. But, having confided so much to me, he went on to tell me that, if I persisted in attempting to discharge my mission, my days were numbered. If, on the other hand, I should change into his service, all would be well. He began to speak of money. When Ricardo Romero begins to speak of money…well, it is almost a proverb…even the angels fly low from heaven to listen to his terms. And I, *señores,* am not an angel.

"To be brief, I accepted his terms. I sailed not for Spain but for the United States. Ricardo Romero, wiser than his partner, had tracked every move you had made. 'An enemy whose grudge has not been paid is a sword of Damocles hanging above my head!' said the great Romero to me. I went, therefore, directly to your place. I took with me, on the trip, a certain comrade of mine, an excellent man with weapons. He died on that luckless night when he and I and two others attacked you, *Señor* Cordoba, and when the two Hargess brothers came by in the nick of time to save your life.

143

"Then I changed my plans. I attracted with a small bribe the nurse who had charge of you, *señor*. I planned with her everything that followed. You must agree, everything was going well until God chose to destroy my clever work." He sighed, and then, turning toward Jargan, there flashed into his eyes, for a fraction of a second, a glance of the most unspeakable rage and hatred. "There," he said, "is the instrument which He chose for His work. And here, *señores,* sit I, beaten by Providence and bad fortune. I am about to land on a shore where the malignity of the terrible Ricardo Romero will now meet me. You, *señores,* are about to land on a shore where the immense fortune of Solis is ready to be placed in your hands. Have I spoken enough? Am I believed?"

"And where do we go," said Jargan, "to make sure of all this from Solis?"

"We?" echoed Mendoza, picking out the one word for his comment.

"Exactly. You stay with us, Mendoza."

"I am a dead man, then."

"Very likely. But there is a chance, eh?"

Mendoza lit another cigarette, still thoughtful. "Kismet," he said at last. "Only fools rebel against fate and manifest destiny. I shall go. I shall be your guide."

"Where?"

"To the great Solis house, which is now about to become your home."

The four horsemen had ridden long and steadily in the dark of the cloud shadows, but when the moon suddenly broke through the clouds, it showed, first of all, upon the silver mane of the gray stallion that Jargan bestrode—none other than *Asesinato*. Mendoza and the two Cordobas had kept with difficulty beside him, pressing their horses steadily with their spurs. Now, moving up from one of the rare elevations in that vast plain, they could look far off and see the moonlight making a haze about a noble cluster of trees and, loftier than these, glimmering upon the roofs of a number of large buildings.

Don José held up his arms and wept. Jargan gazed upon him in wonder but not in scorn. He knew the fine old man too well to despise his emotion. Upon his other side, Juan clasped his hand

"It is the old home," he said. "Now our home is yours, dear Jargan, until death parts us."

The Trail to Crazy Man

Louis L'Amour

Louis Dearborn LaMoore (1908–1988) was born in Jamestown, North Dakota. He left home at fifteen and subse-
quently held a wide variety of jobs although he worked mostly
as a merchant seaman. From his earliest youth, L'Amour had
a love of verse. His first published work was a poem, "The
Chap Worth While," appearing when he was eighteen years
old in his former hometown's newspaper, the *Jamestown Sun*.
It is the only poem from his early years that he left out of
SMOKE FROM THIS ALTAR that appeared in 1939 from
Lusk Publishers in Oklahoma City, a book that L'Amour
published himself; however, this poem is reproduced in THE
LOUIS L'AMOUR COMPANION (Andrews and McMeel,
1992) edited by Robert Weinberg. L'Amour wrote poems
and articles for a number of small circulation arts magazines
all through the early 1930s and, after hundreds of rejection
slips, finally had his first story accepted, "Anything for a Pal"
in *True Gang Life* (10/35). He returned in 1938 to live with
his family where they had settled in Choctaw, Oklahoma, determined to make writing his career. He wrote a fight story
bought by Standard Magazines that year and became acquainted with editor Leo Margulies who was to play an important role later in L'Amour's life. "The Town No Guns
Could Tame" in *New Western* (3/40) was his first published
Western story.

During the Second World War, L'Amour was drafted and
ultimately served with the U.S. Army Transportation Corps
in Europe. However, in the two years before he was shipped

out, he managed to write a great many adventure stories for Standard Magazines. The first story he published in 1946, the year of his discharge, was a Western, "Law of the Desert Born," in *Dime Western* (4/46). A call to Leo Margulies resulted in L'Amour's agreeing to write Western stories for the various Western pulp magazines published by Standard Magazines, a third of which appeared under the byline Jim Mayo, the name of a character in L'Amour's earlier adventure fiction. The proposal for L'Amour to write new Hopalong Cassidy novels came from Margulies who wanted to launch *Hopalong Cassidy's Western Magazine* to take advantage of the popularity William Boyd's old films and new television series were enjoying with a new generation. Doubleday & Company agreed to publish the pulp novelettes in hard cover books. L'Amour was paid $500 a story, no royalties, and he was assigned the house name Tex Burns. L'Amour read Clarence E. Mulford's books about the Bar-20 and based his Hopalong Cassidy on Mulford's original creation. Only two issues of the magazine appeared before it ceased publication. Doubleday felt that the Hopalong character had to appear exactly as William Boyd did in the films and on television, and thus even the first two novels had to be revamped to meet with this requirement prior to publication in book form.

L'Amour's first Western novel under his own byline was WESTWARD THE TIDE (World's Work, 1950). It was rejected by every American publisher to which it was submitted. World's Work paid a flat £75 without royalties for British Empire rights in perpetuity. L'Amour sold his first Western short story to a slick magazine a year later, "The Gift of Cochise," in *Collier's* (7/5/52). Robert Fellows and John Wayne purchased screen rights to this story from L'Amour for $4,000, and James Edward Grant, one of Wayne's favorite screenwriters, developed a script from it, changing

Louis L'Amour

L'Amour's Ches Lane to Hondo Lane. L'Amour retained the right to novelize Grant's screenplay, which differs substantially from his short story, and he was able to get an endorsement from Wayne to be used as a blurb, stating that HONDO was the finest Western Wayne had ever read. HONDO (Fawcett Gold Medal, 1953) by Louis L'Amour was released on the same day as the film, HONDO (Warner, 1953), with a first printing of 320,000 copies.

With SHOWDOWN AT YELLOW BUTTE (Ace, 1953) by Jim Mayo, L'Amour began a series of short Western novels for Don Wollheim that could be doubled with other short novels by other authors in Ace Publishing's paperback two-fers. Advances on these were $800, and usually the author never earned any royalties. HELLER WITH A GUN (Fawcett Gold Medal, 1955) was the first of a series of original Westerns L'Amour had agreed to write under his own name following the success of HONDO for Fawcett. L'Amour wanted even this early to have his Western novels published in hardcover editions. He expanded "Guns of the Timberland" by Jim Mayo in *West* (9/50) for GUNS OF THE TIMBERLANDS (Jason Press, 1955), a hardcover Western for which he was paid an advance of $250. Another novel for Jason Press followed and then SILVER CANYON (Avalon Books, 1956) for Thomas Bouregy & Company. These were basically lending library publishers, and the books seldom earned much money above the small advances paid.

The great turn in L'Amour's fortunes came about because of problems Saul David was having with his original paperback Westerns program at Bantam Books. Fred Glidden had been signed to a contract to produce two original paperback Luke Short Western novels a year for an advance of $15,000 each. It was a long-term contract, but, in the first ten years of

148

it, Fred only wrote six novels. Literary agent Marguerite E. Harper then persuaded Bantam that Fred's brother, Jon, could help fulfill the contract, and Jon was signed for eight Peter Dawson Western novels. When Jon died suddenly before completing even one book for Bantam, Harper managed to engage a ghost writer at the Disney studios to write these eight "Peter Dawson" novels, beginning with THE SAVAGES (Bantam, 1959). They proved inferior to anything Jon had ever written, and what sales they had seemed to be due only to the Peter Dawson name.

Saul David wanted to know from L'Amour if *he* could deliver two Western novels a year. L'Amour said he could, and he did. In fact, by 1962 this number was increased to three original paperback novels a year. The first L'Amour novel to appear under the Bantam contract was RADIGAN (Bantam, 1958). It seemed to me, after I read all of the Western stories L'Amour ever wrote in preparation for my essay, "Louis L'Amour's Western Fiction" in A VARIABLE HARVEST (McFarland, 1990), that by the time L'Amour wrote "Riders of the Dawn" in *Giant Western* (6/51), the short novel he later expanded to form SILVER CANYON, he had almost burned out on the Western story, and this was years before his fame, wealth, and tremendous sales figures. He had developed seven basic plot situations in his pulp Western stories, and he used them over and over again in writing his original paperback Westerns. FLINT (Bantam, 1960), considered by many to be one of L'Amour's better efforts, is basically a reprise of the range war plot which, of the seven, is the one L'Amour used most often. L'Amour's hero, Flint, knows about a hideout in the badlands (where, depending on the story, something is hidden: cattle, horses, outlaws, etc.). Even certain episodes within his basic plots are repeated again and again. Flint scales a sharp V in a cañon wall to escape a tight spot as

Louis L'Amour

Jim Gatlin had before him in L'Amour's "The Black Rock Coffin Makers" in .44 *Western* (2/50) and many a L'Amour hero would again.

Basic to this range war plot is the villain's means for crowding out the other ranchers in a district. He brings in a giant herd that requires all the available grass and forces all the smaller ranchers out of business. It was this same strategy Bantam used in marketing L'Amour. *All* of his Western titles were continuously kept in print. Independent distributors were required to buy titles in lots of 10,000 copies if they wanted access to other Bantam titles at significantly discounted prices. In time L'Amour's paperbacks forced almost everyone else off the racks in the Western sections. L'Amour himself comprised the other half of this successful strategy. He dressed up in cowboy outfits, traveled about the country in a motor home, visiting with independent distributors, taking them to dinner and charming them, making them personal friends. He promoted himself at every available opportunity. L'Amour insisted that he was telling the stories of the people who had made America a great nation, and he appealed to patriotism as much as to commercialism in his rhetoric.

His fiction suffered, of course, stories written hurriedly and submitted in their first draft and published as he wrote them. A character would have a rifle in his hand, a model not yet invented in the period in which the story was set, and, when he crossed a street, the rifle would vanish without explanation. A scene would begin in a saloon and suddenly the setting would be a hotel dining room. Characters would die once and, a few pages later, die again. An old man for most of a story would turn out to be in his twenties.

Once, when we were talking and Louis had showed me his topographical maps and his library of thousands of volumes that he claimed he used for research, he asserted that, if he claimed there was a rock in a road at a certain point in a story, his readers knew that, if they went to that spot, they would find the rock just as he described it. I told him that might be so, but I personally was troubled by the many inconsistencies in his stories. Take LAST STAND AT PAPAGO WELLS (Fawcett Gold Medal, 1957). Five characters are killed during an Indian raid. One of the surviving characters emerges from seclusion after the attack and counts *six* corpses.

"I'll have to go back and count them again," L'Amour said, and smiled. "But, you know, I don't think the people who read my books would really care."

All of this notwithstanding, there are many fine, and some spectacular, moments in Louis L'Amour's Western fiction. I think he was at his best in the shorter forms, especially his magazine stories, and the two best stories he ever wrote appeared in the 1950s, "The Gift of Cochise" early in the decade and "War Party" in *The Saturday Evening Post* in 1959. The latter was later expanded by L'Amour to serve as the opening chapters for BENDIGO SHAFTER (Dutton, 1979). That book is so poorly structured that Harold Kuebler, senior editor at Doubleday & Company to whom it was first offered, said he would not publish it unless L'Amour undertook extensive revisions. This L'Amour refused to do, and, eventually, Bantam started a hardcover publishing program to accommodate him when no other hardcover publisher proved willing to accept his books as he wrote them. Yet the short novel that follows possesses several of the characteristics in purest form that, I suspect, no matter how diluted they ultimately would become, account in largest measure for the loyal following Louis L'Amour won from his readers: a strong male character who is single and hence marriageable; and the powerful, romantic, strangely compelling vision of the American West that invests L'Amour's Western fiction and makes it such a delightful escape from the cares of a later time—in this author's words: "It was a land where nothing was small, nothing was simple. Everything, the lives of men and the stories they told, ran to extremes."

I

In the dark, odorous forecastle a big man with wide shoulders sat at a scarred mess table, his feet spread to brace himself against the roll of the ship. A brass hurricane lantern, its light turned low, swung from a beam overhead, and in the vague light the big man studied a worn and sweat-stained chart. There was no sound in the forecastle but the distant rustle of the bow wash about the hull, the lazy creak of the square rigger's timbers, a few snores from sleeping men, and the hoarse, rasping breath of a man who was dying in the lower bunk.

The big man who bent over the chart wore a slipover jersey with alternate red and white stripes, a broad leather belt with a brass buckle, and coarse jeans. On his feet were woven leather sandals of soft, much-oiled leather. His hair was shaggy and uncut, but he was clean-shaven except for a mustache and burns ides. The chart he studied showed the coast of northern California. He marked a point on it with the tip of his knife, then checked the time with a heavy gold watch. After a swift calculation, he folded the chart and replaced it in an oilskin packet with other papers, and tucked the packet under his jersey above his belt.

Rising, he stood for an instant, canting to the roll of the ship, staring down at the white-haired man in the lower bunk. There was that about the big man to make him stand out in any crowd. He was a man born to command, not only because of his splendid physique and the strength of his character, but because of his personality. He knelt beside the bunk and touched the dying man's wrist. The pulse was feeble. Rafe Caradec crouched there, waiting, watching, thinking.

In a few hours at most, possibly even in a few minutes, this man would die. In the long year at sea his health had broken down under forced labor and constant beatings, and this last one had broken him up internally. When Charles Rodney was dead he, Rafe Caradec, would do what he must.

The ship rolled slightly, and the older man sighed and his lids opened suddenly. For a moment he stared upward into the ill-smelling darkness, then his head turned. He saw the big man crouched beside him. He smiled. His hand fumbled for Rafe's.

"Yuh...yuh've got the papers? Yuh won't forget?"

"I won't forget."

"Yuh must be careful."

"I know."

"See my wife, Carol. Explain to her that I didn't run away, that I wasn't afraid. Tell her I had the money, was comin' back. I'm worried about the mortgage I paid. I don't trust Barkow." Then the man lay silently, breathing deeply, hoarsely. For the first time in three days he was conscious and aware. "Take care of 'em, Rafe," he continued, rising up slightly. "I've got to trust yuh! Yuh're the only chance I have! Dyin' ain't bad, except for them. And to think...a whole year has gone by. Anything may have happened."

"You'd better rest," Rafe said gently.

"It's late for that. He's done me in this time. Why did this happen to me, Rafe? To us?"

Caradec shrugged his powerful shoulders. "I don't know. No reason, I guess. We were just there at the wrong time. We took a drink we shouldn't have taken."

The old man's voice lowered. "Yuh're goin' to try...to-night?"

Rafe smiled then. "Try? Tonight we're goin' ashore,

Rodney. This is our only chance. I'm goin' to see the captain first."

Rodney smiled, and lay back, his face a shade whiter, his breathing more gentle.

A year they had been together, a brutal, ugly, awful year of labor, blood, and bitterness. It had begun, that year, one night in San Francisco in Hongkong Bohl's place on the Barbary Coast. Rafe Caradec was just back from Central America with a pocketful of money, his latest revolution cleaned up, and the proceeds in his pocket, and some of it in the bank. The months just past had been jungle months, dripping jungle, fever-ridden and stifling with heat and humidity. It had been a period of raids and battles, but finally it was over, and Rafe had taken his payment in cash and moved on. He had been on the town, making up for lost time—Rafe Caradec, gambler, soldier of fortune, wanderer of the far places.

Somewhere along the route that night he had met Charles Rodney, a sun-browned cattleman who had come to San Francisco to raise money for his ranch in Wyoming. They had had a couple of drinks and dropped in at Hongkong Bohl's dive. They'd had a drink there, too, and, when they awakened, it had been to the slow, long roll of the sea and the brutal voice of Bully Borger, skipper of the *Mary S.* Rafe had cursed himself for a tenderfoot and a fool. To have been shanghaied like any drunken farmer! He had shrugged it off, knowing the uselessness of resistance. After all, it was not his first trip to sea. Rodney had been wild. He had rushed to the captain and demanded to be put ashore, and Bully Borger had knocked him down and booted him senseless while the mate stood by with a pistol. That had happened twice more until Rodney returned to work almost a cripple, and frantic with worry over his wife and daughter.

155

As always, the crew had split into cliques. One of these consisted of Rafe, Rodney, Roy Penn, Rock Mullaney, and Tex Brisco. Penn had been a law student and occasional prospector. Mullaney was an able-bodied seaman, hardrock miner, and cowhand. They had been shanghaied in San Francisco in the same lot with Rafe and Rodney. Tex Brisco was a Texas cowhand who had been shanghaied from a waterfront dive in Galveston where he had gone to look at the sea.

Finding a friend in Rafe, Rodney had told him the whole story of his coming to Wyoming with his wife and daughter, of what drought and Indians had done to his herd, and how finally he had mortgaged his ranch to a man named Barkow. Rustlers had invaded the country, and he had lost cattle. Finally reaching the end of his rope, he had gone to San Francisco to get a loan from an old friend. In San Francisco, surprisingly, he had met Barkow and some others, and paid off the mortgage. A few hours later, wandering into Hongkong Bohl's place, which had been recommended to him by Barkow's friends, he had been doped, robbed, and shanghaied.

When the ship returned to San Francisco after a year, Rodney had demanded to be put ashore, and Borger had laughed at him. Then Charles Rodney had tackled the big man again, and that time the beating had been final. With Rodney dying, the *Mary S.* had finished her loading and slipped out of port so he could be conveniently "lost at sea."

The cattleman's breathing had grown gentler, and Rafe leaned his head on the edge of the bunk, dozing. Rodney had given him the deed to the ranch, a deed that gave him half a share, the other half belonging to Rodney's wife and daughter. Caradec had promised to save the ranch if he possibly could. Rodney had also given him Barkow's signed receipt for the money.

The Trail to Crazy Man

*   *   *   *   *

Rafe's head came up with a jerk. How long he had slept he did not know. He stiffened as he glanced at Charles Rodney. The hoarse, rasping breath was gone; the even, gentle breath was no more. Rodney was dead.

For an instant, Rafe held the old man's wrist, then drew the blanket over Rodney's face. Abruptly then, he got up. A quick glance at his watch told him they had only a few minutes until they would sight Cape Mendocino. Grabbing a small bag of things off the upper bunk, he turned quickly to the companionway.

Two big feet and two hairy ankles were visible on the top step. They moved, and step by step a man came down the ladder. He was a big man, bigger than Rafe, and his small, cruel eyes stared at him, then at Rodney's bunk.

"Dead?"

"Yes."

The big man rubbed a fist along his unshaven jowl. He grinned at Rafe. "I heerd him speak aboot the ranch. It could be a nice thing, that. I heerd aboot them ranches. Money in 'em." His eyes brightened with cupidity and cunning. "We share an' share alike, eh?"

"No." Caradec's voice was flat. "The deed is made out to his daughter and me. His wife is to share, also. I aim to keep nothin' for myself."

The big man chuckled hoarsely. "I can see that," he said. "Josh Briggs is no fool, Caradec! You're intendin' to get it *all* for yourself. I want mine." He leaned on the hand rail of the ladder. "We can have a nice thing, Caradec. They said there was trouble over there, huh? I guess we can handle any trouble, an' make some ourselves."

"The Rodneys get it all," Rafe said. "Stand aside. I'm in a hurry."

Briggs's face was ugly. "Don't get high an' mighty with me!" he said roughly. "Unless you split even with me, you don't get away. I know aboot the boat you've got ready. I can stop you there, or here."

Rafe Caradec knew the futility of words. There are some natures to whom only violence is an argument. His left hand shot up suddenly, his stiffened fingers and thumb making a V that caught Briggs where his jawbone joined his throat. The blow was short, vicious, unexpected. Briggs's head jerked back, and Rafe hooked short and hard with his right, then followed through with a smashing elbow that flattened Briggs's nose and showered him with blood.

Rafe dropped his bag, then struck, left and right to the body, then left and right to the chin. The last two blows cracked like pistol shots. Josh Briggs hit the foot of the ladder in a heap, rolled over, and lay still, his head partly under the table. Rafe picked up his bag and went up the ladder without so much as a backward glance.

II

On the dark deck Rafe Caradec moved aft along the starboard side. A shadow moved out from the mainmast.

"You ready?"

"Ready, Rock."

Two more men got up from the darkness near the foot of the mast, and all four hauled the boat from its place and got it to the side.

"This the right place?" Penn asked.

"Almost." Caradec straightened. "Get her ready. I'm going to call on the Old Man."

The Trail to Crazy Man

In the darkness he could feel their eyes on him. "You think that's wise?"

"No, but he killed Rodney. I've got to see him."

"You goin' to kill Borger?"

It was like them that they did not doubt he could if he wished. Somehow he had always impressed men so that what he wanted to accomplish, he would accomplish. "No, just a good beatin'. He's had it comin' for a long time."

Mullaney spat. He was a stocky, muscular man. "Yuh cusséd right he has! I'd like to help."

"No, there'll be no help for either of us. Stand by and watch for the mate."

Penn chuckled. "He's tied up aft, by the wheel."

Rafe Caradec turned and walked forward. His soft leather sandals made no noise on the hardwood deck, or on the companionway as he descended. He moved like a shadow along the bulkhead, and saw the door of the captain's cabin standing open. He was inside and had taken two steps before the captain looked up.

Bully Borger was big, almost a giant. He had a red beard around his jaw bone under his chin. He squinted from cold, gray eyes at Rafe. "What's wrong?" he demanded. "Trouble on deck?"

"No, Captain," Rafe said shortly, "there's trouble here. I've come to beat you within an inch of your life, Captain. Charles Rodney is dead. You ruined his life, Captain, and then you killed him."

Borger was on his feet, cat-like. Somehow he had always known this moment would come. A dozen times he had told himself he should kill Caradec, but the man was a seaman, and in the lot of shanghaied crews there were few. So he had delayed.

He lunged at the drawer for his brass knuckles. Rafe had

159

been waiting for that, poised on the balls of his feet. His left hand dropped to the captain's wrist in a grip like steel, and his right hand sank to the wrist in the captain's middle. It stopped Borger, that punch did, stopped him flat-footed for only an instant, but that instant was enough. Rafe's head darted forward, butting the bigger man in the face, as Rafe felt the bones crunch under his hard skull.

Yet the agony gave Borger a burst of strength, and he tore the hand with the knuckles loose and got his fingers through their holes. He lunged, swinging a roundhouse blow that would have dropped a bull elephant. Rafe went under the swing, his movements timed perfectly, his actions almost negligent. He smashed left and right to the wind, and the punches drove hard at Borger's stomach, and he doubled up, gasping. Rafe dropped a palm to the back of the man's head and shoved him down, hard. At the same instant, his knee came up, smashing Borger's face into a gory pulp.

Bully Borger, the dirtiest fighter on many a waterfront, staggered back, moaning with pain. His face expressionless, Rafe Caradec stepped in and threw punches with both hands, driving, wicked punches that had the power of those broad shoulders behind them, and timed with the rolling of the ship. Left, right, left, right, blows that cut and chopped like meat cleavers. Borger tottered and fell back across the settee.

Rafe wheeled to see Penn's blond head in the doorway. Roy Penn stared at the bloody hulk, then at Rafe. "Better come on. The cape's showing off the starb'rd bow."

When they had the boat in the water, they slid down the rope one after the other, then Rafe slashed it with his belt knife, and the boat dropped back. The black hulk of the ship swept by them. Her stern lifted, then sank, and Rafe, at the tiller, turned the bow of the boat toward the monstrous black-ness of the cape.

Mullaney and Penn got the sail up, when the mast was stepped, then Penn looked around at Rafe.

"That was mutiny, you know."

"It was," Rafe said calmly. "I didn't ask to go aboard, and knockout drops in a Barbary Coast dive ain't my way of askin' for a year's job!"

"A year?" Penn swore. "Two years and more for me. For Tex, too."

"Yuh know this coast?" Mullaney asked.

Rafe nodded. "Not well, but there's a place just north of the cape where we can run in. To the south the sunken ledges and rocks might tear our bottom out, but I think we can make this other place. Can you all swim?"

The mountainous headland loomed black against the gray-turning sky of the hours before daybreak. The seaward face of the cape was rocky and water-worn along the shore-line. Rafe, studying the currents and the rocks, brought the boat neatly in among them and headed for a boulder-strewn gray beach where water curled and left a white ruffle of surf. They scrambled out of the boat and threw their gear on the narrow beach.

"How about the boat?" Texas demanded. "Do we leave it?"

"Shove her off, cut a hole in the bottom, and let her sink," Rafe said.

When the hole had been cut, they let the sea take the boat offshore a little, watching it fill and sink. Then they picked up their gear, and Rafe Caradec led them inland, working along the shoulder of the mountain. The northern slope was cov-ered with brush and trees and afforded some concealment. Fog was rolling in from the sea, and soon the gray, cottony shroud of it settled over the countryside.

When they had several miles behind them, Rafe drew to a halt. Penn opened the sack he was carrying and got out some bread, figs, coffee, and a pot.

"Stole 'em out of the captain's stores," he said. "Figured we might as well eat."

"Got anything to drink?" Mullaney rubbed the dark stubble on his wide jaws.

"Uhn-huh. Two bottles of rum. Good stuff from Jamaica."

"Yuh'll do to ride the river with," Tex said, squatting on his heels. He glanced up at Rafe. "What comes now?"

"Wyomin', for me." Rafe broke some sticks and put them into the fire Rock was kindling. "I made my promise to Rodney, and I'll keep it."

"He trusted yuh." Tex studied him thoughtfully.

"Yes. I'm not goin' to let him down. Anyway," he added, smiling, "Wyomin's a long way from here, and we should be as far away as we can. They may try to find us. Mutiny's a hangin' offense."

"Ever run any cattle?" Tex wanted to know.

"Not since I was a kid. I was born in New Orleans, grew up near San Antonio. Rodney tried to tell me all he could."

"I been over the trail to Dodge twice," Tex said, "and to Wyomin' once. I'll be needin' a job."

"You're hired," Rafe said, "if we ever get the money to pay you."

"I'll chance it," Tex Brisco agreed. "I like the way yuh do things."

"Me for the gold fields in Nevady," Rock said.

"That's good for me," Penn said. "If me and Rock don't strike it rich, we may come huntin' a feed."

There was no trail through the tall grass but the one the

mind could make, or the instinct of the cattle moving toward water, yet as the long-legged zebra dun moved along the flank of the little herd, Rafe Caradec thought he was coming home. This was a land for a man to love, a long, beautiful land of rolling grass and trees, of towering mountains pushing their dark peaks against the sky and the straight, slim beauty of lodgepole pines.

He sat easy in the saddle, more at home than in many months, for almost half his life had been lived astride a horse, and he liked the dun, which had an easy, space-eating stride. He had won the horse in a poker game in Ogden, and won the saddle and bridle in the same game. The new Winchester '73, newest and finest gun on the market, he had bought in San Francisco.

A breeze whispered in the grass, turning it to green and shifting silver as the wind stirred along the bottomland. Rafe heard the gallop of a horse behind him and reined in, turning. Tex Brisco rode up alongside.

"We should be about there, Rafe," he said, digging in his pocket for the makings. "Tell me about that business again, will yuh?"

Rafe nodded. "Rodney's brand was one he bought from an *hombre* named Shafter Mason. It was the Bar M. He had two thousand acres in Long Valley that he bought from Red Cloud, paid him good for it, and he was runnin' cattle on that, and some four thousand acres outside the valley. His cabin was built in the entrance to Crazy Man Cañon. He borrowed money, and mortgaged the land to a man named Bruce Barkow. Barkow's a big cattleman there, tied in with three or four others. He has several gunmen workin' for him, but he was the only man around who could loan him the money he needed."

"What's yore plan?" Brisco asked, his eyes following the cattle.

"Tex, I haven't got one. I couldn't plan until I saw the lay of the land. The first thing will be to find Missus Rodney and her daughter and, from them, learn what the situation is. Then we can go to work. In the meantime, I aim to sell these cattle and hunt up Red Cloud."

"That'll be tough," Tex suggested. "There's been some Injun trouble, and he's a Sioux. Mostly, they're on the prod right now."

"I can't help it, Tex," Rafe said. "I've got to see him, tell him I have the deed, and explain so's he'll understand. He might turn out to be a good friend, and he would certainly make a bad enemy."

"There may be some question about these cattle," Tex suggested dryly.

"What of it?" Rafe shrugged. "They are all strays, and we culled them out of cañons where no white man has been in years, and slapped our own brand on 'em. We've driven them two hundred miles, so nobody here has any claim on them. Whoever started cattle where we found these left the country a long time ago. You remember what that old trapper told us?"

"Yeah," Tex agreed, "our claim's good enough." He glanced again at the brand, then looked curiously at Rafe. "Man, why didn't yuh tell me yore old man owned the C Bar? My uncle rode for 'em a while! I heard a lot about 'em! When yuh said to put the C Bar on these cattle, yuh could have knocked me over with a axe! Why, Uncle Joe used to tell me all about the C Bar outfit. The old man had a son who was a ring-tailed terror as a kid. Slick with a gun...say!" Tex Brisco stared at Rafe. "You wouldn't be the same one, would yuh?"

"I'm afraid I am," Rafe said. "For a kid I was too slick with a gun. Had a run-in with some old enemies of Dad's, and, when it was over, I hightailed for Mexico."

"Heard about it."

164

The Trail to Crazy Man

Tex turned his sorrel out in a tight circle to cut a steer back into the herd, and they moved on. Rafe Caradec rode warily, with an eye on the country. This was all Indian country, and the Sioux and Cheyennes had been hunting trouble ever since Custer had ridden into the Black Hills, which was the heart of the Indian country and almost sacred to the plains tribes. This was the near end of Long Valley where Rodney's range had begun, and it could be no more than a few miles to Crazy Man Cañon and his cabin.

Rafe touched a spur to the dun and cantered toward the head of the drive. There were three hundred head of cattle in this bunch, and, when the old trapper had told him about them, curiosity had impelled him to have a look. In the green bottom of several adjoining cañons these cattle, remnants of a herd brought into the country several years before, had looked fat and fine. It had been brutal, bitter work, but he and Tex had rounded up and branded the cattle, then hired two drifting cowhands to help them with the drive.

He passed the man riding point and headed for the strip of trees where Crazy Man Creek curved out of the cañon and turned in a long, sweeping semicircle out to the middle of the valley, then down its center, irrigating some of the finest grassland he had ever seen. Much of it, he noted, was sub-irrigated from the mountains that lifted on both sides of the valley. The air was fresh and cool after the long, hot drive over the mountains and desert. The heavy fragrance of the pines and the smell of the long grass shimmering with dew lifted to his nostrils. He moved the dun down to the stream, and sat his saddle while the horse dipped its muzzle into the clear, cold water of the Crazy Man. When the gelding lifted its head, Rafe waded him across the stream and climbed the opposite bank, then turned upstream toward the cañon.

165

III

The bench beside the stream, backed by its stand of lodgepole pines, looked just as Rodney had described it. Yet, as the cabin came into sight, Rafe's lips tightened with apprehension, for there was no sign of life. The dun, feeling his anxiety, broke into a canter. One glance sufficed. The cabin was empty, and evidently had been so for a long time.

Rafe was standing in the door when Tex rode up. Brisco glanced around, then at Rafe. "Well," he said, "looks like we've had a long ride for nothin'."

The other two hands rode up—Johnny Gill and Bo Marsh, both Texans. With restless saddles, they had finished a drive in the Wyoming country, then headed west and had ridden clear to Salt Lake. On their return they had run into Rafe and Tex, and hired on to work the herd east to Long Valley.

Gill, a short, leather-faced man of thirty, stared around. "I know this place," he said. "Used to be the Rodney Ranch. Feller name of Dan Shute took over. Rancher."

"Shute, eh?" Tex glanced at Caradec. "Not Barkow?"

Gill shook his head. "Barkow made out to be helpin' Rodney's women folks, but he didn't do much good. Personal, I never figgered he cut no great swath a-tryin'. Anyway, this here Dan Shute is a bad *hombre*."

"Well," Rafe said casually, "mebbe we'll find out how bad. I aim to settle right here."

Gill looked at him thoughtfully. "Yuh're buyin' yoreself a piece of trouble, mister," he said. "But I never cottoned to Dan Shute myself. Yuh got any rightful claim to this range? This is where yuh was headed, ain't it?"

"That's right," Rafe said, "and I have a claim."

166

The Trail to Crazy Man

"Well, Bo," Gill said, hooking a leg over the saddle horn, "want to drift on, or do we stay and see how this gent stacks up with Dan Shute?"

Marsh grinned. He had a reckless, infectious grin. "Shore, Johnny," he said. "I'm for stayin' on. Shute's got him a big, red-headed hand ridin' for him that I never liked, no ways."

"Thanks, boys," Rafe said. "Looks like I've got an outfit. Keep the cattle in pretty close the next few days. I'm ridin' in to Painted Rock."

"That town belongs to Barkow," Gill advised. "Might pay yuh to kind of check up on Barkow and Shute. Some of the boys talkin' around the chuck wagon sort of figgered there was more to that than met the eye. That Bruce Barkow is a right important gent around here, but when yuh read his sign, it don't always add up."

"Mebbe," Rafe suggested thoughtfully, "you'd better come along. Let Tex and Marsh worry with the cattle."

Rafe Caradec turned the dun toward Painted Rock. Despite himself, he was worried. His liking for the little cattleman, Rodney, had been very real, and he had come to know and respect the man while aboard the *Mary S.* In the weeks that had followed the flight from the ship, he had been considering the problem of Rodney's ranch so much that it had become much his own problem. Now, Rodney's worst fears seemed to have been realized. The family had evidently been run off their ranch, and Dan Shute had taken possession. Whether there was any connection between Shute and Barkow remained to be seen, but Caradec knew that chuck wagon gossip can often come close to the truth, and that cowhands could many times see men more clearly than people who saw them only on their good behavior or when in town.

As he rode through the country toward Painted Rock, he studied it curiously and listened to Johnny Gill's comments.

167

The little Texan had punched cattle in here two seasons, and knew the area better than most.

Painted Rock was the usual cowtown. A double row of weather-beaten, false-fronted buildings, most of which had never been painted, and a few scattered dwellings, some of logs, most of stone. There was a two-story hotel, and a stone building, squat and solid, whose sign identified it as the **Painted Rock Bank.**

Two buckboards and a spring wagon stood on the street, and a dozen saddle horses stood three-hoofed at hitching rails. A sign ahead of them and cater-cornered across from the stage station told them that here was the **National Bar.**

Gill swung his horse in toward the hitching rail and dropped to the ground. He glanced across his saddle at Caradec. "The big *hombre* lookin' us over is the redhead Bo didn't like," he said in a low voice.

Rafe did not look around until he had tied his own horse with a slipknot. Then he hitched his guns into place on his hips. He was wearing two walnut-stocked pistols, purchased in San Francisco. He wore jeans, star boots, and a buckskin jacket. Stepping up on the boardwalk, Rafe glanced at the burly redhead. The man was studying them with frank curiosity.

"Howdy, Gill!" he said. "Long time no see."

"Is that bad?" Gill said, and shoved through the doors into the dim, cool interior of the National.

At the bar, Rafe glanced around. Two men stood nearby, drinking. Several others were scattered around at tables.

"Red-eye," Gill said, then in a lower tone: "Bruce Barkow is the big man with the black mustache, wearin' black and playin' poker. The Mexican-lookin' *hombre* across from him is Dan Shute's gun-slingin' *segundo,* Gee Bonaro."

Rafe nodded, and lifted his glass. Suddenly he grinned.

"To Charles Rodney!" he said clearly.

Barkow jerked sharply and looked up, his face a shade paler. Bonaro turned his head slowly, like a lizard watching a fly. Gill and Rafe both tossed off their drinks and ignored the stares.

"Man," Gill said, grinning, his eyes dancing, "yuh don't waste no time, do yuh?"

Rafe Caradec turned. "By the way, Barkow," he said, "where can I find Missus Rodney and her daughter?"

Bruce Barkow put down his cards. "If yuh've got any business," he said smoothly, "I'll handle it for 'em."

"Thanks," Rafe said. "My business is personal, and with them."

"Then," Barkow said, his eyes hardening, "yuh'll have trouble. Missus Rodney is dead. Died three months ago."

Rafe's lips tightened. "And her daughter?"

"Ann Rodney," Barkow said carefully, "is here in town. She is to be my wife soon. If yuh've got any business...."

"I'll transact it with her!" Rafe said sharply.

Turning abruptly, he walked out the door, Gill following. The little cowhand grinned, his leathery face folding into wrinkles that belied his thirty-odd years. "Like I say, boss," he chuckled, "yuh shore throw the hooks into 'em." He nodded toward a building across the street. "Let's try the Emporium. Rodney used to trade there, and Gene Baker who runs it was a friend of his."

The Emporium smelled of leather, dry goods, and all the varied and exciting smells of the general store. Rafe rounded a bale of jeans and walked back to the long counter, backed by shelves holding everything from pepper to rifle shells.

"Where am I to find Ann Rodney?" he asked.

The white-haired proprietor gave him a quick glance, then nodded to his right. Rafe turned and found himself looking into the large, soft dark eyes of a slender, yet beautifully shaped, girl in a print dress. Her lips were delicately lovely; her dark hair was gathered in a loose knot at the nape of her neck. She was so lovely that it left him a little breathless.

She smiled, and her eyes were questioning. "I'm Ann Rodney," she said. "What is it you want?"

"My name is Rafe Caradec," he said gently. "Your father sent me."

Her face went white to the lips, and she stepped back suddenly, dropping one hand to the counter as though for support. "You come...from *my father?* Why, I...."

Bruce Barkow, who had apparently followed them from the saloon, stepped in front of Rafe, his face flushed with anger. "Yuh've scared her to death," he snapped. "What do yuh mean, comin' in here with such a story? Charles Rodney has been dead for almost a year."

Rafe's eyes measured Barkow, his thoughts racing. "He has? How did he die?"

"He was killed," Barkow said, "for the money he was carryin', it looked like." Barkow's eyes suddenly turned triumphant. "Did you kill him?"

Rafe was suddenly aware that Johnny Gill was staring at him, his brows drawn together, puzzled and wondering. Gill, he realized, knew him but slightly and might easily become suspicious of his motives. Gene Baker, also, was studying him coldly, his eyes alive with suspicion. Ann Rodney stared at him, as if stunned by what he had said, and somehow uncertain.

"No," Rafe said coolly, "I didn't kill him, but I'd be plumb interested to know who made yuh believe he was dead."

"Believe he was dead?" Barkow laughed harshly. "I was with him when he died. We found him beside the trail, shot through the body by bandits. I brought back his belongings to Miss Rodney."

"Miss Rodney," Rafe began, "if I could talk to you a few minutes...."

"No," she whispered. "I don't want to talk to you. What can you be thinking of? Coming to me with such a story? What is it you want from me?"

"Somehow," Rafe said quietly, "you've got hold of some false information. Your father has been dead for no more than two months."

"Get out of here!" Barkow ordered, his hand on his gun. "Yuh're torturin' that poor young lady! Get out, I say! I don't know what scheme yuh've cooked up, but it won't work! If yuh know what's good for yuh, yuh'll leave this town while the goin' is good!"

Ann Rodney turned sharply around and ran from the store, heading for the storekeeper's living quarters.

"Yuh'd better get out, mister," Gene Baker said harshly. "We know how Rodney died. Yuh can't work no underhanded schemes on that young lady. Her pa died, and he talked before he died. Three men heard him."

Rafe Caradec turned and walked outside, standing on the boardwalk, frowning at the skyline. He was aware that Gill had moved up beside him.

"Boss," Gill said, "I ain't no lily, but neither am I takin' part in no deal to skin a young lady out of what is hers by rights. Yuh'd better throw a leg over yore saddle and get."

"Don't jump to conclusions, Johnny," Rafe advised, "and before you make any change in your plans, suppose you talk to Tex about this? He was with me, an' he knows all about Rodney's death as well as I do. If they brought any belongin's of his back here, there's somethin' more to this than we believed."

Gill kicked his boot toe against a loose board. "Tex was with yuh? Damn it, man! What of that yarn of theirs? It don't make sense."

171

"That's right," Caradec replied, "it don't, and before it will, we've got to do some diggin'." He added: "Suppose I told you that Barkow back there held a mortgage on the Rodney Ranch, and Rodney went to Frisco, got the money, and paid it in Frisco…then never got home?"

Gill stared at Rafe, his mouth tightening. "Then nobody here would know he ever paid that mortgage but Barkow? The man he paid it to?"

"That's right."

"Then I'd say this Barkow was a sneakin' polecat," Gill said harshly. "Let's brace him!"

"Not yet, Johnny. Not yet!"

A horrible thought had occurred to him. He had anticipated no such trouble, yet if he explained the circumstances of Rodney's death and was compelled to prove them, he would be arrested for mutiny on the high seas—a hanging offense! Not only his own life depended on silence, but the lives of Brisco, Penn, and Mullaney. There must be a way out. There had to be.

IV

As Rafe Caradec stood there in the bright sunlight, he began to understand a lot of things and wonder about them. If some of the possessions of Charles Rodney had been returned to Painted Rock, it implied that those who returned them knew something of the shanghaiing of Rodney. How else could they have come by his belongings? Bully Borger had shanghaied his own crew with the connivance of Hongkong Bohl. Had he taken Rodney by suggestion? Had the man been marked for him? Certainly it would not be the first time somebody had got rid of a man in such a manner. If that was the true story, it would account for some of Borger's animosity when he had beaten Rodney.

No doubt they had all been part of a plan to make sure that Charles Rodney never returned to San Francisco alive, or to Painted Rock. Yet believing such a thing and proving it were two vastly different things. Also, it presented a problem of motive. Land was not scarce in the West, and much of it could be had for the taking. Why, then, people would ask, would Barkow go to such efforts to get one piece of land? Rafe had Barkow's signature on the receipt, but that could be claimed to be a forgery. First, a motive beyond the mere value of two thousand acres of land and the money paid on the debt must be established. That might be all, and certainly men had been killed for less, but Bruce Barkow was no fool, nor was he a man who played for small stakes.

Rafe lit a cigarette and stared down the street. He must face another fact. Barkow was warned. Whatever he was gambling for, including the girl, was in danger now and would remain in peril as long as Rafe Caradec remained alive or in the country. That fact stood out cold and clear. Barkow knew by now that he must kill Rafe Caradec.

Rafe understood the situation perfectly. His life had been lived among men who played ruthlessly for the highest stakes. It was no shock to him that men would stoop to killing, or a dozen killings, if they could gain a desired end. From now on he must ride with cat eyes, always aware, and always ready.

Sending Gill to find and buy two pack horses, Rafe turned on his heel and went into the store. Barkow was gone, and Ann Rodney was still out of sight.

Baker looked up and his eyes held no welcome. "If yuh've got any business here," he said, "state it and get out. Charles Rodney was a friend of mine."

"He needed some smarter friends," Rafe replied shortly.

"I came here to buy supplies, but if you want to, start askin' yourself some questions. Who profits by Rodney's death? What evidence have you got besides a few of his belongings, that might have been stolen, that he was killed a year ago? How reliable were the three men who were with him? If he went to San Francisco for the money, what were Barkow and the others doin' on the trail?"

"That's neither here nor there," Baker said roughly. "What do yuh want? I'll refuse no man food."

Coolly Caradec ordered what he wanted, aware that Baker was studying him. The man seemed puzzled.

"Where yuh livin'?" Baker asked suddenly. Some of the animosity seemed to have gone from his voice.

"At the Rodney cabin on the Crazy Man," Caradec said. "I'm stayin', too, till I get the straight of this. If Ann Rodney is wise, she won't get married or get rid of any rights to her property till this is cleared up."

"Shute won't let yuh stay there."

"I'll stay." Rafe gathered up the boxes of shells and stowed them in his pockets. "I'll be right there. While you're askin' yourself questions, ask why Barkow, who holds a mortgage that he claims is unpaid on the Rodney place, lets Dan Shute take over?"

"He didn't want trouble because of Ann," Baker said defensively. "He was right nice about it. He wouldn't foreclose. Givin' her a chance to pay up."

"As long as he's goin' to marry her, why should he foreclose?" Rafe turned away from the counter. "If Ann Rodney wants to see me, I'll tell her all about it, any time. I promised her father I'd take care of her, and I will, whether she likes it or not! Also," he added, "any man who says he talked to Rodney as he was dyin' *lies!*"

The door closed at the front of the store, and Rafe

174

Caradec turned to see the dark, Mexican-looking gunman Gill had indicated in the National Saloon, the man known as Gee Bonaro. The gunman came toward him, smiling and showing even white teeth under a thread of mustache.

"Would you repeat that to me, *señor?*" he asked pleasantly, a thumb hooked in his belt.

"Why not?" Rafe said sharply. He let his eyes, their contempt unveiled, go over the man slowly from head to foot, then back. "If you was one of 'em that said that, you're a liar. And if you touch that gun, I'll kill you."

Gee Bonaro's spread fingers hovered over the gun butt, and he stood flat-footed, an uncomfortable realization breaking over him. This big stranger was not frightened. In the green eyes was a coldness that turned Bonaro a little sick inside. He was uncomfortably aware that he stood, perilously, on the brink of death.

"Were you one of 'em?" Rafe demanded.

"*Sí, señor.*" Bonaro's tongue touched his lips.

"Where was this supposed to be?"

"Where he died, near Pilot Peak, on the trail."

"You're a white-livered liar, Bonaro. Rodney never got back to Pilot Peak. You're bein' trapped for somebody else's gain, and, if I were you, I'd back up and look the trail over again." Rafe's eyes held the man. "You say you saw him. How was he dressed?"

"Dressed?" Bonaro was startled and confused. Nobody had asked such a thing. He had no idea what to say. Suppose the same question was answered in a different way by one of the others? He wavered and was lost. "I...I don't know. I...."

He looked from Baker to Caradec and took a step back, his tongue at his lips, his eyes like those of a trapped animal. He was confused. The big man facing him somehow robbed him

175

of his sureness, his poise, and he had come here to kill him.

"Rodney talked to me only a few weeks ago, Bonaro," Rafe said coldly. "Think! How many others did he talk to? You're bein' mixed up in a cold-blooded killin', Bonaro! Now turn around and get out! And get out fast!"

Bonaro backed up, and Rafe took a forward step. Wheeling, the man scrambled for the door.

Rafe turned and glanced at Baker. "Think that over," he said coolly. "You'll take the word of a coyote like that about an honest man! Somebody's tryin' to rob Miss Rodney, and because you're believin' that cock-and-bull story, you're helpin' it along."

Gene Baker stood stockstill, his hands flat on the counter. What he had seen he would not have believed. Gee Bonaro had slain two men since coming to Painted Rock, and here a stranger had backed him down without lifting a hand or moving toward a gun. Baker rubbed his ear thoughtfully.

Johnny Gill met Rafe in front of the store with two pack horses. A glance told Caradec that the little cowhand had bought well.

Gill glanced questioningly at Rafe. "Did I miss somethin'? I seen that gun hand *segundo* of Shute's come out of that store like he was chased by the devil. You and him have a run-in?"

"I called him, and he backed down," Rafe told Gill. "He said he was one of the three who heard Rodney's last words. I told him he was a liar."

Johnny drew the rope tighter. He glanced out of the corner of his eye at Rafe. This man had come into town and put himself on record for what he was and what he planned faster than anybody he had ever seen. *Shucks,* Johnny thought, grinning at the horse, *why go back to Texas? There'll be ruckus enough here, ridin' for that* hombre.

176

The Trail to Crazy Man

* * * * *

The town of Painted Rock numbered exactly eighty-nine inhabitants, and by sundown the arrival of Rafe Caradec and his challenge to Gee Bonaro was the talk of all of them. It was a behind-the-hand talking, but the story was going the rounds. Also, that Charles Rodney was alive—or had been alive until recently.

By nightfall Dan Shute heard that Caradec had moved into the Rodney house on Crazy Man, and an hour later he had stormed furiously into his bunkhouse and given Bonaro a tongue-lashing that turned the gunman livid with anger. Bruce Barkow was worried, and he made no pretense about it in his conference with Shute. The only hopeful note was that Caradec had said that Rodney was dead.

Gene Baker, sitting in his easy chair in his living quarters behind the store, was uneasy. He was aware that his silence was worrying his wife. He was also aware that Ann was silent herself, an unusual thing, for the girl was usually gay and full of fun and laughter. The idea that there could have been anything wrong about the story told by Barkow, Weber, and Bonaro had never entered the storekeeper's head. He had accepted the story as others had, for many men had been killed along the trails or had died in fights with Indians. It was another tragedy of the westward march, and he had done what he could—he and his wife had taken Ann Rodney into their home and loved her as their own child.

Now this stranger had come with his questions. Despite Baker's irritation that the matter had come up at all, and despite his outward denials of truth in what Caradec had said, he was aware of an inner doubt that gnawed at the walls of his confidence in Bruce Barkow. Whatever else he might be, Gene Baker was a fair man. He was forced to admit that Bonaro was not a man in whom reliance could be placed. He

177

was a known gunman, and a suspected outlaw. That Shute hired him was bad enough in itself, yet when he thought of Shute, Baker was again uneasy. The twin ranches of Barkow and Shute surrounded the town on three sides. Their purchases represented no less than fifty percent of the store-keeper's business, and that did not include what the hands bought on their own. The drinking of the hands from the ranches supported the National Saloon, too, and Gene Baker, who for all his willingness to live and let live was a good citizen, or believed himself to be, found himself examining a situation he did not like. It was not a new situation in Painted Rock, and he had been unconsciously aware of it for some time, yet, while aware of it, he had tacitly accepted it. Now there seemed to be someone in the woodpile, or several of them.

As Baker smoked his pipe, he found himself realizing with some discomfort and growing doubt that Painted Rock was completely subservient to Barkow and Shute. Pod Gomer, who was town marshal, had been nominated for the job by Barkow at the council meeting. Joe Benson of the National had seconded the motion, and Dan Shute had calmly suggested that the nomination be closed, and Gomer was voted in. Gene Baker had never liked Gomer, but the man was a good gun hand and certainly unafraid. Baker had voted with the others, as had Pat Higley, another responsible citizen of the town. In the same manner, Benson had been elected mayor of the town, and Roy Gargan had been made judge.

Remembering that the town was actually in the hands of Barkow and Shute, Baker also recalled that at first the tactics of the two big ranchers had caused grumbling among the smaller holders of land. Nothing had ever been done, largely because one of them, Stu Martin, who talked the loudest, had been killed in a fall from a cliff. A few weeks later another small rancher, Al Chase, had mistakenly tried to draw against Bonaro, and had died. Looked at in that light, the situation made Baker uneasy. Little things began to occur to him that had remained unconsidered, and he began to wonder just what could be done about it, even if he knew for sure that Rodney had been killed. Not only was he dependent on Shute and Barkow for business, but Benson, their partner and friend, owned the freight line that brought in his supplies.

Law was still largely a local matter. The Army maintained a fort not too far away, but the soldiers were busy keeping an eye on the Sioux and their allies who were becoming increasingly restive, what with the blooming gold camps at Bannock and Alder Gulch, Custer's invasion of the Black Hills, and the steady roll of wagon trains over the Bozeman and Laramie Trails. If there were trouble here, Baker realized with a sudden, sickening fear, it would be settled locally, and that meant it would be settled by Dan Shute and Bruce Barkow. Yet, even as he thought of that, Baker recalled the tall man in the black, flat-crowned hat and buckskin jacket. There was something about Rafe Caradec that was convincing, something that made a man doubt he would be controlled by anybody or anything, at any time, or anywhere.

V

Rafe Caradec rode silently alongside Johnny Gill when they moved out of Painted Rock, trailing the two pack horses. The trail turned west by south and crossed the north fork of Clear Creek. They turned then along a narrow path that skirted the huge boulders fringing the mountains.

Gill turned his head slightly. "Might not be a bad idea to take to the hills, boss," he said carelessly. "There's a trail up that-a-way…ain't much used, either."

Caradec glanced quickly at the little 'puncher, then nodded. "All right," he said, "lead off, if you want."

Johnny was riding with his rifle across his saddle, and his eyes were alert. That, Rafe decided, was not a bad idea. He jerked his head back toward Painted Rock. "What you think Barkow will do?"

Gill shrugged. "No tellin', but Dan Shute will know what to do. He'll be gunnin' for yuh, if yuh've shore enough got the straight of this. What yuh figger happened?"

Rafe hesitated, then he said carefully: "What happened to Charles Rodney wasn't any accident. It was planned and carried out mighty smooth." He waited while the horse took a half dozen steps, then looked up suddenly. "Gill, you size up like a man to ride the river with. Here's the story, and if you ever tell it, you'll hang four good men."

Briefly and concisely, he outlined the shanghaiing of Rodney and himself, the events aboard ship, the escape.

"See?" he added. "It must have looked foolproof to them. Rodney goes away to sea and never comes back. Nobody but Barkow knows that mortgage was paid, and what did happen was somethin' they couldn't plan for, and probably didn't even think about."

Gil nodded. "Rodney must have been tougher'n anybody figgered," he said admiringly. "He never quit tryin', yuh say?"

"Right. He had only one idea, it looked like, and that was to live to get home to his wife and daughter. If," Rafe added, "the wife was anything like the daughter, I don't blame him."

The cowhand chuckled. "Yeah, I know what yuh mean. She's purty as a papoose in a red hat."

"You know, Gill," Rafe said speculatively, "there's one thing that bothers me. Why do they want that ranch so bad?"

The Trail to Crazy Man

"That's got me wonderin', too," Gill agreed. "It's a good ranch, mostly, except for that land at the mouth of the valley. Rises there to a sort of a dome, and the Crazy Man swings around it. Nothin' much grows there. The rest of it's a good ranch."

"Say anything about Tex or Bo?" Caradec asked.

"No," Gill said. "It figgers like war, now. No use lettin' the enemy know what you're holdin'."

The trail they followed left the grasslands of the creek bottom and turned back up into the hills to a long plateau. They rode on among the tall pines, scattered here and there with birch or aspen along the slopes. A cool breeze stirred among the pines, and the horses walked along slowly, taking their time, their hoof beats soundless on the cushion of pine needles. Once the trail wound down the steep side of a shadowy cañon, weaving back and forth, finally to reach bottom in a brawling, swift-running stream. Willows skirted the banks, and, while the horses were drinking, Rafe saw a trout leap in a pool above the rapids. A brown thrasher swept like a darting red-brown arrow past his head, and he could hear yellow warblers gossiping among the willows.

He himself was drinking when he saw the sand crumble from a spot on the bank and fall with a tiny splash into the creek. Carefully he got to his feet. His rifle was in his saddle boot, but his pistols were good enough for anything he could see in this narrow place. He glanced casually at Gill, and the cowhand was tightening his cinch, all unawares.

Caradec drew a long breath and hitched up his trousers, then hooked his thumbs in his belt near the gun butts. He had no idea who was there, but that sand did not fall without a reason. In his own mind he was sure that someone was standing in the willow thicket across and downstream, above where the sand had fallen. Someone was watching them.

181

"Ready?" Johnny suggested, looking at him curiously.

"Almost," Rafe drawled casually. "Sort of like this little place. It's cool and pleasant. Sort of place a man might like to rest a while, and where a body could watch his back trail, too." He was talking at random, hoping Gill would catch on. The 'puncher was looking at him intently now. "At least," Rafe added, "it would be nice here if a man *was* alone. He could think better."

It was then that his eye caught the color in the willows. It was a tiny corner of red, a bright, flaming crimson, and it lay where no such color should be. That was not likely to be a cowhand unless he was a Mexican or a dude, and they were scarce in this country. It could be an Indian. If whoever it was had planned to fire, a good chance had been missed while he and Gill drank. Two well-placed shots would have done for them both. Therefore, it was logical to discount the person in the willows as an enemy, or, if so, a patient enemy. To all appearances whoever lay in the willows preferred to remain unseen. It had all the earmarks of being someone or something trying to avoid trouble.

Gill was quiet and puzzled. Cat-like, he watched Rafe for some sign to indicate what the trouble was. A quick scanning of the brush had revealed nothing, but Caradec was not the man to be spooked by a shadow.

"You speak Sioux?" Rafe asked casually.

Gill's mouth tightened. "A mite. Not so good, mebbe."

"Speak loud and say we are friends."

Johnny Gill's eyes were wary as he spoke. There was no sound, no reply.

"Try it again," Rafe suggested. "Tell him we want to talk. Tell him we want to talk to Red Cloud, the great chief."

Gill complied, and there was still no sound.

Rafe looked up at him. "I'm goin' to go over into those willows," he said softly. "Something's wrong."

"You watch yoreself!" Gill warned. "The Sioux are plenty smart."

Moving slowly, so as to excite no hostility, Rafe Caradec walked his horse across the stream, then swung down. There was neither sound nor movement from the willows. He walked back among the slender trees, glancing around, yet even then, close as he was, he might not have seen her had it not been for the red stripes. Her clothing blended perfectly with the willows and flowers along the stream bank.

She was a young squaw, slender and dark, with large, intelligent eyes. One look told Rafe that she was frightened speechless, and, knowing what had happened to squaws found by some of the white men, he could understand. Her legs were outstretched, and from the marks on the grass and the bank of the stream he could see she had been dragging herself. The reason was plain to see. One leg was broken just below the knee.

"Johnny," he said, not too loudly, "here's a young squaw. She's got a busted leg."

"Better get away quick!" Gill advised. "The Sioux are pretty mean where squaws are concerned."

"Not till I set that leg," Rafe said.

"Boss," Gill advised worriedly, "don't do it. She's liable to yell like blazes if yuh lay a hand on her. Our lives won't be worth a nickel. We've got troubles enough, without askin' for more."

Rafe walked a step nearer, and smiled at the girl. "I want to fix your leg," he said gently, motioning to it. "Don't be afraid."

She said nothing, staring at him, yet he walked up and knelt down. She drew back from his touch, and he saw then she had a knife. He smiled and touched the break with gentle fingers.

"Better cut some splints, Gill," he said. "She's got a bad break. Just a little jolt and it might pop right through the skin."

Working carefully, he set the leg. There was no sound from the girl, no sign of pain. Gill shook his head wonderingly.

"Nervy, ain't she?" Rafe suggested.

Taking the splints Gill had cut, he bound them on her leg.

"Better take the pack off that paint and split it between the two of us and the other hoss," he said. "We'll put her up on the hoss."

When they had her on the paint's back, Gill asked her, in Sioux: "How far to Indian camp?"

She looked at him, then at Rafe. Then she spoke quickly to him.

Gill grinned. "She says she talks to the chief. That means you. Her camp is about an hour south and west, in the hills."

"Tell her we'll take her most of the way."

Rafe swung into saddle, and they turned their horses back into the trail. Rafe rode ahead, the squaw and the pack horse following, and Johnny Gill, rifle still across the saddle bows, bringing up the rear.

They had gone no more than a mile when they heard voices, then three riders swung around a bend in the trail, reining in sharply. Tough-looking, bearded men, they stared from Rafe to the Indian girl. She gasped suddenly, and Rafe's eyes narrowed a little.

"See yuh got our pigeon!" A red-bearded man rode toward them, grinning. "We been a-chasin' her for a couple of hours. Purty thing, ain't she?"

"Yeah." A slim, wiry man with a hatchet face and a cigarette dangling from his lips was speaking. "Glad yuh found her. We'll take her off yore hands now."

"That's all right," Rafe said quietly. "We're taking her back to her village. She's got a broken leg."

"Takin' her back to the village?" the red-bearded man exclaimed. "Why, we cut that squaw out for ourselves, and we're slappin' our own brand on her. You get yore own squaws." He nodded toward the hatchet-faced man. "Get that lead rope, Boyne."

"Keep your hands off that rope!" Rafe's voice was cold. "You blasted fools will get us all killed. This girl's tribe would be down on your ears before night."

"We'll take care of that," Red persisted. "Get her, Boyne!"

Rafe smiled suddenly. "If you boys are lookin' for trouble, I reckon you've found it. I don't know how many of you want to die for this squaw, but any time you figger to take her away from us, some of you'd better start sizing up grave space."

Boyne's eyes narrowed wickedly. "Why, he's askin' for a ruckus, Red! Which eye shall I shoot him through?"

Rafe Caradec sat his horse calmly, smiling a little. "I reckon," he said, "you boys ain't any too battle wise. You're bunched too much. Now, from where I sit, all three of you are dead in range and grouped nice for even one gun shootin', and I'm figurin' to use two." He spoke to Gill. "Johnny," he said quietly, "suppose these *hombres* start smokin' it, you take that fat one. Leave the redhead and this Boyne for me."

The fat cowhand shifted in his saddle uncomfortably. He was unpleasantly aware that he had turned his horse so he was sideward to Gill and, while presenting a fair target himself, would have to turn half around in the saddle to fire.

Boyne's eyes were hard and reckless. Rafe knew he was the one to watch. He wore his gun slung low, and that he fancied himself as a gun hand was obvious. Suddenly Rafe knew the man was going to draw.

185

"Hold it!" The voice cut sharply across the air like the crack of a whip. "Boyne, keep yore hand shoulder high! You, too, Red! Now turn yore horses with yore knees and start down the trail. If one of yuh even looks like yuh wanted to use a gun, I'll open up with this Henry and cut yuh into little pieces."

Boyne cursed wickedly. "Yuh're gettin' out of it easy this time!" he said viciously. "I'll see yuh again!"

Rafe smiled. "Why, shore, Boyne! Only next time you'd better take the rawhide lashin' off the butt of your Colt. Mighty handy when ridin' over rough country, but mighty unhandy when you need your gun in a hurry."

With a startled gasp, Boyne glanced down. The rawhide thong was tied over his gun to hold it in place. His face two shades whiter than a snake's belly, he turned his horse with his knees and started the trek down trail.

Bo Marsh stepped out of the brush with his rifle in his hands. He was grinning.

"Hey, boss! If I'd known that six-gun was tied down, I'd 'a' let yuh mow him down! That skunk needs it. That's Lem Boyne. He's a gunslinger for Dan Shute."

Gill laughed. "Man! Will our ears burn tonight! Rafe's run two of Shute's boys into the ground today!"

Marsh grinned. "Figgered yuh'd be headed home soon, and I was out after deer." He glanced at the squaw with the broken leg. "Got more trouble?"

"No," Rafe said. "Those *hombres* had been runnin' this girl down. She busted her leg gettin' away, so we fixed it up. Let's ride."

VI

The trail was smoother now and drifted casually from one cañon to another. Obviously it had been a game trail that had been found and used by Indians, trappers, and wandering buffalo hunters before the coming of the cowhands and trail drivers.

When they were still several miles from the cabin on the Crazy Man, the squaw spoke up suddenly. Gill looked over at Rafe.

"Her camp's just over that rise in a draw," he said.

Caradec nodded. Then he turned to the girl. She was looking at him, expecting him to speak.

"Tell her," he said, "that we share the land Rodney bought from Red Cloud. That we share it with the daughter of Rodney. Get her to tell Red Cloud we will live on the Crazy Man, and we are friends to the Sioux, that their women are safe with us, their horses will not be stolen, that we are friends to the warriors of Red Cloud and the great chiefs of the Sioux people."

Gill spoke slowly, emphatically, and the girl nodded. Then she turned her horse and rode up through the trees.

"Boss," Johnny said, "she's got our best hoss. That's the one I give the most money for!"

Rafe grinned. "Forget it. The girl was scared silly but wouldn't show it for anything. It's a cheap price to pay to get her home safe. Like I said, the Sioux make better friends than enemies."

When the three men rode up, Tex Brisco was carrying two buckets of water to the house. He grinned at them. "That grub looks good," he told them. "I've eaten so much antelope meat, the next thing you know I'll be boundin' along over the prairie myself."

While Marsh got busy with the grub, Johnny told Tex about the events of the trip.

"Nobody been around here," Brisco said. "I seen three In- juns, but they was off a couple of miles and didn't come this way. There hasn't been nobody else around."

During the three days that followed the trip to Painted Rock, Rafe Caradec scouted the range. There were a lot of Bar M cattle around, and most of them were in fairly good shape. His own cattle were mingling freely with them. The range would support many more head than it carried, and the upper end of Long Valley was almost untouched. There was much good grass in the mountain meadows, also, and in sev- eral cañons south of the Crazy Man.

Johnny Gill and Bo Marsh explained the lay of the land as they knew it.

"North of here," Gill said, "back of Painted Rock, and mostly west of there, the mountains rise up nigh onto nine thousand feet. Good huntin' country, some of the best I ever seen. South, toward the end of the valley, the mountains thin out. There's a pass through to the head of Otter Creek, and that country west of the mountains is good grazin' land, and nobody much in there yet. Injuns got a big powwow grounds over there. Still farther south there's a long road wall, runnin' purty much north and south. Only one entrance in thirty-five miles. Regular hole in the wall. A few men could get into that hole and stand off an army, and, if they wanted to hightail it, they could lose themselves in that back country."

Rafe scouted the crossing toward the head of Otter Creek, and rode down the creek to the grasslands below. This would be good grazing land, and mentally he made a note to make some plans for it.

He rode back to the ranch that night, and, when he was sitting on the stoop after the sun was down, he looked around at Tex Brisco. "You been over the trail from Texas?" he asked.

"Uhn-huh."

"Once aboard ship you were tellin' me about a stampede you had. Only got back about sixteen hundred head of a two-thousand-head herd. That sort of thing happen often?"

Tex laughed. "Shucks, yes! Stampedes are regular things along the trail. Yuh lose some cattle, yuh mebbe get more back, but there's plenty of maverick stock runnin' on the plains south of the Platte...all the way to the Canadian, as far as that goes."

"Reckon a few men could slip over there and round up some of that stock?"

Brisco sat up and glanced at Rafe. "Shore could. Wild stuff, though, and it would be a man-sized job."

"Mebbe," Caradec suggested, "we'll try and do it. It would be one way of gettin' a herd pretty fast, or turnin' some quick money."

There followed days of hard, driving labor. Always one man stayed at the cabin keeping a sharp look-out for any of the Shute or Barkow riders. Caradec knew they would come and, when they did, they would be riding with only one idea in mind—to get rid of him.

In the visit to Painted Rock he had laid his cards on the table, and they had no idea how much he knew, or what his story of Charles Rodney could be. Rafe Caradec knew Barkow was worried, and that pleased him. Yet while the delayed attack was a concern, it was also a help.

There was some grumbling from the hands, but he kept them busy, cutting hay in the meadows and stacking it.

189

Winter in this country was going to be bad—he needed no weather prophet to tell him that—and he had no intention of losing a lot of stock.

In a cañon that branched off from the head of Crazy Man, he had found a warm spring. There was small chance of it freezing, yet the water was not too hot to drink. In severe cold it would freeze, but otherwise it would offer an excellent watering place for his stock. They made no effort to bring hay back to the ranch, but arranged it in huge stacks back in the cañons and meadows.

There had been no sign of Indians, and Rafe avoided their camp, yet once, when he did pass nearby, there was no sign of them. It seemed as if they had moved out and left the country.

Then one night he heard a noise at the corral, and the snorting of a horse. Instantly he was out of bed and had his boots on when he heard Brisco swearing in the next room. They got outside in a hurry, fearing someone was rustling their stock. In the corral they could see the horses, and there was no one nearby.

Bo Marsh had walked over to the corral, and suddenly he called out.

"Boss! Look it here!"

They all trooped over, then stopped. Instead of five horses in the corral there were ten! One of them was the paint they had loaned the young squaw, but the others were strange horses, and every one was a picked animal.

"Well, I'll be damned!" Gill exploded. "Brung our own hoss and an extra for each of us. Reckon that big black is for you, boss."

By daylight, when they could examine the horses, Tex Brisco walked around them admiringly.

"Man," he said, "that was the best horse trade I ever heard of! There's four of the purtiest horses I ever laid an eye on! I always did say the Sioux knowed hossflesh, and this proves it. Reckon yore bread cast on the water shore come back to yuh, boss!"

Rafe studied the valley thoughtfully. They would have another month of good haying weather if there was no rain. Four men could not work much harder than they were, but the beaver were building their houses bigger and in deeper water, and from that and all other indications the winter was going to be hard.

He made his decision suddenly, and mentioned it that night at the supper table. "I'm ridin' to Painted Rock. Want to go along, Tex?"

"Yeah." The Texan looked at him calculatingly. "Yeah, I'd like that."

"How about me?" Bo asked, grinning. "Johnny went last time. I could shore use a belt of that red-eye the National peddles, and mebbe a look around town."

"Take him along, boss," Johnny said. "I can hold this end. If he stays, he'll be ridin' me all the time, anyway."

"All right. Saddle up first thing in the mornin'."

"Boss...." Johnny threw one leg over the other, and lit his smoke. "One thing I better tell yuh. I hadn't said a word before, but two, three days ago, when I was down to the bend of the Crazy Man, I run into a couple fellers. One of 'em was Red Blazer, that big galoot who was with Boyne. Remember?"

Rafe turned around and looked down at the little, leatherfaced cowhand. "Well," he said, "what about him?"

Gill took a long drag on his cigarette. "He told me he was carryin' a message from Trigger Boyne, and that Trigger was goin' to shoot on sight, next time yuh showed up in Painted Rock."

Rafe reached over on the table and picked up a piece of

cold cornbread. "Then I reckon that's what he'll do," he said. "If he gets into action fast enough."

"Boss," Marsh pleaded, "if that red-headed Tom Blazer, brother to the one yuh had the run-in with...if he's there, I want him."

"That the one we saw on the National stoop?" Rafe asked Gill.

"Uhn-huh. There's five of them brothers. All gun-toters."

Gill got up and stretched. "Well, I'll have it purty lazy while you *hombres* are down there dustin' lead." He added: "It would be a good idea to sort of keep an eye out. Gee Bonaro's probably in town and could be feelin' mighty mad."

Rafe walked outside, strolling toward the corral. Behind him, Marsh turned to Gill. "Reckon he can sling a gun?"

Tex chuckled. "Mister, that *hombre* killed one of the fastest, slickest gun throwers that ever came out of Texas, and done it when he was no more'n sixteen, down on the C Bar. Also, while I've never seen him shoot, if he can shoot like he can fist fight, Mister Trigger Boyne had better grab hisself an armful of hossflesh and start makin' tracks for the blackest pan of the Black Hills...*fast!*"

VII

Nothing about the town of Painted Rock suggested drama or excitement. It lay sprawled comfortably in the morning sunlight in an elbow of Rock Creek. A normally roaring and plunging stream, the creek had decided here to loiter a while, enjoying the warm sun and the graceful willows that lined the banks. Behind and among the willows the white, slender trunks of the birch trees marched in neat ranks, each tree so like its neighbor that it was almost impossible to distinguish between them. Clumps of mountain alder, yellow rose, puffed clematis, and antelope bush were scattered along the far bank of the stream and advanced up the hill beyond in skirmishing formation. In a few weeks now the aspen leaves would be changing, and Painted Rock would take on a background of flaming color—a bank of trees, rising toward the darker growth of spruce and fir along the higher mountainside.

Painted Rock's one street was the only thing about the town that was ordered. It lay between two neat rows of buildings that stared at each other down across a long lane of dust and, during the rainy periods, of mud. At any time of day or night a dozen saddle horses would be standing three-legged at the hitching rails, usually in front of Joe Benson's National Saloon. A buckboard or a spring wagon would also be present, usually driven by some small rancher in for his supplies. The two big outfits sent two wagons together, drawn by mules.

Bruce Barkow sat in front of the sheriff's office this morning, deep in conversation with Pod Gomer. It was a conversation that had begun over an hour before. Gomer was a short, thick-set man, almost as deep from chest to spine as from shoulder to shoulder. He was not fat and was considered a tough man to tangle with. He was also a man who liked to play on the winning side, and long ago he had decided there was only one side to consider in this light—the side of Dan Shute and Bruce Barkow. Yet he was a man who was sensitive to the way the wind blew, and he frequently found himself puzzled when he considered his two bosses. There was no good feeling between them. They met on business or pleasure, saw things through much the same eyes, but each wanted to be kingpin. Sooner or later, Gomer knew, he must make a choice between them.

Barkow was shrewd, cunning. He was a planner and a conniver. He was a man who would use any method to win,

Louis L'Amour

but in most cases he kept himself in the background of anything smacking of crime or wrongdoing. Otherwise, he was much in the foreground. Dan Shute was another type of man. He was tall and broad of shoulder. Normally he was sullen, hard-eyed, and surly. He had little to say to anyone and was more inclined to settle matters with a blow or a gun than with words. He was utterly cold-blooded, felt slightly about anything, and would kill a man as quickly and with as little excitement as he would brand a calf.

Barkow might carve a notch on his gun butt. Shute wouldn't even understand such a thing. Shute was a man who seemed to be without vanity, and such men are dangerous. For the vanity is there, only submerged, and the slow-burning, deep fires of hatred for the vain smolder within them until suddenly they burst into flame and end in sudden, dramatic climax and ugly violence.

Pod Gomer understood little of Dan Shute. He understood the man's complex character just enough to know that he was dangerous, that as long as Shute rode along, Barkow would be top dog, but that if ever Barkow incurred Shute's resentment, the deep-seated fury of the gunman would brush his partner aside as he would swat a fly. In a sense, both men were using each other, but of the two Dan Shute was the man to be reckoned with. Yet Gomer had seen Barkow at work. He had seen how deviously the big rancher planned, how carefully he made friends. At the fort, they knew and liked him, and what little law there was outside the town of Painted Rock was in the hands of the commanding officer at the fort. Knowing this, Bruce Barkow had made it a point to know the personnel there, and to plan accordingly.

The big black that Rafe was riding was a powerful horse, and he let the animal have its head. Behind him in single file

194

trailed Tex Brisco and Bo Marsh. Rafe Caradec was thinking as he rode. He had seen too much of violence and struggle to fail to understand men who lived lives along the frontier. He had correctly gauged the kind of courage Gee Bonaro possessed, yet he knew the man was dangerous and, if the opportunity offered, would shoot and shoot instantly.

Trigger Boyne was another proposition. Boyne was reckless, wickedly fast with a gun, and the type of man who would fight at the drop of a hat, and had his own ready to drop on the slightest pretext. Boyne liked the name of being a gunman, and he liked being top dog. If Boyne had sent a warning to Caradec, it would be only because he intended to back up that warning.

Rafe took the black along the mountain trail, riding swiftly. The big horse was the finest he had ever had between his knees. When a Sioux gave gifts, he apparently went all the way. A gift had been sent to each of the men on the Crazy Man, which was evidence that the Sioux had looked them over at the cabin. The black had a long, space-eating stride that seemed to put no strain on his endurance. The horses given to the others were almost as good. There were not four men in the mountains mounted as well, Rafe knew.

He rounded the big horse into the dusty street of Painted Rock and rode down toward the hitching rail at a spanking trot. He pulled up and swung down, and the other men swung down alongside him.

"Just keep your eyes open," Rafe said guardedly. "I don't want trouble. But if Boyne starts anything, he's my meat."

Marsh nodded, and walked up on the boardwalk alongside of Brisco, who was sweeping the street with quick, observant eyes.

"Have a drink?" Rafe suggested, and led the way inside the National.

Joe Benson was behind the bar. He looked up warily as the three men entered. He spoke to Bo, then glanced at Tex Brisco. He placed Tex as a stranger, and his mind leaped ahead. It took no long study to see that Tex was a hard character and a fighting man.

Joe was cautious and shrewd. Unless he was mistaken, Barkow and Shute had their work cut out for them. These men didn't look like the sort to back water for anything or anyone. The town's saloonkeeper-mayor had an uncomfortable feeling that a change was in the offing, yet he pushed the feeling aside with irritation. That must not happen. His own failure and his own interests were too closely allied to those of Barkow and Shute. Of course, when Barkow married the Rodney girl that would give them complete title to the ranch. That would leave them in the clear, and these men, if alive, could be run off the ranch with every claim to legal process.

Caradec tossed off his whisky and looked up sharply. His glance pinned Joe Benson to the spot. "Trigger Boyne sent word he was looking for me," he said abruptly. "Tell him I'm in town…ready."

"How should I know Trigger better'n any other man who comes into this bar?" Benson demanded.

"You know him. Tell him."

Rafe hitched his guns into a comfortable position and strode through the swinging doors. There were a dozen men in sight, but none of them resembled Boyne or either of the Blazers he had seen.

He started for the Emporium. Behind him, Tex stopped by one of the posts that supported the wooden awning over the walk, and leaned a negligent shoulder against it, a cigarette drooping from the corner of his mouth.

Bo Marsh sat back in a chair against the wall, his interested eyes sweeping the street. Several men who passed spoke to him and glanced at Tex Brisco's tall, lean figure.

Rafe opened the door of the Emporium and strode inside. Gene Baker looked up, frowning when he saw him. He was not glad to see Rafe, for the man's words on his previous visit had been responsible for some doubts and speculations.

"Is Ann Rodney in?"

Baker hesitated. "Yes," he said finally. "She's back there."

Rafe went around the counter toward the door, hat in his left hand.

"I don't think she wants to see yuh," Baker advised.

"All right," Rafe said, "we'll see."

He pushed past the screen, and stepped into the living room beyond.

Ann Rodney was sewing, and, when the quick step sounded, she glanced up. Her eyes changed. Something inside her seemed to turn over slowly. This big man who had brought such disturbing news affected her as no man ever had. Considering her engagement to Bruce Barkow, she didn't like to feel that way about any man. Since he had last been here, she had worried a good deal about what he had said and her reaction to it. Why would he come with such a tale? Shouldn't she have heard him out?

Bruce said no, that the man was an imposter and someone who hoped to get money from her. Yet she knew something of Johnny Gill, and she had danced with Bo Marsh, and knew that these men were honest and had been so as long as she had known of them. They were liked and respected in Painted Rock.

"Oh," she said, rising. "It's you?"

Rafe stopped in the center of the room, a tall, picturesque figure in his buckskin coat and with his waving black hair. He was, she thought, a handsome man. He wore his guns low and tied down, and she knew what that meant.

197

"I was goin' to wait," he said abruptly, "and let you come to me and ask questions, if you ever did, but when I thought it over, rememberin' what I'd promised your father, I decided I must come back now, lay all my cards on the table, and tell you what happened."

She started to speak, and he lifted his hand. "Wait. I'm goin' to talk quick, because in a few minutes I have an appointment outside that I must keep. Your father did not die on the trail back from California. He was shanghaied in San Francisco, taken aboard a ship while unconscious, and forced to work as a seaman. I was shanghaied at the same time and place. Your father and I in the months that followed were together a lot. He asked me to come here, to take care of you and his wife, and to protect you. He died of beatin's he got aboard ship, just before the rest of us got away from the ship. I was with him when he died, settin' beside his bed. Almost his last words were about you."

Ann Rodney stood very still, staring at him. There was a ring of truth in the rapidly spoken words, yet how could she believe this? Three men had told her they saw her father die, and one of them was the man she was to marry, the man who had befriended her, who had refused to foreclose on the mortgage he held and take from her the last thing she possessed in the world.

"What was my father like?" she asked.

"Like?" Rafe's brow furrowed. "How can anybody say what any man is like? I'd say he was about five feet eight or nine. When he died, his hair was almost white, but when I first saw him, he had only a few gray hairs. His face was a heap like yours. So were his eyes, except they weren't so large nor so beautiful. He was a kind man who wasn't used to violence, I think, and he didn't like it. He planned well, and thought well, but the West was not the country for him, yet. Ten years

198

from now, when it has settled more, he'd have been a leadin' citizen. He was a good man, and a sincere man."

"It sounds like him," Ann said hesitantly, "but there is nothing you could not have learned here, or from someone who knew him."

"No," he said frankly. "That's so. But there's somethin' else you should know. The mortgage your father had against his place was paid."

"What?" Ann stiffened. "Paid? How can you say that?"

"He borrowed the money in Frisco and paid Barkow with it. He got a receipt for it."

"Oh, I can't believe that! Why, Bruce would have…."

"Would he?" Rafe asked gently. "You shore?"

She looked at him. "What was the other thing?"

"I have a deed," he said, "to the ranch made out to you and to me."

Her eyes widened, then hardened with suspicion. "So? Now things become clearer. A deed to my father's ranch made out to you and to me! In other words, you are laying claim to half of my ranch?"

"Please…," Rafe said. "I…."

She smiled. "You needn't say anything more, Mister Caradec. I admit I was almost coming to believe there was something in your story. At least, I was wondering about it, for I couldn't understand how you hoped to profit from any such tale. Now it becomes clear. You are trying to get half my ranch. You have even moved into my house without asking permission." She stepped to one side of the door and pulled back the curtain. "I'm sorry, but I must ask you to leave. I must also ask you to vacate the house on Crazy Man at once. I must ask you to refrain from calling on me again, or from approaching me."

"Please," Rafe said, "you're jumping to conclusions. I

never aimed to claim any part of the ranch. I came here only because your father asked me to."

"Good day, Mister Caradec!" Ann still held the curtain.

He looked at her, and for an instant their eyes held. She was first to look away. He turned abruptly and stepped through the curtain, and, as he did, the door opened and he saw Bo Marsh.

Marsh's eyes were excited and anxious. "Rafe," he said, "that Boyne *hombre's* in front of the National. He wants yuh!"

"Why, shore," Rafe said quietly. "I'm ready."

He walked to the front door, hitching his guns into place. Behind him, he heard Ann Rodney asking Baker: "What did he mean? That Boyne was waiting for him?"

Baker's reply came to Rafe as he stepped out into the morning light. "Trigger Boyne's goin' to kill him, Ann. Yuh'd better go back inside."

Rafe smiled slightly. Kill him? Would that be it? No man knew better than he the tricks that Destiny plays on a man, or how often the right man dies at the wrong time and place. A man never wore a gun without inviting trouble; he never stepped into a street and began the gunman's walk without the full knowledge that he might be a shade too slow, that some small thing might disturb him just long enough.

VIII

Morning sun was bright, and the street lay empty of horses or vehicles. A few idlers loafed in front of the stage station, but all of them were on their feet.

Rafe Caradec saw his black horse switch his tail at a fly, and he stepped down into the street. Trigger Boyne stepped off the boardwalk to face him, some distance off. Rafe did not walk slowly; he made no measured, quiet approach. He started to walk toward Boyne, going fast.

Trigger walked down the street easily, casually. He was smiling. Inside, his heart was throbbing, and there was a wild reckless eagerness within him. This one he would finish off fast. This would be simple, easy. He squared in the street, and suddenly the smile was wiped from his face. Caradec was coming toward him, shortening the distance at a fast walk. That rapid approach did something to the calm on Boyne's face and in his mind. It was wrong. Caradec should have come slowly; he should have come poised and ready to draw. Knowing his own deadly marksmanship, Boyne felt sure he could kill this man at any distance. But as soon as he saw that walk, he knew that Caradec was going to be so close in a few more steps that he himself would be killed. It is one thing to know you are to kill another man, quite a different thing to know you are to die yourself. Why, if Caradec walked that way, he would be so close he couldn't miss!

Boyne's legs spread and the wolf sprang into his eyes, but there was panic there, too. He had to stop his man, get him now. His hand swept down for his gun. Yet something was wrong. For all his speed he seemed incredibly slow, because that other man, that tall, moving figure in the buckskin coat and black hat, was already shooting.

Trigger's own hand moved first, his own hand gripped the gun butt first, and then he was staring into a smashing, blossoming rose of flame that seemed to bloom beyond the muzzle of that big black gun in the hand of Rafe Caradec. Something stabbed at his stomach, and he went numb to his toes. Stupidly he swung his gun up, staring over it. The gun seemed awfully heavy. He must get a smaller one. That gun opposite him blossomed with rose again, and something struck him again in the stomach. He started to speak, half turning toward the men in front of the stage station, his mouth opening and closing.

Something was wrong with him, he tried to say. Why, everyone knew he was the fastest man in Wyoming, unless it was Shute! Everyone knew that! The heavy gun in his hand bucked, and he saw the flame stab at the ground. He dropped the gun, swayed, then fell flat on his face.

He would have to get up. He was going to kill that stranger, that Rafe Caradec. He would have to get up. The numbness from his stomach climbed higher, and he suddenly felt himself in the saddle of a bucking horse, a monstrous and awful horse that leaped and plunged, and it was going up! Up! Up! Then it came down hard, and he felt himself leave the saddle, all sprawled out. The horse had thrown him. Bucked off into the dust. He closed his hands spasmodically.

Rafe Caradec stood tall in the middle of the gunman's walk, the black, walnut-stocked pistol in his right hand. He glanced once at the still figure sprawled in the street, then his eyes lifted, sweeping the walks in swift, accurate, appraisal. Only then, some instinct prodded his unconscious and warned him. The merest flicker of a curtain, and in the space between the curtain and the edge of the window the black muzzle of a rifle! His .44 lifted, and the heavy gun bucked in his hand just as flame leaped from the rifle barrel, and he felt quick, urgent fingers pluck at his sleeve. The .44 jolted again, and a rifle rattled on the shingled porch roof. The curtain made a tearing sound, and the head and shoulders of a man fell through, toppling over the sill. Overbalanced, the heels came up, and the man's body rolled over slowly, seemed to hesitate, then rolled over again, poised an instant on the edge of the roof, and dropped suddenly into the street. Dust lifted from around the body, settled back. Gee Bonaro thrust hard with one leg, and his face twisted a little. In the quiet street there was no sound, no movement.

For the space of a full half-minute the watchers held themselves, shocked by the sudden climax, stunned with disbelief. Trigger Boyne had been beaten to the draw and killed; Gee Bonaro had made his try, and died.

Rafe Caradec turned slowly and walked back to his horse. Without a word he swung into saddle. He turned the horse and, sitting tall in the saddle, swept the street with a cold, hard eye that seemed to stare at each man there. Then, as if by his own wish, the black horse turned. Walking slowly, his head held proudly, he carried his rider down the street and out of town.

Behind him, coolly and without smiles, Bo Marsh and Tex Brisco followed. Like him, they rode slowly; like him they rode proudly. Something in their bearing seemed to say: *We were challenged. We came. You see the result.*

In the window of the National, Joe Benson chewed his mustache. He stared at the figure of Trigger Boyne with vague disquiet, then irritation. "Cuss it!" he muttered under his breath. "You was supposed to be a gunman? What in thunder was wrong with yuh?"

A bullet from Boyne's gun, or from Bonaro's, for that matter, could have ended it all. A bullet now could settle the whole thing, quiet the gossip, remove the doubts, and leave Barkow free to marry Ann, and the whole business could go forward. Instead, they had failed. It would be a long time now, Benson knew, before it was all over. A long time. Barkow was slipping. The man had better think fast and get something done. Rafe Caradec must die.

The Fort Laramie Treaty of 1868 had forbidden white men to enter the Powder River country, yet gold discoveries had brought prospectors north in increasing numbers. Small villages and mining camps had come into existence. Following them, cattlemen discovered the rich grasses of northern Wyoming, and a few herds came over what later was to be known as the Texas Trail.

Indian attacks and general hostility caused many of these pioneers to retreat to more stable localities, but a few of the more courageous had stayed on. Prospectors had entered the Black Hills, following the Custer expedition in 1874, and the Sioux, always resentful of any incursion upon their hunting grounds or any flaunting of their rights, were preparing to do something more than talk.

The names of such chiefs as Red Cloud, Dull Knife, Crazy Horse, and the medicine man, Sitting Bull, came more and more into frontier gossip. A steamboat was reported to be *en route* up the turbulent Yellowstone, and river traffic on the upper Mississippi was an accepted fact. There were increasing reports of gatherings of Indians in the hills, and white men rode warily, never without arms.

Cut off from contact with the few scattered ranchers, Rafe Caradec and his riders heard little of the gossip except what they gleaned from an occasional prospector or wandering hunter. Yet no gossip was needed to tell them how the land lay.

Twice they heard sounds of rifle fire, and once the Sioux ran off a number of cattle from Shute's ranch, taking them from a herd kept not far from Long Valley. Two of Shute's riders were killed. None of Caradec's men was molested. He was left strictly alone. Indians avoided his place, no matter what their mission.

Twice, riders from the ranch went to Painted Rock. Each time they returned, they brought stories of an impending Indian outbreak. A few of the less courageous ranchers sold out and left the country. In all this time, Rafe Caradec lived in the saddle, riding often from dawn until dusk, avoiding the tangled brakes, but studying the lay of the land with care. There was, he knew, some particular reason for Bruce Barkow's interest in the ranch that belonged to Ann Rodney. What that reason was, he must know. Without it, he knew he could offer no real reason why Barkow would go to the lengths he had gone to get a ranch that was on the face of things of no more value than any piece of land in the country, most of which could be had for the taking....

Ann spent much of her time alone. Business at the store was thriving, and Gene Baker and his wife, and often Ann as well, were busy. In her spare time the thought kept returning to her that Rafe Caradec might be honest. Yet she dismissed the thought as unworthy. If she admitted even for an instant that he was honest, she must also admit that Bruce Barkow was dishonest, a thief, and possibly a killer. Yet somehow the picture of her father kept returning to her mind. It was present there on one of the occasions when Bruce Barkow came to call.

A handsome man, Barkow understood how to appeal to a woman. He carried himself well, and his clothes were always the best in Painted Rock. He called this evening, looking even better than he had on the last occasion, his black suit neatly pressed, his mustache carefully trimmed.

They had been talking for some time when Ann mentioned Rafe Caradec. "His story sounded so sincere!" she said, after a minute. "He said he had been shanghaied in San Francisco with Father, and that they had become acquainted on the ship."

"He's a careful man," Barkow commented, "and a dangerous one. He showed that when he killed Trigger Boyne and Bonaro. He met Boyne on the range, and they had some trouble over an Indian girl."

"An Indian girl?" Ann looked at him questioningly.

"Yes." Barkow frowned as if the subject was distasteful to him. "You know how some of the cowhands are…always running after some squaw. They have stolen squaws, kept them for a while, then turned them loose or killed them. Caradec had a young squaw, and Boyne tried to argue with him to let her go. They had words, and there'd have been a shooting then if one of Caradec's other men hadn't come up with a rifle, and Shute's boys went away."

Ann was shocked. She had heard of such things happening and was well aware of how much trouble they caused. That Rafe Caradec would be a man like that was hard to believe. Yet, what did she know of the man? He disturbed her more than she allowed herself to believe. Despite the fact that he seemed to be trying to work some scheme to get all or part of her ranch, and despite all she had heard of him at one time or another from Bruce, she couldn't make herself believe that all she heard was true.

That he appealed to her, she refused to admit. Yet when with him, she felt drawn to him. She liked his rugged masculinity, his looks, his voice, and was impressed with his sincerity. Yet the killing of Boyne and Bonaro was the talk of the town. The Bonaro phase of the incident she could understand from the previous episode in the store. But no one had any idea of why Boyne should be looking for Caradec. The solution now offered by Barkow was the only one. A fight over a squaw! Without understanding why, Ann felt vaguely resentful.

For days a dozen of Shute's riders had hung around town. There had been talk of lynching Caradec, but nothing came of it. Ann had heard the talk, and asked Baker about it.

The old storekeeper looked up, nodding.

The Trail to Crazy Man

"There's talk, but it'll come to nothin'. None of these boys aim to ride out there to Crazy Man and tackle that crowd. You know what Gill and Marsh are like. They'll fight, and they can. Well, Caradec's showed what he could do with a gun when he killed those two in the street. I don't know whether yuh saw that other feller with Caradec or not. The one from Texas. Well, if he ain't tougher than either Marsh or Gill, I'll pay off! Notice how he wore his guns? Nope, nobody'll go looking for them. If they got their hands on Caradec, that would be somethin' else."

Baker rubbed his jaw thoughtfully. "Unless they are powerful lucky, they won't last long, anyway. That's Injun country, and Red Cloud or Man-Afraid-Of-His-Hoss won't take kindly to white men livin' there. They liked yore pa, and he was friendly to 'em."

As a result of his conversations with Barkow, Sheriff Pod Gomer had sent messages south by stage to Cheyenne and the telegraph. Rafe Caradec had come from San Francisco, and Bruce Barkow wanted to know who and what he was. More than that, he wanted to find out how he had been allowed to escape the *Mary S.* With that in mind he wrote to Bully Borger.

Barkow had known nothing about Caradec when the deal was made, but Borger had agreed to take Charles Rodney to sea and let him die there, silencing the truth forever. Allowing Rafe Caradec to come ashore with his story was not keeping the terms of the bargain. If Caradec had actually been aboard the ship and left it, there might be something in that to make him liable to the law. Barkow intended to leave no stone unturned, and in the meanwhile he spread his stories around about Caradec's reason for killing Boyne.

IX

Caradec went on with his haying. The nights were already growing chillier. At odd times, when not haying or handling cattle, he and the boys built another room onto the cabin, and banked the house against the wind. Fortunately its position was sheltered. Wind would not bother them greatly where they were, but there would be snow and lots of it.

Rafe rode out each day, and several times brought back deer or elk. The meat was jerked and stored away. Gill got the old wagon Rodney had brought from Missouri and made some repairs. It would be the easiest way to get supplies out from Painted Rock. He worked over it and soon had it in excellent shape.

On the last morning of the month, Rafe walked out to where Gill was hitching a team to the wagon.

"Looks good," he agreed. "You've done a job on it, Johnny."

Gill looked pleased. He nodded at the hubs of the wheels. "Notice 'em? No squeak!"

"Well, I'll be hanged." Rafe looked at the grease on the hubs. "Where'd you get the grease?"

"Sort of a spring back over in the hills. I brung back a bucket of it."

Rafe Caradec looked up sharply. "Johnny, where'd you find that spring?"

"Why,"—Gil looked puzzled—"it's just a sort of hole, back over next to that mound. You know, in that bad range. Ain't much account down there, but I was down there once and found this here spring. This stuff works as well as the grease yuh buy."

"It should," Rafe said dryly. "It's the same stuff!"

He caught up the black and threw a saddle on it. Within an hour he was riding down toward the barren knoll Gill had mentioned. What he found was not a spring, but a hole among some sparse rushes, dead and sick-looking. It was an oil seepage.

Oil! Swiftly his mind leaped ahead. This, then, could be the reason why Barkow and Shute were so anxious to acquire title to this piece of land, so anxious that they would have a man shanghaied and killed. Caradec recalled that Bonneville had reported oil seepages on his trip through the state some forty years or so before, and there had been a well drilled in the previous decade. One of the largest markets for oil was the patent medicine business, for it was the main ingredient in so-called "British Oil."

The hole in which the oil was seeping in a thick stream might be shallow, but sounding with a six-foot stick found no bottom. Rafe doubted if it was much deeper. Still, there would be several barrels here, and he seemed to recall some talk of selling oil for twenty dollars the barrel.

Swinging into the saddle, he turned the big black down the draw and rode rapidly toward the hills. This could be the reason, for certainly it was reason enough. The medicine business was only one possible market, for machinery of all kinds needed lubricants. There was every chance that the oil industry might really mean something in time. If the hole was emptied, how fast would it refill? How constant was the supply? On one point he could soon find out.

He swung the horse up out of the draw, forded the Crazy Man, and cantered up the hill to the cabin. As he reined in and swung down at the door, he noticed two strange horses.

Tex Brisco stepped to the door, his face hard. "Watch it, boss!" he said sharply.

Pod Gomer's thick-set body thrust into the doorway. "Caradec," he said calmly, "yuh're under arrest."

Rafe swung down, facing him. Two horses. Who had ridden the other one?

"For what?" he demanded.

His mind was racing. *The mutiny? Have they found out about that?*

"For killin'. Shootin' Bonaro."

"Bonaro?" Rafe laughed. "You mean for defendin' myself? Bonaro had a rifle in that window. He was all set to shoot me."

Gomer nodded coolly. "That was most folks' opinion, but it seems nobody *saw* him aim any gun at yuh. We've only got yore say-so. When we got to askin' around, it begun to look sort of funny-like. It appears to a lot of folks that yuh just took that chance to shoot him and get away with it. Anyway, yuh'd be better off to stand trial."

"Don't go, boss," Brisco said. "They don't ever aim to have a trial."

"Yuh'd better not resist," Gomer replied calmly. "I've got twenty Shute riders down in the valley. I made 'em stay back. The minute any shootin' starts, they'll come a-runnin', and yuh all know what that would mean."

Rafe knew. It would mean the death of all four of them and the end to any opposition to Barkow's plans. Probably that was what the rancher hoped would happen.

"Why, shore, Gomer," Caradec said calmly, "I'll go."

Tex started to protest, and Rafe saw Gill hurl his hat into the dust.

"Give me yore guns, then," Gomer said, "and mount up."

"No." Rafe's voice was flat. "I keep my guns till I get to town. If that bunch of Shute's starts anything, the first one I'll kill will be you, Gomer."

Pod Gomer's face turned sullen. "Yuh ain't goin' to be bothered. I'm the law here. Let's go!"

"Gomer," Tex Brisco said viciously, "if anything happens to him, I'll kill you and Barkow both!"

"That goes for me, too!" Gill said harshly.

"And me," Marsh put in. "I'll get you if I have to dry-gulch yuh, Gomer."

"Well, all right!" Gomer said angrily. "It's just a trial. I told 'em I didn't think much of it, but the judge issued this warrant."

He was scowling blackly. It was all right for them to issue warrants, but if they thought he was going to get killed for them, they were bloody well wrong. Pod Gomer jammed his hat down on his head. This was a far cry from the coal mines of Lancashire, but sometimes he wished he was back in England. There was a look in Brisco's eyes he didn't like. *No,* he told himself, *he'll be turned loose before I take a chance. Let Barkow kill his own pigeons. I don't want these Bar M hands gunnin' for me!*

The man who had ridden the other horse stepped out of the cabin, followed closely by Bo Marsh. There was no smile on the young cowhand's face. The man was Bruce Barkow. For an instant, his eyes met Caradec's. "This is just a formality," Barkow said smoothly. "There's been some talk around Painted Rock, and a trial will clear the air a lot, and, of course, if yuh're innocent, Caradec, yuh'll be freed."

"You shore of that?" Rafe's eyes smiled cynically. "Barkow, you hate me and you know it. If I ever leave that jail alive, it won't be your fault."

Barkow shrugged. "Think what you want," he said indifferently. "I believe in law and order. We've got a nice little community at Painted Rock, and we want to keep it that way.

211

Boyne had challenged yuh, and that was different. Bonaro had no part in the fight."

"No use arguin' that here," Gomer protested. "Court's the place for that. Let's go."

Tex Brisco lounged down the steps, his thumbs hooked in his belt. He stared at Gomer. "I don't like you," he said coolly. "I don't like you a bit. I think yuh're yeller as a coyote. I think yuh bob ever' time this here Barkow says bob."

Gomer's face whitened, and his eyes shifted. "Yuh've got no call to start trouble," he said. "I'm doin' my duty."

"Let it ride," Caradec told Tex. "There's plenty of time."

"Yeah," Tex drawled, his hard eyes on Gomer, "but just for luck I'm goin' to mount and trail yuh into town, keepin' to the hills. If that bunch of Shute riders gets fancy, I'm goin' to get myself a sheriff, and"—his eyes shifted—"mebbe another *hombre*."

"Is that a threat?" Barkow asked contemptuously. "Talk is cheap."

"Want to see how cheap?" Tex prodded. His eyes were ugly, and he was itching for a fight. It showed in every line of him. "Want to make it expensive?"

Bruce Barkow was no fool. He had not seen Tex Brisco in action, yet there was something chill and deadly about the tall Texan. Barkow shrugged. "We came here to enforce the law. Is this resistance, Caradec?"

"No," Rafe said. "Let's go."

The three men turned their horses and walked them down the trail toward Long Valley. Tex Brisco threw a saddle on his horse, then mounted. Glancing back, Pod Gomer saw the Texan turn his horse up a trail into the trees. He swore viciously.

Caradec sat his horse easily. The trouble would not come now. He was quite sure the plan had been to get him away,

212

then claim the Shute riders had taken him from the law. Yet he was sure it would not come to that now. Pod Gomer would know that Brisco's Winchester was within range. Also, Rafe was still wearing his guns.

Rafe rode warily, lagging a trifle behind the sheriff. He glanced at Barkow, but the rancher's face was expressionless. Ahead of them, in a tight bunch, waited the Shute riders. The first he recognized were the Blazers. There was another man, known as Joe Gorman, whom he also recognized.

Red Blazer started forward abruptly. "He come, did he?" he shouted. "Now we'll show him!"

"Get back!" Gomer ordered sharply.

"Huh?" Red glared at Gomer. "Who says I'll get back! I'm stringin' this *hombre* to the first tree we get to."

"You stay back!" Gomer ordered. "We're takin' this man in for trial!"

Red Blazer laughed. "Come on, boys!" he yelled. "Let's hang the skunk!"

"I wouldn't, Red," Rafe Caradec said calmly. "You've overlooked somethin'. I'm wearin' my guns. Are you faster than Trigger Boyne?"

Blazer jerked his horse's head around, his face pale but furious. "Hey!" he yelled. "What the devil is this? I thought...."

"That you'd have an easy time of it?" Rafe shoved the black horse between Gomer and Barkow, pushing ahead of them. He rode right up to Blazer and let the big black shove into the other horse. "Well, get this, Blazer, any time you kill me, you'll do it with a gun in your hand, savvy? You're nothin' but a lot of lynch-crazy coyotes! Try it, damn it! Try it now, and I'll blow you out of that saddle so full of lead you'll sink a foot into the ground!" Rafe's eyes swept the crowd. "Think this is a joke? That goes for any of you. As for Gomer,

213

he knows that if you *hombres* want any trouble, he gets it, too. There's a man up in the hills with a Winchester, and, if you don't think he can empty saddles, start somethin'. That Winchester carries sixteen shots, and I've seen him empty it and get that many rabbits! I'm packing two guns. I'm askin' you now so, if you want any of what I've got, start the ball rollin'. Mebbe you'd get me, but I'm tellin' you there'll be more dead men around here than you can shake a stick at."

Joe Gorman spoke quickly. "Watch it, boys! There is an *hombre* up on the mountain with a rifle. I seen him."

"What the hell is this?" Red Blazer repeated.

"The fun's over," Rafe replied shortly. "You might as well head for home and tell Dan Shute to kill his own wolves. I'm wearin' my guns, and I'm goin' to keep 'em. I'll stand trial, but you know and I know that Bonaro got what he was askin' for." Caradec turned his eyes on Blazer. "As for you, stay out of my sight. You're too blasted willin' to throw your hemp over a man you think is helpless. I don't like skunks and never did."

"Yuh can't call me a skunk!" Blazer bellowed.

Rafe stared at him. "I just did," he said calmly.

X

For a full minute their eyes held. Rafe's hand was on his thigh within inches of his gun. If it came to gun play now, he would be killed, but Blazer and Barkow would go down, too, and there would be others. He had not exaggerated when he spoke of Tex Brisco's shooting. The man was a wizard with the rifle.

Red Blazer was trapped. White to the lips, he stared at Rafe and could see cold, certain death looking back at him.

He could stand it no longer. "Why don't some of yuh do somethin'?" he bellowed.

Joe Gorman spat: "You done the talkin', Red."

"Tarnation with it!"

Blazer swung his horse around, touched spurs to the animal, and raced off at top speed.

Bruce Barkow's hand hovered close to his gun. A quick draw, a shot, and the man would be dead. Just like that. His lips tightened, and his elbow crooked.

Gomer grabbed his wrist. "Don't, Bruce! Don't! That *hombre* up there…look!"

Barkow's head swung. Brisco was in plain sight, his rifle resting over the limb of a tree. At that distance, he could not miss. Yet he was beyond pistol range, and, while some of the riders had rifles, they were out in the open without a bit of cover.

Barkow jerked his arm away and turned his horse toward town. Rafe turned the black and rode beside him. He said nothing, but Barkow was seething at the big man's obvious contempt. Rafe Caradec had outfaced the lot of them. He had made them look fools. Yet Barkow remembered as well as each of the riders remembered that Rafe had fired but three shots in the street battle, that all the shots had scored, and two men had died.

When the cavalcade reached the National, Rafe turned to Pod Gomer. "Get your court goin'," he said calmly. "We'll have this trial now."

"Listen here!" Gomer burst out, infuriated. "Yuh can do things like that too often! We'll have our court when we get blamed good and ready!"

"No," Rafe said, "you'll hold court this afternoon…now. You haven't got any calendar to interfere. I have business to attend to that can't wait, and I won't. You'll have yore trial today, or I'll leave, and you can come and get me."

"Who you tellin' what to do?" Gomer said angrily. "I'll have you know...."

"Then you tell him, Barkow...or does he take his orders from Shute? Call that judge of yours and let's get this over."

Bruce Barkow's lips tightened. He could see that Gene Baker and Ann Rodney were standing in the doorway of the store, listening.

"All right," Barkow said savagely. "Call him down here."

Not much later Judge Roy Gargan walked into the stage station and looked around. He was a tall, slightly stooped man with a lean, hangdog face and round eyes. He walked up to the table and sat down in the chair behind it. Bruce Barkow took a chair to one side where he could see the judge.

Noting the move, Rafe Caradec sat down where both men were visible. Barkow, nettled, shifted his chair irritably. He glanced up and saw Ann Rodney come in, accompanied by Baker and Pat Higley. He scowled again. *Why couldn't they stay out of this?*

Slowly the hangers-on around town filed in. Joe Benson came in and sat down close to Barkow. They exchanged looks. Benson's questioning glance made Barkow furious. If they wanted so much done, why didn't someone do something besides him?

"I'll watch from here," drawled a voice.

Barkow's head came up. Standing in the window behind and to the right of the judge was Tex Brisco. At the same instant Barkow noted him, the Texan lifted a hand.

"Hi, Johnny! Glad to see you."

Bruce Barkow's face went hard. Johnny Gill and, beside him, Bo Marsh. If anything rusty was pulled in this courtroom, the place would be a shambles. Maybe Dan Shute was right, after all. If they were going to be crooked, why not dry-

216

gulch the fellow and get it over? All Barkow's carefully worked-out plans to get Caradec had failed.

There had been three good chances. Resistance, that would warrant killing in attempting an arrest; attempted escape, if he so much as made a wrong move; or lynching by the Shute riders. At every point they had been outguessed.

Judge Gargan slammed a six-shooter on the table.

"Order!" he proclaimed. "Court's in session! Reckon I'll appoint a jury. Six men will do. I'll have Joe Benson, Tom Blazer, Sam Mawson, Doe Otto, and...."

"Joe Benson's not eligible," Caradec interrupted.

Gargan frowned. "Who's runnin' this court?"

"Supposedly," Rafe said quietly, "the law, supposedly the interests of justice. Joe Benson was a witness to the shootin', so he'll be called on to give testimony."

"Who yuh tellin' how to run this court?" Gargan demanded belligerently.

"Doesn't the defendant even have a chance to defend himself?" Caradec asked gently. He glanced around at the crowd. "I think you'll all agree that a man on trial for his life should have a chance to defend himself, that he should be allowed to call and question witnesses, and that he should have an attorney. But since this court hasn't provided an attorney, and because I want to, I'll act for myself. Now,"—he looked around—"the judge picked out three members of the jury. I'd like to pick out three more. I'd like Pat Higley, Gene Baker, and Ann Rodney as members of the jury."

"What?" Gargan roared. "I'll have no woman settin' on the jury in my court! Why, of all the...."

Rafe said smoothly: "It kind of looks like Your Honor does not know the law in Wyomin'. By an act approved in December Eighteen Sixty-Nine, the first Territorial Legislature granted equal rights to women. Women served on juries in

217

Laramie in Eighteen Seventy, and one was servin' as justice of the peace that year."

Gargan swallowed and looked uncomfortable. Barkow sat up, started to say something, but before he could open his mouth, Caradec was speaking again.

"As I understand, the attorney for the State and the defense attorney usually select a jury. As the Court has taken it upon himself to appoint a jury, I was just suggestin' the names of three responsible citizens I respect. I'm shore none of these three can be considered friends of mine, sorry as I am to say it. Of course," he added, "if the court objects to these three people...if there's somethin' about their characters I don't know, or if they are not good citizens...then I take back my suggestion." He turned to look at Bruce Barkow. "Or mebbe Mister Barkow objects to Ann Rodney servin' on the jury?"

Barkow sat up, flushing. Suddenly he was burning with rage. This whole thing had got out of hand. What had happened to bring this about? He was acutely conscious that Ann was staring at him, her eyes wide, a flush mounting in her cheeks at his hesitation. "No!" he said violently. "No, of course, no. Let her sit, but let's get this business started."

Pod Gomer was slumped in his chair, watching cynically. His eyes shifted to Barkow with a faintly curious expression. The planner and schemer had missed out on this trial. It had been his idea to condemn the man in public, then see to it that he was hanged.

"Yuh're actin' as prosecutin' attorney?" Gargan asked Barkow.

The rancher got to his feet, cursing the thought that had given rise to this situation. That Rafe Caradec had won the first round he was unpleasantly aware. Somehow they had never contemplated any trouble on the score of the jury. In the few trials held thus far the judge had appointed the jury, and there had been no complaint. All the cases had gone off as planned.

"Yore Honor," he began, "and gentlemen of the jury. Yuh all know none of us here are lawyers. This court is bein' held only so's we can keep law and order in this community, and that's the way it will be till the county is organized. This prisoner was in a gunfight with Lemuel Boyne, known as Trigger. Boyne challenged him...some of yuh know the reason for that...and Caradec accepted. In the fight out in the street, Caradec shot Boyne and killed him. In almost the same instant, he lifted his gun and shot Gee Bonaro, who was innocently watchin' the battle from his window. If a thing like this isn't punished, any gunfighter is apt to shoot anybody he don't like at any time, and nothin' done about it. We've all heard that Caradec claims Bonaro had a rifle and was about to shoot at him, which was a plumb good excuse, but a right weak one. We know this Caradec had words with Bonaro at the Emporium, and almost got into a fight then and there. I say Caradec is guilty of murder in the first degree, and should be hung." Barkow turned his head and motioned to Red Blazer. "Red, you get up there and tell the jury what yuh know."

Red strode up to the chair that was doing duty for a witness stand and slouched down in the seat. He was unshaven, and his hair was uncombed. He sprawled his legs out and stuck his thumbs in his belt. He rolled his quid in his jaws, and spat. "I seen this here Caradec shoot Boyne," he said, "then he ups with his pistol and cut down on Bonaro, who was a-standin' in the window, just a-lookin'."

"Did Bonaro make any threatening moves toward Caradec?"

"Him?" Red's eyes opened wide. "Shucks, no. Gee was

just a-standin' there. Caradec was afeerd of him, an' seen a chance to kill him and get plumb away."

Rafe looked thoughtfully at Barkow. "Is the fact that the witness was not sworn in the regular way in this court? Or is his conscience delicate on the subject of perjury?"

"Huh?" Blazer sat up. "What'd he say?"

Barkow flushed. "It hasn't usually been the way here, but..."

"Swear him in," Caradec said calmly, "and have him say under oath what he's just said."

He waited until this was done, and then, as Red started to get up, Rafe motioned him back. "I've got a few questions," he said.

"Huh?" Red demanded belligerently. "I don't have to answer no more questions."

"Yes, you do." Rafe's voice was quiet. "Get back on that witness stand."

"Do I have to?" Blazer demanded of Barkow, who nodded.

If there had been any easy way out, he would have taken it, but there was none. He was beginning to look at Rafe Caradec with new eyes.

Rafe got up and walked over to the jury. "Gentlemen," he said, "none of you know me well. None of us, as Barkow said, knows much about how court business should be handled. All we want to do is get at the truth. I know that all of you here are busy men. You're willin' and anxious to help along justice and the beginnin's of law hereabouts, and all of you are honest men. You want to do the right thing. Red Blazer has just testified that I shot a man who was makin' no threatenin' moves, that Bonaro was standing in a window, just watching."

Caradec turned around and looked at Blazer thoughtfully.

220

He walked over to him, squatted on his haunches, and peered into his eyes, shifting first to one side, then the other.

Red Blazer's face flamed. "What's the matter?" he blared. "Yuh gone crazy?"

"No," Caradec said, "just lookin' at your eyes. I was curious to see what kind of eyes a man had who could see through a shingle roof and a ceilin'."

"Huh?" Blazer glared.

The jury sat up, and Barkow's eyes narrowed. The courtroom crowd leaned forward.

"Why, Red, you must have forgot," Rafe said. "You were in the National when I killed Boyne. You were standin' behind Joe Benson. You were the first person I saw when I looked around. You could see me, and you could see Boyne...but you couldn't see the second-story window across the street."

Somebody whooped, and Pat Higley grinned.

"I reckon he's right," Pat said coolly. "I was standin' right alongside of Red."

"That's right!" somebody from back in the courtroom shouted. "Blazer tried to duck out without payin' for his drink, and Joe Benson stopped him!"

Everybody laughed, and Blazer turned fiery red, glaring back into the room to see who the speaker was, and not finding him.

Rafe turned to Barkow, and smiled. "Have you got another witness?"

XI

Despite herself, Ann Rodney found herself admiring Rafe Caradec's composure, his easy manner. Her curiosity was stirred. What manner of man was he? Where was he from?

221

What background had he? Was he only a wanderer, or was he something different? His language, aside from his characteristic Texas drawl, and his manner spoke of refinement, yet she knew of his gun skill as exhibited in the Boyne fight.

"Tom Blazer's my next witness," Barkow said. "Swear him in."

Tom Blazer, a hulking redhead even bigger than Red, took the stand. Animosity glared from his eyes.

"Did you see the shootin'?" Barkow asked.

"Yuh're darned right I did!" Tom declared, staring at Rafe. "I seen it, and I wasn't inside no saloon! I was right out in the street!"

"Was Bonaro where yuh could see him?"

"He shore was!"

"Did he make any threatenin' moves?"

"Not any!"

"Did he lift a gun?"

"He shore didn't!"

"Did he make any move that would give an idea he was goin' to shoot?"

"Nope. Not any." As Tom Blazer answered each question, he glared triumphantly at Caradec.

Barkow turned to the jury. "Well, there yuh are. I think that's enough evidence. I think...."

"Let's hear Caradec ask his questions," Pat Higley said. "I want both sides of this yarn."

Rafe got up and walked over to Tom Blazer, then looked at the judge. "Your Honor, I'd like permission to ask one question of a man in the audience. He can be sworn or not, just as you say."

Gargan hesitated uncertainly. Always before things had gone smoothly. Trials had been railroaded through, objections swept aside, and the wordless little ranchers or other ob-

222

jectors to the rule of Barkow and Shute had been helpless. This time preparations should have been more complete. He didn't know what to do. "All right," he said, his misgiving showing in his expression and tone.

Caradec turned to look at a short, stocky man with a brown mustache streaked with gray. "Grant," he said, "what kind of a curtain have you got over that window above your harness and saddle shop?"

Grant looked up. "Why, it ain't rightly no curtain," he said frankly. "It's a blanket."

"You keep it down all the time? The window covered?"

"Uhn-huh. Shore do. Sun gets in there otherwise and makes the floor hot and she heats up the store thataway. Keepin' that window covered keeps her cooler."

"It was covered the day of the shooting?"

"Shore was."

"Where did you find the blanket after the shootin'?"

"Well, she laid over the sill, partly inside, partly outside."

Rafe turned to the jury. "Miss Rodney and gentlemen, I believe the evidence is clear. The window was covered by a blanket. When Bonaro fell after I shot him, he tumbled across the sill, tearin' down the blanket. Do you agree?"

"Shore!" Gene Baker found his voice. The whole case was only too obviously a frame-up to get Caradec. It was like Bonaro to try a sneak killing, anyway. "If that blanket hadn't been over the window, then he couldn't have fallen against it and carried part out with him."

"That's right." Rafe turned on Tom Blazer. "Your eyes seem to be as amazin' as your brother's. You can see through a wool blanket!"

Blazer sat up with a jerk, his face dark with sullen rage. "Listen!" he said, "I'll tell yuh...."

"Wait a minute!" Rafe whirled on him and thrust a finger

Louis L'Amour

in his face. "You're not only a perjurer but a thief! What did you do with that Winchester Bonaro dropped out of the window?"

"It wa'n't no Winchester!" Blazer blared furiously. "It was a Henry!" Then, seeing the expression on Barkow's face, and hearing the low murmur that swept the court, he realized what he had said. He started to get up, then sat back, angry and confused.

Rafe Caradec turned toward the jury. "The witness swore that Bonaro had no gun, yet he testified that the rifle Bonaro dropped was a Henry. Gentlemen and Miss Rodney, I'm goin' to ask that you recommend the case be dismissed, and also that Red and Tom Blazer be held in jail to answer charges of perjury."

"What?" Tom Blazer came out of the witness chair with a lunge. "Jail? Me? Why, you…."

He leaped, hurling a huge red-haired fist in a roundhouse swing. Rafe Caradec stepped in with a left that smashed Blazer's lips, then a solid right that sent him crashing to the floor.

He glanced at the judge. "And that, I think," he said quietly "is contempt of court."

Pat Higley got up abruptly. "Gargan, I reckon yuh better dismiss this case. Yuh haven't got any evidence or anything that sounds like evidence, and I guess ever'body here heard about Caradec facin' Bonaro down in the store. If he wanted to shoot him, there was his chance."

Gargan swallowed. "Case dismissed," he said.

He looked up at Bruce Barkow, but the rancher was walking toward Ann Rodney. She glanced at him, then her eyes lifted, and beyond him she saw Rafe Caradec. How fine his face was! It was a rugged, strong face. There was character in it, and sincerity. She came to with a start. Bruce was speaking to her.

224

"Gomer told me he had a case," Barkow said, "or I'd never have been a party to this. He's guilty as can be, but he's smooth."

Ann looked down at Bruce Barkow, and suddenly his eyes looked different to her than they ever had before. "He may be guilty of a lot of things," she said tartly, "but if ever there was a cooked-up, dishonest case, it was this one. And everyone in town knew it. If I were you, Bruce Barkow, I'd be ashamed of myself."

Abruptly she turned her back on him and started for the door, yet, as she went, she glanced up, and for a brief instant her eyes met those of Rafe Caradec's, and something within her leaped. Her throat seemed to catch. Head high, she hurried past him into the street. The store seemed a long distance away.

When Bruce Barkow walked into Pod Gomer's office, the sheriff was sitting in his swivel chair. In the big leather armchair across the room Dan Shute was waiting. He was a big man, with massive shoulders, powerfully muscled arms, and great hands. A shock of dusky blond hair covered the top of his head, and his eyebrows were the color of corn silk. He looked up as Barkow came in, and, when he spoke, his voice was rough. "You shore played hob!"

"The man's smart, that's all," Barkow said. "Next time we'll have a better case."

"Next time?" Dan Shute lounged back in the big chair, the contempt in his eyes unconcealed. "There ain't goin' to be a next time. Yuh're through, Barkow. From now on, this is my show, and we run it my way. Caradec needs killin', and we'll kill him. Also, yuh're goin' to foreclose that mortgage on the Rodney place." He held up a hand as Barkow started to speak. "No, you wait. Yuh was all for pullin' this slick stuff.

225

Winnin' the girl, gettin' the property the easy way, the legal way. To blazes with that! This Caradec is makin' a monkey of yuh! Yuh're not slick! Yuh're just a country boy playin' with a real smooth lad! To blazes with that smooth stuff! You fore-close on that mortgage and do it plumb quick. I'll take care of Mister Rafe Caradec! With my own hands, or guns if neces-sary. We'll clean that country down there so slick of his hands and cattle they won't know what happened."

"That won't get it," Barkow protested. "You let me handle this. I'll take care of things."

Dan Shute looked up at Barkow, his eyes sardonic. "I'll run this show. You're takin' the back seat, Barkow, from now on. All yuh've done is make us out fumblin' fools. Also," he added calmly, "I'm takin' over that girl."

"What?" Barkow whirled, his face livid. In his wildest doubts of Shute, and he had had many of them, this was one thing that had never entered his mind.

"You heard me," Shute replied. "She's a neat little lady, and I can make a place for her out to my ranch. You messed up all around, so I'm takin' over."

Barkow laughed, but his laugh was hollow with something of fear in it. Always before Dan Shute had been big, silent, and surly, saying little, letting Barkow plan and plot and take the lead. Bruce Barkow had always thought of the man as a sort of strong-arm squad to use in a pinch. Suddenly he was shockingly aware that this big man was completely sure of himself, that he held him, Barkow, in contempt. He would ride roughshod over everything. "Dan," Barkow protested, trying to keep his thoughts ordered, "yuh can't play with a girl's affections. She's in love with me. Yuh can't do anything about that. Yuh think she'd fall out of love with one man, and...?"

Dan Shute grinned. "Who said anything about love? You

talk about that all yuh want. Talk it to yoreself. I want the girl, and I'm goin' to have her. It doesn't make any difference who says no, and that goes for Gene Baker, her, or you."

Bruce Barkow stood flat-footed and pale. Suddenly he felt sick and empty. Here it was, then. He was through. Dan Shute had told him off, and in front of Pod Gomer. Out of the tail of his eye he could see the calm, yet cynical, expression on Gomer's face. He looked up, and he felt small under the flat, ironic gaze of Shute's eyes. "All right, Dan, if that's the way yuh feel. I expect we'd better part company."

Shute chuckled, and his voice was rough when he spoke. "No," he said, "we don't part company. You sit tight. Yuh're holdin' that mortgage, and I want that land. Yuh had a good idea there, Barkow, but yuh're too weak-kneed to swing it. I'll swing it, and mebbe, if yuh're quiet and obey orders, I'll see yuh get some of it."

Bruce Barkow glared at Shute. For the first time he knew what hatred was. Here, in a few minutes, he had been destroyed. This story would go the rounds, and before nightfall everyone in town would know it. Dan Shute, big, slow-talking Dan Shute with his hard fists and his guns had crushed Barkow. He stared at Shute with hatred livid in his eyes. "Yuh'll go too far!" he said viciously.

Shute shrugged. "Yuh can live, an' come out of this with a few dollars," he said calmly, "or yuh can die. I'd just as soon kill yuh, Barkow, as look at yuh." He picked up his hat. "We had a nice thing. That shanghaiin' idea was yores. Why yuh didn't shoot him, I'll never know. If yuh had, this Caradec would never have run into him at all and would never have come in here, stirrin' things up. Yuh could have foreclosed that mortgage, and we could be makin' a deal on that oil now."

"Caradec don't know anything about that," Barkow protested.

"Like sin he don't!" Dan Shute sneered. "Caradec's been watched by my men for days. He's been wise there was somethin' in the wind, and he's scouted all over that place. Well, he was down to the knob the other day, and he took a long look at that oil seepage. He's no fool, Barkow."

Bruce Barkow looked up. "No," he replied suddenly, "he's not, and he's a hand with a gun, too, Dan. He's a hand with a gun. He took Boyne."

Shute shrugged. "Boyne was nothin'. I could have spanked him with his own gun. I'll kill Caradec someday, but first I want to beat him, to beat him with my own hands."

He heaved himself out of the chair and stalked outside. For an instant, Barkow stared after him, then his gaze shifted to Pod Gomer.

The sheriff was absently whittling a small stick. "Well," he said, "he told yuh."

XII

Hard and grim, Barkow's mouth tightened. So Gomer was in it, too. He started to speak, then hesitated. Like Caradec, Gomer was no fool, and he, too, was a good hand with a gun. Barkow shrugged. "Dan sees things wrong," he said. "I've still got an ace in the hole." He looked at Gomer. "I'd like it better if you were on my side."

Pod Gomer shrugged. "I'm with the winner. My health is good. All I need is more money."

"Yuh think Shute's the winner?"

"Don't you?" Gomer asked. "He told yuh plenty, and yuh took it."

"Yes, I did, because I know I'm no match for him with a gun. Nor for you." He studied the sheriff thoughtfully. "This

228

is goin' to be a nice thing, Pod. It would split well, two ways."

Gomer got up and snapped his knife shut. "You show me the color of some money," he said, "and how Dan Shute's out, and we might talk. Also," he added, "if yuh mention this to Dan, I'll call yuh a liar in the street or in the National. I'll make you use that gun."

"I won't talk," Barkow said. "Only I've been learnin' a few things. When we get answers to some of the messages yuh sent, and some I sent, we should know more. Borger wouldn't let Caradec off that ship willin'ly after he knew Rodney. I think he deserted. I think we can get something on him for mutiny, and that means hangin'."

"Mebbe yuh can," Gomer agreed. "You show me yuh're holdin' good cards, and I'll back yuh to the limit."

Bruce Barkow walked out on the street. Gomer, at least, he understood. He knew the man had no use for him, but if he could show evidence that he was to win, then Gomer would be a powerful ally. Judge Gargan would go as Gomer went, and would always adopt the less violent means. The cards were on the table now. Dan Shute was running things. What he could do, Barkow was not sure. He realized suddenly, with no little trepidation, that after all his association with Shute he knew little of what went on behind the hard brutality of the rancher's face. Yet he was not a man to lag or linger. What he did would be sudden, brutal, and thorough, but it would make a perfect shield under which he, Barkow, could operate and carry to fulfillment his own plans.

Dan Shute's abrupt statement of his purpose in regard to Ann Rodney had jolted Barkow. Somehow, he had taken Ann for granted. He had always planned a marriage. That he wanted her land was true. Perhaps better than Shute he knew what oil might mean in the future, and Barkow was a far-sighted man. But Ann Rodney was lovely and interesting. She would be a good wife for him. There was one way he could defeat Dan Shute on that score. To marry Ann at once.

True, it might precipitate a killing, but already Bruce Barkow was getting ideas on that score. He was suddenly less disturbed about Rafe Caradec than Dan Shute. The rancher loomed large and formidable in his mind. He knew the brutality of the man, had seen him kill, and knew with what coldness he regarded people or animals. Bruce Barkow made up his mind. Come what may, he was going to marry Ann Rodney.

He could, he realized, marry her and get her clear away from here. His mind leaped ahead. Flight to the northwest to the gold camps would be foolhardy. To the Utah country would be as bad. In either case, Shute might and probably would overtake him. There remained another way out, and one that Shute probably would never suspect—he could strike for Fort Phil Kearney not far distant, and then, with or without a scouting party for escort, could head across country and reach the Yellowstone. Or he might even try the nearer Powder River. A steamer had ascended the Yellowstone earlier that year, and there was every chance that another would come. If not, with a canoe or barge they could head downstream until they encountered such a boat, and buy passage to St. Louis.

Ann and full title to her land would be in his hands then, and he could negotiate a sale or the leasing of the land from a safe distance. The more he thought of this, the more he was positive it remained the only solution for him.

Let Gomer think what he would. Let Dan Shute believe him content with a minor role. He would go ahead with his plans, then strike suddenly and swiftly and be well on his way before Shute realized what had happened. Once he made the fort, he would be in the clear. Knowing the officers as well as

230

he did, he was sure he could get an escort to the river. He had never seen the Yellowstone, nor did he know much about either that river or Powder River. But they had been used by many men as a high road to the West, and he could use a river as an escape to the East.

Carefully he considered the plan. There were preparations to be made. Every angle must be considered. At his ranch were horses enough. He would borrow Baker's buckboard to take Ann for a ride, then at his ranch they would mount and be off. With luck they would be well on their way before anyone so much as guessed what had happened.

Stopping by the store, he bought ammunition from Baker. He glanced up to find the storekeeper's eyes studying him, and he didn't like the expression.

"Is Ann in?" he asked.

Baker nodded, and jerked a thumb toward the curtain. Turning, Barkow walked behind the curtain and looked at Ann, who arose as he entered. Quickly he sensed a coolness that had not been there before. This was no time to talk of marriage. First things first.

He shrugged shamefacedly. "I suppose yuh're thinkin' pretty bad of me," he suggested ruefully. "I know now I shouldn't have listened to Dan Shute or to Gomer. Pod swore he had a case, and Shute claims Caradec is a crook and a rustler. If I had realized, I wouldn't have had any hand in it."

"It was pretty bad," Ann agreed as she sat down and began knitting. "What will happen now?"

"I don't know," he admitted, "but I wish I could spare you all this. Before it's over I'm afraid there'll be more killin's and trouble. Dan Shute is plenty roused up. He'll kill Caradec."

She looked at him. "You think that will be easy?"

Surprised, he nodded. "Yes. Dan's a dangerous man, and a cruel and brutal one. He's fast with a gun, too."

231

Louis L'Amour

"I thought you were a friend to Dan Shute?" she asked, looking at him hard. "What's changed you, Bruce?"

He shrugged. "Oh, little things. He showed himself up today. He's brutal, unfeelin'. He'll stop at nothin' to gain his ends."

"I think he will," Ann said composedly. "I think he'll stop at Rafe Caradec."

Barkow stared at her. "He seems to have impressed yuh. What makes yuh think that?"

"I never really saw him until today, Bruce," she admitted. "Whatever his motives, he is shrewd and capable. I think he is a much more dangerous man than Dan Shute. There's something behind him, too. He has background. I could see it in his manner more than his words. I wish I knew more about him."

Nettled at her defense of the man, and her apparent respect for him, Bruce shrugged his shoulders. "Don't forget, he probably killed your father."

She looked up. "Did he, Bruce?"

Her question struck fear into him. Veiling his eyes, he shrugged again. "Yuh never know. I'm worried about you, Ann. This country's going to be flamin' within a few days or weeks. If it ain't the fight here, it'll be the Indians. I wish I could get yuh out of it."

"But this is my home," Ann protested. "It is all I have."

"Not quite all." Her eyes fell before his gaze. "Ann, how would yuh like to go to Saint Louis?"

She looked up, startled. "To Saint Louis? But how...?"

"Not so loud." He glanced apprehensively at the door. There was no telling who might be listening. "I don't want anybody to know about it unless yuh decide, and nobody to know till after we're gone. But Ann, we *could* go. I've always wanted to marry yuh, and there's no time better than now."

232

She got up and walked to the window. St. Louis. It was another world. She hadn't seen a city in six years, and, after all, they had been engaged for several months now. "How would we get there?" she asked, turning to face him.

"That's a secret." He laughed. "Don't tell anybody about it, but I've got a wonderful trip planned for yuh. I always wanted to do things for yuh, Ann. We could go away and be married within a few hours."

"Where?"

"By the chaplain, at the fort. One of the officers would stand up with me, and there are a couple of officers' wives there, too."

"I don't know, Bruce," she said hesitantly. "I'll have to think about it."

He smiled and kissed her lightly. "Then think fast, honey. I want to get yuh away from all this trouble, and quick."

When he got outside in the street, he paused, smiling with satisfaction. *I'll show that Dan Shute a thing or two,* he told himself grimly. *I'll leave him standin' here flat-footed, holdin' the bag. I'll have the girl and the ranch, and won't be within miles of this place.* Abruptly he turned toward the cabin where he lived.

Dan Shute stood on the boardwalk, staring into the dust, big hands on his hips above the heavy guns, his gray hat pulled low, a stubble of corn-white beard along his hard jaws. *I think,* he said to himself, looking up, *that I'll kill Bruce Barkow. And I'm goin' to like the doin' of it.*

XIII

Gene Baker was sweeping his store and the stoop in front of it when he saw a tight little cavalcade of horsemen trot around the corner into the street. It was the morning after the fiasco

233

of the trial, and he had been worried and irritated while wondering what the reaction would be from Barkow and Shute. Then word had come to him of the break between the two at Gomer's office.

Dan Shute, riding a powerful gray, was in the van of the bunch of horsemen. He rode up to the stoop of Baker's store, and reined in. Behind him were Red and Tom Blazer, Joe Gorman, Fritz Handl, Fats McCabe, and others of the hard bunch that trailed with Shute.

"Gene," Shute said abruptly, resting his big hands on the pommel of the saddle, "don't sell any more supplies to Caradec or any of his crowd." He added harshly: "I'm not askin' yuh. I'm tellin' yuh. And if yuh do, I'll put you out of business and run you out of the country. You know I don't make threats. The chances are Caradec won't be alive by daybreak, anyway, but, just in case, yuh've been told."

Without giving Baker a chance to reply, Dan Shute touched spurs to his horse and led off down the south trail toward the Crazy Man. The door slammed behind Baker.

"Where are they going?" Ann wanted to know, her eyes wide. "What are they going to do?"

Gene stared after them bleakly. This was the end of something.

"They are goin' after Caradec and his crowd, Ann."

"What will they do to him?" Something inside her went sick and frightened. She had always been afraid of Dan Shute. The way he looked at her made her shrink. He was the only human being of whom she had ever been afraid. He seemed without feeling, without decency, without regard for anything but his own immediate desires.

"Kill him," Baker said. "They'll kill him. Shute's a hard man, and with him that's a mighty wicked lot of men."

"But can't someone warn him?" Ann protested.

The Trail to Crazy Man

Baker glanced at her. "So far as we know, that Caradec is a crook, and mebbe a killer, Ann. You ain't gettin' soft on him, are yuh?"

"No!" she exclaimed, startled. "Of course not! What an idea! Why, I've scarcely talked to him."

Yet there was a heavy, sinking feeling in her heart as she watched the riders disappear in the dust along the southward trail. If there were only something she could do! If she could warn them!

Suddenly she remembered the bay horse her father had given her. Because of the Indians, she had not been riding in a long time, but if she took the mountain trail....Hurrying through the door, she swiftly saddled the bay. There was no thought in her mind. She was acting strictly on impulse, prompted by some memory of the way the hair swept back from Rafe's brow, and the look in his eyes when he met her gaze. She told herself she wanted to see no man killed, that Bo Marsh and Johnny Gill were her friends. Yet even in her heart she knew the excuse would not do. She was thinking of Rafe, and only of Rafe.

The bay was in fine shape and impatient after his long restraint in the corral. He started for the trail, eagerly, and his ears pricked up at every sound. The leaves had turned to red and gold now, and in the air there was a hint of frost. Winter was coming. Soon the country would be blanketed, inches deep, under a thick covering of snow.

Hastily Ann's mind leaped ahead. The prairie trail, which the Shute riders had taken, swept wide into the valley, then crossed the Crazy Man, and turned to follow the stream up the cañon. By cutting across over the mountain trail, there was every chance she could beat them to the ranch. In any case, her lead would be slight due to the start the bunch had had.

Louis L'Amour

The trail crossed the mountainside through a long grove of quaking aspens, their leaves shimmering in the cool wind, dark green above, a gray below. Now with oncoming autumn, most of the leaves had turned to bright yellow intermixed with crimson, and here and there among the forest of mounting color were the darker arrowheads of spruce and lodgepole pine.

Once, coming out in a small clearing, she got a view of the valley below. She had gained a little, but only a little. Frightened, she touched spurs to the bay, and the little horse leaped ahead and swept down through the woods at a rapid gallop. Ahead, there was a ledge. It was a good six miles off yet, but from there she would be able to see the cañon of the Crazy Man and the upper cañon. A rider had told her that Caradec had been putting up hay in the wind-sheltered upper cañon and was obviously planning on feeding his stock there near the warm spring.

She recalled it because she remembered it was something her father had spoken of doing. There was room in the upper valley for many cattle, and, if there was hay enough for them, the warm water would be a help, and with only that little help the cattle should survive even the coldest weather.

Fording the stream where Caradec had encountered the young squaw, she rode higher on the mountain, angling across the slope under a magnificent stand of lodgepole pine. It was a splendid avenue of trees, all seemingly of the same size and shape as though cast from a mold. Once she glimpsed a deer, and another time in the distance in a small, branching valley she saw a small bunch of elk. This was her country. No wonder her father had loved it, wanted it, worked to get and to keep it.

Had her father paid the mortgage? Wouldn't Bruce have told her if he had? She could not believe Bruce dishonest or

236

deceitful, and certainly he had made no effort to foreclose, but had been most patient and thoughtful with her. What would he think of this ride? To warn a man he regarded as an enemy. But she could never forgive herself if Rafe Caradec were killed, and she had made no effort to avert it.

Too often she had listened to her father discourse on the necessity for peace and consideration of the problems of others. She believed in that policy whole-heartedly, and the fact that occasionally violence was necessary did not alter her convictions one whit. No system of philosophy or ethics, no growth of government, no improvement in living came without trial and struggle. Struggle, she had often heard her father say, quoting Hegel, was the law of growth.

Without giving too much thought to it, she understood that such men as Rafe Caradec, Tex Brisco, and others of their ilk were needed. For all their violence, their occasional heedlessness and the desire to go their own way, they were men building a new world in a rough and violent land where everything tended to extremes. Mountains were high, the prairies wide, the streams roaring, the buffalo by the thousand and tens of thousands. It was a land where nothing was small, nothing was simple. Everything, the lives of men and the stories they told, ran to extremes.

The bay pony trotted down the trail, then around a stand of lodgepole. Ann brought him up sharply on the lip of the ledge that had been her first goal. Below her, a vast and magnificent panorama, lay the ranch her father had pioneered. The silver curve of the Crazy Man lay below and east of her, and opposite the ledge was the mighty wall of the cañon. From below, a faint thread of smoke among the trees marked the cabin.

Turning her head, she looked west and south into the upper cañon. Far away, she seemed to see a horseman

237

moving, and the black dot of a herd. Turning the bay, she started west, riding fast. If they were working the upper cañon, she still had a chance.

An hour later, the little bay showing signs of his rough traveling, she came down to the floor of the cañon. Not far away, she could see Rafe Caradec, moving a bunch of cattle into the trees.

He looked around at her approach, and the black, flat-crowned hat came off his head. His dark, wavy hair was plastered to his brow with sweat, and his eyes were gray and curious.

"Good mornin'!" he said. "This is a surprise!"

"Please!" she burst out. "This isn't a social call! Dan Shute's riding this way with twenty men or more. He's going to wipe you out!"

"You shore?" She could see the quick wonder in his eyes at her warning, then he wheeled his horse and yelled: "Johnny! Johnny Gill! Come a-runnin'!"

Jerking his rifle from his boot, he looked at her again. He put his hand over hers suddenly, and she started at his touch. "Thanks, Ann," he said simply. "You're regular."

Then he was gone, and Johnny Gill was streaking after him. As Gill swept by, he lifted a hand and waved.

There they went, and below were twenty men, all armed. Would they come through alive? She turned the bay and, letting the pony take his own time, started him back over the mountain trail.

Rafe Caradec gave no thought to Ann's reason for warning him. There was no time for that. Tex Brisco and Bo Marsh were at the cabin. They were probably working outside, and their rifles would probably be in the cabin and beyond them. If they were cut off from their guns, the Shute riders would mow them down and kill them one by one at long range with rifle fire.

238

The Trail to Crazy Man

Rafe heard Gill coming up, and slacked off a little to let the little cowhand draw alongside.

"Shute!" he said. "And about twenty men. I guess this is the pay-ofif!"

"Yeah!" Gill yelled.

Rifle fire came to them suddenly. A burst of shots, then a shot that might have been from a pistol. Yet that was sheer guesswork, Rafe knew, for distinguishing the two was not easy and especially at this distance.

Their horses rounded the entrance and raced down the main cañon toward the cabin on the Crazy Man, running neck and neck. A column of smoke greeted them, and they could see riders circling and firing.

"The trees on the slope!" Rafe yelled, and raced for them.

He reached the trees with the black at a dead run and hit the ground before the animal had ceased to move. He raced to the rocks at the edge of the trees. His rifle lifted, settled, his breath steadied. Then the rifle spoke.

A man shouted and waved an arm, and at the same moment Gill fired. A horse went down. Two men, or possibly three, lay sprawled in the clearing before the cabin. Were Tex and Bo already down? Rafe steadied himself and squeezed off another shot. A saddle emptied. He saw the fallen man lunge to his feet, then spill over on his face. Coolly then, and taking their time, he and Gill began to fire. Another man went down, and rifles began to smoke in their direction. A bullet clipped the leaves overhead, but too high.

Rafe knocked the hat from a man's head and, as the fellow sprinted for shelter, dropped him. Suddenly the attack broke, and he saw the horses sweeping away from them in a ragged line. Mounting, Rafe and Gill rode cautiously toward the cabin.

There was no cabin. There was only a roaring inferno of

239

flames. There were five sprawled bodies now, and Rafe ran toward them. A Shute rider—another. Then he saw Bo. The boy was lying on his face with dark, spreading stain on the back of his shirt. There was no sign of Tex.

Rafe dropped to his knees and put a hand over the young cowhand's heart. It was still beating! Gently, with Johnny lending a hand, he turned the boy over. Then, working with the crude but efficient skill picked up in war and struggle in a half dozen countries, he examined the wounds.

"Four times," he said grimly. He felt something mount and swell within him, a tide of fierce, uncontrollable anger. Around one bullet hole in the stomach the cloth of the cowhand's shirt was still smoldering!

"I seen that!" It was Tex Brisco, his face haggard and smoke-grimed. "I saw it! I know who done it! He walked up where the kid was laying, stuck a gun against his stomach, and shot! He didn't want the kid to go quick. He wanted him to die slow and hard!"

"Who done it?" Gill demanded fiercely. "I'll git him now! Rightnow!"

Brisco's eyes were red and inflamed. "Nobody gets him but me. This kid was your pard, but I *seen* it!" He turned abruptly on Rafe. "Boss, let me go to town. I want to kill a man!"

"It won't do, Tex," Caradec said quietly. "I know how you feel, but the town will be full of 'em. They'll be celebratin'. They burned our cabin, ran off some cattle, and they got Bo. It wouldn't do."

"Yeah." Tex spat. "I know. But they won't be expectin' any trouble now. We've been together a long time, boss, and if yuh don't let me go, I'll quit."

Rafe looked up from the wounded man. "All right, Tex. I told you I know how you feel. But if somethin' should happen ...who did it?"

240

The Trail to Crazy Man

"Tom Blazer. That big redhead. He always hated the kid. The kid was shot down and left lay. I was out back in the woods, lookin' for a pole to cut. They rode up so fast the kid never had a chance. He was hit twice before he knew what was goin' on. Then, again, when he started toward the house. After the house was afire, Tom Blazer walked up, and the kid was conscious. Tom said somethin' to Bo, shoved the gun against him, and pulled the trigger." He stared miserably at Bo. "I was out of pistol range. Took me a few minutes to get closer, then I got me two men before you rode up."

Wheeling, he headed toward the corral.

Rafe had stopped the flow of blood, and Johnny had returned with a blanket from a line back of the house.

"Reckon we better get him over in the trees, boss," Gill said.

Easing the cowboy to the blanket with care, Rafe and Johnny carried Bo into the shade in a quiet place under the pines. Caradec glanced up as they put him down. Tex Brisco was riding out of the cañon. Johnny Gill watched him go.

"Boss," Gill said, "I wanted like blazes to go, but I ain't the man Brisco is. Rightly I'm a quiet man, but that Texan is a wolf on the prowl. I'm some glad I'm not Tom Blazer right now." He looked down at Bo Marsh. The young cowhand's face was flushed, his breathing hoarse. "Will he live, Rafe?" Johnny asked softly.

Caradec shrugged. "I don't know," he said hoarsely. "He needs better care than I can give him." He studied the situation thoughtfully. "Johnny," he said, "you stay with him. Better take time to build a lean-to for cover in case of rain or snow. Get some fuel, too."

"What about you?" Johnny asked. "Where you goin'?"

"To the fort. There's an Army doctor there, and I'll go get him."

241

"Reckon he'll come this far?" Johnny asked doubtingly.

"He'll come."

Rafe Caradec mounted the black and rode slowly away into the dusk. It was a long ride to the fort, and, even if he got the doctor, it might be too late. That was the chance he would have to take. There was small danger of an attack now. Yet it was not really a return of Dan Shute's riders that disturbed him, but a subtle coolness in the air, a chill that was of more than autumn. Winters in this country could be bitterly cold, and all the signs gave evidence this one would be the worst in years, and they were without a cabin. He rode on toward the fort, with a thought that Tex Brisco now must be nearing town.

XIV

It was growing late, and Painted Rock was swathed in velvety darkness when Tex Brisco walked his horse to the edge of town. He stopped across the bend of the stream from town and planned to leave his horse among the trees there. He would have a better chance of escape from across the stream than from the street, and by leaving town on foot he could create some doubt as to his whereabouts. He was under no misapprehension as to the problem he faced. Painted Rock would be filled to overflowing with Shute and Barkow riders, many of whom knew him by sight. Yet, although he could envision their certainty of victory, their numbers, and was well aware of the reckless task he had chosen, he knew they would not be expecting him, or any riders from Crazy Man.

He tied his horse loosely to a bush among the trees, and crossed the stream on a log. Once across, he thought of his spurs. Kneeling down, he unfastened them from his boots and hung them over a root near the end of the log. He wanted no jingling spurs to give his presence away at an inopportune moment.

Carefully avoiding any dwellings with lights, he made his way through the scattered houses to the back of the row of buildings across the street. He was wearing the gun he usually wore, and for luck he had taken another from his saddlebags and thrust it in to his waistband.

Tex Brisco was a man of the frontier. From riding the range in South and West Texas, he had drifted north with trail herds. He had seen some of the days around the beginning of Dodge and Ellsworth, and some hard fighting down in the Nations, and with rustlers along the Mexican border. He was an honest man, a sincere man. He had a quality to be found in many men of his kind and period—a quality of deep-seated loyalty that was his outstanding trait. Hard and reckless in demeanor, he rode with dash and acted with a flair. He had at times been called a hardcase. Yet no man lived long in a dangerous country, if he were reckless. There was a place always for courage, but intelligent courage, not the heedlessness of a harebrained youngster. Tex Brisco was twenty-five years old, but he had been doing a man's work since he was eleven. He had walked with men, ridden with men, fought with men as one of them. He had asked no favors and had been granted none. Now, at twenty-five, he was a seasoned veteran. He was a man who knew the plains and the mountains, knew cattle, horses, and guns. He possessed a fierce loyalty to his outfit and to his friends.

Shanghaied, he had quickly seen that the sea was not his element. He had concealed his resentment and gone to work, realizing that safety lay along that route. He had known his time would come. It had come when Rafe Caradec came aboard, and all his need for friendship, for loyalty, and for a cause had been tied to the big, soft-spoken stranger.

Now Painted Rock was vibrant with danger. The men who did not hate him in Painted Rock were men who would not speak for him, or act for him. It was like Tex Brisco that he did not think in terms of help. He had his job, he knew his problem, and he knew he was the man to do it.

The National Saloon was booming with sound. The tinny jangle of an out-of-tune piano mingled with hoarse laughter, shouts, and the rattle of glasses. The hitching rail was lined with horses.

Tex walked between the buildings to the edge of the dark and empty street. Then he walked up to the horses and, speaking softly, made his way along the hitching rail, turning every slipknot into a hard knot.

The Emporium was dark, except for a light in Baker's living quarters where he sat with his wife and Ann Rodney. The stage station was lit by a feeble glow of a light over a desk as a station agent worked late over his books.

It was a moonless night, and the stars were bright. Tex lit a cigarette, loosened his guns in his holsters, and studied the situation. The National was full. To step into that saloon was suicide, and Tex had no such idea in mind. It was early, and he would have to wait. Yet might it be the best way, if he stepped in? There would be a moment of confusion. In that instant he could act.

Working his way back to a window, he studied the interior. It took him several minutes to locate Tom Blazer. The big man was standing by the bar with Fats McCabe. Slipping to the other end of the window, Tex could see that no one was between them and the rear door. He stepped back into the darkest shadows and, leaning against the building, finished his cigarette. When it was down to a stub, he threw it on the ground and carefully rubbed it out with the toe of his boot.

Then he pulled his hat low, and walked around to the rear of the saloon.

There was some scrap lumber there, and he skirted the rough pile, avoiding some bottles. It was cool out here, and he rubbed his fingers a little, working his hands to keep the circulation going. Then he stepped up to the door and turned the knob. It opened under his hand, and, if it made a sound, it went unheard. Stepping inside, he closed the door after him, pleased that it opened outward.

In the hurly-burly of the interior one more cowhand went unseen. Nobody even glanced his way. He sidled up to the bar, then reached over under Tom Blazer's nose, drew the whisky bottle toward him, and poured a drink into a glass just rinsed by the bartender.

Tom Blazer scarcely glanced at the bottle, for other bottles were being passed back and forth. Fats McCabe stood beside Tom and, without noticing Tex, went on talking.

"That blasted Marsh!" Tom said thickly. "I got him! I been wantin' him a long time! Yuh should have seen the look in his eyes when I shoved that pistol against him and pulled the trigger!"

Tex's lips tightened, and he poured his glass full once more. He left it sitting on the bar in front of him. His eyes swept the room. Bruce Barkow was here, and Pod Gomer. Tex moved over a little closer to McCabe.

"That'll finish 'em off," McCabe was saying. "When Shute took over, I knew they wouldn't last long. If they get out of the country, they'll be lucky. They've no supplies now, and it will be snowin' within a few days. The winter will get 'em, if we don't, or the Injuns."

Tex Brisco smiled grimly. *Not before I get you!* he thought. *That comes first.*

The piano was banging away with "Oh, Susanna!" and a

245

bunch of cowhands were trying to sing it. Joe Benson leaned on his bar talking to Pod Gomer. Barkow sat at a table in the corner, staring morosely into a glass. Joe Gorman and Fritz Handl were watching a poker game.

Tex glanced again at the back door. No one stood between the door and himself. Well, why wait?

Just then Tom Blazer reached for the bottle in front of Tex, and Tex pulled it away from his hand. Tom stared. "Hey, what yuh tryin' to do?" he demanded belligerently.

"I've come for yuh, Blazer," Tex said. "I've come to kill a skunk that shoots a helpless man when he's on his back. How are yuh against standin' men, Blazer?"

"Huh?" Tom Blazer said stupidly. Then he realized what had been said, and he thrust his big face forward for a closer look. The gray eyes he saw were icy, the lantern-jawed Texan's face was chill as death, and Tom Blazer jerked back. Slowly, his face white, Fats McCabe drew aside.

To neither man came the realization that Tex Brisco was alone. All they felt was the shock of his sudden appearance, here, among them. Brisco turned, stepping one pace away from the bar. "Well, Tom," he said quietly, his voice just loud enough to carry over the sound of the music, "I've come for yuh."

Riveted to the spot, Tom Blazer felt an instant of panic. Brisco's presence here had the air of magic, and Tom was half frightened by the sheer unexpectedness of it. Sounds in the saloon seemed to die out, although they still went full blast, and Tom stared across that short space like a man in a trance, trapped and faced with a fight to the death. There would be no escaping this issue, he knew. He might win, and he might lose, but it was here, now, and he had to face it. He realized suddenly that it was a chance he had no desire to make. Wouldn't anyone notice? Why didn't Fats say something?

246

The Trail to Crazy Man

Tex Brisco stood there, staring at him.

"Yuh've had yore chance," Tex said gently. "Now I'm goin' to kill yuh!"

The shock of the word *kill* snapped Tom Blazer out of it. He dropped into a half crouch, and his lips curled in a snarl of mingled rage and fear. His clawed hand swept back for his gun.

In the throbbing and rattle of the room the guns boomed like a crash of thunder. Heads whirled, and liquor-befuddled brains tried to focus eyes. All they saw was Tom Blazer, sagging back against the bar, his shirt darkening with blood, and the strained, foolish expression on his face like that of a man who had been shocked beyond reason.

Facing the room was a lean, broad-shouldered man with two guns, and, as they looked, he swung a gun at Fats McCabe. Instinctively, at the *boom* of guns, McCabe's brain had reacted, but a shade slow. His hand started for his gun. It was an involuntary movement that, had he had but a moment's thought, would never have been made. He had no intention of drawing. All he wanted was out, but the movement of his hand was enough. It was too much.

Tex Brisco's gun *boomed* again, and Fats toppled over on his face. Then Tex opened up, and three shots, blasting into the brightly lit room, brought it to complete darkness. Brisco faded into that darkness, swung the door open, and vanished as a shot clipped the air over his head.

He ran hard for fifty feet, then ducked into the shadow of a barn, threw himself over a low corral fence, and ran across the corral in a low crouch. Shouts and orders, then the *crash* of glass, came from the saloon.

The door burst open again, and he could have got another man, but only by betraying his position. He crawled through the fence and, keeping close to a dark house, ran swiftly to its far corner. He paused there, breathing heavily. So far, so good.

From here on he would be in comparative light, but the distance was enough now. He ran on swiftly for the river. Behind him he heard curses and yells as men found their knotted bridle reins. At the end of the log, Tex retrieved his spurs. Then, gasping for breath from his hard run, he ran across the log and started for his horse. He saw it suddenly, and then he saw something else.

XV

In the dim light, Tex recognized Joe Gorman by his hat. Joe wore his hat brim rolled to a point in front.

"Hi, Texas!" Gorman said. Tex could see the gun in his hand, waist high and leveled on him.

"Hi, Joe. Looks like yuh smelled somethin'."

"Yeah"—Joe nodded—"I did at that. Happened to see somebody ride up here in the dark, and got curious. When yuh headed for the saloon, I got around yuh and went in. Then I saw yuh come in the back door. I slipped out just before the shootin' started, so's I could beat yuh back here in case yuh got away."

"Too bad yuh missed the fun," Brisco said quietly.

Behind Tex the pursuit seemed to have gained no direction as yet. His mind was on a hair trigger, watching for a break. Which of his guns was still loaded? He had forgotten whether he put the loaded gun in the holster or in his belt.

"Who'd yuh get?" asked Gorman.

"Tom Blazer. Fats McCabe, too."

"I figgered Tom. I told him he shouldn't have shot the kid. That was a low-down trick. But why shoot Fats?"

"He acted like he was reachin' for a gun."

"Huh. Don't take a lot to get a man killed, does it?"

Brisco could see in the dark enough to realize that Gorman was smiling a little.

"How do yuh want it, Tex? Should I let yuh have it now, or save yuh for Shute? He's a bad man, Tex."

"I think yuh'd better slip yore gun in yore holster and go back home, Joe," Tex said. "Yuh're the most decent one of a bad lot."

"Mebbe I want the money I'd get for you, Tex. I can use some."

"Think yuh'd live to collect?"

"Yuh mean Caradec? He's through, Brisco. Through. We got Bo. Now we got you. That leaves only Caradec and Johnny Gill. They won't be so tough."

"Yuh're wrong, Joe," Tex said quietly. "Rafe could take the lot of yuh, and he will. But you bought into my game yoreself. I wouldn't ask for help, Joe. I'd kill yuh myself."

"You?" Gorman chuckled with real humor. "And me with the drop on yuh? Not a chance! Why, Tex, *one* of these slugs would get yuh, and, if I have to start blastin', I'm goin' to empty the gun before I quit."

"Uhn-huh," Tex agreed, "yuh mean, get me before I could shoot?" He repeated: "Not a chance."

The sounds of pursuit were coming now. The men had a light and had found his tracks.

"Toward the river, I'll be a 'coon!" a voice yelled. "Let's go!"

Here it was! Joe Gorman started to yell, then saw the black figure ahead of him move, and his gun blazed. Tex felt the shocking jolt of a slug, and his knees buckled, but his gun was out, and he triggered two shots, fast. Joe started to fall, and he fired again, but the hammer fell on an empty chamber.

249

Tex jerked the slipknot in his reins loose and dragged himself into the saddle. He was bleeding badly. His mind felt hazy, but he saw Joe Gorman move on the ground, and heard him say: "Yuh did it, damn yuh! Yuh did it!"

"So long, Joe," Tex whispered hoarsely.

He walked the horse for twenty feet, then started moving faster. His brain was singing with a strange noise, and his blood seemed to drum in his brain. He headed up the tree-covered slope, and the numbness crawled up his legs. He fought like a cornered wolf against the darkness that crept over him. *I can't die...I can't!* he kept saying in his brain. *Rafe'll need help! I can't!*

Fighting the blackness and numbness, he tied the bridle reins to the saddle horn, and thrust both feet clear through the stirrups. Sagging in the saddle, he got his handkerchief out and fumbled a knot, tying his wrists to the saddle horn.

The light glowed and died, and the horse walked on, weaving in the awful darkness, weaving through a world of agony and the soft, clutching hands that seemed to be pulling Tex down, pulling him down. The darkness closed in around him, but under him he seemed still to feel the slow plodding of the horse....

Roughly, the distance to the fort was seventy miles, a shade less, perhaps. Rafe Caradec rode steadily into the increasing cold of the wind. There was no mistaking the seriousness of Bo's condition. The young cowhand was badly shot up, weak from loss of blood, and despite the amazing vitality of frontier men, his chance was slight unless his wounds had proper care.

Bowing his head to the wind, Rafe headed the horse down a draw and its partial shelter. There was no use thinking of Tex. Whatever had happened in Painted Rock had happened now, or was happening. Brisco might be dead. He might be alive and safe, even now heading back to the Crazy Man, or he might be wounded and in need of help. Tex Brisco was an uncertainty, but Bo Marsh hung between life and death, hence there was no choice. The friendship and under-standing between the lean, hard-faced Texan and Rafe Caradec had grown aboard ship. Rafe was not one to take lightly the Texan's loyalty in joining him in his foray into Wy-oming. Now Brisco might be dead, killed in a fight he would never have known but for Rafe. Yet Tex would have had it no other way. His destinies were guided by his loyalties. Those loyalties were his life, his religion, his reason for living.

Yet despite his worries over Marsh and Brisco, Rafe found his thoughts returning again and again to Ann Rodney. Why had she ridden to warn them of the impending attack? Had it not been for that warning the riders would have wiped out Brisco at the same time they got Marsh, and would have fol-lowed it up to find Rafe and Johnny back in the cañon. It would have been, or could have been, a clean sweep.

Why had Ann warned them? Was it because of her dislike of violence and killing? Or was there some other, some deeper, feeling? Yet how could that be? What feeling could Ann have for any of them, believing as she seemed to believe that he was a thief, or worse? The fact remained that she had come, that she had warned them. Remembering her, he re-called the flash of her eyes, the proud lift of her chin, the way she walked. He stared grimly into the night and swore softly. Was he in love?

"Who knows?" he demanded viciously of the night. "And what good would it do if I was?"

He had never been to the fort, yet knew it lay between the forks of the Piney and its approximate location. His way led across the billowing hills and through a country marked by small streams lined with cottonwood, box elder, willow, chokeberry, and wild plum. That this was the Indian country, he knew. The unrest of the tribes was about to break into open warfare, and already there had been sporadic attacks on haying or wood-cutting parties, and constant attacks were being made on the Missouri steamboats far to the north.

Red Cloud, most influential chieftain among the Sioux, had tried to hold the tribes together and, despite the continued betrayal of treaties by the white man, had sought to abide by the code he had laid down for his people. With Man-Afraid-Of-His-Horse, the Oglala chief, Red Cloud was the strongest of all the Sioux leaders, or had been. With Custer's march into the Black Hills and the increasing travel over the Laramie and Bozeman Trails, the Sioux were growing restless. The Sioux medicine man, Sitting Bull, was indulging in war talk, and he was aided and abetted by two powerful warriors—Crazy Horse and Gall. No one in the West but understood that an outbreak of serious nature was overdue.

Rafe Caradec was aware of all this. He was aware, too, that it would not be an easy thing to prevail upon the doctor to leave the fort, or upon the commander to allow him to leave. In the face of impending trouble, his place was with the Army....

News of the battle on the Crazy Man, after Ann's warning, reached her that evening. The return of the triumphant Shute riders was enough to tell her what had happened. She heard them ride into the street, heard their yells and their shouts. She heard that Bo Marsh was definitely dead, even though some of the Shute riders were harsh in their criticism of Tom Blazer for that action.

While the Shute outfit had ridden away, following their attack, fearful of the effects of snapshooting from the timber, they were satisfied. Winter was coming on, and they had destroyed the cabin on the Crazy Man and killed Bo Marsh. Mistakenly they also believed they had killed Brisco and wounded at least one other man.

Sick at heart, Ann had walked back into her room and stood by the window. Suddenly she was overwhelmed by the desire to get away, to escape all this sickening violence, the guns, the killings, the problems of frontier life. Back East there were lovely homes along quiet streets, slow-running streams, men who walked quietly on Sunday mornings. There were parties, theaters, friends, homes.

Her long ride had tired her. The touch of Rafe Caradec's hand, the look in his eyes, had given her a lift. Something had sparked within her, and she felt herself drawn to him, yearning toward him with everything feminine that was in her. Riding away, she had heard the crash of guns, shouts, and yells. Had she been too late?

There had been no turning back. She had known there was nothing she could do. Her natural good sense had told her that she would only complicate matters if she tried to stay. Nor did she know now what she would have done if she had stayed. Where was her sympathy? With Shute's riders, or with this strange, tall young man who had come to claim half her ranch and tell fantastic stories of knowing her father aboard a ship? Every iota of intelligence she had told her the man was all wrong, that his story could not be true. Bruce Barkow's story of her father's death had been the true one. What reason for him to lie? Why would he want to claim her land when there was so much more to be had for the taking? Her father had told her, and Gene Baker agreed, that soon all this country would be open to settlement, and there would be towns and railroads here. Why choose one piece of land, a large section of it worthless, when the hills lay bare for the taking?

Standing by the window and looking out into the darkness, Ann knew suddenly she was sick of it all. She would get away, go back East. Bruce was right. It was time she left here, and, when he came again, she would tell him she was ready. He had been thoughtful and considerate. He had protected her, been attentive and affectionate. He was a man of intelligence. He was handsome. She could be proud of him.

She stifled her misgivings with a sudden resolution, and hurriedly began to pack.

XVI

Vaguely Ann had sensed Barkow's fear of something, but she believed it was fear of an attack by Indians. Word had come earlier that day that the Oglalas were gathering in the hills, and there was much war talk among them. That it could be Dan Shute whom Barkow feared Ann had no idea.

She had completed the packing of the few items she would need for the trip when she heard the sound of gunfire from the National. The shots brought her to her feet with a start, her face pale. Running into the living room, she found that Gene Baker had caught up his rifle. She ran to Mrs. Baker, and the two women stood together, listening.

Baker looked at them. "Can't be Indians," he said after a moment. "Mebbe some wild cowhand celebratin'."

They heard excited voices, yells. Baker went to the door, hesitated, then went out. He was gone several minutes before he returned. His face was grave.

"It was that Texas rider from the Crazy Man," he said. "He stepped into the back door of the National and shot it out with Tom Blazer and Fats McCabe. They're both dead."

"Was he alone?" Ann asked quickly.

Baker nodded, looking at her somberly. "They're huntin' him now. He won't get away, I'm afeerd."

"You're *afraid* he won't?"

"Yes, Ann," Baker said, "I am. That Blazer outfit's poison. All of the Shute bunch, far's that goes. Tom killed young Bo Marsh by stickin' a pistol against him whilst he was lyin' down."

The flat bark of a shot cut across the night air, and they went rigid. Two more shots rang out.

"Guess they got him," Baker said. "There's so many of them, I figgered they would."

Before the news reached them of what had actually happened, daylight had come. Ann Rodney was awake after an almost sleepless night. Tex Brisco, she heard, had killed Joe Gorman when Gorman had caught him at his horse. Tex had escaped, but from all the evidence he was badly wounded. They were trailing him by the blood from his wounds. Bo Marsh, now Brisco. Was Johnny Gill alive? Was Rafe? If Rafe were alive, then he must be alone, harried like a rabbit by hounds.

Restless, Ann paced the floor. Shute riders came and went in the store. They were buying supplies and going out in groups of four and five, scouring the hills for Brisco or any of the others of the Crazy Man crowd.

Bruce Barkow came shortly after breakfast. He walked into the store. He looked tired, worried.

"Ann," he said abruptly, "if we're goin', it'll have to be today. This country is goin' to the wolves. All they think about now is killin'. Let's get out."

She hesitated only an instant. Something inside her seemed lost and dead. "All right, Bruce. We've planned it for a long time. It might as well be now."

255

Louis L'Amour

There was no fire in her, no spark. Barkow scarcely heeded that. She would go, and, once away from here and married, he would have title to the land, and Dan Shute for all his talk and harsh ways would be helpless. "All right," he said. "We'll leave in an hour. Don't tell anybody. We'll take the buckboard like we were goin' for a drive, as we often do."

She was ready, so there was nothing to do after he had gone.

Baker seemed older, worried. Twice riders came in, and each time Ann heard that Tex Brisco was still at large. His horse had been trailed, seemingly wandering without guidance, to a place on a mountain creek. There the horse had walked into the water, and no trail had been found to show where he had left it. He was apparently headed for the high ridges, south by west, nor had anything been found of Marsh or Gill. Shute riders had returned to the Crazy Man, torn down the corral, and hunted through the woods, but no sign had been found beyond a crude lean-to where the wounded man had evidently been sheltered. Marsh, if dead, had been buried, and the grave concealed. Nothing had been found of any of them, although one horse had ridden off to the northeast, mostly east.

One horse had gone east! Ann Rodney's heart gave a queer leap. East would mean toward the fort! Perhaps....But she was being foolish. Why should it be Caradec rather than Gill, and why to the fort? She expressed the thought, and Baker looked at her.

"Likely enough one of 'em's gone there. If Marsh ain't dead, and the riders didn't find his body, chances are he's mighty bad off. The only doctor around is at the fort."

The door to the store opened, and Baker went in, leaving the living room. There was a brief altercation, then the curtain was pushed aside, and Ann looked up. A start of fear went through her.

The Trail to Crazy Man

Dan Shute was standing in the door. For a wonder, he was clean-shaven except for his mustache. He looked at her with his queer, gray-white eyes. "Don't you do nothin' foolish," he said, "like tryin' to leave here. I don't aim to let yuh."

Ann got up, amazed and angry. "You don't aim to let me?" she flared. "What business is it of yours?"

Shute stood there with his big hands on his hips, staring at her insolently. "Because I want to make it my business," he said. "I've told Barkow where he stands with you. If he don't like it, he can say so and die. I ain't particular. I just wanted yuh should know that from here on yuh're my woman."

"Listen here, Shute," Baker flared. "You can't talk to a decent woman that way!"

"Shut yore mouth," Shute said, staring at Baker. "I talk the way I please. I'm tellin' her. If she tries to get away from here, I'll take her out to the ranch now. If she waits…"—he looked her up and down coolly—"I may marry her. Don't know why I should." He added, glaring at Baker: "You butt into this and I'll smash yuh. She ain't no woman for a weak sister like Barkow. I guess she'll come to like me all right. Anyway, she'd better." He turned toward the door. "Don't get any ideas. I'm the law here, and the only law."

"I'll appeal to the Army," Baker declared.

"You do," Shute said, "and I'll kill yuh. Anyway, the Army's goin' to be some busy. A bunch of Sioux raided a stage station way south of here last night and killed three men, then ran off the stock. Two men were killed hayin' over on Otter last night. A bunch of soldiers hayin' not far from the Piney were fired on and one man wounded. The Army's too busy to bother with the likes of you. Besides," he added, grinning, "the commandin' officer said that in case of Injun trouble, I was to take command at Painted Rock and make all preparations for defense."

He turned and walked out of the room. They heard the front door slam, and Ann sat down suddenly.

Gene Baker walked to the desk and got out his gun. His face was stiff and old.

"No, not that," Ann said. "I'm leaving, Uncle Gene."

"Leaving How?" He turned on her, his eyes alert.

"With Bruce. He's asked me several times. I was going to tell you, but nobody else. I'm all packed."

"Barkow, eh?" Gene Baker stared at her. "Well, why not? He's half a gentleman, anyway. Shute is an animal and a brute."

The back door opened gently. Bruce Barkow stepped in.

"Was Dan here?"

Baker explained quickly. "Better forget that buckboard idea," he said, once Barkow had outlined the plan. "Take the hosses and go by the river trail. Leave at noon when everybody will be eatin'. Take the Bannock Trail, then swing north and east and cut around toward the fort. They'll think yuh're tryin' for the gold fields."

Barkow nodded. He looked stiff and pale, and he was wearing a gun. It was almost noon.

When the streets were empty, Bruce Barkow went out back to the barn and saddled the horses. There was no one in sight. The woods along the creek were only a hundred yards away.

Walking outside, the two got into their saddles and rode at a walk to the trees, the dust muffling the beat of horses' hoofs, then they took the Bannock Trail. Two miles out, Barkow rode into a stream, then led the way north.

Once away from the trail they rode swiftly, keeping the horses at a rapid trot. Barkow was silent, and his eyes kept straying to the back trail. Twice they saw Indian sign, but their escape had evidently been made successfully, for there was no immediate sound of pursuit.

Bruce Barkow kept moving, and, as he rode, his irritation, doubt, and fear began to grow more and more obvious. He rode like a man in the grip of deadly terror. Ann, watching him, wondered. Before, Shute had tolerated Barkow. Now a definite break had been made, and with each mile of their escape Barkow became more frightened. There was no way back now. He would be killed on sight, for Dan Shute was not a man to forgive or tolerate such a thing.

It was only on the girl's insistence that he stopped for a rest, and to give the horses a much needed blow. They took it, while Ann sat on the grass, and Bruce paced the ground, his eyes searching the trail over which they had come. When they were in the saddle again, he seemed to relax, to come to himself. Then he looked at her. "Yuh must think I'm a coward," he said, "but it's just that I'm afraid of what Shute would do if he got his hands on you, and I'm no gunfighter. He'd kill us both."

"I know." She nodded gravely.

This man who was to be her husband impressed her less at every moment. Somehow, his claim that he was thinking of her failed to ring with sincerity. Yet with all his faults, he was probably only a weak man, a man cut out for civilization, and not for the frontier. They rode on, and the miles piled up behind them....

Rafe Caradec awakened with a start to the sound of a bugle. It took him several seconds to realize that he was in bed at the fort. Then he remembered. The commanding officer had refused to allow the surgeon to leave before morning, and then only with an escort. With Lieutenant Bryson and eight men they would form a scouting patrol,

259

would circle around by Crazy Man, then cut back toward the fort.

The party at the fort was small, for the place had been abandoned several years before, and had been utilized only for a few weeks as a base for scouting parties when fear of an Indian outbreak began to grow. It was no longer an established post but merely a camp. Further to the south there was a post at Fort Fetterman, named for the leader of the troops trapped in the Fetterman Massacre. A wagon train had been attacked within a short distance of Fort Phil Kearney, and a group of seventy-nine soldiers and two civilians were to march out to relieve them under command of Major James Powell, a skilled Indian fighter. However, Brevet Lieutenant Colonel Fetterman had used his rank to take over command, and had ridden out. Holding the fighting ability of the Indians in contempt, Fetterman had pursued some of them beyond a ridge. Firing had been heard, and, when other troops were sent out from the fort, they had discovered Fetterman and his entire command wiped out, about halfway down the ridge. The wagon train they had gone to relieve had reached the fort later, unaware of the encounter on the ridge.

Getting into his clothes, Rafe hurried outside. The first person he met was Bryson.

"Good morning, Caradec!" Bryson said, grinning. "Bugle wake you up?"

Caradec nodded. "It isn't the first time."

"You've been in the service, then?" Bryson asked, glancing at him quickly.

"Yes." Rafe glanced around the stockade. "I was with Sully. In Mexico for a while, too, and Guatemala."

Bryson glanced at him. "Then you're *that* Caradec? Man, I've heard of you! Major Skehan will be pleased to know. He's an admirer of yours, sir." He nodded toward two weary, dust-covered horses. "You're not the only arrival from Painted Rock," Bryson said. "Those horses came in last night, almost daylight, in fact, with two riders. A chap named Barkow, and a girl. Pretty, too, the lucky dog."

Rafe turned on him, his eyes sharp. "A woman? A girl?"

Bryson looked surprised. "Why, yes! Her name's Rodney. She..."

"Where is she?" Rafe snapped. "Where is she now?"

Bryson smiled slightly. "Why, that's her over there! A friend of yours?"

But Rafe was gone.

Ann was standing in the door of one of the partly reconstructed buildings, and, when she saw him, her eyes widened.

"Rafe! You, here? Then you got away!"

"I came after a doctor for Marsh. He's in a bad way." He tossed the remark aside, studying her face. "Ann, what are you doing here with Barkow?"

His tone nettled her. "Why? How does it concern you?"

"Your father asked me to take care of you," he said, "and, if you married Bruce Barkow, I certainly wouldn't be doin' it."

"Oh?" Her voice was icy. "Still claiming you knew my father? Well, Mister Caradec, I think you'd be much better off to forget that story. I don't know where you got the idea, or how, or what made you believe you could get away with it, but it won't do. I've been engaged to Bruce for months. I intend to marry him now. There's a chaplain here. Then we'll go on to the river and down to Saint Louis. There's a steamer on the way up that we can meet."

"I won't let you do it, Ann," Rafe said harshly.

Her weariness, her irritation, and something else brought quick anger to her face and lips. "You won't let me? You have nothing to do with it! It simply isn't any of your business!

261

Louis L'Amour

Now, if you please, I'm waiting for Bruce. Will you go?"

"No," he said violently, "I won't. I'll say again what I said before. I knew your father. He gave me a deed givin' us the ranch. He asked me to care for you. He also gave me the receipt that Bruce Barkow gave him for the mortgage money. I wanted things to be different, Ann. I...."

"Caradec!" Bryson called. "We're ready!"

He glanced around. The small column awaited him, and his horse was ready. For an instant he glanced back at the girl. Her jaw was set, her eyes blazing. "Oh, what's the use?" he flared. "Marry who you blasted well please!"

Wheeling, he walked to his horse and swung into the saddle, riding away without a backward glance.

XVII

Lips parted to speak, Ann Rodney stared after the disappearing riders. Suddenly all her anger was gone. She found herself gazing at the closing gate of the stockade and fighting a mounting sense of panic. What had she done? Suppose what Rafe had said was the truth? What had he ever done to make her doubt him?

Confused, puzzled by her own feelings for this stranger of whom she knew so little, yet who stirred her so deeply, she was standing there, one hand partly upraised when she saw two men come around the corner of the building. Both wore the rough clothing of miners. They paused near her, one a stocky, thick-set man with a broad, hard jaw, the other a slender blond young man.

"Miss," the younger man said, "we just come in from the river. The major was tellin' us you were goin' back that way?" She nodded dumbly, then forced herself to speak. "Yes,

262

we are going to the river with some of the troops. Or that has been our plan."

"We come up the Powder from the Yellowstone, miss," the young man said, "and, if yuh could tell us where to find yore husband, we might sell him our boats."

She shook her head. "I'm not married yet. You will have to see my fiancé, Bruce Barkow. He's in the mess hall."

The fellow hesitated, turning his hat in his hand. "Miss, they said yuh was from Painted Rock. Ever hear tell of a man named Rafe Caradec over there?"

She stiffened. "Rafe Caradec?" She looked at him quickly. "You know him?"

He nodded, pleased by her sudden interest. "Yes, miss. We were shipmates of his. Me and my partner over there, Rock Mullaney. My name is Penn, miss…Roy Penn."

Suddenly her heart was pounding. She looked at him and bit her lip. Then she said carefully: "You were on a ship with him?"

"That's right."

Penn was puzzled, and he was growing wary. After all, there was the manner of their leaving. Of course, that was months ago, and they were far from the sea now, but that still hung over them.

"Was there . . . aboard that ship . . . a man named Rodney?"

Ann couldn't look at them now. She stared at the stockade, almost afraid to hear their reply. Vaguely she realized that Bruce Barkow was approaching.

"Rodney? Shorest thing yuh know! Charles Rodney. Nice feller, too. He died off the California coast after…." He hesitated. "Miss, you ain't no relation of his now?"

"I'm Charles Rodney's daughter."

"Oh?" Then Penn's eyes brightened. "Say, then you're the

263

girl Rafe came here to see! You know, Charlie's daughter!"

Bruce Barkow stopped dead still. His dark face was suddenly wary.

"What was that?" he said sharply. "What did yuh say?"

Penn stared at him. "No reason to get excited, mister. Yeah, we knew this young lady's father aboard ship. He was shanghaied out of San Francisco."

Bruce Barkow's face was cold. Here it was, at the last minute. He could see in Ann's face the growing realization of how he had lied, how he had betrayed her, and even—he could see that coming into her eyes, too—the idea that he had killed her father. Veins swelled in his forehead and throat. He glared at Penn, half crouching, like some cornered animal. "Yuh're a liar," he snarled.

"Don't call me that," Penn said fiercely. "I'm not wearing a gun, mister."

If Barkow heard the last words, they made no impression. His hand was already sweeping down. Penn stepped back, throwing his arms wide, and Bruce Barkow, his face livid with the fury of frustration, whipped up a gun and shot him twice through the body. Penn staggered back, uncomprehending, staring.

"No...gun!" he gasped. "I don't...gun."

He staggered into an Army wagon, reeled, and fell headlong.

Bruce Barkow stared at the fallen man, then his contorted face turned upward. On the verge of escape and success he had been trapped, and now he had become a killer. Wheeling, he sprang into saddle. The gate was open for a wood wagon, and he whipped the horse through it, shouting hoarsely.

Men had rushed from everywhere, and Rock Mullaney, staring in shocked surprise, could only fumble at his belt. He wore no gun, either. He looked up at Ann. "We carried rifles," he muttered. "We never figgered on no trouble!" Then he rubbed his face, sense returning to his eyes. "Miss, what did he shoot him for?"

She stared at him, humbled by the grief written on the man's hard, lonely face. "That man, Barkow, killed my father," she said.

"No, miss. If yuh're Charlie Rodney's daughter, Charlie died aboard ship with us."

She nodded. "I know, but Barkow was responsible. Oh, I've been a fool! An awful fool!"

An officer was kneeling over Penn's body. He got up, glanced at Mullaney, then at Ann. "This man is dead," he said.

Resolution came suddenly to Ann. "Major," she said, "I'm going to catch the patrol. Will you lend me a fresh horse? Ours will still be badly worn out after last night."

"It wouldn't be safe, Miss Rodney," he protested. "It wouldn't at all. There's Indians out there. How Caradec got through, or you and Barkow, is beyond me." He gestured to the body. "What you know about this?"

Briefly, concisely she explained, telling all. She made no attempt to spare herself or to leave anything out. She outlined the entire affair, taking only a few minutes.

"I see." He looked thoughtfully at the gate. "If I could give you an escort, I would, but…."

"If she knows the way," Mullaney said, "I'll go with her. We came down the river from Fort Benton, then up the Yellowstone and the Powder. We thought we would come and see how Rafe was getting along. If we'd knowed there was trouble, we'd have come before."

"It's as much as your life is worth, man," the major warned.

Mullaney shrugged. "Like as not, but my life has had

chances taken with it before. Besides,"—he ran his fingers over his bald head—"there's no scalp here to attract Indians."

Well-mounted, Ann and Mullaney rode swiftly. The patrol would be hurrying because of Bo Marsh's serious condition, but they should overtake them, and following was no immediate problem. Mullaney knew the West and had fought before in his life as a wandering jack-of-all-trades, and he was not upset by the chance they were taking. He glanced from time to time at Ann, then, rambling along, he began to give her an account of their life aboard ship, of the friendship that had grown between her father and Rafe Caradec, and all Rafe had done to spare the older man work and trouble. He told her how Rafe had treated Rodney's wounds when he had been beaten, how he had saved food for him, and how close the two had grown. Twice, noting her grief and shame, he ceased talking, but each time she insisted on his continuing.

"Caradec?" Mullaney said finally. "Well, I'd say he was one of the finest men I've known. A fighter, he is. The lad's a fighter from 'way back. Yuh should have seen the beatin' he gave that Borger! I got only a glimpse, but Penn told me about it. And if it hadn't been for Rafe, none us would have got away. He planned it, and he carried it out. He planned it before yore father's last trouble...the trouble that killed him ...but when he saw yore father would die, he carried on with it."

They rode on in silence. All the time, Ann knew now, she should have trusted her instincts. Always they had warned her about Bruce Barkow, always they had been sure of Rafe Caradec. As she had sat in the jury box and watched him talk, handling his case, it had been his sincerity that had impressed her, even more than his shrewd handling of questions. He

The Trail to Crazy Man

had killed men, yes. But what men! Bonaro and Trigger Boyne, both acknowledged and boastful killers of men themselves, men unfit to walk in the tracks of such as Rafe. She had to find him! She must!

The wind was chill, and she glanced at Mullaney. "It's cold!" she said. "It feels like snow!"

He nodded grimly. "It does that," he said. "Early for it, but it's happened before. If we get a norther now...." He shook his head.

They made camp while it was still light, and Mullaney built a fire of dry sticks that gave off almost no smoke. Water was heated, and they made coffee. While Ann was fixing the little food they had, he rubbed the horses down with handfuls of dry grass.

"Can yuh find yore way in the dark?" he asked her.

"Yes, I think so. It is fairly easy from here, for we have the mountains. That highest peak will serve as a landmark unless there are too many clouds."

"All right," he said, "we'll try to keep movin'."

She found herself liking the burly seaman and cowhand. He helped her smother the fire and wipe out traces of it.

"If we stick to the trail of the soldiers," he said, "it'll confuse the Injuns. They'll think we're with their party."

They started on. Ann led off, keeping the horses at a fast walk. Dusk came, and with it the wind grew stronger. After an hour of travel, Ann reined in.

Mullaney rode up beside her. "What's the matter?"

She indicated the tracks of a single horse crossing the route of the soldiers.

"Yuh think this is Barkow?" He nodded as an idea came. "It could be. The soldiers don't know what happened back there. He might ride with 'em for protection."

Another thought came to him. He looked at Ann keenly.

267

"Suppose he'd try to kill Caradec?"

Her heart jumped. "Oh, no!" She was saying no to the thought, not to the possibility. She knew it was a possibility. What did Bruce have to lose? He was already a fugitive, and another killing would make it no worse. And Rafe Caradec had been the cause of it all.

"He might," she agreed. "He might, at that...."

Miles to the west, Bruce Barkow, his rifle across his saddle, leaned into the wind. He had followed the soldiers for a way, and the idea of a snipe shot at Caradec stayed in his mind. He could do it, and they would think the Indians had done it. But there was a better way, a way to get at them all. If he could ride on ahead, reach Gill and Marsh before the patrol did, he might kill them, then get Caradec when he approached. If then he could get rid of Shute, Gomer would have to swing with him to save something from the mess. Maybe Dan Shute's idea was right, after all! Maybe killing was the solution.

Absorbed by the possibilities of the idea, Barkow turned off the route followed by the soldiers. There was a way that could make it safer, and somewhat faster. He headed for the old Bozeman Trail, now abandoned.

He gathered his coat around him to protect him from the increasing cold. His mind was fevered with worry, doubt of himself, and mingled with it was hatred of Caradec, Shute, Ann Rodney, and everyone and everything. He drove on into the night.

Twice, he stopped to rest. The second time he started on, it was turning gray with morning, and, as he swung into the saddle, a snowflake touched his cheek. He thought little of it. His horse was uneasy, though, and anxious for the trail. Snow was not a new thing, and Barkow scarcely noticed as the flakes began to come down thicker and faster.

Gill and the wounded man had disappeared, he knew. Shute's searchers had not found them near the house. Bruce Barkow had visited that house many times before the coming of Caradec, and he knew the surrounding hills well. About a half mile back from the house, sheltered by a thick growth of lodgepole pine, was a deep cave among some rocks. If Johnny Gill had found that cave, he might have moved Marsh there. It was, at least, a chance.

Bruce Barkow was not worried about the tracks he was leaving. Few Indians would be moving in this inclement weather, nor would the party from the fort have come this far north. From the route they had taken, he knew they were keeping to the low country. He was nearing the first range of foothills now, the hills that divided Long Valley from the open plain that sloped gradually away to the Powder and the old Bozeman Trail. He rode into the pines and started up the trail, intent upon death. His mind was sharpened like that of a hungry coyote. Cornered and defeated for the prize himself, his only way out, either for victory or revenge, lay in massacre, wholesale killing.

It was like him that having killed once, he did not hesitate to accept the idea of killing again. He did not see the big man on the gray horse who fell in behind him. He did not glance back over his trail, although by now the thickening snow obscured the background so much the rider, gaining slowly on him through the storm, would have been no more than a shadow.

To the right, behind the once bald and now snow-covered dome, was the black smear of seeping oil. Drawing abreast of it, Bruce Barkow reined in and glanced down. Here it was, the cause of it all. The key to wealth, to everything a man could want. Men had killed for less; he could kill for this. He knew where there were four other such seepages, and the oil sold from twenty dollars to thirty dollars a barrel.

He got down and stirred it with a stick. It was thick now, thickened by cold. Well, he still might win. Then he heard a shuffle of hoofs in the snow, and looked up. Dan Shute's figure was gigantic in the heavy coat he wore, sitting astride the big horse. He looked down at Barkow, and his lips parted.

"Tried to get away with her, did yuh? I knew yuh had coyote in yuh, Barkow."

His hand came up, and in the gloved hand was a pistol. In a sort of shocked disbelief, Bruce Barkow saw the gun lift. His own gun was under his short, thick coat.

"No!" he gasped hoarsely. "Not that! *Dan!*"

The last word was a scream, cut sharply off by the hard *bark* of the gun. Bruce Barkow folded slowly and, clutching his stomach, toppled across the black seepage, staining it with a slow shading of red.

For a minute, Dan Shute sat his horse, staring down. Then he turned the horse and moved on. He had an idea of his own. Before the storm began, from a mountain ridge he had picked out the moving patrol. Behind it were two figures. He had a hunch about those two riders, striving to overtake the patrol. He would see.

XVIII

Pushing rapidly ahead through the falling snow, the patrol came up to the ruins of the cabin on the Crazy Man on the morning of the second day out from the fort. Steam rose from the horses, and the breath of horses and men fogged the air. There was no sign of life. Rafe swung down, and stared about. The smooth surface of the snow was unbroken, yet he

270

could see that much had happened since he started his trek to the fort for help. The lean-to, not quite complete, was abandoned.

Lieutenant Bryson surveyed the scene thoughtfully. "Are we too late?" he asked.

Caradec hesitated, staring around. There was no hope in what he saw. "I don't think so," he said. "Johnny Gill was a smart hand. He would figger out somethin', and, besides, I don't see any bodies."

In his mind, he surveyed the cañon. Certainly Gill could not have gone far with the wounded man. Also, it would have to be in the direction of possible shelter. The grove of lodgepoles offered the best chance. Turning, he walked toward them. Bryson dismounted his men, and they started fires.

Milton Waitt, the surgeon, stared after Rafe, then walked in his tracks. When he came up with him, he suggested: "Any caves around?"

Caradec paused, considering that. "There may be. None that I know of, though. Still, Johnny prowled in these rocks a lot and may have found one. Let's have a look." Then a thought occurred to him. "They'd have to have water, Doc. Let's go to the spring."

There was ice over it, but the ice had been broken and had frozen again. Rafe indicated it.

"Somebody drank here after the cold set in."

He knelt and felt of the snow with his fingers, working his way slowly around the spring. Suddenly he stopped.

"Found something?" Waitt watched curiously. This made no sense to him.

"Yes. Whoever got water from the spring splashed some on this side. It froze. I can feel the ice it made. That's a fair indication that whoever got water came from that side of the spring." Moving around, he kept feeling of the snow. "Here." He felt again. "There's an icy ring where he set the bucket for a minute. Water left on the bottom froze." He straightened, studying the mountainside. "He's up here, somewheres. He's got a bucket, and he's able to come down here for water, but findin' him'll be the devil's own job. He'll need fuel, though. Somewhere he's been breakin' sticks and collectin' wood, but wherever he does, it won't be close to his shelter. Gill's too smart for that."

Studying the hillside, Rafe indicated the nearest clump of trees.

"He wouldn't want to be out in the open on this snow any longer than he had to," he said thoughtfully, "and the chances are he'd head for the shelter of those trees. When he got there, he would probably set the bucket down while he studied the back trail and made shore he hadn't been seen."

Waitt nodded, his interest aroused. "Good reasoning, man. Let's see."

They walked to the clump of trees, and, after a few minutes' search, Waitt found the same icy frozen place just under the thin skimming of snow. "Where do we go from here?" he asked.

Rafe hesitated, studying the trees. A man would automatically follow the line of easiest travel, and there was an opening between the trees. He started on, then stopped. "This is right. See? There's not so much snow on this branch. There's a good chance he brushed it off in passin'."

It was mostly guesswork, he knew. Yet, after they had gone three hundred yards, Rafe looked up and saw the cliff pushing its rocky shoulder in among the trees. At its base was a tumbled cluster of gigantic boulders and broken slabs. He led off for the rocks, and almost the first thing he saw was a fragment of loose bark lying on the snow, and a few crumbs of dust such as is sometimes found between the bark and tree. He pointed it out to Waitt.

"He carried wood this way."

They paused there, and Rafe sniffed the air. There was no smell of wood smoke. Were they dead? Had cold done what rifle bullets couldn't do? No, he decided, Johnny Gill knew too well how to take care of himself.

Rafe walked between the rocks, turning where it felt natural to turn. Suddenly he saw a tipped-up slab of granite leaning against a larger boulder. It looked dry underneath. He stooped and glanced in. It was dark and silent, yet some instinct seemed to tell him it was not so empty as it appeared.

He crouched in the opening, leaving light from outside to come in first along one wall, then another. His keen eyes picked out a damp spot on the leaves. There was no place for a leak, and the wind had been in the wrong direction to blow in here.

"Snow," he said. "Probably fell off a boot."

They moved into the cave, bending over to walk. Yet it was not really a cave at first, merely a slab of rock offering partial shelter. About fifteen feet farther along the slab ended under a thick growth of pine boughs and brush that formed a canopy overhead, offering almost as solid shelter as the stone itself. Then, in the rock face of the cliff, they saw a cave, a place gouged by wind and water long since and completely obscured behind the boulders and brush from any view but from where they stood.

They walked up to the entrance. The overhang of the cliff offered a shelter that was all of fifty feet deep, running along one wall of a diagonal gash in the cliff that was invisible from outside. They stepped in on the dry sand, and had taken only a step when they smelled wood smoke. At almost the same instant, Johnny Gill spoke.

"Hi, Rafe!" He stepped down from behind a heap of debris against one wall of the rock fissure. "I couldn't see who yuh were till now. I had my rifle ready so's if yuh was the wrong one, I could plumb discourage yuh." His face looked drawn and tired. "He's over here, Doc," Gill continued, "and he's been delirious all night."

While Waitt was busy over the wounded man, Gill walked back up the cave with Rafe.

"What's happened," Gill asked. "I thought they'd got yuh."

"No, they haven't, but I don't know much of what's been goin' on. Ann's at the fort with Barkow, says she's goin' to marry him."

"What about Tex?" Gill asked quickly.

Rafe shook his head, scowling. "No sign of him. I don't know what's come off at Painted Rock. I'm leavin' for there as soon as I've told the lieutenant and his patrol where Doc is. You'll have to stick here because the Doc has to get back to the fort."

"You goin' to Painted Rock?"

"Yes. I'm goin' to kill Dan Shute."

"I'd like to see that," Gill said grimly, "but watch yoreself!" The little cowhand looked at him seriously. "Boss, what about that girl?"

Rafe's lips tightened, and he stared at the bare wall of the cave. "I don't know," he said grimly. "I tried to talk her out of it, but I guess I wasn't what you'd call tactful."

Gill stuck his thumbs in his belt. "Tell her yuh're in love with her yoreself?"

Caradec stared at him. "Where'd yuh get that idea?"

"Readin' signs. Yuh ain't been the same since yuh ran into her the first time. She's yore kind of people, boss."

"Mebbe. But looks like she reckoned she wasn't. Never

274

would listen to me give the straight story on her father. Both of us flew off the handle this time."

"Well, I ain't no hand at ridin' herd on women folks, but I've seen a thing or two, boss. The chances are, if yuh'd a told her yuh're in love with her, she'd never have gone with Bruce Barkow."

Rafe was remembering those words when he rode down the trail toward Painted Rock. What lay ahead of him could not be planned. He had no idea when or where he would encounter Dan Shute. He knew only that he must find him.

After reporting to Bryson so he wouldn't worry about the doctor, Rafe had hit the trail for Painted Rock alone. By now he knew that mountain trail well, and even the steady fall of snow failed to make him change his mind about making the ride.

He was burning up inside. The old, driving recklessness was in him, the urge to be in and shooting. His enemies were in the clear, and all the cards were on the table in plain sight. Barkow he discounted. Dan Shute was the man to get, and Pod Gomer the man to watch. What he intended to do was as high-handed in its way as what Shute and Barkow had attempted, but in Rafe's case the cause was just.

Mullaney stopped in a wooded draw short of the hills. The pause was for a short rest just before daybreak on that fatal second morning. The single rider had turned off from the trail and was no longer with the patrol. Both he and the girl needed rest, aside from the horses.

He kicked snow away from the grass, then swept some of it clear with a branch. In most places it was already much too thick for that. After he made coffee, and they had eaten, he got up.

"Get ready," he said, "and I'll get the hosses."

All night he had been thinking of what he would do when he found Barkow. He had seen the man draw on Penn, and he was not fast. That made it an even break, for Mullaney knew that he was not fast himself.

When he found the horses missing, he stopped. Evidently they had pulled their picket pins and wandered off. He started on, keeping in their tracks. He did not see the big man in the heavy coat who stood in the brush and watched him go.

Dan Shute threaded his way down to the campfire. When Ann looked up at his approach, she thought it was Mullaney, and then she saw Shute. Eyes wide, she came to her feet. "Why, hello! What are you doing here?"

He smiled at her, his eyes sleepy and yet wary. "Huntin' you. Reckoned this was you. When I seen Barkow, I reckoned somethin' had gone wrong."

"You saw Bruce? Where?"

"North a ways. He won't bother yuh none." Shute smiled. "Barkow was spineless. Thought he was smart. He never was half as smart as that Caradec, nor as tough as me."

"What happened?" Ann's heart was pounding. Mullaney should be coming now. He would hear their voices and be warned.

"I killed him." Shute was grinning cynically. "He wasn't much good. Don't be wonderin' about that *hombre* with yuh. I led the hosses off and turned his adrift. He'll be hours catchin' it, if he ever does. However, he might come back, so we'd better drift."

"No," Ann said, "I'll wait."

He smiled. "Better come quiet. If he came back, I'd have to kill him. Yuh don't want him killed, do yuh?"

She hesitated only a moment. This man would stop at

nothing. He was going to take her if he had to knock her out and tie her. Better anything than that. If she appeared to play along, she might have a chance. "I'll go," she said simply. "You have a horse?"

"I kept yores," he said. "Mount up."

XIX

By the time Rafe Caradec was *en route* to Painted Rock, Dan Shute was riding with his prisoner into the ranch yard of his place near Painted Rock. Far to the south and west, Rock Mullaney long since had come up to the place where Shute had finally turned his horse loose and ridden on, leading the other. Mullaney kept on the trail of the lone horse and came up with it almost a mile farther.

Lost and alone in the thickly falling snow, the animal hesitated at his call, then waited for him to catch up. When he was mounted once more, he turned back to his camp, and the tracks, nearly covered, told him little. The girl, accompanied by another rider, had ridden away. She would never have gone willingly.

Mullaney was worried. During the travel they had talked little, yet Ann had supplied a few of the details, and he knew vaguely about Dan Shute, about Bruce Barkow. He also knew, having heard all about it long before reaching the fort, that an Indian outbreak was feared.

Mullaney knew something about Indians, and doubted any trouble until spring or summer. There might be occasional shootings, but Indians were not as a rule cold-weather fighters. For that, he didn't blame them. Yet any wandering, hunting, or foraging parties must be avoided, and it was probable that any warrior or group of them coming along a fresh

277

trail would fail to follow it and count coup on an enemy if possible.

He knew roughly the direction of Painted Rock, yet instinct told him he'd better stick to the tangible and near, so he swung back to the trail of the Army patrol and headed for the pass into Lone Valley.

Painted Rock lay still under the falling snow when Rafe Caradec drifted down the street in front of the Emporium, and went in. Baker looked up, and his eyes grew alert when he saw Rafe. At Caradec's question, he told him of what had happened to Tex Brisco so far as he knew, of the killing of Blazer, McCabe, and Gorman, and Brisco's escape while apparently wounded. He also told him of Dan Shute's arrival and threat to Ann, and her subsequent escape with Barkow. Baker was relieved to know they were at the fort.

A wind was beginning to moan around the eaves, and they listened a moment.

"Won't be good to be out in that," the storekeeper said gravely. "Sounds like a blizzard comin'. If Brisco's found shelter, he might be all right."

"Not in this cold," Caradec said, scowling. "No man with his resistance lowered by a wound is going to last in this. It's going to be worse before it's better."

Standing there at the counter, letting the warmth of the big potbellied stove work through his system, Rafe assayed his position. Bo Marsh, while in bad shape, had been tended by a doctor and would have Gill's care. There was nothing more to be done there for the time being. Ann had made her choice. She had gone off with Barkow, and in his heart he knew that if there was any choice between the two—Barkow or Shute—she had made the better. Yet there had been another choice. Or had there? Yes, she

278

could at least have listened to him.

The fort was not far away, and all he could do now was trust to Ann's innate good sense to change her mind before it was too late. In any event, he could not get back there in time to do anything about it.

"Where's Shute?" he demanded.

"Ain't seen him," Baker said worriedly. "Ain't seen hide nor hair of him. But I can promise yuh one thing, Caradec. He won't take Barkow's runnin' out with Ann lyin' down. He'll be on their trail."

The door opened in a flurry of snow, and Pat Higley pushed in. He pulled off his mittens and extended stiff fingers toward the red swell of the stove. He glanced at Rafe.

"Hear yuh askin' about Shute?" he asked. "I just seen him, headed for the ranch. He wasn't alone, neither." He rubbed his fingers. "Looked to me like a woman ridin' along."

Rafe looked around. "A woman?" he asked carefully. "Now who would that be?"

"He's found Ann!" Baker exclaimed.

"She was at the fort," Rafe said, "with Barkow. He couldn't take her away from the soldiers."

"No, he couldn't," Baker agreed, "but she might have left on her own. She's a stubborn girl when she takes a notion. After you left, she may have changed her mind." .

Rafe pushed the thought away. The chance was too slight. And where was Tex Brisco? "Baker," he suggested, "you and Higley know this country. You know about Tex. Where do you reckon he'd wind up?"

Higley shrugged. "There's no tellin'. It ain't as if he knew the country, too. They trailed him for a while, and they said it looked like his hoss was wanderin' loose without no hand on the bridle. Then the hoss took to the water, so Brisco must have come to his senses somewhat. Anyway, they lost his trail when he was ridin' west along a fork of Clear Creek. If he held to that direction, it would take him over some plumb high, rough country south of the big peak. If he did get across, he'd wind up somewheres down along Tensleep Cañon, mebbe. But that's all guesswork."

"Any shelter that way?"

"Nary a mite. Not if yuh mean human shelter. There's plenty of shelter there, but wolves, too. There's also plenty of shelter in the rocks. The only humans over that way are the Sioux, and they ain't in what yuh'd call a friendly mood. That's where Man-Afraid-Of-His-Hoss has been holed up."

Finding Tex Brisco would be like hunting a needle in a haystack and worse, but it was what Rafe Caradec had to do. He had to make an effort, anyway. Yet the thought of Dan Shute and the girl returned to him. Suppose it was Ann? He shuddered to think of her in Shute's hands. The man was without a spark of decency or mercy. Not even his best friends would deny that.

"No use goin' out in this storm," Baker said. "Yuh can stay with us, Caradec."

"You've changed your tune some, Baker," Rafe suggested grimly.

"A man can be wrong, can't he?" Baker inquired testily. "Mebbe I was. I don't know. Things have gone to perdition around here fast, ever since you came in here with that story about Rodney."

"Well, I'm not stayin'," Rafe told him. "I'm going to look for Tex Brisco."

The door was pushed open, and they looked around. It was Pod Gomer. The sheriff looked even squarer and more bulky in a heavy buffalo coat. He cast a bleak look at Caradec, then walked to the fire, sliding out of his overcoat. "You still

280

here?" he asked, glancing at Rafe out of the corners of his eyes.

"Yes, I'm still here, Gomer, but you're traveling."

"What?"

"You heard me. You can wait till the storm is over, then get out, and keep movin'.."

Gomer turned, his square, hard face dark with angry blood. "You...tellin' me?" he said furiously. "I'm sheriff here!"

"You were," Caradec said calmly. "Ever since you've been hand in glove with Barkow and Shute, runnin' their dirty errands for them, pickin' up the scraps they tossed you. Well, the fun's over. You slope out of here when the storm's over. Barkow's gone, and within a few hours Shute will be, too."

"Shute?" Gomer was incredulous. "Yuh'd go up against Dan Shute? Why, man, yuh're insane!"

"Am I?" Rafe shrugged. "That's neither here nor there. I'm talkin' to you. Get out and stay out. You can take your tinhorn judge with you."

Gomer laughed. "You're the one who's through! Marsh dead, Brisco either dead or on the dodge, and Gill mebbe dead. What chance have you got?"

"Gill's in as good a shape as I am," Rafe said calmly, "and Bo Marsh is gettin' Army care, and he'll be out of the woods, too. As for Tex, I don't know. He got away, and I'm bankin' on that Texan to come out walkin'. How much stomach are your boys goin' to have for the fight when Gill and I ride in here? Tom Blazer's gone, and so are a half dozen more. Take your coat"—Rafe picked it up with his left hand—"and get out. If I see you after this storm, I'm shootin' on sight. Now, get!"

He heaved the heavy coat at Gomer, and the sheriff ducked, his face livid. Yet, surprisingly, he did not reach for a gun. He lunged and swung with his fist. A shorter man than Caradec, he was wider and thicker, a powerfully built man who was known in mining and trail camps as a rough-and-tumble fighter.

Caradec turned, catching Gomer's right on the cheek bone, but bringing up a solid punch to Gomer's midsection. The sheriff lunged close and tried to butt, and Rafe stabbed him in the face with a left, then smeared him with a hard right.

It was no match. Pod Gomer had fancied himself as a fighter, but Caradec had too much experience. He knocked Gomer back into a heap of sacks, then walked in on him, and slugged him wickedly in the middle with both hands. Gomer went to his knees.

"All right, Pod," Rafe said, panting, "I told you. Get goin'."

The sheriff stayed on his knees, breathing heavily, blood dripping from his smashed nose. Rafe Caradec slipped on his coat and walked to the door.

Outside, he took the horse to the livery stable, brushed him off, then gave him a rub-down and some oats.

He did not return to the store but, after a meal, saddled his horse and headed for Dan Shute's ranch. He couldn't escape the idea that the rider with Shute may have been Ann, despite the seeming impossibility of her being this far west. If she had left the fort within a short time after the patrol, then it might be, but there was small chance of that. Barkow would never return, having managed to get that far away. There was no one else at the fort to bring her. Scouts had said that a party of travelers was coming up from the river, but there would be small chance that any of them would push on to Painted Rock in this weather.

Dan Shute's ranch lay in a hollow of the hills near a

curving stream. Not far away, the timber ran down to the plain's edge and dwindled away into a few scattered groves, blanketed now in snow. A thin trail of smoke lifted from the chimney of the house, and another from the bunkhouse. Rafe Caradec decided on boldness as the best course and his muffled, snow-covered appearance to disguise him until within gun range. He opened a button on the front of his coat so he could get at a gun thrust into his waistband. He removed his right hand from the glove and thrust it deeply in his pocket. There it would be warm and at the same time free to grasp the six-gun when he needed it.

No one showed. It was very cold, and, if there was anyone around and they noticed his approach, their curiosity did not extend to the point where they would come outside to investigate. Rafe strode directly to the house, walked up on the porch, and rapped on the door with his left hand. There was no response. He rapped again, much harder.

All was silence. The mounting wind made hearing difficult, but he put his ear to the door and listened. There was no sound.

He dropped his left hand to the door and turned the knob. The door opened easily, and he let it swing wide, standing well out of line. The wind howled in, and a few flakes of snow, but there was no sound. He stepped inside and closed the door after him.

His ears tingled with cold, and he resisted a desire to rub them, then let his eyes sweep the wide room. A fire burned on the huge stone fireplace, but there was no one in the long room. Two exits from the room were hung with blankets. There was a table, littered with odds and ends, and one end held some dirty dishes where a hasty meal had been eaten. Beneath that spot was a place showing dampness as though a pair of boots had shed melting snow.

Louis L'Amour

There was no sound in the living room but the crackle of the fire and the low moan of the wind around the eaves. Walking warily, Rafe stepped over a saddle and some bits of harness and walked across to the opposite room. He pushed the blanket aside. Empty. There was an unmade bed of tumbled blankets and a lamp standing on a table by the bed.

Rafe turned and stared at the other door, then looked back into the bedroom. There was a pair of dirty socks lying there, and he stepped over and felt of them. They were damp. Someone, within the last hour or less, had changed socks here. Walking outside, he noticed something he had not seen before. Below a chair near the table was another spot of dampness. Apparently two people had been here.

He stepped back into the shadow of the bedroom door and put his hand in the front of his coat. He hadn't wanted to reach for that gun in case anyone was watching. Now, with his hand on the gun, he stepped out of the bedroom and walked to the other blanket-covered door. He pushed it aside.

A large kitchen. A fire glowed in the huge sheet-metal stove, and there was a coffee pot filled with boiling coffee. Seeing, it, Rafe let go of his gun and picked up a cup. When he had filled it, he looked around the unkempt room. Like the rest of the house it was strongly built, but poorly kept inside. The floor was dirty, and dirty dishes and scraps of food were around.

He lifted the coffee cup, then his eyes saw a bit of white. He put down the cup and stepped over to the end of the woodpile. His heart jumped. It was a woman's handkerchief!

XX

Quickly Rafe Caradec glanced around. Again he looked at the handkerchief in his hand, and lifted it to his nostrils. There was a faint whiff of perfume—a perfume he remembered only too well. She had been here, then. The other rider with Dan Shute had been Ann Rodney. But where was she now? Where could she be? What had happened?

He gulped a mouthful of the hot coffee, and stared around again. The handkerchief had been near the back door. He put down the coffee, and eased the door open. Beyond were the barn and a corral. He walked outside and, pushing through the curtain of blowing snow, reached the corral, and then the barn.

Several horses were there. Hurrying along, he found two with dampness marking the places where their saddles had been. There were no saddles showing any evidence of having been ridden, and the saddles would be sweaty underneath if they had been. Evidently two horses had been saddled and ridden away from this barn.

Scowling, Rafe stared around. In the dust of the floor he found a small track, almost obliterated by a larger one. Had Shute saddled two horses and taken the girl away? If so, where would he take her, and why? He decided suddenly that Shute had not taken Ann from here. She must have slipped away, saddled a horse, and escaped. It was a far-fetched conclusion, but it offered not only the solution he wanted, but one that fitted with the few facts available or, at least, with the logic of the situation. Why would Shute take the girl away from his home ranch? There was no logical reason. Especially in such a storm as this when so far as Shute knew there would be no pursuit? Rafe himself would not have done it. Perhaps he had been overconfident, believing that Ann would rather share the warmth and security of the house than the mounting blizzard.

Only the bunkhouse remained unexplored. There was a chance they had gone there. Turning, Rafe walked to the bunkhouse. Shoving the door open, he stepped inside. Four men sat on bunks, and one, his boots off and his socks propped toward the stove, stared glumly at him from a chair made of a barrel. The faces of all the men were familiar, but he could put a name to none of them. They had seen the right hand in the front of his coat, and they sat quietly appreciating its significance.

"Where's Dan Shute?" he demanded.

"Ain't seen him," said the man in the barrel chair.

"That go for all of you?" Rafe's eyes swung from one to the other.

A lean, hard-faced man with a scar on his jaw bone grinned, showing yellow teeth. He raised himself on his elbow. "Why, no. It shore don't, pilgrim. I seen him. He rode up here nigh onto an hour ago with that there girl from the store. They went inside. S'pose you want to get killed, you go to the house."

"I've been there. It's empty."

The lean-faced man sat up. "That right? That don't make sense. Why would a man with a filly like that go off into the storm?"

Rafe Caradec studied them coldly. "You men," he said, "had better get out of here when the storm's over. Dan Shute's through."

"Ain't yuh countin' unbranded stock, pardner?" the lean-faced man said, smiling tauntingly. "Dan Shute's able to handle his own troubles. He took care of Barkow."

286

This was news to Rafe. "He did! How'd you know that?"

"He done told me. Barkow was with this girl, and Shute trailed him. I didn't only see Shute come back, I talked some with him, and I unsaddled his hosses." He picked up a boot and pulled it on. "This here Rodney girl, she left the fort, runnin' away from Barkow and takin' after the Army patrol that rode out with you. Shute, he seen 'em. He also seen Barkow. He hunted Bruce down and shot him near that bare dome in your lower valley, and then he left Barkow and caught up with the girl and this strange *hombre* with her. Shute led their hosses off, then got the girl while this *hombre* was huntin' the hosses."

The explanation cleared up several points for Rafe. He stared thoughtfully around. "You didn't see 'em leave here?"

"Not us," the lean-faced 'puncher said dryly. "None of us hired on for punchin' cows or ridin' herd on women in blizzards. Come a storm, we hole up and set her out. We aim to keep on doin' just that."

Rafe backed to the door and stepped out. The wind tore at his garments, and he backed away from the building. Within twenty feet it was lost behind a curtain of blowing snow. He stumbled back to the house.

More than ever, he was convinced that somehow Ann had escaped. Yet where to look? In this storm there was no direction, nothing. If she headed for town, she might make it. However, safety for her would more likely lie toward the mountains, for there she could improvise shelter, and probably could last the storm out. Knowing the country, she would know how long such storms lasted. It was rarely more than three days.

He had little hope of finding Ann, yet he knew she would never return here. Seated in the ranch house, he coolly ate a hastily picked-up meal and drank more coffee. Then he returned to his horse that he had led to the stable. Mounting, he rode out into the storm on the way to town.

Gene Baker and Pat Higley looked up when Rafe Caradec came in. Baker's face paled when he saw that Rafe was alone. "Did yuh find out?" he asked. "Was it Ann?"

Briefly Rafe explained, telling all he had learned and his own speculations as to what had happened.

"She must have plumb got away," Higley agreed. "Shute would never take her away from his ranch in this storm. But where could she have gone?"

Rafe explained his own theories on that. "She probably took it for granted he would think she would head for town," he suggested, "so she may have taken to the mountains. After all, she would know that Shute would kill anybody who tried to stop him."

Gene Baker nodded miserably. "That's right, and what can a body do?"

"Wait," Higley said. "Just wait."

"I won't wait," Rafe said. "If she shows up here, hold her. Shoot Dan if you have to, dry-gulch him or anything. Get him out of the way. I'm goin' into the mountains. I can at least be lookin', and I might stumble onto some kind of a trail...."

Two hours later, shivering with cold, Rafe Caradec acknowledged how foolhardy he had been. His black horse was walking steadily through a snow-covered avenue among the pines, weaving around fallen logs and clumps of brush. He had found nothing that resembled a trail, and twice he had crossed the stream. This, he knew, was also the direction that had been taken by the wounded Tex Brisco.

No track could last more than a minute in the whirling snow-filled world in which Rafe now rode. The wind howled and tore at his garments, even here, within the partial shelter of the lodgepoles. Yet he rode on, then dismounted, and walked ahead, resting the horse. It was growing worse instead of better, yet he pushed on, taking the line of least resistance, sure that this was what the fleeing Ann would have done.

The icy wind ripped at his clothing, at times faced him like a solid, moving wall. The black stumbled wearily, and Rafe was suddenly contrite. The big horse had taken a brutal beating in these last few days, and even its great strength was weakening.

Squinting his eyes against the blowing snow, he remounted and stared ahead. He could see nothing, but he was aware that the wall of the mountain was on his left. Bearing in that direction, he came up to a thicker stand of trees and some scattered boulders. He rode on, alert for some possible shelter for himself and his horse.

Almost an hour later, he found it, a dry, sandy place under the overhang of the cliff, sheltered from the wind and protected from the snow by the overhang and by the trees and brush that fronted it. Swinging down, Rafe led the horse into the shelter and hastily built a fire.

From the underside of a log he got some bark, great sheets of it, and some fibrous, rotting wood. Then he broke some low branches on the trees, dead and dry. In a few minutes his fire was burning nicely. Then he stripped the saddle from the horse and rubbed him down with a handful of crushed bark. When that was done, he got out the nosebag and fed the horse some of the oats he had appropriated from Shute's barn.

The next hour he occupied himself in gathering fuel. Luckily there were a number of dead trees close by, debris left from some landslide from up the mountain. He settled down by the fire, made coffee. Dozing against the rock, he fed the blaze intermittently, his mind far away.

Somehow, sometime, he fell asleep. Around the rocks the wind, moaning and whining, sought with icy fingers for a grasp at his shoulder, at his hands. But the log burned well, and the big horse stood close, stamping in the sand and dozing beside the man on the ground.

Once, starting from his sleep, Rafe noticed that the log had burned until it was out of the fire, so he dragged it around, then laid another across it. Soon he was again asleep.

He awakened suddenly. It was daylight, and the storm was still raging. His fire blazed among the charred embers of his logs, and he lifted his eyes. Six Indians faced him beyond the fire, and their rifles and bows covered him. Their faces were hard and unreadable. Two stepped forward and jerked him to his feet, stripped his guns from him, and motioned for him to saddle his horse.

Numb with cold, he could scarcely realize what had happened to him. One of the Indians, wrapped in a worn red blanket, jabbered at the others and kept pointing to the horse, making threatening gestures. Yet when Rafe had the animal saddled, they motioned to him to mount. Two of the Indians rode up then, leading the horses of the others. So this was the way it ended. He was a prisoner.

XXI

Uncomprehending, Rafe Caradec opened his eyes to darkness. He sat up abruptly and stared around. Then, after a long minute, it came to him. He was a prisoner in a village of the Oglala Sioux, and he had just awakened. Two days before they had brought him here, bound him hand and foot, and left him in the teepee he now occupied. Several times squaws had entered the teepee and departed. They had given him food and water.

It was night, and his wrists were swollen from the tightness of the bonds. It was warm in the teepee, for there was a fire, but smoke filled the skin wigwam and filtered out at the top. He had a feeling it was almost morning.

What had happened at Painted Rock? Where was Ann? And where was Tex Brisco? Had Dan Shute returned?

He was rolling over toward the entrance to catch a breath of fresh air when the flap was drawn back and a squaw came in. She spoke rapidly in Sioux, then picked a brand from the fire, and, as it blazed up, held it close to his face. He drew back, thinking she meant to sear his eyes. Then, looking beyond the blaze, he saw that the squaw holding it was the Indian girl he had saved from Trigger Boyne!

With a burst of excited talk, she bent over him. A knife slid under his bonds, and they were cut. Chafing his ankles, he looked up. In the flare of the torchlight he could now see the face of a male Indian.

He spoke, gutturally, but in fair English. "My daughter say you man help her," he said.

"Yes," Rafe replied. "The Sioux are not my enemies, nor am I theirs."

"Your name Caradec." The Indian's statement was flat, not to be contradicted.

"Yes." Rafe stumbled to his feet, rubbing his wrists.

"We know your horse, also the horses of the others."

"Others?" Rafe asked quickly. "There are others here?"

"Yes, a woman and a man. The man is much better. He had been injured."

Ann and Tex! Rafe's heart leaped.

"May I see them?" he asked. "They are my friends."

The Indian nodded. He studied Rafe for a minute. "I

291

think you are good man. My name Man-Afraid-Of-His-Horse."

The Oglala chief. Rafe looked again at the Indian. "I know the name. With Red Cloud you are the greatest of the Sioux."

The chief nodded. "There are others. John Grass, Gall, Crazy Horse, many others. The Sioux have many great men."

The girl led Rafe away to the tent where he found Tex Brisco, lying on a pile of skins and blankets. Tex was pale, but he grinned when Rafe came in.

"Man," he said, "it's good to see yuh! And here's Ann?"

Rafe turned to look at her, and she smiled, then held out her hand. "I have learned how foolish I was. First from Penn, and then from Mullaney and Tex."

"Penn? Mullaney?" Rafe squinted his eyes. "Are they here?"

Quickly Ann explained about Barkow's killing of Penn, and her subsequent attempt to overtake Bruce, guided and helped by Rock Mullaney.

"Barkow's dead," Rafe said. "Shute killed him."

"Ann told me," Tex said. "He had it comin'. Where's Dan Shute now?"

Caradec shrugged. "I don't know, but I'm goin' to find out."

"Please." Ann came to him. "Don't fight with him, Rafe. There has been enough killing. You might be hurt, and I couldn't stand that."

He looked at her. "Does it matter so much?"

Her eyes fell. "Yes," she said simply, "it does...."

Painted Rock lay quietly in a world of white, its shabbiness lost under the purity of freshly fallen snow. Escorted by a band of Oglalas, Ann, Rafe, and Tex rode to the edge of street was empty, and the town seemed to have no word of their coming.

Tex Brisco, still weak from loss of blood and looking pale, brought up the rear. With Ann, he headed right for the Emporium. Rafe Caradec rode ahead until they neared the National Saloon, then swung toward the boardwalk, and waited until they had gone by.

Baker came rushing from the store and, with Ann's help, got Tex down from the horse and inside.

Rafe Caradec led his own horse down the street and tied it to the hitching rail. Then he glanced up and down the street, looking for Shute. Within a matter of minutes Dan would know he was back, and, once he was aware of it, there would be trouble.

Pat Higley was inside the store when Rafe entered. He nodded at Rafe's story of what had taken place.

"Shute's been back in town," Higley said. "I reckon after he lost Ann in the snowstorm he figgered she would circle around and come back here."

"Where's Pod Gomer?" Rafe inquired.

"If yuh mean has he taken out, why I can tell yuh he hasn't," Baker said. "He's been around with Shute, and he's wearin' double hardware right now."

Higley nodded. "They ain't goin' to give up without a fight," he warned. "They're keepin' some men in town, quite a bunch of 'em."

Rafe also nodded. "That will end as soon Shute's out of the way."

He looked up as the door pushed open, and started to his feet when Johnny Gill walked in with Rock Mullaney.

"The soldiers rigged a sled," Gill announced at once. "They're takin' Bo back to the fort, so we reckoned it might be a good idea to come down here and stand by in case of trouble."

Ann came to the door, and stood there by the curtain, watching them. Her eyes continually strayed to Rafe, and he looked up, meeting their glance. Ann flushed and looked away, then invited him to join her for coffee.

Excusing himself, he got up and went inside. Gravely Ann showed him to a chair, brought him a napkin, then poured coffee for him, and put sugar and cream beside his cup. He took the sugar, then looked up at her.

"Can you ever forgive me?" she asked.

"There's nothin' to forgive," he said. "I couldn't blame you. You were sure your father was dead."

"I didn't know why the property should cause all that trouble until I heard of the oil. Is it really worth so much?"

"Quite a lot. Shippin' is a problem now, but that will be taken care of soon. So it could be worth a great deal of money. I expect they knew more about that end of it than we did." Rafe looked at her. "I never aimed to claim my half of the ranch," he said, "and I don't now. I accepted it just to give me some kind of a legal basis for workin' with you, but now that the trouble is over, I'll give you the deed, the will your father made out, and the other papers."

"Oh, no!" she exclaimed quickly. "You mustn't! I'll need your help to handle things, and you must accept your part of the ranch and stay on. That is," she added, "if you don't think I'm too awful for the way I acted."

He flushed. "I don't think you're awful, Ann," he said clumsily, getting to his feet. "I think you're wonderful. I guess I always have, ever since that first day when I came into the store and saw you." His eyes strayed, and carried their glance out the window. He came to with a start and got to his feet. "There's Dan Shute," he said. "I got to go."

Ann arose with him, white to the lips. He avoided her

glance, then turned abruptly toward the door. The girl made no protest, but as he started through the curtain, she said: "Come back, Rafe. I'll be waiting."

He walked to the street door, and the others saw him go, then something in his manner apprised them of what was about to happen. Mullaney caught up his rifle and started for the door, also, and Baker reached for a scattergun.

Rafe Caradec glanced quickly at the snow-covered street. One wagon had been down the center of the street about daybreak, and there had been no other traffic except for a few passing riders. Horses stood in front of the National and the Emporium and had kicked up the snow, but otherwise it was an even, unbroken expanse of pure white.

Rafe stepped out on the porch of the Emporium. Dan Shute's gray was tied at the National's hitching rail, but Shute was nowhere in sight. Rafe walked to the corner of the store, his feet crunching on the snow. The sun was coming out, and the snow might soon be gone. As he thought of that, a drop fell from the roof overhead and touched him on the neck.

Dan Shute would be in the National. Rafe walked slowly down the walk to the saloon and pushed open the door. Joe Benson looked up from behind his bar, and hastily moved down toward the other end. Pod Gomer, slumped in a chair at a table across the room, sat up abruptly, his eyes shifting to the big man at the bar.

Dan Shute's back was to the room. In his short, thick coat he looked enormous. His hat was off, and his shock of blond hair, coarse and uncombed, glinted in the sunlight.

Rafe stopped inside the door, his gaze sweeping the room in one all-encompassing glance. Then his eyes riveted on the big man at the bar.

"All right, Shute," he said calmly. "Turn around and take

it."

Dan Shute turned, and he was grinning. He was grinning widely, but there was a wicked light dancing in his eyes. He stared at Caradec, letting his slow, insolent gaze go over him from head to foot.

"Killin' yuh would be too easy," he said. "I promised myself that when the time came I would take yuh apart with my hands, and then, if there was anything left, shoot it full of holes. I'm goin' to kill yuh, Caradec."

Out of the tail of his eye, Rafe saw that Johnny Gill was leaning against the jamb of the back door, and that Rock Mullaney was just inside of that same door.

"Take off your guns, Caradec, and I'll kill yuh," Shute said softly.

"It's their fight," Gill said suddenly. "Let 'em have it the way they want it!"

The voice startled Gomer so that he jerked, and he glanced over his shoulder, his face white. Then the front door pushed open, and Higley came in with Baker. Pod Gomer touched his lips with his tongue and shot a sidelong glance at Benson. The saloonkeeper looked unhappy.

Carefully Dan Shute reached for his belt buckle and unbuckled the twin belts, laying the big guns on the bar, butts toward him. At the opposite end of the bar, Rafe Caradec did the same. Then, as one man, they shed their coats.

Lithe and broad-shouldered, Rafe was an inch shorter and forty pounds lighter than the other man. Narrow-hipped and lean as a greyhound, he was built for speed, but the powerful shoulders and powerful hands and arms spoke of years of training as well as hard work with a double jack, axe, or heaving at heavy, wet lines of a ship.

Dan Shute's neck was thick, his chest broad and massive. His stomach was flat and hard. His hands were big, and he reeked of sheer animal strength and power. Licking his lips like a hungry wolf, he started forward. He was grinning, and the light was dancing in his hard gray-white eyes. He did not rush or leap. He walked right up to Rafe, with that grin on his lips, and Caradec stood flat-footed, waiting for him. But as Shute stepped in close, Rafe suddenly whipped up a left to the wind that beat the man to the punch. Shute winced at the blow, and his eyes narrowed. Then he smashed forward with his hard skull, trying for a butt. Rafe clipped him with an elbow and swung away, keeping out of the corner.

XXII

Still grinning, Dan Shute moved in. The big man was deceptively fast, and, as he moved in, suddenly he left his feet and hurled himself feet foremost at Rafe. Caradec sprang back, but too slowly. The legs jack-knifed around him, and Rafe staggered arid went to the floor. He hit hard, and Dan was the first to move. Throwing himself over, he caught his weight on his left hand and swung with his right. It was a wicked, half-arm blow, and it caught Rafe on the chin. Lights exploded in his brain, and he felt himself go down. Then Shute sprang for him.

Rafe rolled his head more by instinct than knowledge, and the blow clipped his ear. He threw his feet high, and tipped Dan over on his head and off his body. Both men came to their feet like cats and hurled themselves at each other. They struck like two charging bulls with an impact that shook the room.

Rafe slugged a right to the wind and took a smashing blow to the head. They backed off, then charged together, and both men started pitching them—short, wicked hooks

297

thrown from the hips with everything they had in the world in every punch. Rafe's head was roaring, and he felt the smashing blows rocking his head from side to side. He smashed an inside right to the face, and saw a thin streak of blood on Shute's cheek. He fired his right down the same groove, and it might well have been on a track. The split in the skin widened, and a trickle of blood started. Rafe let go another one to the same spot, then whipped a wicked left uppercut to the wind.

Shute took it coming in and never lost stride. He ducked and lunged, knocking Rafe off balance with his shoulder, then swinging an overhand punch that caught Rafe on the cheek bone. Rafe tried to sidestep and failed, slipping on a wet spot on the floor. As he went down, Dan Shute aimed a terrific kick at his head that would have ended the fight right there but, half off balance, Rafe hurled himself at the pivot leg and knocked Dan sprawling.

Both men came up and walked into each other, slugging. Rafe evaded a kick aimed for his stomach and slapped a palm under the man's heel, lifting it high. Shute went over on his back, and Rafe left the floor in a dive and lit right in the middle of Dan Shute and knocked the wind out of him, but not enough so that Dan's thumb failed to stab him in the eye.

Blinded by pain, Rafe jerked his head away from that stabbing thumb and felt it rip along his cheek. Then he slammed two blows to the head before Shute heaved him off. They came up together.

Dan Shute was bleeding from the cut on his cheek, but he was still smiling. His gray shirt was torn, revealing bulging white muscles. He was not even breathing hard, and he walked into Rafe with a queer little bounce in his step. Rafe weaved right to left, then straightened suddenly and left-handed a stiff one into Shute's mouth. Dan went under a duplicate punch and slammed a right to the wind that lifted Rafe off the floor. They went into a clinch then, and Rafe was the faster, throwing Dan with a rolling hillock. He came off the floor fast, and the two went over like a pinwheel, gouging, slugging, ripping, and tearing at each other with fists, thumbs, and elbows.

Shute was up first, and Rafe followed, lunging in, but Dan stepped back and whipped a right uppercut that smashed every bit of sense in Rafe's head into a blinding pinwheel of white light. But he was moving fast and went on in with the impetus of his rush, and both men crashed to the floor.

Up again and swinging, they stood toe to toe and slugged viciously, wickedly, each punch a killing blow. Jaws set, they lashed at each other like madmen. Then Rafe let his right go down the groove to the cut cheek. He sidestepped and let go again, then again and again. Five times straight he hit that split cheek. It was cut deeply now and streaming blood.

Dan rushed and grabbed Rafe around the knees, heaving him clear of the floor. He brought him down with a thunderous crash that would have killed a lesser man. Rafe got up, panting, and was set for Shute as he rushed. He split Dan's lips with another left, then threw a right that missed and caught a punch in the middle that jerked his mouth open and brought his breath out of his lungs in one great gasp.

All reason gone, the two men fought like animals, yet worse than animals for in each man was the experience of years of accumulated brawling and slugging in the hard, tough, wild places of the world. They lived by their strength and their hands and the fierce animal drive that was within them, the drive of the fight for survival.

Rafe stepped in, punching Shute with a wicked, cutting, stabbing left, and his right went down the line again, and blood streamed from the cut cheek. They stood then, facing each other, shirts in ribbons, blood-streaked, with arms a-swing. They started to circle, and suddenly Shute lunged. Rafe took one step back and let go a kick from the hips. An inch or so lower down and he would have caught the bigger man in the solar plexus. As it was, the kick struck him on the chest and lifted him clear of the floor. He came down hard, but his powerful arms grabbed Rafe's leg as they swung down, and both men hit the floor together.

Shute sank his teeth into Rafe's leg, and Rafe stabbed at his eye with a thumb. Shute let go and got up, grabbing a chair. Rafe went under it, heard the chair splinter, and scarcely realized in the heat of battle that his back had taken the force of the blow. He shoved Dan back and smashed both hands into the big man's body, then rolled aside and spilled him with a rolling hillock.

Dan Shute came up, and Rafe walked in. He stabbed a left to the face, and Shute's teeth showed through his lip, broken and ugly. Rafe set himself and whipped an uppercut that stood Shute on his toes.

Tottering and punch-drunk, the light of battle still flamed in Shute's eyes. He grabbed at a bottle and lunged at Rafe, smashing it down on his shoulders. Rafe rolled with the blow and felt the bottle shatter over the compact mass of the deltoid at the end of his shoulder, then he hooked a left with that same numb arm, and felt the fist sink into Shute's body.

The strong muscles of that rock-ribbed stomach were yielding now. Rafe set himself and threw a right from the hip to the same place, and Shute staggered, his face greenish-white. Rafe walked in and stabbed three times with a powerful, cutting left that left Shute's lips in shreds. Then, suddenly calling on some hidden well of strength, Dan dived for Rafe's legs, got him around the knees, and jerked back. Rafe hit the floor on the side of his head, and his world splintered

300

into fragments of broken glass and light, flickering and exploding in a flaming chain reaction. He rolled over, took a kick on the chest, then staggered up as Shute stepped in, drunk with a chance of victory. Heavy, brutal punches smashed him to his knees, but Rafe staggered up. A powerful blow brought him down again, and he lunged to his feet.

Again he went to his knees, and again, he came up. Then he uncorked one of his own, and Dan Shute staggered. But Dan had shot his bolt. Head ringing, Rafe Caradec walked in, grabbed the bigger man by the shirt collar and belt, right hand at the belt, then turned his back on him and jerked down with his left hand at the collar and heaved up with the right. He got his back under him, and then hurled the big man like a sack of wheat.

Dan Shute hit the table beside which Gene Baker was standing, and both went down in a heap. Suddenly Shute rolled over and came to his knees, his eyes blazing. Blood streamed from the gash in his cheek, open now from mouth to ear, his lips were shreds, and a huge blue lump concealed one eye. His face was scarcely human, yet in the remaining eye gleamed a wild, killing, insane light. And in his hands he held Gene Baker's double-barreled shotgun! He did not speak— just swept the gun up and squeezed down on both triggers.

Yet at the very instant that he squeezed those triggers, Rafe's left hand had dropped to the table near him, and with one terrific heave he spun it toward the kneeling man. The gun belched flame and thunder as Rafe hit the floor flat on his stomach, and rolled over to see an awful sight.

Joe Benson, crouched over the bar, took the full blast of buckshot in the face and went over backward with a queer, choking scream.

Rafe heaved himself erect, and suddenly the room was deathly still. Pod Gomer's face was a blank sheet of white

Louis L'Amoor

horror as he stared at the spot where Benson had vanished.

Staggering, Caradec walked toward Dan Shute. The man lay on his back, arms outflung, head lying at a queer angle.

Mullaney pointed. "The table," he said. "It busted his neck."

Rafe turned and staggered toward the door. Johnny Gill caught him there. He slid an arm under Rafe's shoulders and strapped his guns to his waist.

"What about Gomer?" he asked.

Caradec shook his head. Pod Gomer was getting up to face him, and he lifted a hand. "Don't start anything. I've had enough. I'll go."

Somebody brought a bucket of water, and Rafe fell on his knees and began splashing the ice-cold water over his head and face. When he had dried himself on a towel someone had handed him, he started for a coat. Baker had come in with a clean shirt from the store.

"I'm sorry about that shotgun," he said. "It happened so fast I didn't know."

Rafe tried to smile, and couldn't. His face was stiff and swollen. "Forget it," he said. "Let's get out of here."

"Yuh ain't goin' to leave, are yuh?" Baker asked. "Ann said that she...."

"Leave? Shucks, no! We've got an oil business here, and there's a ranch. While I was at the fort, I had a wire sent to the C Bar down in Texas for some more cattle."

Ann was waiting for him, wide-eyed when she saw his face. He walked past her toward the bed and fell across it. "Don't let it get you, honey," he said. "We'll talk about it when I wake up next week."

She stared at him, started to speak, and a snore sounded in the room. Ma Baker smiled. "When a man wants to sleep, let him sleep, and I'd say he'd earned it."

302